"All of you, listen to m[...] [...] as her expression. "Ben[...] pick up your detectors, then start walking backward to the fence."

Delbert snorted. "What are you jabber—"

"Hush, fool." IdaClare nodded to her left. "Look yonder."

A horned locomotive on legs stood not five yards behind them. Twelve hundred pounds of nostril-flared, devil-horned steak on the hoof.

IdaClare said, "He has a herd to protect and the racket we made didn't set well with him."

Let me live, Hannah whimpered silently, and I'll never eat beef again, I swear. Veggies all the way.

Walt stammered, "Wh-what are we going to do?"

"Take our leave nice and easy and quiet. As long as we don't rile him, I don't think he'll charge." IdaClare looked from one frightened face to the next. "Unless he does, whatever you do, *don't turn tail and run.*"

Jelly-muscled and stiff-kneed, their machines gripped like flagstaffs, they backward marched over rain-slick rocks and grass tufts.

Hannah tromped her shoelace. Staggered. Caught herself an instant before she fell. *Klutz.*

The bull broke into a trot.

SUZANN LEDBETTER

South of Sanity

MIRA

ISBN 1-55166-797-5

SOUTH OF SANITY

Copyright © 2001 by Suzann Ledbetter.

Visit us at www.mirabooks.com

Printed in U.S.A.

For Daddy, who I will miss for all the days of my life,
and for Mom, who has always been there for me
in ways I wasn't smart enough to realize,
much less appreciate for too long.

A writer may work alone, but the end result wouldn't be possible without the help of an army of mighty fine and generous folks.

Many thanks are due:

Christian County (MO) Sheriff Steve Whitney; Christian County (MO) Deputy Joey Matlock; Detective (ret.) Gary Smith, Crime Unit, Kansas City, MO; Springfield (MO) Police Chief Lynn Rowe; Corporal Todd Revelle, S.P.D.; Patrol Officer Casey Cornelius, S.P.D. and all unit commanders and officers who participated in the 3rd Civilian Police Academy; Patrol Officers Josh Ledbetter and Kurt Hermann, Tulsa Police Dept.; Attorney Gene Andereck, Andereck, Evans, Milne, Peace & Baumhoer, LLC, Springfield, MO; the Every Friday Pizza Lunch Bunch; Ellen Recknor, writer extraordinaire and separated-at-birth twin, regardless of what our mothers say; Ellen Wade, R.N.; Paul W. Johns, first reader and superb glitch-finder; Ray Rosenbaum, who keeps me humble, as if I need any assistance; and my hardworking, patient and much admired partners in crime: Martha Keenan and Dianne Moggy, MIRA Books, and Robin Rue, Writers House.

1

In less than twenty-four hours, Hannah Garvey had survived an assault with a deadly weapon, almost made love with Kinderhook County Sheriff David Hendrickson and was about to console her boss's sixty-seven-year-old mother who'd just been busted for distributing marijuana to members of her bridge club.

Not bad for a Wednesday, and it wasn't even noon yet.

Leaning against his patrol car, Hannah watched David's eyes slide from her bruised neck to her bruised cheek, then to the puffy shiner not camouflaged by liquid makeup—the purplish souvenirs of the previous evening's near-death experience.

Sunlight did not become her. It was six months too early for Halloween. Three months too late for a ski mask. Five minutes too late for an orgasm. Timing had never been one of her best things.

"You're as wobbly as a foal," David said. "Will you *please* go back to bed and let me handle this mess at the community center?"

She grinned up at him. "Hypocrite."

"Say what?"

"Funny how my health wasn't an issue a few

minutes ago, when you were rounding first base and advancing to second.''

His arm tightened around her waist, drawing her snug against his chest. She fit as if her body had been designed for that purpose. ''Well, sugar, as I recall, you were doing a fine job of warming up the ol' batter yourself.''

Dangerous. The same warning she'd issued seconds before Detective Marlin Andrik's radio call stopped her from finding out exactly how dangerous the sheriff could be.

Safer if I never do, she reasoned.

Just because he's six foot three, and his killer grin and ''Aw, shucks'' manner send your libido screaming into overdrive, you vowed on a stack of packing boxes not to screw up your new life as badly as you did most of your old one.

An excellent promise. Mature. Prudent. Empowering. A no-sweat no-brainer, except for when she was in the throes of pure unadulterated horniness.

Like now, for instance.

''I *am* this retirement community's operations manager,'' she reminded him and eased from his embrace. ''It isn't part of my job description, but something tells me I ought to be around when my employer's mother is about to be arrested on a couple of misdemeanor charges.''

David blew out a resigned sigh and swung open his patrol car's door. Easing into the seat, she turned away to hide a wince.

He was right, as he'd been too many times during their short relationship. She should be in bed. Alone. Popping painkillers like candy. Except IdaClare Clancy was in trouble. The irrepressible, pink-haired widow wouldn't use a little thing like recovering from assault and battery for an excuse, had their situations been reversed.

Hannah surveyed her surroundings. Enough electronic gadgets and gizmos to delight the *Starship Enterprise's* navigator arrayed the Crown Victoria's dashboard, floor hump and console. A shotgun's cold, smooth barrel brushed Hannah's sandaled heel.

The car's interior smelled of vinyl cleaner, dust and David's brand of aftershave. In her recent, former life as an account executive at Friedlich & Friedlich in Chicago, she'd spearheaded advertising campaigns for some of the world's most expensive colognes, but there really *was* something about an Aqua Velva man.

David keyed the ignition. "You've never been in a patrol unit before, huh?"

"Not in the front."

His crooked eyebrow begged a question. Hers said, "No comment." Keeping the sheriff off balance was a helluva lot more fun than spilling secrets like jelly beans from a jar.

Musty, warm blasts from the air-conditioning vents changed to musty, arctic blasts. The gooseflesh on Hannah's arms did an "Atten-*hut*" and forward marched.

Locked inside a mobile freezer with a guy whose metabolism rivaled a polar bear's, she gazed longingly at the seventy-degree late-April day drifting past the window.

Sunshine enveloped the bowlegged duffers cheating each other out of quarters on the development's golf course. Johnboats skimmed the surface of the adjacent spring-fed lake. Other anglers tried their luck along its sloped, grassy banks.

Three hundred and sixty healthy and moderately wealthy senior citizens lived in Valhalla Springs, a retirement community described in promotional brochures as "East of Peculiar and the closest thing to paradise this side of Sanity."

Persnickety types with Missouri maps would say it was actually east-southeast of Peculiar, a bedroom community near Kansas City. City dwellers who loved mass transit, crowded sidewalks and a Starbucks on every corner would say the Ozarks terrain surrounding Sanity, the Kinderhook County seat, was too hardscrabble to fit anyone's definition of paradise.

After three burglaries, two murders and an attempted homicide occurred during Hannah's brief tenure as operations manager, she took "paradise" with a grain of salt, too. Still, she admired Jack Clancy, the owner of Valhalla Springs, for preserving the land's natural beauty rather than bulldozing the trees and naming streets after them.

She rejoiced when they turned into the parking lot of the elongated, cedar-sided community center. If IdaClare had run afoul of the law, at least she'd done it where open windows promised relief from frostbite.

At ground level, the hub of Valhalla Springs's indoor activities featured a banquet room, six meeting rooms and commercial-grade kitchen. The basement's swimming pool and workout room gave residents no reason not to get or stay in shape, whatever the season or weather.

A hand-lettered Closed sign was taped to the center's door. Hannah made a mental note to clean her answering machine's heads. They'd need it, poor babies, with all the complaints they'd record, before the center was cleared as a crime scene.

Hannah expected a cross between a Gray Panther rally and a riot. She wasn't disappointed. A platoon of matronly bridge players surrounded Detective Marlin Andrik like magpies pecking at a wounded wren.

Chin bobbing, mouth working and hands raised in an attempt to stem the tide, the craggy-faced detective was as besieged and beleaguered as a Libertarian at a Democratic National Committee luncheon.

"There's Sheriff Hendrickson," Andrik shouted. "He's the ranking officer."

The horde pivoted en masse, shaking fingers and fists like a hair-sprayed, heavily perfumed, human tsunami.

David backpedaled. "Holy Moses."

Wedging a pinkie and thumb at the corners of her lips, Hannah cut loose a piercing whistle, a skill learned in childhood and honed by hailing taxis for twenty-five years.

The stampede halted. Invectives were bitten off mid-syllable. Andrik's jaw dropped as if its bone hinges had snapped.

"If you ladies would please retake your seats," Hannah said, "Detective Andrik and Sheriff Hendrickson will finish their business as quickly as possible."

Nods and murmured assents accompanied the sea of protest's deployment. Andrik crossed the room as metal folding chairs thumped, rattled and squeaked. "How in the devil did you *do* that?"

Hannah licked her lips for an encore.

"Not the whistle." He jerked his head at the tables.

"The sit-down and shut-up part. Those old biddies have been harassing my ass nonstop for a half hour."

David said, "She's something else, isn't she?" as if he had assembled Hannah à la Dr. Frankenstein.

She said, "Before the natives get restless again, Detective, would you mind telling me *where you get off* raiding private property without notifying the manager?"

"Much less the sheriff," David added.

"I did, as soon as I knew I had something. And what did I get in return for my friggin' thoughtfulness? My superior officer yells 'This, by God, had *better* be an emergency' into his handset." Andrik cupped his ear. "Still sounds like the ocean in there. Could be permanent."

Hannah chuckled. A grudging respect had developed between her and the chief of detectives in the course of the recent homicide investigations. She hadn't forgiven him for putting her name at the top of his suspect list or for the interrogation she'd endured, but his surliness had a certain charm.

"Complaint noted and round-filed," David said. "Now, how's about cutting to the chase?"

Andrik shifted his weight. "I got a tip from a lineman who was out here during yesterday's power outage. The pole he was hanging from gave a bird's-eye view of a greenhouse at 2404 Sumac Drive and the healthiest crop of cannabis he'd seen in a coon's age.

"The same guy reported that pot patch in the National Forest last fall, so it was no problem obtaining a search warrant. Since nobody answered the door, I nosed around outside. The informant was dead-on. I rang a couple of chimes until a neighbor told me it was

IdaClare Clancy's residence and she was up here playing bridge.''

Andrik pulled a zip-top bag from his sport-coat pocket. He pinched Exhibit A's dried, dull green leaves. "I guarantee, this ain't oregano, children. Neither is the dope Clancy was doling out like party favors when I bopped in.''

Hannah bit her lip. A few days earlier, IdaClare mentioned the greenhouse she'd had built without her son's knowledge or consent. When Hannah had asked to see it, IdaClare stammered something about exotic plants from Borneo needing unrelieved darkness to bloom.

The evasion had tripped Hannah's internal lie detector, but she'd been preoccupied with figuring out why someone had bludgeoned a retired spinster schoolteacher to death.

Prioritizing. Great strategy, but minor problems had a nasty habit of falling through the cracks. Like the possibility your employer's mother was the Cannabis Queen of Valhalla Springs.

"What's with the uh-oh look?" David asked her. "Did you know about Miz Clancy's secret garden?"

From the moment they'd met—a roadside interlude whereby Hannah was nailed with a five-hundred-and-sixty-dollar fine and court costs for speeding—the sheriff had demonstrated an uncanny knack for reading her mind.

Having lived so independently throughout her forty-three years she should be licensed to print her own currency, his psychic flair had proven to be a real pain in the patoot.

"The greenhouse I was aware of," she said. "What IdaClare was growing in it? Not a clue." Scanning the tables, she added, "Where is our master gardener, anyway?"

Andrik's elbow jutted at a couch and wing chairs grouped in front of a windowed wall at the room's far end. "Over there with your physical fitness instructor. Maybe you can talk some sense into her. When I tried, she waved a bustcard under my nose."

"What's a bustcard?"

David cursed under his breath. "The American Civil Liberties Union distributes wallet cards listing rights and responsibilities for individuals to use when they're stopped by the police."

Hannah frowned. "So? What's wrong with that?"

"Nothing, except they're advertised as a deterrent to police abuse."

Andrik said, "Could be, us law enforcement types are too sensitive, but the ninety-nine-point-nine percent of us who don't make a habit of knocking heads together sort of resent the insinuation we're dirtbags with badges."

"I see…" And she did, although her understanding was tempered by memories of her hometown's chief of police. Vic Brummit had thrown his beer belly around Effindale, Illinois, with impunity. Without a doubt, he'd have responded to an A.C.L.U. bustcard with the fat end of his whomp-ass stick.

She looked at David. "Any objections to me talking to IdaClare?"

He passed the buck to Andrik. "All the formalities dispensed with?"

"Duly Mirandized and etcetera-ed, only I don't think the old girl savvies how much trouble she's in." He

scratched a graying sideburn. "If there ever was such a thing as an open-and-shut case, this is it."

IdaClare was attired, as always, in her one-note color scheme—on this occasion, a pink, light-wool skort-suit and matching shell. Sitting with her purse in her lap like a patient awaiting a distasteful medical procedure, the hand not clutching her pocketbook clasped Willard Johnson's larger, brown one. The physical fitness instructor slumped in the adjacent wing chair as though his bones had been surgically removed.

Willard graced Hannah with a beatific smile. "Hiya."

IdaClare gasped. "Your face—those bruises. I heard about last night, but I had no idea... My stars and garters, child, are you all right?"

"I'm fine," Hannah lied. "What I want to know is what's wrong with Willard?"

"Well, it's his own fault. I told him to help himself to our refreshments, *except* for the brownies on the green tray." IdaClare tossed a disgusted look in Willard's direction. "Why, he must have eaten a dozen before I caught him."

"Better'n my mom bakes by a mile." He giggled. "Man, I gotta get her the recipe."

Hannah massaged a temple to ward off the migraine she was due to have any second. "Don't tell me, let me guess. The brownies on the green tray were spiked with marijuana."

"Just a teensy pinch or two," IdaClare said. "If he hadn't gotten greedy, he'd probably never have noticed." Her thumb caressed Willard's knuckles. "It isn't as if I *poisoned* him or anything."

"But IdaClare..." Hannah's shoulders slumped. She

looked back at the refreshment table. No green tray. Andrik must have confiscated it. Damn. Snorking wacky-snacks might relieve the urge to throw something. Like a tantrum. Or perhaps that lovely candlestick lamp, through the plate-glass window located so handily behind it.

A majority of the detained card players filed out the door, their chins aloft, wattles taut with indignation. Smoke would rise from the development's telephone lines within minutes. Marge Rosenbaum, the president of the Every-Other-Tuesday Bridge Club, and the six ladies still at the tables were pictures of serenity, much like Willard. Imagine that.

Hannah gazed wistfully at David's broad shoulders, his tapered waist, his sculpted jeans-clad butt. Alas, poor Yorrick, I didn't know him well. Or biblically.

Quitting the ad agency had been as impulsive as it had been abrupt. Maybe if she groveled, pled temporary insanity and accepted a pay cut, Tom and Rob Friedlich would hire her back, starting tomorrow.

On the other hand, as her great-uncle Mort Garvey had often said, "It ain't wise to burn your house down just to kill a rat," a homily that made actual sense, as opposed to most of his repertoire. With age had come Hannah's realization that her elder relation's elevator hadn't gone all the way to the top, but Socrates was considered a crackpot in his day, too.

IdaClare clucked her tongue. "I'm truly sorry to cause such a ruckus, dear. I wouldn't blame you if you never spoke to me again."

Hannah knelt beside her chair. "I'm not angry. Well, I'm not as angry as I am worried. Ye gods, IdaClare.

If you're convicted of selling homegrown marijuana—''

"Sell it? I have never charged a plug nickel for my herbs. It wouldn't be Christian to take advantage of people that way."

Willard's fist punched the air. "Right on, soul sister."

Hannah glared at him. "Oh, why don't you take a nap or something?"

He smacked his lips. "B'lieve I will." His eyelids drooped like a pair of cheap window shades. He looked so young. So innocent. So stoned out of his mind. She'd apologize for being snappish when he was lucid enough to comprehend.

"Does Detective Andrik know you don't sell your, uh, herbs?"

"Yes, and he was glad to hear it—not that you could tell by looking at him." IdaClare sniffed. "Have you noticed how his nostrils pinch? I suspect he was colicky as a child and never entirely recovered."

Hannah tried, but couldn't stifle a laugh at the image of Baby Marlin belching on his mother's shoulder.

Misinterpreting Hannah's laughter, IdaClare sat up straighter in her chair. "I know the three of you think I'm a bubble-brained old fool, but I'm not. I knew exactly what I was doing when I started growing my herbs, and I'm not one iota sorry I did. If a judge can't find it in his heart to understand the why of it, he can kiss my keister in the middle of the courthouse square at high noon."

A flush mottled her aged-cherub face. "It's hard getting old, dear. Harder for some than others. Harder on

some days than on others. It's true, Hannah. The spirit's willing, but the body won't obey.

"I won't bore you with an organ recital," she went on, "but if I can ease my friends' ailings with a cookie, a poultice, a cup of tea or a pipe, there's no one short of Almighty God Himself who's going to stop me."

The speech and the passion with which it was delivered defeated any argument Hannah might have launched. "All right, then, do you want to call Jack or would you rather I did?"

IdaClare gnawed at her lipstick. Her expression said she'd rather while away her golden years on Riker's Island than confess her sins to her only child. "What do you think he'll say?"

Hannah had known Jack Clancy for over fifteen years, both as a client and a cherished friend. A gambler by nature, he'd parlayed a commercial construction/excavation company into one of the country's premier resort development firms.

Jack was a shrewd, brilliant, kind, adorable, funny, second-generation Irish teddy bear. With nuclear capabilities.

"He'll say a lot of one-syllable words," Hannah answered. "None Chase Wingate will be able to quote in next week's edition of the *Sanity Examiner*."

"The boy does take after his daddy—God rest him—in that respect." IdaClare patted Hannah's knee. "Maybe it's best if you talked to him first, dear."

Surprise, surprise. At least Jack couldn't kill the messenger from his Saint Louis office. Drive-time would allow a four-hour stay of execution. "What about a lawyer?"

IdaClare waved a dismissal. "There's no sense pay-

ing some twit I don't know from Methuselah's grampa to lock the barn door after the horse has run off.''

Great-uncle Mort would have loved that one.

IdaClare looked at her watch. ''I do wish that detective and your sheriff would quit piddling around. Kathleen Osborn's memorial service is at four and we are *not* going to miss it.''

Before Hannah could refute ownership of the hunky, thirty-six-year-old county mountie, he called her name and crooked a finger. Deliberating what wonderful news he had for her now, Hannah nearly jumped out of her sandals when something *ka-whammed* into the center's front door.

The face attached to a roly-poly, uniformed deputy was squashed against the glass, his nose flattened and mouth distorted into a grotesque sneer. He peeled himself off the obstruction, shook like a wet dog, adjusted his tie, then pulled on the door, in keeping with the large, instructional placard beside the handle.

''What's Moody doing here?'' David asked.

''Making our day,'' Andrik said. ''That's what I get for requesting a patrol unit to help transport our string to the courthouse.''

Hannah watched as the newcomer smiled and fawned over the bridge players like a table-hopping emcee. ''He's one of your deputies?''

''A reserve deputy,'' David corrected. ''Rudy managed to graduate from the academy, but isn't and never will be on the payroll. He's a bad example of a good recruitment program.''

''World's worst example,'' Andrik said. ''I'm gonna get Claudina for this.''

''After I'm through with her.'' David added for Hannah's benefit, "Claudina Burkholtz is our chief dispatcher. Sending Moody out on our calls is her idea of high comedy."

The Schmoo in Blue snapped a salute, then his hand whipped to his service revolver, as though ready for a quick-draw. "I understand we have a 10–15 at this location, sir."

He rolled his shoulders and jeered at Hannah. "Too bad you're learning the hard way, we have zero tolerance for drug activity in this county."

David groaned. "For Christ's sake, Moody. Leave it to you to pick on the only person in this room who isn't involved."

The reservist's eyes wagged between his prime suspect and the sheriff. "You sure about that, sir?"

"Yes, Rudy. This is Hannah Garvey, Valhalla Springs's operations manager."

"Oh—oh my *gosh.*" He pumped Hannah's hand as if expecting water to gush out. "I'm awful sorry, Ms. Garvey—and about your face, too."

Poor guy. Bruises fade, but dumb is usually permanent.

"That's all right, Officer Moody. You had no way of knowing who I am."

His off-the-hook smile deflated into a scowl. "Except if she isn't...I mean...well, sir, who is the 10–15?" He nodded toward Willard Johnson. "Him?"

A buzzer-like noise sounded in Andrik's throat. "Wrong again. At this rate, you don't have a prayer of making it to the lightning round."

David gave the detective a "back-off" look. "You're familiar with medicinal marijuana, aren't you, Rudy?"

"Oh, sure. Groups all over the place are trying to legalize it for folks with cancer and AIDS and such."

"Well, I'm afraid the lady in pink over yonder and those at the tables jumped the gun a trifle."

Rudy's expression resembled that of a goldfish who'd leaped from its bowl without fully considering the ramifications. "But sir, they're older than my mama."

"Don't let those sweet-ol'-lady faces fool you," Andrik warned. "They're vicious. Every last one of 'em."

David clasped Hannah's arm. "While you two sort out the logistics, I'll take Hannah back to her cottage."

"Oh no you won't," she said.

"Oh yes I will." He steered her to the door. "You're pale as a ghost and there's nothing you can do at the courthouse anyway."

"I can lend moral support."

"Nope."

"Fine." She shrugged. "I'll drive myself into Sanity."

The eyes probing hers were more gray than blue. Not a good omen. "Why? Just to show me and everybody else how tough you are?"

"No."

"Bull."

Yes, it was, but he didn't need to be rude about it.

"Okay, I'm lousy at doing what's best for me, especially when someone tells me what's best for me."

"Is that a fact?" David pulled the door open for her.

Hannah looked back. "What about Willard? He isn't under arrest, is he?"

"Uh-uh. Being slipped a marijuana mickey isn't illegal. I'm working on the assumption he didn't know the brownies were spiked.''

"Well, I can't just leave him here and he's in no shape to drive."

"I'll get his keys and lock up the building," David said. "Then one of us can drop him off at home on the way to the courthouse."

"What about his car?" Hannah indicated a white compact in a shady corner of the lot.

"Call Willard this evening after he's had time to come back to earth. Between the two of you, you'll figure something out."

"You have an answer for everything, don't you, Hendrickson?"

"Sugar, like my daddy always says, I don't even know most of the questions yet."

Sugar. Gloria Steinem would probably call the word demeaning, but Gloria Steinem had never heard David say it in that low, slow drawl.

During the short ride, as much as Hannah hated to admit it, she began to feel borderline wretched.

"Are you okay?" David asked, his tone concerned.

"I will be, as soon as I have a bologna, mustard and potato-chip sandwich and a nap."

Having seen the reaction before, Hannah knew his curdled expression didn't pertain to the nap. Besides chocolate, everyone had a personal comfort food. As the only child of an unwed, alcoholic mother, Hannah never had the luxury of being a picky eater.

Then again, rich people missed out on trailer-trash delicacies such as her favorite sandwich, or refried-bean dip and Cheez Whiz on crackers, toasted at 350 degrees until gooey and golden.

The check-and-balance system. It's what made America great.

The index finger curled around the cruiser's steering wheel pointed out the windshield. "Your nap may have to wait a while."

Bob Davies, the development's Maintenance Department supervisor and an equally blond, burly assistant were repairing the damage wrought on her cottage's front door the previous night. She couldn't hear their hammers, but felt them pound, like the anvil chorus in vintage Anacin commercials.

David turned into the circle drive, shifted into park and laid his arm across the seat back. "I wish I could stay, but I can't."

"I know." She groped for the door handle.

"Remember me telling you about my buddy in Tulsa?"

She nodded. Mike Rivera, David's best friend since they trained together at the police academy, was recovering from a gunshot wound received during a convenience-store holdup.

David said, "Well, soon as IdaClare and her girl-gang are booked and post bond, I'm heading for Oklahoma to see him." His forehead corduroyed. "I don't know how long I'll be gone. Could be two, maybe three days."

A soldier shipping out to parts unknown and maybe fatal wouldn't have looked more solemn. Hannah clasped her hands to her bosom. "I'll count the hours till your return."

He threw back his head and laughed. "You do beat all I've ever seen, woman." Leaning closer, he glanced at the workmen. "Mind if I kiss you goodbye in front of witnesses?"

Past—albeit limited—experience had proven the man kissed finer than a fantasy lover. Thorough. Paralyzing. *Dangerous.* Hannah edged away. "I'm not keen on public displays of affection."

David studied her a moment. "Second thoughts, huh?"

"Some." Rough estimate, forty-two thousand since their lovemaking had been interrupted that morning.

His lazy grin banished thoughts of emergency liposuction, chemical peels and breast implants, replacing them with images of how godlike he'd look naked. How much she wanted to see him naked. Whether the Crown Vic's back seat was as spacious as it appeared.

"Will you promise me something, then?" he asked.

Anything. Everything. "Depends on what it is."

"Dinner at my house the night I get home. The one we've already had to postpone twice."

Better judgment and forty-two thousand second thoughts voted no. "Okay."

"Promise?"

She shivered. Subzero air-conditioning always had that effect on her. "Promise."

2

He spotted her the instant she stepped through the pneumatic doors. Blonde. Blue eyes. Five-ten. Slender. Self-assured.

Pregnant?

He scooted down on the bench and tented Friday's *Tulsa World* in front of him. The smell of soy-ink melded with the inside-of-a-multivitamin-bottle odor peculiar to hospitals.

Leather-soled high heels tapped against the tile, the cadence brisk and firm, a universal Morse code slackers heard as "Gangway, or get run over."

The sound grew louder. Slowed. Stopped. "David?"

Lowering the newspaper barricade, he said, "Cynthia? How did you know it was me?"

"We were married for almost ten years, remember? I could pick you out of the crowd at Chapman Music Hall."

David stared up at her, an uncustomed position for a man of his height. He didn't like it. "If you're here to visit Mike, they're getting ready to dismiss him."

Dodging a hospitality cart and the trollish woman pushing it, Cynthia hesitated, then sat down beside him. "So soon?"

"Five days is longer than I'd have bet they'd keep him without chaining him to the bed rails."

His gaze slid from the marquise-cut diamond on her ring finger to the bulge at her waist. Once upon a time, Cynthia told him big solitaires looked fake even if they were real and she didn't want children. "Congratulations."

Following his eyes, she said, "Oh," then smiled and patted her belly. "Thank you. Brandon Archibald Montgomery the Third, if the tests are accurate."

The kid better latch on to a nickname before he started school or learn how to fight.

Silence stretched between them, intensified by public-address-system pages, snippets of passing conversations and foot traffic. Coral-polished toenails at the tip of Cynthia's shoe flashed in and out of David's peripheral vision.

Down the corridor, an elevator bell dinged a farewell to its occupants and an all-aboard to passengers scuttling up to the doors.

Go on, Cynthia. Go upstairs and ruin Mike's day. He's on morphine. I haven't even had a cup of coffee yet.

"Your parents," she blurted. "How are they?"

Christ. "On the way to Toronto, last I heard. They bought a condo in Florida, but spend most of their time wandering around in their motorhome." He paused before the obligatory, "Yours?"

Cynthia wriggled backward on the cushion. "Oh, you know Mother. Still running from one club or charitable foundation meeting to the next." A frown deepened lines a weekly facial and twenty-dollar-an-ounce moisturizer couldn't stave off forever. "Daddy had a quadruple bypass a few months ago. He tires more easily, but other than that, you'd never know he was so ill."

"Glad he's all right." David's fingernail traced the seam of his jeans. Tiny stitches, straight as a die. Must be torture bending over a sewing machine to keep a roof over your head.

"So," she said, "you're staying with Mike until he's back on his feet?"

"Just acting as the delivery boy today. A home-health nurse will visit twice a day for a while. Change the bandages. Help him shave and shower." Pushing the bounds of small talk, he said, "The divorce is off, you know."

"Postponed is not the same as off, David. Under the circumstances, what else could Vanessa do besides agree to try one last time?"

She tossed her head. A blond wisp escaped her chignon.

"God, she could do *so* much better for herself."

"Than Mike? Or a cop?"

"Both."

"Like you did." The words slipped out before David could stop them. For a moment he wasn't sure he'd said them aloud. Cynthia's face, as rigid as porcelain, assured him he had.

"*Exactly* like I did." Her left hand, fingers splayed, reached ever-so slowly to tuck the stray hair behind her ear. The headlamp diamond winked "Fuck you, David" in sundry rainbow hues.

He expected anger, the return of that punched-in-the-balls-and-split-up-the-middle feeling he'd had when Cynthia left him. Instead, a grin jumped up, spread, and

he laughed. Not at her, but…well, okay, it *was* at her.
After all the misery they'd inflicted on each other, he
could finally laugh at the daggers shooting from those
beautiful cornflower eyes, instead of duck, run or just
stand and bleed.

Her lips parted, quivering with fury or the effort to
suppress her own laughter. "You are *such* a bastard."

"I believe my folks'd take exception to that remark,
Miz Montgomery."

"You haven't changed a bit."

"Nope. Neither have you."

Right on cue, she delivered the final line of a dog-
eared script. "How in God's name we *ever* thought we
were in love with each other, I'll never know."

David had asked himself the same question a thousand times—as recently as last week, in fact, when her
telephone call about Mike's injury set off the usual
pissing contest. The answer was always the same.

"Because we *were* in love, Cynthia. Stone-deaf, hog-
tied and blind-staggered."

The temptation to add *until you started sleeping with
your second husband a couple of years before you
bothered to divorce me* was like looking skyward when
thunder rumbled in the distance. Nothing more than a
reflex.

She turned her head away, took a deep breath and
exhaled. "Yes," she conceded, "we were, weren't we?
Fresh out of college and ready to save the world."

Best David could recall, it was closer to her wanting
to decorate it while he played cops and robbers, but if
that's how she chose to remember it, fine. It had been
many a year since he'd seen her smile all the way to
her eyes.

"Are you, er, dating anyone?" she asked.

"Yeah." Case closed. Smile or no smile, Hannah Garvey was a subject he wasn't about to discuss with his ex-wife.

"Well. As long as I'm here, I guess I'll go up and wish Mike a speedy recovery." She stood, smoothed the wrinkles from her dress and tucked her purse under her arm. "It was nice seeing you again, David."

"You too, Cynthia."

And it was, he realized as he watched her walk away. He had loved her, a part of him always would and it didn't hurt to admit it. Tossing the newspaper in the seat she'd vacated, he crossed his arms at his chest. No, it *didn't* hurt to admit it at all.

After another two hours on that devil-take-it lobby bench, what did hurt was his hind-end. He told those who plopped down beside him that his name should be stenciled on the cushion, like a director's chair in movies about making movies.

Hospital visitors were a tough crowd to pry a laugh from, until a little girl with brown eyes and auburn pigtails sat down to wait, while her mommy "got stuck with needles 'cause she's got heema-goblins."

Katy gave David a loop-handled sucker and told a slew of knock-knock jokes, fracturing the punch lines with motorboat giggles. David caught himself thinking how much Hannah must have looked like her when she was a kid and how much he missed the grown-up model.

Not that he'd ever tell Hannah he'd met her five-year-old alter ego. She'd tease him about taking candy from babies, then remind him she'd been in the second grade when he was born.

The way David figured it, since a woman's average life expectancy was eight years longer than a man's, the two of them were pretty much even-steven. All he had to do was sell Hannah on the idea.

"Puh-leeez releeze me, lemme go..." funneled down the corridor in an off-key tenor David wished he didn't recognize.

"I don' wanna be here anymo-r-e..."

Pedestrians laughed and cleared a path for a nurse pushing a wheelchair occupied by the tone-deaf, Hispanic Engelbert Humperdinck. Behind her an auxiliary volunteer guided a cart laden with flowers, cards and the plastic claptrap that health-care facilities bestow on survivors.

"Mr. Rivera," the nurse said. "This is a hospital, not a cocktail lounge."

Before she rerouted her patient to the psychiatric ward where he belonged, David intervened. "I'll be glad to take him off your hands, ma'am."

"Oh no you don't," Mike said. "She's gotta give me curb service." He craned his neck. "Isn't that right, angel?"

The nurse minced, "If you haven't brought your car around yet, Mr. Hendrickson, now would be an excellent time."

"It's ready and waiting, ma'am."

The woman wouldn't have looked happier if David had offered her the title, keys and twenty bucks for gas.

Loading a weak, wounded, five-foot-ten-inch, hundred-and-eighty-pound man with his left arm bound to his chest into the cab of a pickup was akin to loading a handcuffed, shit-faced Bubba into a patrol unit, except drunks don't gnash their teeth and go white around the mouth.

Garth Brooks's *Double Live* cassette sufficed as conversation as David battled midday traffic. It reminded him—as if he needed it—why he'd given up on calling a city the size of Tulsa home. He'd grown up on the northwestern edge of Missouri, but Kinderhook County smelled, looked and felt like the land he hadn't appreciated until he'd left it.

Unlearning his academy training and relearning four hundred and seventy hours' worth of Missouri's brand of law enforcement was tougher than David had anticipated. Nor had he expected Sheriff Larry Beauford to hire him as chief deputy, or within six months be appointed sheriff when Beauford suffered a stroke.

Change. The only constant in life, but it didn't always sit well with folks. David wished he had a dollar for every sentence that had begun with, "Now, son, when Larry was sheriff…"

Before the same could ever be said of David, he had to win the August primary and November's general election to secure a full four-year term. Doubt and dread hummed in his bones. A politician, he wasn't. Beauford had campaigned every day of his fifteen-year tenure and loved it the way P.T. Barnum loved gate receipts.

He'd chosen David to replace his retiring chief deputy to stifle criticism. The sheriff's department's upper echelon was considered a good old boys' club, rife with patronage and nepotism. To be fair, small counties thrived on both by virtue of their size. Shake a family tree and cousins drop from the branches like walnuts in October.

Lacking any family ties to Kinderhook County, David had to win the election on merit or be immortalized as the first technical incumbent to lose.

Garth Brooks howled the previously censored last chorus to "I've Got Friends In Low Places" as David turned into the Cherokee Ridge apartment complex's lot. A breezeway verged by railed wooden stairways divided each two-story, eight-unit building. The abandoned Big Wheels, bicycles and toys cluttering the walkways were a docketful of personal-injury lawsuits waiting to happen.

David looked from the steps to his groggy passenger. "You didn't tell the doc you lived on the second floor, did you?"

"He didn't ask."

"You'd have lied if he had."

"Damn right I would've."

David whistled. "Getting you up there is gonna be a bitch."

Mike angled his head. "You're never going to learn to think positive, are you, Hendrickson?"

"Okay. Getting you up there is *positively* gonna be a bitch."

They mounted the stairs like sailors on shore leave. David wrapped an arm around Mike's waist; Mike's free hand clamped David's belt as much to channel pain as for support.

Mike shuffled into the apartment, then halted on the foyer's wedge of linoleum. "What the…where's my… Sainted Mother of Jesus, you destroyed the place!"

David drawled, "Flat outdid myself, didn't I?" He motioned as if showing it to a prospective tenant. "Five trash bags full of crap and corruption to the Dumpster, four loads of clothes washed, folded and put away, clean sheets on the bed and a spit-shined bathroom.''

Mike snarled at a basket centered on the dinette table.

"What the hell is that?"

"It's called fresh fruit." David opened the refrigerator and freezer doors, displaying their well-stocked interiors. "Here's some more stuff you might not recognize, aka real food." The doors snicked shut. "Man cannot live by beer and What-A-Burgers alone, Rivera."

Muttering bilingual curses, Mike tottered to a recliner with stuffing leaking from the seams, salvaged from the garage when he and his wife separated. "Get me drugs or my service revolver. I don't give a rat's ass which."

After David made two trips to the pickup, the kitchen sink was abloom with flowers. Balloons moored to the utility closet's doorknob swayed like belly dancers. Mike hadn't moved a muscle.

David took a can of diet soda from the fridge, filled a glass with ice and water, then fished two pharmacy sacks from Mike's duffel bag. Setting the glass on the lamp table, he tossed the prescriptions in the patient's lap. "Hope one of those is a chill-pill."

Mike gave him a glare renowned for stopping fleeing felons in their tracks. His eyes averted to an outlet where the lamp cord was plugged into a small plastic box. "That's an air freshener, isn't it?"

"The place smelled like a jockstrap recycling center when I got here," David said. "I didn't want Vanessa to hurl when she brought your supper tonight."

"Hey, no problem-o with *me* chokin' on that pine-

tree shit. Suck down enough of it and I might quit the
T.P.D. and join the friggin' Forest Service.''

Mike's personality could use a tune-up, but his color
had improved. Nothing like cussedness to put the roses
in a man's cheeks.

Paper ripped. Mike shook out a tablet and washed it
down. ''I figure it's fifty-fifty whether Vanessa shows
or not, anyway.'' The glass smacked the tabletop. ''Not
sure I want her to.''

David sat down on the couch, cracked the tab on his
soda and took a long pull. One of the doctors had mentioned post-trauma depression. A wounded cop with
marital problems was a prime candidate.

Not to discount the internist's professional opinion,
but David had known Mike Rivera for nearly fifteen
years and was best man at his wedding. They'd covered
each other's backs on Tulsa's crime-rich north side for
over a decade.

He could be wrong, but instinct said Mike suspected
Vanessa withdrawing the divorce petition was a stall,
not a genuine desire for reconciliation. If Cynthia had
hinted as much when she'd visited Mike...

Nah. His ex-wife ranked cops a notch above serial
killers as husband material, but she wouldn't kick Mike
when he was down. She'd wait until he was on his feet,
then saw him off at the knees.

David set his drink on the floor. ''When I heard you
and Vanessa had separated, I didn't believe it. I still
don't.''

''Think I moved here for the scenery, huh?''

''Physically, you're apart. Emotionally?'' David
shook his head. ''Vanessa didn't take Joel and Jacob
to her mom's and practically live at the hospital out of

pity, or duty, or because there'd be talk if she didn't. She loves you, you jerk."

"My wife loves the man she married. According to her, that ain't me."

"Vanessa isn't the gal you married, either."

"Took the words right out of my mouth, amigo, except I said 'em to her. *Big* mistake."

"I know."

"What do you mean, *you know?*"

David leaned back. "Same way I know she's cooking up her chicken cacciatore, garlic bread and an apple cobbler to bring over here in, um—" he checked his watch "—'bout four hours, give or take."

Mike made a "keep talking" gesture.

"Last night, me and your bride had a heart-to-heart in the coffee shop. I'm not about to say something stupid like getting shot was a blessing, but I reckon it gave you both a kick in the complaint department."

"I don't know about her," Mike said, "but it did me. Vanessa and my boys are why I'm not six feet under counting off a twenty-one-gun salute."

"Then I'll tell you the same as I told her when we got to the 'he's changed, she's changed' shinola. Y'all can't hold up how things used to be as a standard to meet. What you think you remember is nine-tenths bullshit starring Meg Ryan and Tom Hanks. Besides, a never-ending honeymoon would get boring as hell."

Mike laughed, then clutched at the sling binding his chest. "No way, no how. Ours was incredible."

"Oh? Seems I recollect something about you upchucking the entire flight to Acapulco, relay races to the toilet when you both got Montezuma's revenge and one of you breaking out in hives."

Mike's eyebrows veed above the bridge of his nose.

"Trust me, Rivera. If somebody'd videotaped your honeymoon, you could sell it to a funniest-video show for ten grand."

"So, maybe I forgot some details. What's your point? You usually have one, but take longer to get there than anyone I've ever known."

Hannah had mentioned David's roundaboutness a time or six as well. Wouldn't hurt either of them to learn a little patience. "Forget this 'start over' routine. Take the ball you have and figure out how to run with it, instead of whining about what you had and trying to get it back. It won't work."

"Been there?"

David looked him straight in the eye. "You ought to know. So should Vanessa."

Mike's expression went from skeptical to pensive to amused. "You told Vanessa all that?"

"Yep."

"What'd she say?"

"That I'm a big, stupid, *divorced* sheriff who hasn't dated the same woman twice in years, and not a goddamn marriage counselor."

Mike chuckled. "Then she said, 'Go screw yourself sideways' and stormed out of the coffee shop."

"Dang-near knocked the door off its hinges." David ran the tip of his tongue over his teeth. "Then she called first thing this morning, told me tonight's menu and hinted that three would be a crowd."

"She did?"

"But...since you and her can't seem to talk to *each other,* I'll hang around a few more days, seeing as how I have this mediator thing down pat."

"Uh-huh. Sure." Mike reached for the cordless phone on the table and punched a button with his thumb.

"What are you doing?"

"Rule number one, basic patrol procedure. Never draw your weapon unless you're prepared to—" Mike grinned up at the ceiling. "Ms. Garvey? Hey, Mike Rivera, down in Tulsa. Yeah, yeah, I'm doin' great, thanks. Listen, the reason I called was to ask what time our mutual friend is picking you up for dinner tonight. Uh-huh. Seven, seven-thirty sounds—"

Mutual Friend snatched the phone and clapped it to his ear. A robotic voice informed *The number you have dialed is not a working number....* David hauled back the handset as if to throw a third-and-long. "Cute, Rivera. Real cute."

"C'mon, admit it." A toed-off tennis shoe hit the floor. "I had you going for a minute."

David returned the phone to its charger. "Ten seconds, max, before I remembered I've been using my calling card and you can't hit redial and repeat the entire sequence."

The right sneaker thumped a yard from its mate. Mike flexed his socked feet and sighed, his shoulders slumping into a Naugahyde embrace. Hope and painkillers were a powerful combination.

"You want me to hit the road, don't you?" David said.

Mike blinked up at him. "What makes you say that?"

"'Cause I'd want to be alone if I'd been cut on, sewed up, poked, jabbed and visited by everybody and their uncle Bob for five solid days."

"10–4, all frequencies," Mike said. "You've got more faults than California, but there's nobody else I could send packing without them taking it personally."

"Same here, except it doesn't mean I'm comfortable leaving you here by your lonesome."

"No, but—" Mike stuck out his hand "—you're going to."

David clasped it, a tightness constricting his chest. He hated goodbyes. The weight of things unsaid that should be, the platitudes that rattled out instead. "Take care of yourself, you hear?"

"You, too."

David laid the apartment's spare key on top of the television. "Fair warning, I'll put your Latino ass in I.C.U. for a month if you and Vanessa don't get back together."

"Soon as we are, you have to bring Hannah down here so we can check her out." Mike grinned. "And so Vanessa can report the findings to Cynthia."

David rolled his eyes. "Like I told you, between Hannah's job and mine, we haven't even had an honest-to-God first date yet."

A wadded pharmacy sack sailed across the room. "*No hablas Inglés?* Think *positive,* man. Tonight's the night."

3

Hannah glared at the clothes piled on the foot of the sleigh bed, then at the walk-in closet. She yanked on the belt to her tatty chenille robe, the womanly equivalent of a toddler's security blanket.

Life after high school is still high school. As it was in the beginning, it is now and ever shall be. Puberty without end. Amen.

All she wanted was to look good. Something between Bidda-boom, Bidda-bah—only in her dreams—and Nearly Menopausal Frump.

Slacks, silk blouse and jacket? Too dressy. Sweatshirt and jeans? Too casual, not to mention sloppy. Oxford shirt, slacks and sweater tied at her neck?

Right. Next thing, she'd whip up a batch of potpourri, build a barbecue pit, then go shear a sheep.

T-shirt, designer overalls, jean jacket? As if Caroline Garvey were beside her, Hannah heard her mother say, "You're having dinner with a man, not fixin' to plow the back forty behind a mule."

Hannah raked the shower-damp hair from her face. Valhalla Springs's former operations manager, Owen McCutcheon, heard voices in his head, too, but his were of the extraterrestrial persuasion. Hers belonged to fam-

ily members, all surnamed Garvey, who were only ru-
mored to have beamed down from another planet.

Had she agonized the what-to-wear question when
she and Jarrod Amberley were together? Not that she
could recall. It seemed significant in a depressingly
hindsighted way.

Jarrod, a European antiques dealer based in London,
had breezed into and out of her life for a decade—a
charming, witty Captain Bligh who docked between
ports of call for a pint, a few turns at the trough and
to get his barnacles off.

Transatlantic love affairs were cutting-edge chic, and
absence had made Hannah's heart fonder when she
wasn't hating him for never being there when she
needed a laugh or a shoulder to cry on. Someone to
share a pot of coffee and the Sunday *Tribune* with. A
sunrise walk along the lake. An orgasm on a Tuesday
in a month not ending in Y.

When they did occupy the same continent, Hannah
wanted to rock Jarrod's world, not the boat, which explained why it took so long to see him for what he truly
was: an arrogant, two-timing, psuedosophisticated dick-
head.

"Care to hazard a guess *why* you didn't wonder what
to wear back then?" She shook a gabardine blazer by
its padded shoulders. "Because you never bought anything you weren't sure he'd like."

Hangers *skreed* across the metal closet-rod. "You
haven't seen Jarrod the Jerk-off in three years." Hannah's lip curled. "Ancient history." A ribbed tunic was
considered and rejected. "Not the kind that bears repeating." She tugged a cotton-knit, V-necked top off a
hanger. "Ever."

A far corner of the closet yielded a pair of jeans she wore sparingly. Even she knew they didn't make her butt look big. Only God knew if or when she'd find another pair like them.

Hannah added an off-white satin demi-bra and matching bikinis to the pile draped over her arm. "Look, Ma," she said to a framed snapshot of a woman with sad eyes and long, coppery hair, "I'm finally learning how to dress myself."

When she emerged from the bathroom, the woods beyond the oak-slatted double windows were steeped in twilight. Shadows grayed the bedroom's cream walls, carpet and pillow shams. Head resting against the door, Hannah sighed and clasped her hands in front of her.

IdaClare would accuse her of being "house proud." Hannah supposed she was, though all she'd done was accept Jack Clancy's job offer, sell almost everything she owned, buy a used four-wheel drive vehicle and watch Chicago's skyline shrink in its side mirrors.

Weeks before she resigned from Friedlich & Friedlich, Jack had contacted Owen McCutcheon's brother and two sisters and offered to buy Owen's furniture and housegoods to help defray the cost of his psychiatric care—treatment his siblings denied he needed until he suffered a complete breakdown.

Knowing Jack, he'd paid triple what the cottage's contents were worth. Hannah also discovered while slogging through her first attempt at payroll clerk that McCutcheon received a five-hundred-dollar monthly stipend as a "managerial consultant."

Generous Jack Clancy. He hadn't yelled when she'd called him about IdaClare's homegrown pharmacy. Just made strangling sounds, then told Hannah she'd better not ever again bitch about being an orphan.

She refused to dwell on or analyze why a fifty-two-year-old bachelor's decor suited her to the ground, particularly since she hadn't been aware she'd harbored any desire for mission oak interspersed with the living room's oxblood-leather seating group, brass-fitted ceiling fans, ceiling beams or fieldstone fireplace.

Whenever the spirit had moved her, Hannah had spent tens of thousands of dollars remodeling and refurnishing her Chicago apartment, but had never achieved the sense of homecoming she'd felt that Sunday afternoon when she first crossed the cottage's threshold.

"House proud?" She eyed the powdery golden pollen dulling the dresser top, the Ozarks' inescapable harbinger of spring. Smiling, she hoisted herself away from the doorjamb. "Damn right I am."

The mirror above the bathroom's vanity had given head-to-crotch approval of her outfit. The cheval's full-length, three-hundred-and-sixty-degree review would be the acid test.

Ivory sweater and herringbone gold chain? The feminine touch. British-tan leather jacket, miracle jeans, woven belt and blunt-toed boots? Snazzy, if Hannah didn't say so herself. Sort of Cheryl Tiegs does the Australian outback without the California-girl overtones or wild dingoes circling in the background.

Sliding her hands into her back pockets, she tipped back on her heels. "So, Ms. Crockashit Dundee, now that you've gotten your act together, why are you going out with David Hendrickson? He's only two days older than he was two days ago and you haven't done a Dorian Gray while he was gone."

Good question, that. After all, just yesterday she'd sworn on a stack of Valhalla Springs's promotional brochures that friendship must be the extent of their involvement.

But hey. Friends are known to scarf down a meal together, aren't they? No big deal, no strings, no complications.

Her inner Jiminy Cricket warned *Get real. After the other morning's interrupted touchy-feely, ooh-baby-ooh session, David must assume you're going to his house for the sizzle, not just the steak.*

"Well, then," she told her reflection, "I'll just have to make it perfectly clear—"

The front-door chime bing-bonged. She sucked in a breath, coughed, then grabbed her shoulder bag.

Her not-really-a-date stood on the porch, black Stetson in hand, a boot propping the screen and grinning like a shy boy on prom night. "Sorry I'm a little late, but—"

"I am *not* going to bed with you, David. Tonight, or any other night."

He favored his left ear, as if what he'd heard and what she'd said couldn't possibly be the same.

Hannah fidgeted, heat scalding her cheeks. "I mean it."

He grunted, his expression one part sober and two parts pissed. "Oh, you do, huh?"

"Yes. I most certainly do."

"Well, in that case..." David settled the Stetson on his head and tapped the brim. "I expect I'll see ya around, Miz Garvey."

Her jaw dropped when he started toward the steps. "What?" The screen door banged shut an inch from her nose. "Of all the…you're just going to *leave?*"

"Yep." His boots thudded on the planks. Pausing, he shot an angry glare over his shoulder. "I told you a while back I wasn't out to get myself laid. Told you before *that* I'd never lie to you."

His eyes resembled molten lead. "Guess I might as well have been whistling in the wind."

Hannah stared at his denim-clad back. Her mouth worked, formed words, but no sound. "You…I…" She stamped a foot. "Will you wait a minute?"

David put another stride between them, then swiveled half around. "Why should I?"

Hinges yipped. The screen door rat-tatted behind her. She curled an arm around the porch post, the fragrant hewn cedar stout enough to hold up the roof and the foolish, tactless woman under it. "So I can apologize for confusing you with someone else."

She wished his face wasn't veiled in shadows cast by his hat brim, yet was glad it was. "The truth is, I've trusted you since the first—well, the second time we met. For me, that's the worst kind of bad karma. I don't trust 'trust.'"

A corner of David's mouth puckered. "Scary."

"What is?"

"That convoluted mess of an explanation making sense." He tipped back his head. "Mind my asking who you're confusing me with?"

Names tramped through her mind to the beat of Janis Joplin wailing "Piece of My Heart." Jarrod, of course. Cody Wyrick, the urban cowboy who was neither. Before that, Dirk…uh, Dirk What's-his-name, the wanna-be hippie with the sitar, then—

Damp air filled Hannah's lungs. "How about we forgo the specifics and leave it at the majority of the adult male population?"

David studied her, thumbs hooked in his pockets, fingers playing riffs on the fabric. "That's a lot of confusion for one man to overcome, Hannah."

She looked away. Misery stabbed, then twisted her heart at the nicest, most gentle brush-off she'd ever received.

Leather soles scraped the flagstone walk, closing the distance between them. "But, I reckon if we take things slow and easy…"

His baritone softened and dropped an octave. "Which ain't gonna *be* easy, since I want to make love to you in the worst way…but there's a lot to be said for keeping the nookie monster in his cage until the time's right to cut him loose."

Blinking, trying to digest another of his trademark soliloquies, a chuckle gurgled up Hannah's throat and burst into laughter. Through a sheen of tears she saw him standing there, tall as a tree, scowling at her like a…a…

Nookie monster. A second wave hit. She doubled over, snorting, gasping for air, knees chafing, threatening collapse. "Hendrickson, you're…you're—"

"Wastin' my gol-danged breath?" he suggested, a snide edge to his tone. "Crazy for being honest with you?"

"On," she stammered. "You're on."

"Huh?"

Stepping down on the first riser, equalizing her five

foot seven to his six foot three, her arms draped his shoulders, encircling his neck. "Where I come from, 'You're on' means *okay*, Sheriff. You win, heaven help us both. We'll take things slow and easy."

"Real slow."

"Whatever." Hannah moistened her lips and leaned forward to kiss him.

David clasped her upper arms and eased her back. "Nah-ah-ah. We'll have none of that on a first date, young lady. 'Specially before it's even started."

All right, buster. Just because only one of us is dying of embarrassment, two can play the game. She tossed her head and sniffed. "Well, since we're establishing ground rules, I don't think dinner at your house is appropriate for a first date."

"Nope, it isn't. That's why I'm taking you to Bubba Lou's. His steaks are a poor second to mine, but most anybody's are."

"Bubba Lou's?" Hannah envisioned a kettle-bellied cook with *Mom* tattooed on a bicep, champing on a stogie. Flypaper hula-dancing in ceiling corners. Long-necked Budweisers sweating on tables with penknifed graffiti and cigarette burns. Elvis, Hank Williams Sr. and Patsy Cline on the jukebox.

"It isn't fancy," David said, confirming her suspicions, "but you won't leave hungry."

In the Ozarks, the recommendation was equivalent to, if not rungs above, a Michelin five-star rating. Restaurants with belt-busting reputations didn't include fat grams, sodium, calories, "high-fiber" or "heart-smart" references on their menus. Hannah's mouth watered at the prospect.

Earlier, she'd been too distracted by romantic angst to notice David was driving his county car, not his chrome and candy-apple-red Dodge Ram.

"My pickup tried to overheat about midway between Tulsa and home," he explained as they whisked through Valhalla Springs's brick-and-wrought-iron gates. "I dropped my patrol unit at the dealership for maintenance on my way out of town and wound up having to leave my truck there when I got back."

Muted, intermittent voices sputtered from the police radio. Hannah scrutinized the console's array of colored buttons, electronic displays and backlit knobs. What had been an intriguing assortment by daylight was mesmerizing at night.

She couldn't imagine how a cop could simultaneously flip switches, adjust controls, handle two-way radio transmissions and drive.

Knowing the limits of her own eye-hand coordination, Hannah was perhaps the only person in America whose vehicle—and person—had never been mobile phone booths. It was a privacy issue. She liked hers.

"Do you?" she asked.

"Do I what?"

"Have a cell phone?"

"I will in a day or so. The county commissioners can't find the money to replace three patrol cars with a couple of hundred thousand miles on 'em, but gadgets? There's always cash in the kitty for toys."

The dashboard lights revealed a hint of cop-face tightening his features. "Don't get me started on shoptalk. I don't know when to quit."

"At risk of sounding like a ten-year-old, I think this law enforcement stuff is fascinating."

"You do?" David snickered, a throaty growl rife with lechery. "Aw, now, you just want to play with my siren."

"Can I?" The shoulder harness pulled taut as Hannah's fingertip hovered over the controls. "Which button is it? The square red one?"

"Quit it, knucklehead." David swatted her hand away.

"I can't let you kick up the siren for the fun of it."

"Do you expect me to believe you don't, when you're stuck in traffic or something?"

"No." His hand closed over hers—whether defensively or merely to hold, Hannah wasn't sure. "But I'm the sheriff. You aren't."

"Spoilspo—"

His hand jerked away. He plied a knob and grabbed the microphone in one blurry motion. "Adam–101. What's up, Tony?"

Hannah looked from the radio to David. She hadn't heard anything but static and garble. The man must have satellite dishes for ears.

Citizen's complaint. Possible 10–97 at 5406 Skyline Drive. White male, late thirties, light-colored shirt, blue or black trousers. Refused to pay for a pizza delivery. The driver says the individual had a gun and ordered him off the property.

The Crown Vic accelerated with a rumbling surge of horsepower. David said, "Nobody else, 10–8?"

No other units available, Sheriff. Sorry.

"Not necessary," David said. "It was a dumb question to begin with."

FYI, the manager at Mama Leoni's thinks his driver is mistaken about the weapon. They've delivered to that address before without incident. Resident's name, Quince. The driver is a new hire and he's out thirty bucks on the deal. Clear.

David peered out the windshield. "My 10–20 is approximately four miles north of Sanity on VV."

10–4. Will send first available for backup. Clear.

"Adam–101, clear." The microphone snicked into its holder.

A childish voice nattered in Hannah's mind, "What's a 10–97? Where's Skyline Drive? Are we almost there yet?"

David reached for the console, paused, then pointed. "Okay, Cadet Garvey, flip that toggle and turn the knob right of it."

Red, white and blue light splashed the pavement. The siren ascended its five-note octave, not as loud inside the cruiser as Hannah assumed it would be.

The sports car ahead of them and an oncoming van braked and pulled over on opposing shoulders, like the Red Sea parting for Moses.

"Our date just turned into a ride-along," David said.

"I was afraid that might happen. One of my deputies got banged up at softball practice last night and another caught chicken pox from his daughter."

"A ride-along?" City lights haloed the horizon. "Does that mean I can go with you?"

No answer. Hannah's pulse stepped up to the clack of the lightbar's revolutions. Should she keep still and hope he forgot she was there? Or beg to be Hutch to his Starsky?

"Maybe I'd better drop you off at Bubba Lou's," David said. "You can hold us a table while I have a talk with the pizza bandito."

"Oh, c'mon, let me go with you. I promise I'll stay in the car." Her mouth clapped shut before she tacked on, "Pretty please?"

David's eyebrows pinched above his aquiline nose. The Crown Vic zigzagged around traffic halted along First Street, Sanity's aptly named main drag and only three-lane thoroughfare. Hannah knew this was no joyride, but it didn't lessen her excitement.

The sense of power thrilled her. With the flick of a button, a law enforcement officer snapped the rest of the world to attention. Made it stand still, if only for a few seconds. Transcended speed limits, traffic signals and lane divisions mere mortals had to abide.

Fate had wisely steered Hannah toward a career in advertising. She knew herself well enough to admit she'd have made a lousy cop. Power trips and fast cars were an intoxicating combination. Besides, navy polyester uniform pants would make even a skinny woman's rear end look as broad as a Volvo station wagon.

"You will sit tight when we get there," David said. A nerve stitched in his jaw. "I mean it, Hannah."

Her belly fluttered. "Have I ever ignored a direct order, Sheriff?"

"Yes."

"Oh. Well, I've reformed."

"You better have."

Cop-face, cop-tone. She'd seen and heard both before, but didn't remember the transition from David Hendrickson to Sheriff Hendrickson being so rapid or complete.

He cut the siren, turned left at a wye intersection onto a secondary road, then wheeled into one right and another. First Street's white-way vanished as fast as it had appeared. Beyond knowing they were outside Sanity's city limits and inside Kinderhook County's, Hannah was lost.

Cattle stood along a fence dividing pastureland from a two-story farmhouse the owner had remodeled into an imitation Tara. A blue glow pulsed from a television in a corner of the front room. Across the road, a dreary mobile-home village resembled a company of battle-fatigued soldiers.

Hannah shuddered. She'd grown up in a trailer park the classier citizens of Effindale had dubbed Tin Can Alley. The standing joke among the resident trailer trash was that a guy couldn't crack open a beer lest the neighbors on both sides belched.

With Caroline's bevy of Mr. Wrongs, whiskey bottles and broken promises cluttering up the place, a rented ten-by-forty Fleetwood was too small for a mother and daughter to peaceably coexist, no matter how much they loved each other.

Hannah dug her nails into her palm to keep the curtain from rising on flashbacks she'd rather forget and the orchestra from striking up a medley of "if onlys."

The cruiser's headlights swept a peeling billboard with triangles in shades of weathered green. Faded, slashed lettering announced Whispering Pines—Country Living, City Convenience. Lots Available.

David switched off the lightbar. Crumbling asphalt crunched under tires maneuvering around potholes and heaves.

"I'll bet there are lots of lots available," Hannah said.

He agreed. "It could have been a nice subdivision, if the developer had put it somewhere else. Back in the late 1960s, Sanity had a little industrial revolution, thanks to a federal economic development program.

"A builder named Pat Conrad got a tip that Rawlings Industries and an engine remanufacturer were building plants here. He bought this parcel for three hundred bucks an acre, sold a raft of spec houses and had down payments on most of the remaining lots."

Hannah said, "Then Conrad caught the next plane to Rio."

"More like the next train to the state pokey. Until buyers started having septic-tank trouble, all he was guilty of was taking advantage of a tip and a tight housing market."

David motioned. "This ridge is pure hardpan. Get a good rain and the wells test positive for fecal coliform contamination."

Hannah's nose wrinkled at the lopsided, half-bricked homes centered on spacious, pine tree-shaded lots. As ordained by the law of There's No Accounting for Taste, several were painted marine blue, pea green or lavender. For Sale by Owner signs, as well as the Realtor variety, were as common as basketball hoops drooping above garage doors.

Strands of barbed wire paralleled Skyline Drive, the development's last cross-street. A distant barn indicated the property had remained agricultural.

David slowed the car to a crawl, its spotlight strafing a sallow brick house with brown siding. A mauled stock car and a tractor-trailer cab dominated the driveway.

He U-turned at the dead end, and parked in front of one of two vacant lots neighboring 5406. Thumbing the trunk-release button, he said, "Be right back."

The semi blocked Hannah's view of all but a small patch of the ranch house's roof. She propped her elbow on the window ledge and rested her chin in her hand. Well, hell. She didn't know where Bubba Lou's was, but she could probably have seen as much from there as from the Crown Vic's passenger seat.

The trunk lid shut with a soft whump. Mr. Protective slid backward into the car. He'd exchanged his denim jacket for a navy windbreaker with Sheriff emblazoned on it in bright yellow letters. Light sparked off the badge clipped to his Sam Browne belt.

"Adam–101," he said into the mike.

Go ahead, 101.

"10–20, 5406 Skyline Drive."

10–4, Sheriff. Charlie 3–14 is en route, your location, from County Line Road. Clear.

"101, clear." The microphone hit the dashboard. "Shit."

With reluctance, Hannah asked, "Is something wrong?"

"No backup to speak of. Charlie 3–14 could be anywhere from fifteen to twenty-five miles from here."

Muttering to himself, he looked up and down the street. "And I'm not inclined to sit here and wait on him."

He exited the car, then stuck his head back inside and gave Hannah a tight-lipped smile.

She flapped a hand. "I'm sitting tight, already."

"Atta girl." Pressing the lock button, he shut the door as quietly as he had the trunk.

She stuck out her tongue at his departing, broad-shouldered back. When had Starsky ever told Hutch to wait in the stupid car?

4

Instinct. A sixth sense. Bad vibes. Experience.

Whatever you call the feeling that things weren't as they appeared, David had been under its influence since dispatch radioed the pizza parlor manager's complaint.

For the tenth and final time, he told himself he was just road-weary, hungry and a mite torqued about being here.

Yeah, well, want to have a social life? Turn in your badge and get a job selling insurance.

He kicked up a combination wrench. Vise grips and a socket nib glinted in the clumped grass as if thrown there. An accordion toolbox lay open on what was left of the stock car's rear fender.

David heard his father lecture, "Take care of your tools and they'll take care of you." Ed Hendrickson didn't think much of those who broke the rule. Neither did his eldest son.

Gutters bowed from the house's eaves—force of habit fighting gravitational pull. Instead of curtains, thermal blankets were tacked over the windows. Blisters welted the sun-bleached front door's veneer; dry rot consuming the frame.

A handyman's special in progress. David didn't bother to speculate how the place looked on the inside.

The door swung open. A man of medium build and height, dressed in an undershirt and dark trousers, stood in the threshold. Backlit by the interior light, he bore an eerie resemblance to a firing-range target.

His face expressionless and his right arm behind his back, he said, "You're the sheriff."

Hannah's palms chafed her thighs. She closed her eyes and gave in to the power of suggestion. Thick-crust, Chicago-style pizza, hot and fresh from a brick-lined oven. Cheese bubbling like miniature volcanoes. A smothering layer of genuine Italian pepperoni.

What was Hendrickson *doing?* Helping the guy count pennies to pay off the delivery kid?

He could have been thoughtful enough to leave the keys in the ignition. The radio's crackles were getting on her nerves. It was too dark to make out which was the volume knob. With her luck, she'd activate the P.A. system by mistake and a Humphrey Bogart-like voice would warn, "This is the police! Throw down your weapons and come out with your hands up."

That'd get David's attention. It was a heck of a long walk home though.

Fat lot of good the REO Speedwagon and James Taylor cassettes in the glove compartment did her, with no way to switch on juice from the battery to play them.

David didn't trust her. How obvious can he get? Just because she couldn't roll down the window without the keys didn't mean she *would* have if he'd left them.

Well, an inch or two maybe. For air. But not all the way. It was too creepy sitting here alone. The back side of the house on the next street looked as hermetically sealed as she felt.

What was taking David so long?

"Yes, sir. I'm Sheriff Hendrickson." David palm-grazed the butt of his service revolver. His ring finger curled under the holster's safety strap. "Are you Mr. Quince?" The leather strip unsnapped with a *tick.*

The man nodded. The motion robotic, deliberate, as if confirming more than his identity.

In the distance, a child wheedled, "I'll be in in a minute, Mom, okay?" Leaves rustled to David's left, along the property line. Prickles at the base of his neck crawled upward, like ants on a hill.

The man in the doorway didn't move.

"How 'bout you put both hands where I can see them, Mr. Quince."

"I need to die. This is the only way."

The statement iced David's veins. Fifteen feet of open ground separated them. Reflex pulled his leg back a half step. Knee flexed, he leveled his Smith & Wesson at the man's chest. "Both hands, Quince. *Now.*"

"I'm sorry, Sheriff." The calm monotone sounded rehearsed, as if he'd practiced his and his unwitting executioner's lines. "I don't want to hurt you, but I will if I have to."

The neighbor kid David had heard. He prayed the boy had minded his mother and gone inside. Hannah. Lord God Almighty, please don't let her out of the car.

"I won't tell you again, mister. *Put your hands where I can see them.*"

"I can't do it myself, Sheriff. I've tried." Quince's mouth stretched into a mocking smile. "This is the only way."

David's eyes stung for want of a blink. It seemed like an hour since he'd radioed dispatch. Where the hell was Charlie 3–14? Gotta keep Quince talking until his backup got there.

Quince's elbow jerked. Left hand met right in a two-fisted grip.

Gun.

Kuh-kuh-crack-kuh.

Hannah jumped. Her head swung side to side. Echoes dispersed around her, skewing direction. Hands flattened on the dashboard, she peered through the windshield, straining to hear, her nails digging into the padded vinyl.

Her heart tried, failed, to convince herself that a car had backfired. The door lever thwacked in the armrest's molded niche. Her thumb jabbed the inoperative window toggle. Wrenching sideward, her fingertips pecked at the lock's slick chrome nub.

"Damn it, damn it, damn it!" She pummeled the glass with her fist. "Da-a-vid." Panic throttled her.

A hum and a garbled voice sliced through her fear. She grabbed the microphone off the dash. Pressing the button on the side of the casing, she shouted, "Adam–101. Emergency."

No voice. No static. Dead silence.

"Answer me. I think David—the sheriff—has been shot."

Nothing. She choked back a sob. Why wasn't the dispatcher saying anything? "For God's sake, can't you hear—"

The button. She had to release the transmit button to allow two-way communication.

Adam–101, identify yourself.

Relief shuddered through her. "This is Hannah Garvey. Send an ambulance to…" The address. What was the house number? The street? *Jesus.* The microphone slipped in her sweaty hands.

Slow down, Ms. Garvey. Help's on the way. Push the button to tell me what happened, then let go.

The dispatcher's calm voice was barely audible, but soothing. She swallowed hard. "I'm in the sheriff's car. Locked in it. I can't see him or the house he went to. Can't see anything, but I'm sure I heard a gunshot."

One shot? Or more?

"One—I'm pretty sure it was just one."

Get down on the floorboard and stay there. Keep ahold of the microphone. Hear anything, see anything, let me know right away. Clear.

With a final glance out the windshield, Hannah slid off the seat into a crouch. Knees wedged under her chin, she cradled the microphone like an amulet.

Twenty-five years fell away. She was eighteen again. Listening for an ambulance's siren. Fisting the money she'd earned writing term papers for classmates who had better things to do with their weekends.

Her terminally ill mother had no insurance. Paramedics employed by Effindale's private ambulance company had warned Hannah that Caroline wouldn't be transported to the hospital again, unless the fee was paid upfront, in cash.

A month after Caroline died, leaving her grieving daughter staggering under a mountain of unpaid bills, Hannah found out the drivers had pocketed her money and charged the county for services rendered.

Road grit crunching near the cruiser's front bumper

yanked her back to the present. The footsteps slowed, faltered.

Cheekbones grinding her kneecaps, Hannah wrapped her arms around her shins, trying to make herself smaller. The dashboard's metal underside grated her spine.

Scrape. A pivoting noise, as if the person attached to it was visually searching the area for her.

The microphone gave a horribly false sense of security. Move, and whoever was out there would see her. Talk, and he'd hear her. The good guys were coming, but not fast enough to rescue her.

The steps came closer. Closer. Hannah bit the skin lining her inner cheek to keep from screaming.

Metal rasped metal. The driver's door swung wide.

"Hannah? Are you in there?"

Her temple bashed the radio. Stars orbited David's pallid, sweat-shiny face. Gasping for breath, she stammered his name. "Are you all right?"

An action figure's plastic features would have looked more lifelike than his; the planes and hollows were as sharply defined as caricatures sketched by a sidewalk artist.

Hannah's legs tangled in the mike's pigtail cord. She freed herself and returned it to its hook. Slithering from her hidey-hole, she flexed her toes before the cramp at her instep welded them together.

David fell into the seat. He exhaled, his breath heavy and sour. Staring into the middle distance, a clammy hand sought and found hers. "What a waste." Head bowed, he shook it slowly. "A stupid, goddamn waste."

Pain so rived his voice, Hannah thought he was

wounded. She saw no blood, no dirt, nothing save the waxen cast to his skin, the wooden quality of his movements. "What is, David? What happened?"

If he heard her, he chose not to answer. His hand left hers and reached for the microphone. "Adam–101."

Go ahead.

"Got a 10–18, 5406 Skyline Drive. Need an EMS and notify the coroner."

No, oh please, no, Hannah thought. This can't be happening. A man rips off a delivery boy and now he's dead?

Tears filmed her eyes at the same time her belly knotted in horror. David must have fired the shot she'd heard. She looked down at the black leather holster crammed between his thigh and the console, the grip of the pistol jutting from it. She recoiled, aware she had, but unable to stop herself.

Ambulance already en route, Sheriff, responding to Ms. Garvey's shots-fired report. Charlie 3–14, 3–10, and Baker 2–03 also en route, your 10–20.

David turned his head. "You got on the radio and called in a shots-fired?"

"I don't know what I said. I just told the dispatcher you needed help."

A wan smile played on David's lips. "I had backup all along and didn't know it." Into the microphone, he said, "I'm off this one, Tony. As of now."

Approaching sirens whooped and chirruped, their disharmony identifying an ambulance and at least two patrol cars streaking through Whispering Pines's once-tranquil streets.

10–4, Adam–101. Glad you're okay, Sheriff. Clear.

"Yeah." David snorted. "101, clear."

The microphone banged into its holder. He chafed his face, then jerked his hands away, squinting at them as though they belonged to someone else. "Screw it. Like Andrik's gonna need gunpowder residue from me?"

Hannah wanted to say something. Do something. But what? She wasn't sure he remembered she was there. Wasn't sure he'd want to be reminded.

Sirens squelched in midwail. Light flooded the open field. The brilliance swung across the barbed-wire fence and pasture beyond as an orange-and-white ambulance hurtled around the corner. Two patrol units followed.

Dual high beams and flashing lightbars lanced the parked cruiser. David said, "Sit tight," and elbowed the car door.

"Not this time," Hannah said. "I'll keep out of everyone's way, but I'm not staying in here another second."

"This is a crime scene. A…homicide."

Through gritted teeth, she said, "Unlock my door or I swear I'll climb over the seat and go out yours."

David's arm rested on the steering wheel a moment. "All right." A *thunk* sounded inches from her ear. "Don't step foot past the edge of the driveway or—"

"I won't. I promise."

They exited the cruiser together. David strode toward the house. Hannah breathed in crisp, sweet air to chase away the dregs of claustrophobia. She'd never felt its effect before and hoped she never did again.

Emotions tossed and tumbled within her: relief, concern, residual fear, a dozen others too entwined to name and—God help her—a twinge of revulsion.

Her mind couldn't connect the man whose profession required a gun, and the split-second decisiveness to use it, with the big, gentle guy who teased her unmercifully and, in the course of a ridiculously few days, had become the best friend she'd ever had.

A Jekyll-and-Hyde personality? Pure Hollywood. Totally inappropriate. Too simplistic, too black-and-white for a man of uncommon depth, wisdom and complexity.

She realized early on that for David Hendrickson the oath of office, the pledge to protect and serve the citizens of Kinderhook County, weren't words repeated by ceremonial rote. Judging by the haunted look in his eyes, if anything, he cared too much for his own good.

Hannah thrust her hands in her coat pockets. Chin down, she walked into the kaleidoscopic swirl of light. The sense of reality and surreality were impossible to separate.

A deputy was reeling out yellow crime-scene tape. With the end tied to the semi-cab's grab bar, the Police Line: Do Not Cross boundary extended to shrubs on the opposite side of the yard.

Inside it, one paramedic squatted on the stoop, his gloved hands ghost-white against his dark jacket and trousers. A pair of legs were sprawled just inside the doorway. The other EMT stood beside David, nodding as people do to let the speaker know they're listening.

Hannah wished she could hear what was being said. The shooting's effect was clear. She wanted to know the cause, the sequence of events.

Why? Morbid curiosity? To reassure yourself David had no option? Or because in a ghoulish, awful way, a homicide scene is fascinating, as long as you can't see and don't know the victim?

Multiple-choice questions had always been a bitch. The more sure Hannah always was about which answer was correct, the quicker doubt crept in behind it.

The second paramedic tamped a pack of cigarettes and offered David one. He took it. Leaning into the lighter's flame, he straightened, exhaled, then turned his head and coughed, like a kid toking one of his daddy's Chesterfields behind the barn.

A deputy materialized beside her, startling her. "Unless you have something to report, ma'am, I'd advise you to take yourself home and stay there."

Swallowing her yo-yo heart for the fourth time in the past few minutes and tired of being stage-managed, Hannah snapped, "Believe me, I'd love to, if home weren't twenty-five miles away."

His head cocked in classic you-want-a-hassle-I'll-give-you-a-hassle style.

She speed-read his brass nameplate. "I apologize, Deputy Cahill. I didn't see you and I just..." Her shoulders sagged. "I was with Sheriff Hendrickson, and I'm not quite with the program yet."

"And your name would be...?"

Supplying it changed Cahill's expression from formidable to Officer Friendly. "Why, I'll be. I was responding to the 10–61 when I heard your 10–33. I could tell you were scared, but you did a fine job. Better'n some rookies I won't mention."

From previous, though scant, experience with ten-codes, Hannah translated the first as David's original request for backup and assumed the second referred to her SOS to the dispatcher. "Then you must be Charlie 3–14."

"That's right, ma'am. Tom Cahill. The fella over yonder securing things is Bret Vann, aka Charlie 3–10. He's the watch commander this shift."

Hannah was about to ask what had taken Cahill so ungodly long when a car cut in front of the parked ambulance ramped into the driveway. Blinded by its headlights, she crossed her arms over her face as though they'd ward off a starring role in a vehicular manslaughter. Cahill grabbed her elbow and yanked her to safety.

Brakes squalled. Dust and gravel spewed from the car's rear tires. A chartreuse Toyota Camry skidded to a halt, inches from the semi's fifth wheel. With the lights extinguished and the engine dieseling to a spasmodic death, Reserve Officer Rudy Moody scrambled from the driver's seat.

"I got here as fast as I could." Moody sawed a finger under his nose. "Jiminy, the sheriff shot that dude dead-bang, eh? Wow."

Cahill exploded, "You goddam—er, ding-blasted fool, where do you get off tearing in here like that? You pert-near ran this lady down."

"I did no such a thing." Moody squinted at Hannah. "What's Ms. Garvey doing here anyhow? Not s'posed to be any civilians on the premises."

David loomed over them, visibly trembling with anger.

"You're out of line, Cahill."

"Me? He's the one—"

"As for you, Moody, I've had all the stunts out of you I'm going to take. Got that?"

The reservist's baby face flushed as his eyes lasered a spot below David's jaw. "Yes, sir."

David pointed to a far corner of the yard. "You want to make yourself useful, go see if the neighbors ganging up over there know Quince's wife's name and where she is. If they don't, send 'em home."

Moody blinked, then realized the order was directed at him. He snapped a salute, a "Yes sir, Sheriff" and hastened away.

"Cahill," David said, "you start canvassing the houses on this block and the one behind. Same info, plus anything the neighbors might have seen or heard."

As the deputy pulled a notebook and pen from his shirt pocket, he said, "Me and Iola and others from the church sang carols out here back around Christmastime. I can't be sure it's the same house, but if it is, the wife's name is Lydia. She and Iola knew each other from…"

Cahill frowned and shook his head. "Well, I don't rightly remember where it was now, but Iola said Lydia was Eldredge Randal's secretary down to his insurance office for a number of years."

"Was?" David repeated.

"Lydia quit a few days before we come around singing 'Joy to the World.' Iola said she and hubby weren't getting along. Lydia was dead set to leave him, leave town and start fresh somewhere's else."

David said, "The faster you confirm the name and put an address or phone number with it, the happier I'll be."

"Will do, Sheriff."

Cahill turned and waved at the paramedic behind the wheel of the departing ambulance. The pool of darkness it left refilled with Detective Marlin Andrik's unmarkcd beater Chevy and a hearse driven by funeral-home owner and Kinderhook county coroner Junior Duckworth.

A wood-trimmed minivan with the *Sanity Examiner* painted in Old-English lettering on the door angled in behind Deputy Cahill's patrol unit. Chase Wingate had plenty of lead time to compose what was sure to be next Tuesday's above-the-fold feature.

Hannah hadn't met Wingate, but had spoken to him on the phone after the Kathleen Osborn murder. The middle-aged, lanky, bespectacled man with a huge camera slung around his neck fit the image she'd created from his voice. Wingate's beeline for Detective Andrik met with a rebuff and an unheard but apparent command to back off.

David said, "It's shaping up into one long, devil-dog night. Sorry you're stuck in the middle of it."

"If anyone should apologize, it's me. I'm beginning to think I'm a jinx. Three homi—" Hannah flinched "—*deaths,* in two weeks?"

"Could be the company you keep."

The tease fell flat—if it was a tease. The walls David had erected around himself were real. Hannah would have resented it, maybe have been hurt by it, if instinct hadn't told her they weren't there to shut her out but to hold himself in.

"Well, I happen to like the company I'm keeping, Sheriff Hendrickson. Very much."

He gave her the first genuine grin she'd seen in what seemed like eons. "Thanks, sugar. I needed to hear that. More than you know."

Actually she did know. The recent past had demonstrated that their involvement in the Osborn case had developed an odd type of intimacy between them, a mutual perceptiveness to what the other was thinking and feeling, regardless of what was said or outward appearances. Sharing the same wavelength was comforting in some instances, aggravating in others.

"Wouldn't you know," Andrik grumbled, stalking across the lawn, "the kids are out doing something we'll ground 'em for later, me and Beth were just beginning to remember what we used to do before we had 'em and be damned if duty doesn't call."

He was lugging a heavy plastic equipment case in each hand. Rather than his usual dapper attire, his sport coat, baggy sweat suit, shoulder holster and high-top tennis shoes ensemble was a cross between Dirty Harry and a Little League coach.

"If I hadn't needed you on this one," David said as they started toward the house, "I sure as hell wouldn't have bothered you."

Andrik hesitated a half step. "Okay..." The word comprised two lengthy syllables with an uptick at the end. He grunted, bent double and shuffled under the tape barrier David stepped over with ease.

The watch commander had set up battery-operated tripod lights in the yard. Cletus Orr, another departmental detective, arrived on the scene. Camera flashes marked Andrik's movements both indoors and out.

Film is as cheap as evidence is fragile, temporary and easily contaminated in the process of investigation. Photographs provided irrefutable insurance against faulty memories, keen eyes missing what might be of enormous importance later on and notes that can't be a hundred percent comprehensive.

Hannah retreated to Moody's car and slumped

against it. Listening to the engine ping as it cooled, she wished she could see and hear what was transpiring in the doorway to 5406 Skyline Drive.

Of its own volition, her posterior began to inch along the Toyota's quarter panel until the edge of the front bumper pressed her calves. Hannah paused, studying the road-grimy semi's vertical exhaust pipes, the air-brake hoses dangling in ringlets, the desiccated grease clinging to the slanted fifth wheel.

Next thing she knew, her derriere was nestled in a dent in the stock car's door. At no time had any part of her anatomy "stepped foot" past the driveway or breached the yellow barrier—a technicality David would fail to appreciate, but worth the lecture he was sure to deliver.

She heard Junior Duckworth say, "Body temperature is right at ninety-eight degrees. How long ago did you say this happened?"

"Ten, maybe fifteen minutes," David answered. "He smelled as if he'd crawled out of a whiskey bottle when I checked for a pulse and respiration."

Andrik spat out, "Suicide-by-cop. Like we don't have enough shit messing with our heads."

He took a pack of cigarettes from his pocket, scowled, then crammed them back in. "I heard about a college kid that got himself eyeball deep in gambling debts. The dirtbag hauls ass up and down the street until a uniform pulls him over, then bails out and aims a gun at the cop.

"*Blammo*—the cop blows him away. Turns out the weapon was a BB pistol, but the cop was justified. No doubt about it."

The detective chuckled bitterly. "Know what they

found on the dead guy's dashboard? A goddamn greeting card with 'To the officer who shot me' on the envelope. Son of a bitch wrote inside how *sorry* he was, but jeez, ya know, he *needed* to die."

Hannah's stomach rolled. She clutched at her sweater, balling the fabric in her fist.

"Quince said the same thing, Marlin. He needed to die. Said he didn't want to hurt me, but would if he had to."

"Shoot or be shot," Andrik snarled. *"Christ."*

David paused, his voice tight, higher-pitched than Hannah had ever heard it. "His finger looked as big as a salami on the trigger. Everything went slow-mo. I was here, right here on this spot, watching that fat finger. Squeezing mine back. Saw the muzzle flash…thought I was dead meat. I don't know how he missed."

David's hand clamped his forehead. "Maybe he pulled it at the last second…I can't remember. That *instant*—it's a fuckin' black hole, Marlin. *How the hell did he miss me?* I'm still walkin' around. Quince is *dead.* I don't get it. I just don't get it."

Tears spilled down Hannah's cheeks at the agony, the anger, the guilt lacerating his voice. Swiping the corners of her eyes, she stumbled back to Moody's car, terrified anew at how close David had come to dying at the hands of a suicidal maniac.

Refusing to allow a single what-if to slither into her thoughts, she watched Junior Duckworth's assistant unload a gurney from the back of the hearse, trying not to despise the wretch who'd soon be strapped to it.

David walked toward her, mopping his face with a handkerchief. He carried himself less like a member of a military color-guard, but looked haggard. Exhausted. A thousand years old.

The Toyota rocked with his weight when he leaned against it. Arm cradling Hannah's waist, he pulled her to him.

Standing hip to hip, she rested her head on his chest, listened to the beat of his heart, wished she could think of something to say and content to say nothing at all.

Presently, he murmured, "If it's okay with you, let's count this as our first date. Sure as hell ain't romantic, but the way things keep happening—well, I'm all for getting past one, on to number two."

"Excellent idea."

His eyebrows arched. "I have another one I don't expect you're going to like as much."

"Which is?"

"Marlin needs a statement from you since you're the only witness. As soon as that's done, I'm ordering Rudy to take you home."

She groaned.

"I don't want to, but...you're a distraction, sugar, and I can't let myself be distracted. As for Moody, I can't spare anyone else. After me and him have a little discussion, he'll drive like he's got the pope riding passenger."

"Well, it isn't an excellent idea," Hannah allowed, "but I can live with it."

David gave her ribs a squeeze. "Have I ever told you how much—"

"Aw right, let's break it up." Andrik waved his notebook at them. "While I take dictation from Ms. Garvey, why don't you fetch Quince's gun from your trunk. Maybe we can wrap this up before the wife conks out on the couch.''

Hannah said, ''I really don't have much to—''

''You don't need to send me on a goose chase to talk to her in private,'' David said. ''I was fixing to tell Rudy he's on escort duty anyhow.''

Andrik hesitated, then shrugged. ''Call it what you will, but I have to tag 'n bag that gun.''

It was David's turn to look perplexed. He motioned toward the house. ''So, tag it and bag it. Hannah's not leaving until you're finished with her.''

Andrik craned his neck, looked over his shoulder for a long moment, then slowly back at David. ''You didn't lock the gun in your trunk for safekeeping?''

''No.'' David's skin tone faded to a sickly gray. ''When I went to the car to radio dispatch, it was lying in plain sight. Fourteen, sixteen inches from Quince's right hand.''

Andrik stiffened, his expression as stone-cold as his voice. ''I searched the front room from top to bottom, including under the body. There is no gun, Sheriff. Not inside, not outside. Nowhere.''

5

"I told Mrs. Schnieder," Rudy droned, "I said, 'Mrs. Schnieder, I can't be coming over here all the time to get your cat out of the tree' and then, she said in that funny way she has of talking, she said…"

Hannah stared through her reflection on the Toyota's side window and into the darkness, wondering how much more of Moody's drivel she could endure.

His nasal voice was the equivalent of a fork tapping a dental filling. Compared to his law enforcement exploits, a "Win-win Benefits of Office Micromanagement" seminar was spellbinding.

Besides that, Rudy smelled rank—like canned chicken-noodle soup broth, only strong enough to be lethal. Maybe he confused body odor with body armor, which might explain his empty holster. Assuming he didn't talk the bad guys to death, they couldn't get close enough to shoot him.

Louder than the human white noise, the electronic babble from his police radio and citizens band radio mounted on the hump, *What happened to Quince's gun?* pounded in Hannah's head like a tympanum.

At no time had Detective Andrik or others at the scene accused David of killing an unarmed man. The unspoken damnation had saturated the air, as invisible yet tangible as humidity.

From the moment the gun's existence came into question, Andrik hadn't let Hannah and David within twenty feet of each other. Told them to have no contact with each other, even by telephone, until further notice.

A homicide investigation was under way. Hannah a witness. Hannah had heard the shot. *One* shot, not two or six or sixty. She tried to hedge. Insisted she'd been so frightened for David's safety, she couldn't be sure of anything.

"You reported 'one' to the dispatcher, Ms. Garvey," Andrik had said, his tone formal, knowing as well as she did what a single shot implied.

"I told Tony I *thought* I heard just one. Everything happened so fast, I'm a far cry from positive."

"I know what you're thinking, but you're wrong," Andrik had said. "We're going to find out what happened here tonight. When we're through, what you've told us won't be more than a fraction of the evidence collected."

Hannah had acknowledged the truth in his statement, but it didn't relieve the heartsick feeling she'd betrayed David. Contributed to the skeptical glances she'd seen traded by Andrik, the deputies, Junior Duckworth and Chase Wingate.

The gaze she'd leveled at Andrik was as point-blank as her question. "Do *you* believe David?"

The detective had turned his head, called out, "Moody, you can take the lady home, now," and walked away.

The sleeve of Hannah's leather jacket creaked as she rubbed the bony ridge above her eye. Her thoughts segued to how impossible it seemed that an hour or two earlier she'd been a passenger in David's car.

Starsky and Hutch. Unless Andrik found Quince's gun, those alter egos might become Julius Caesar and Brutus.

"...none of that doctor or astronaut or engineer stuff for me," Rudy said. "All I ever wanted to be my whole life was a law enforcement officer."

"And now you are." Hannah hoped he'd reached the end of his unprovoked autobiography.

"Not that I plan on working here forever. It's a good place to get experience, but the Federal Marshal's Service looks interesting, and then there's the Border Patrol, the Secret Service, ATF—"

His laugh sounded forced. "Gosh, Ms. Garvey, the sky's the limit for a guy like me!"

She smiled at his enthusiasm. It was fairly obvious those brass rings were way beyond Rudy's reach, but then the majority of the population of Effindale, Illinois, would have said the same of Hannah.

Small-town residents weren't prone to letting an absence hinder rehashing gossip. Hannah was certain her name still cropped up in "I wonder whatever happened to" conversations common to high school reunions and beauty shops catering to ladies who rated the invention of Dippity-Do alongside the discovery of penicillin.

Had they known—or cared—that she'd parlayed a high school education, a diploma-mill degree and a bogus résumé into an advertising agency's senior account executive's position, they'd have uttered a collective sniff and sworn Hannah must have fornicated her way to the top.

That's precisely what they'd say, in fact. *Fornicated.*

Not slept or screwed or any other nonbiblical synonym.
Undeserved and provincial to the point of quaint, the
word still delivered the sharpest sting of them all.

The oversize coachlights atop Valhalla Springs's
gated entry winked through the trees just as Rudy
launched into the history of the Federal Marshal's Service. He'd only gotten to day two of its existence when
the Toyota crested the hill and Hannah's beloved brick-
and-cedar cottage sprang into view.

A gleaming, turquoise Edsel occupied the semicir-
cular driveway, much like the *QE II* would occupy the
Thames, had it taken a shortcut to Windsor Castle.

"Wow-wee, ma'am. Is that your car?"

"No, it belongs to a friend of mine. Delbert Bisbee."

As if summoned, Delbert proceeded to emerge from
the vehicle clad in his typical, dressed-in-the-dark style.
Tonight's ensemble was a green turtleneck peeking out
the collar of an orange-and-red plaid flannel shirt, blue
houndstooth-check slacks, yellow socks and black-and-
white sneakers.

Whether Delbert was color-blind or enjoyed looking
like a Picasso painting of a crowd scene, Hannah had
yet to decide.

Rudy made a humming noise as he turned into the
driveway. "Bisbee, eh? That name sounds familiar."

No surprise there. When Kathleen Osborn's battered
body was found in her cottage, the sixty-seven-year-old
retired postal supervisor, together with IdaClare
Clancy, organized a gang of elderly sleuths to track
down the killer. In the process, Delbert "infiltrated" a
local biker bar called Mother Truckers. A Sanity Police
Department officer intervened before Delbert received
a pool cue implant.

Hannah thanked Moody for the ride home and exited the car. The Toyota clunked into reverse, the engine whining as it fishtailed on the curved asphalt ribbon. Squashed jonquils marked the tires' exit but Rudy did miss the hewn post and signboard with Manager wood-burned on either side.

"Ladybug," Delbert said, "if you're going to date a Cub Scout, you ought to latch on to one that knows how to drive."

Hannah shot him a dirty look, then burst out laughing. Maybe she shouldn't have, but it felt good. "For your information, that was Reserve Deputy Rudy Moody of the Kinderhook County Sheriff's Department."

"It was, huh?" Weathered creases in Delbert's face deepened to crevasses. He caught her hand, his palm silken and warm, the backside knobbed and sandpaper rough. "I heard you on the scanner. I can see you're all right, but how about Hendrickson?"

Hannah smiled, could have cried, could have just let her bones go ahead and dissolve, weary as they were of shoring her up when all she wanted to do was lean on someone.

She should have known Delbert had been tuned in to the department's radio frequency. He'd bought a scanner for Hannah and each of his cohorts in crime solving, known alternately as IdaClare and Company and the Mod Squad.

She also should have realized Delbert would have camped in his car all night waiting for her to come home. Knights in shining armor are patient, loyal and not deterred by a little rust in their joints.

And of course, he was champing his dentures to hear

every gory detail of the suicide-by-cop's transition to a suspected homicide-by-cop.

David opened the door to his office on the court-house's third floor and flipped on the overhead light. Coffee slopped over the rim of his cup and scorched his thumb and knuckles. It should have stung like fire.

He sat down at the scarred oak desk that a First National Bank of Sanity loan officer had kept between himself and Depression-whipped farmers begging him not to foreclose. The same kind of desperation clawed at David's gut.

He knew what his men were saying about him. Understood why. Would have done so himself, had it been one of them in his boots. And he resented their Monday-morning quarterbacking so much the gall would choke him if he didn't keep swallowing it down.

Leaning back in his chair, he winged his arms behind his neck and stared out the window at the crenellated rooflines of the buildings on the west side of the square. Like the courthouse at center, the century-old brick-and-mortar dinosaurs looked less forlorn at night. Some had been defaced by well-intended improvements, such as the corrugated-metal false fronts bolted to their original false fronts. They'd probably been snazzier than all get-out, when John Travolta danced in white leisure suits to music only heard in elevators these days.

Traffic and signs of life had been suspended on account of darkness. Even the juveniles who derived the same kick their grandparents had from driving around in circles had scattered like dandelion spores in a breeze.

If not for distant voices from the dispatchers' cubbyholes, muffled telephones ringing and the steel door bonging behind the jailer making his rounds, David would have thought he was alone, rather than just feeling like the departmental's pariah.

He perused the grimy punched-tin ceiling. A sigh billowed up from somewhere near his toes. Maybe this would turn out to be a good thing, by and by. One of those character builders his mother had preached about after his high school team lost a football game they should have won. Or the time Johnny Paul Williams challenged David to a drag race and he totaled the cream-puff Mustang he'd bucked ten million bales of hay to buy.

Having grown up mostly on the right side of the law, and with eleven years' experience enforcing it, learning firsthand how it felt to be on the wrong side might enlarge his perspective. Mix a dollop of gray into what David admitted was a relatively black-and-white point of view.

The squeak of an antique desk chair wrenching sideways reverberated off the plaster walls. On a stand beside David's desk, a computer racketed through its boot-up sequence. David sipped his coffee and reminded himself that work was salvation's stepbrother and that he hadn't come here to sit and feel sorry for himself.

Delbert sat on a bar stool watching Hannah crack eggs in a skillet, drop bread in the toaster, cut a green pepper into strips and dice a wedge of red onion.

"I thought you said you couldn't cook."

She smiled at the inferred compliment. "This isn't

cooking. This is survival. A six-course meal with a flaming dessert is cooking.''

"My fourth wife—Hilda I believe her name was— made whatever she put on a plate into a work of art." He chuckled. "The stuff tasted like the bottom of a paint can, but it looked nice."

Hannah slathered Miracle Whip on the toast, then laid on a thick slice of Velveeta. She'd left all vestiges of an appetite on Skyline Drive, but the thump at her temples demanded food and caffeine.

Sliding the fried egg, sautéed onion and green pepper atop the cheese, she said, "Last chance for halvsies. My specialty of the house isn't pretty, but it meets the minimum daily grease requirement."

Delbert stretched down from his perch. "Mind if I help myself to another cup of coffee instead?"

Mouth decommissioned by a big bite of sandwich, Hannah pointed to a refrigerator magnet. *You're only a guest in my kitchen once. Thereafter, heed Matthew 7:7.* It separated those who recognized "Seek, and ye shall find" by chapter and verse from those who didn't.

Delbert topped off her mug, filled his own and returned the carafe to the coffeemaker. Clambering back onto the stool, he folded his arms on the bar and leaned forward expectantly.

Hannah teased, "Do you think two tablespoons of fresh coffee is all it takes to make me spill my guts?"

"Most women'll tell a man what he wants to hear for less than that."

Accustomed to Delbert's brand of misogyny, she countered, "Except I'm not most women."

"You're stalling."

"I'm eating. After I'm finished and I still don't talk, then I'll be stalling."

He argued, "Detective Andrik put a gag order on you talking to the sheriff. Now, I can see where you'd get us two swashbuckling types confused, but I'm the one without a badge pinned on my chest."

"Delbert—"

"Aw, don't 'Delbert' me. By eight o'clock tomorrow morning, it'll be standing room only at the Short Stack Café on the square and the liars' club won't be cussing and discussing the weather."

Egg, bread and condiments congealed into a concrete-like mass in Hannah's stomach. She laid the half-eaten sandwich on its saucer and pushed it aside.

"It's you I'm worried about, ladybug," Delbert said, "especially with David out of the picture. You've had a special kind of radar since the day you locked eyeballs on Kathleen's front porch." He grimaced. "It's had me fishing for a Di-Gel more than once, I don't mind telling you, but the fact remains, if David were here, you wouldn't have Beelzebub's pitchfork carved above your snoot."

The tip of Hannah's ring finger went to the bridge of her nose. The old fart was right. Poke seeds in there, pour a glass of water over her head and presto—human Chia Pet.

Delbert came up beside her and pulled her arm down. His milky blue eyes searched her brown ones. "You need to talk, Hannah. I don't feature myself a substitute for David, but I am your friend and I'll listen as close as he would, I promise you that."

Feeling her legs melt from under her, Hannah hugged him, wondering how she'd gotten by for forty-three years without a Delbert Bisbee in her life to lean on.

David proofread the sheaf of papers the printer had spewed out. Objectivity wasn't the problem. The report read as though the incident had happened to someone else—someone whose powers of recall weren't quite as sharp as his, who ought to study up on sentence structure.

Lieutenant David Hendrickson of the Tulsa Police Department had received commendations on the conciseness and clarity of his reports. Sheriff David Hendrickson could learn a thing or two from him.

Knuckles rapped the office door. Silhouettes bobbed and weaved on the opaque glass pane. Massaging the crick from his neck, David called, "Come on in."

He'd rather have said, "Go away." Better yet, not moved a muscle and let whoever it was think he'd gone home and forgotten to douse the lights.

Marlin Andrik, Junior Duckworth and Chief Deputy Jimmy Wayne McBride wore the smiles widows and widowers do to comfort other mourners attending the funeral. Being a third-generation mortician, Duckworth's looked the most sincere.

Jimmy Wayne stepped back to grab a chair from the outer room. Marlin and Junior took seats in the visitors' chairs facing David's desk.

Absently, David wondered where McBride had been all evening. Correction: wondered which sweet young thing had been the object of Jimmy Wayne's attention. At six-one and a hard-muscled two hundred pounds, the chief deputy didn't lack for lady friends. David didn't exactly approve of McBride's serial dating, but

Jimmy Wayne was an exemplary law enforcement officer.

The visitors fidgeted. Adjusted their jackets. Fingers stretched shirt collars. Invisible lint was picked off trouser legs. David mutilated a paper clip.

Tension rising to an almost audible buzz, he broke it by waving the printed sheets at Marlin. "I just finished my report. Considering the circumstances, it's a hybrid of a field interview, a preliminary and a witness statement."

The detective skimmed the top page, then glanced up. If the eyes mirrored the soul, his was composed of flywheels, gears and circuit boards. "Are you sure you want to do this?"

"You mean incriminate myself in ten-point Courier?" David stretched back in his chair. "Stuart Quince aimed and fired a gun at me. What happened to it? Damned if I know, but I guarantee he'll test positive for powder residue."

The three exchanged looks. Jimmy Wayne smoothed the tips of his mustache. "I've been on the horn with Theron Pike of the Missouri Highway Patrol. He wants to meet with you tomorrow—uh, well, later on today."

David nodded. Municipal police departments had Internal Affairs divisions, but counties relied on HP investigators to determine whether a sheriff's or deputy's line-of-duty actions were justified.

Contrary to what some civilians believed, the harshest judge a cop came up against—excluding himself—was another cop charged with second-guessing every move made practically since his date of birth.

Theron Pike was a good man and a skilled investigator. Marlin would assist, along with Cletus Orr. Josh

Phelps, the rookie detective Andrik was training, would likely be involved as well, for the experience and to give Andrik someone to harass besides Pike.

To the coroner, David said, "I figured you and the deceased would be at the lab in Columbia by now."

Duckworth gripped the chair's arms and pushed himself straighter in the seat. "No, I have the Kaltenback funeral at ten-thirty in the morning. My assistant is transporting."

"Who's witnessing the autopsy?" David asked.

Marlin answered, "Cletus."

David's eyebrows peaked. There was a reason Marlin was chief of the Detective Division and not Cletus Orr, whose years of service outnumbered Andrik's by a decade.

"I'm in on the meeting with Pike," he said, a note of defensiveness in his tone.

David raised a hand. "Look, I know this is an uncomfortable situation for all of us." He attempted a grin. "Most especially *me*."

Marlin slapped David's report on a knee. "Well, damn it to hell, it's about to get worse."

"For your sake," Junior said, "we must do things by the book from here on out. The August primary is only a couple of months away and I, for one, don't want this...incident to have a negative effect on your reelection."

Jee-sus Christ. It should be David's hindmost concern, but couldn't be if he planned on staying the sheriff of Kinderhook County.

Jimmy Wayne said, "That's why we're here."

Mind still focused on politics, David stammered, "Wh-what is?"

"Like Junior said, we've got to play this out according to protocol."

A hollow wide enough to drive an elephant through yawned in David's gut. He should have known these three particular men hadn't come to give him a pep talk, discuss campaign strategy or brainstorm the Quince case. "Would one of you be kind enough to tell me what this is all about?"

Junior Duckworth's face was as red as the medallions on his necktie. "According to county statute, it's the duty of the coroner to place a sheriff actively under investigation for malfeasance on administrative leave."

He coughed into his fist. "The chief deputy will serve as acting sheriff until such time the elected sheriff is cleared of any and all charges levied against him."

"It's just a formality," Jimmy Wayne stressed. "Public relations, man. Call it a few extra days paid vacation."

David couldn't think. Couldn't move. *Administrative leave* tolled like a demonic bell. Jimmy Wayne, Marlin and Junior were all talking at once. He couldn't hear a word they said.

Dignity. All his life his father had told him he could sell it or give it away, but it was the one thing nobody could take from him. Time had proven Ed Hendrickson right about most everything he'd taught his four sons. What would he do if he were in this chair, feeling everything he'd worked for, as hard as he knew how, turn into a fistful of sand?

David rose, his back ramrod straight, his head as high as the day he'd taken the oath of office. He unclipped his wallet badge and laid it at the center of the desk blotter. Eyes locked on the opposite wall, he unbuckled his utility belt and placed it like a wreath around his badge.

"You already have my Smith & Wesson, Detective Andrik." David's hand slid into his pocket for his keys. He held them up by the ring. "Now, by county statute, after I surrender my car, should I walk home or would one of you gentlemen mind giving me a lift?"

Turning from Hannah's driveway onto Valhalla Springs Boulevard, Delbert saw the lights go off in the front room of her cottage.

She'd sleep like a baby tonight. After she excused herself to use the bathroom, he'd crushed a muscle relaxant into a cup of hot cocoa, then added an extra splash of chocolate syrup to mask the taste.

Slipping someone a mickey was dirty pool, but Hannah was smart and she thought more than was good for a woman. Tomorrow was soon enough for her to put two and two together and realize how much trouble David Hendrickson was really in.

'Twas a blessing, Delbert supposed, that she wasn't the *Law & Order* and Discovery channel fan he was. From what she'd told him, the sheriff had deviated from procedure. As for Detective Andrik...

Well, the kindest thing that could be said of him was he'd broken the second rule of an investigation: Make no assumptions.

Could David have panicked for some reason and shot an unarmed man?

No. More's to the point, *hell* no.

Delbert's eyes slid to the rearview mirror, seeking confirmation. His lips puckered and made a kissy sound.

All right, he could have. He was human. Anybody's judgment can fail for a split second. Those who said otherwise were lying, self-righteous sons of bitches.

As he wheeled onto Sassafras Lane, a soft moan emitted from the Edsel's steering column. He braked to allow the garage door time to open its remote-controlled maw. Ear cocked, he pulled the wheel left, then right.

"Jehoshaphat." Now that he was listening, there was not a peep.

Good. He had enough things to fix without adding his car to the list. First he had to get IdaClare out of the jam she'd gotten herself into, playing witch doctor. Then he'd muster the troops for a strategy session on the Hendrickson case.

If they couldn't pull his fat out of the fire, a good man was going to spend the rest of his natural life wearing a number instead of a badge.

6

"This isn't a social call, Ms. Garvey."

"I realize that," Hannah said to Lieutenant Theron Pike, who had introduced himself as a Missouri Highway Patrol special investigator.

If it were, she'd be leading him to the leather sofa and wing chairs grouped around the fireplace, not toward the railed office nook on the opposite side of the living room.

"Where I come from," she continued, indicating the chair alongside her desk, "business doesn't preclude hospitality."

His mouth rumpled, bemused by her stage-managing. "All right, then. I take my coffee black." A pause. "Just like you do."

Hannah glanced at her mug resting on the blotter, more impressed by his powers of observation than intimidated by them. She'd seen David's in action enough times to know cops absorb details the rest of the population never notices.

She supposed Pike had also identified her shower gel, shampoo and deodorant by their scents. Branded her khaki slacks and silk blouse by their cut. Her Wonderbra's scalloped outline alluded to a belief that underwires could plump a pair of 34B's into bazoomier 36C's.

The atomic halo effect of last week's attempt to banish seventeen gray hairs had faded with repeated washings, but Pike would conclude she'd had a close encounter with a home-coloring kit. And he'd know why.

In the spirit of equal opportunity, Lieutenant Pike's bearing, Marine haircut and old eyes had pegged him as a cop the instant she laid sight on him. The pinstriped suit, a midpriced, off-the-rack model, had been altered by a tailor who knew his trade.

His features bespoke Native-American extraction and he was left-handed, judging by the watch strapped to the opposite wrist and a razor nick on the right side of his jaw. Late thirties/early forties, still wedded to the original Mrs. Pike, and he probably shunned boxers for briefs—colored ones to match his tie's predominant stripe and satisfy the inner bon vivant.

Mug in hand, Hannah excused herself and strolled to the kitchen as if accustomed to state police officers wearing snazzy suits and maroon underpants dropping by for an early Saturday-morning kaffeeklatsch.

Fetching another cup from the cabinet, she smiled at the mucky saucepan in the sink and mouthed a thank-you to Delbert for making her drink the cocoa she'd wanted last night like so-much hemlock.

She hadn't believed in the sleep-inducing power of hot milk, but his concoction knocked her out the instant her head creased the pillow. She'd wakened early, wondrously refreshed and feeling as guilty as homemade sin.

If David had slept at all, it wouldn't have been the poetic "nature's sweet restorer" variety. Some friend

Hannah was, zonked out in a tryptophan coma while he'd dissected the Quince shooting frame by frame and what he should have done differently to change the outcome.

When Hannah returned from the kitchen, Lieutenant Pike was jotting a note in a southpaw-slanted scrawl in a small spiral notebook. He thanked her for the coffee, then said, "Your answering machine is blinking. I can step outside if you need to check the messages."

Unless someone had called while she was in the shower, the indicator must have been flashing since she'd left the cottage for another not-to-be date with David. "No, a few more minutes won't make any difference."

By his frown, Pike took that as a time limit on his interview. She hadn't meant it as such, but if it worked, what the hey.

"My purpose isn't to hang Sheriff Hendrickson out to dry, Ms. Garvey. All I'm after is the truth."

Hannah settled back in her desk chair. The faint-of-heart would be ill advised to call Pike's bluff in a poker game. He was as cool and professional as a palace guard, which she found oddly reassuring. "I suppose you want me to start at the top?"

Another semismile.

Leaving nothing out, yet keeping her account brief, she related everything she'd heard, done or seen, from the dispatcher's original radio transmission to her departure with Reserve Officer Moody.

Pike asked, "How long was it between the time Hendrickson exited the vehicle to when you heard the shot?"

"I don't know." Hannah thought a moment, then

shook her head. "It couldn't have been more than a few minutes, but sitting in the car with nothing to do besides think about how hungry I was, it felt like an hour."

"You didn't exit the vehicle? Stretch your legs?"

"David told me to sit tight." She hitched a shoulder. "Even if I'd been in the mood for civil disobedience, he locked the doors and took the keys with him."

"Did you wonder why he did that?"

"It was for my own protection."

"Is that what he told you?"

"He didn't have to." Hackles unfurling, she issued a stern warning to her temper.

"Did anyone drive by while you were waiting?"

"No."

"A child on a bicycle? A block-walker?"

"No." Realizing what he was really asking, Hannah said, "Sheriff Hendrickson's glove compartment contains two cassette tapes, a travel-size bottle of after-shave, a toothbrush, penlight, an extra set of handcuffs, a screwdriver and an owner's manual.

"He has three dollars and sixty-two cents in change in the ashtray—mostly quarters. Polaroids of three men and a woman your wife would not mistake for door-to-door missionaries are taped to the back side of the driver's-side visor."

Pike may have chuckled. "All right, so you stayed in the car until after the shot. How about the length of time between it and when Hendrickson came back to the unit?"

"I don't know that one, either. I was afraid David—Sheriff Hendrickson—was hurt. I tried everything short of breaking a window to get out, finally figured out how to work the radio, then hid on the floorboard like the dispatcher told me to.''

Pike's pen rhumbaed across the page. ''What did you and the sheriff talk about?''

''After he came back to the car?''

''Yes.''

''I don't...'' Hannah bit off what was becoming a routine response and stared down at the hardwood floor. Images clicked behind her eyes like a disc in a View-Master.

''I asked David what had happened. He didn't answer. I got the gist of it from what he told Tony, the dispatcher. Then David said 'Sit tight' again and started to get out of the car.''

''So, he went back to the house alone.''

''No, I—well, I argued with him. Claustrophobic I'm not, but I'd had all of the inside of that car I wanted.''

Hannah looked up. ''We weren't alone by then, anyway. I think he was still on the radio when the ambulance and two patrol cars arrived.''

Pike said, ''You didn't mention that in your written statement. Are you sure?''

''That's why David unlocked my door. He wouldn't have if the EMTs and his deputies weren't on the scene.''

''Is that speculation? Or did the sheriff say something to that effect?''

Grudgingly, she admitted the former.

Once the chronological sequence was established, Pike's questions became rapid-fire, pointed and hop-scotching all over the timeline. Hannah gripped the chair arms as if she were a kid again, riding the Scrambler at the county fair.

Whoever said "The truth shall set you free" had not been a witness-once-removed in a homicide investigation. Hadn't squirmed and stuttered and felt certain every word etched a black mark against a man's hard-earned reputation and trustworthiness.

By the time Pike pulled back his lapel and slipped his notebook and pen in his shirt pocket, Hannah's blouse clung to her back as though it had been laminated to her skin. He stood, then looked out the window. "I apologize if I've made you late for your golf game."

Leaning over the credenza to see past him, Hannah's eyes widened at the golf carts amassing on the lawn. Her first thought was that the gumshoe gang had expanded its membership, but she didn't recognize any of the drivers or passengers.

"I appreciate your cooperation." Pike offered his hand. "We may need to talk again."

Hannah nodded, distracted by the horde trooping up the porch steps, a grim bunch if ever she'd seen one. Maybe she should ask Pike to stay for another cup of coffee. A highway patrolman on the premises might come in handy.

The incoming females parted to allow the outgoing male to pass, then marched through the door before Hannah could say hello, much less extend an invitation.

From Theron Pike's interrogation to what resembled a female senior citizens' lynch mob. Life was good and getting better every second.

The only face Hannah recognized belonged to Zerelda Sue Connor, the physical fitness instructor she'd fired her first day on the job. Connor's expression was the epitome of smug. It didn't bode well.

A blond woman with frizz sufficing for hair, who must believe one couldn't be too rich or too thin, stepped forward. "We haven't met formally, Ms. Garvey, but I'm Hetta Caldwell. I spoke with you on the telephone when the utilities went out earlier this week."

Spoke? She'd screamed in Hannah's ear, expected her to repair two acts of God—namely a power failure and the thunderstorm that caused it—then slammed down the receiver.

Hannah twitched up a smile as sincere as the apparent spokeswitch's. "I presume you and your cov—er, friends have something to discuss with me?"

"Oh, yes. We most certainly do." Hetta appealed to her groupies. "Don't we, ladies?"

They bobbed their heads, murmuring assent.

Hetta said, "Let's start with the fact that on your very first day as the manager of Valhalla Springs *and* after having brunch with IdaClare Clancy and her little clique, you fired an employee you had not even met. Is that true, Ms. Garvey?"

Hannah's fingers splayed on the railing. "I can understand how you might misinterpret—"

"Oh, really now. What other interpretation could there be? Did you receive any complaints about Zerelda Sue Connor from anyone besides IdaClare and her friends? Did you even know the physical fitness instructor's *name* before your tête-à-tête at Nellie Dunn's Cafe?"

To both questions, the answer was unfortunately no. It *could* appear as though Connor was fired based on IdaClare, Rosemary Marchetti, Velma Billingsly and Marge Rosenbaum's complaints that Connor was managing the community center's fitness programs like a boot camp for seniors.

Then again, whether Hannah would have discharged Zee Connor on their say-so became moot the minute Hannah walked into the exercise room and saw Connor nose-to-nose with a gasping, overweight matron, calling her a slacker for not stair-stepping to the beat of "Stars & Stripes Forever."

"Well?" Hetta sneered. "What do you have to say for yourself, Ms. Garvey?"

Nothing. Zilch, nada, zip. Explaining her motivations and actions would have the same effect as the opening bell in a boxing match.

Hannah replied, "Since Ms. Connor's employment was terminated almost two weeks ago, I'm curious why you waited until now to question it."

Hetta sputtered, her mouth working in strange and unattractive ways. "We...because... It was, uh, it was out of respect for Katherine Osborn. Death isn't taken lightly here, and might I remind you, Katherine was *murdered*."

Muted voices chimed *"Kathleen."*

Hannah graced Hetta with a knowing smile. To her credit, the woman had the decency to blush.

As the sanctimonious are wont to do, Hetta recovered her wits with astonishing speed. "Our timeliness is not the issue, Ms. Garvey. Ms. Connor is a highly qualified, popular employee of this community, who was fired without cause and with no discussion of the complaints lodged against her.

"Unless you reinstate her immediately, we are prepared to support her in an age discrimination lawsuit against you, Jack Clancy and Valhalla Springs, Incorporated.''

Hannah's features arranged themselves into a perfectly doltish "Huh?" while her palms moved side to side as if erasing a chalkboard. "Whoa, whoa, whoa. Did I miss something? How does age discrimination factor into this?"

Hetta folded her arms over a nonexistent bosom. "Zee is fifty-nine years old, Ms. Garvey. The attorney we consulted says age discrimination is easier to prove than improper employment practices.''

Hannah chuckled without the merest trace of humor. From computer chips to zip-top bags, the purpose of advertising was answer a fundamental question everyone asks themselves, whether consciously or subconsciously: What's in it for me?

Intuition said this posse didn't give a damn whether or not Zerelda Sue Connor ever darkened the community center's exercise rooms again. If so, what did they expect to gain?

Demote IdaClare from her unofficial Queen Bee status? Yeah, well, them and what army?

Get Hannah fired for some unspecified reason? Not bloody likely. She wasn't indispensable, but Jack had known her too well for too long to send her packing over a management decision, especially after she explained why she made it.

Okay, if neither IdaClare nor I are the targets, then who is?

Hetta beckoned to a petite brunette with a flawless complexion and enviable hourglass figure. "Eulilly, I believe it's time we show Ms. Garvey how serious we are about this matter."

Floorboards creaked in the sudden hush. A dozen lipsticked mouths flat-lined. Eulilly pinched open a manila envelope's clasp and withdrew two sheets of ruled paper. "If you think we're the only ones concerned about Zee's future, this petition ought to convince you otherwise."

Eulilly's voice, its cadence and her languid embroidery of "petition" resounded in Hannah's mind. She'd only heard them once, but there was no mistaking them.

Six days ago, after she'd introduced Willard Johnson as the new physical fitness instructor during a gathering at the community center, the tenant now known as Eulilly No-Last-Name had left an anonymous message on Hannah's answering machine.

Miz Gah-vey, it's only fair to warn you, the residents are circulatin' a puh-tish-un callin' for your resignation. Nothin' personal and bygones will be bygones if you change your mind about hirin' that—well, surely you know who we mean. His kind don't belong here.

His kind meaning black, though Eulilly and *her* kind thought, if not verbalized, a less socially acceptable noun.

Hannah had no means of identifying the caller or a man who'd left a similar message. Willard's parents, from whom he rented a garage apartment, had brushed off similar calls as one would crumbs from a countertop.

As harassment went, the episode had been a one-act play with no encore. Under Willard's direction, participation in the fitness programs had increased, not decreased. Hannah had assumed—wrongly—that the cowardly racists had slithered back under their rocks.

Mustering every ounce of self-control she possessed,

Hannah took the papers from Eulilly's hand. The columns blurred as she skimmed thirty or forty names and addresses.

Ye gods. Was Valhalla Springs a white supremacists' enclave disguised as a retirement village?

The rational hemisphere of her brain said there was a better-than-even chance the majority had never participated in any fitness programs and had been force-fed the baloney about Zee Connor's "unfair" dismissal. The same could apply to the group shuffling in place in her living room—including Hetta Caldwell.

Yes. Definitely including Hetta Caldwell. She wouldn't have taken Connor's hup-two crap for a New York minute and people with built-in mean streaks are violins in the manipulative hands of a maestro.

Hannah cleared her throat to stifle an ardent desire to spit in Eulilly Who's-it's green eye. "Thank you all for bringing your concerns to my attention. I will inform Mrs. Caldwell of my decision no later than noon on Monday."

Hetta's hand started to rise in protest. Eulilly caught her wrist and stayed it. "That'll be jes' fine, Miz Gahvey." She smiled as wide as a debutante, which she surely had been during the Truman administration.

The visitors filed out, practically stepping on each other's heels. A few finger-waved. Hannah didn't return them. As her great-uncle Mort always said, "Only a fool ventures out on thin ice with fancy skaters."

She perched on the railing and stared out the screen door long after the golf-cart convoy disappeared over the hill.

Choices. A supposed plural, since most decisions connote an *either* and an *or*. Hers was singular. One of those shitty, balls-to-the-walls kind, irrespective of gender. Ovaries-to-the-walls just didn't have the same oomph.

Minutes later, an elbow anchored on the desk and hair bunched in her fist, Hannah listened to Jack Clancy's private office line ring twenty-some times.

On any given Saturday morning, he could be anywhere in the country, hunched over a set of blueprints with investors eager to build a tax shelter complete with a championship golf course.

Hesitant to interrupt with a cell-phone delivered crisis, Hannah tried another Greater Saint Louis-area number. On the third ring, a male voice boomed, "Hi, Hannah. How's it going?"

She reared back. "Stephen? Are you psychic all of a sudden?"

The other man of the Clancy house laughed. "If I say yes, will you shell out four bucks a minute to talk to me?"

She smiled. "Better stick to delivering babies for a living, Dr. Riverton. I just remembered you guys have caller ID, like everyone else in America except me."

"Are you sure? If your system didn't have access, your number wouldn't have scrolled up on my phone's LED. At least I don't think it would."

Hannah scowled at the receiver. If caller ID were available, it couldn't cost more than five or six dollars a month to subscribe, whether she had any need for it or not.

"Generous Jack, the sometimes cheapskate strikes again," she said. "Can we agree the love of your life is a trifle penny-wise, pound foolish?"

"I think it's an occupational hazard. A string of zeros on a prospectus isn't real money. A fifty in Jack's wallet is, and he guards it like he'll never see another one if he spends it.''

Hannah nodded as though Stephen were in the room, rather than in a fabulous loft apartment in downtown Saint Louis. ''With those qualifications, Jack should run for Congress.''

''No, Washington's dirt wouldn't be as much fun to play in as the real thing. Give Jack an earthmover as big as a house and he's a happy man.''

Hannah asked, ''I don't suppose he's home, is he?''

She was beginning to think they'd been disconnected when Stephen said, ''You haven't talked to him? He left at the crack of dawn to drive down there. Didn't you get the message he left on your machine last night?''

The button still blinked with electronic abandon.

''No,'' Hannah admitted. ''I haven't been at my best or brightest the past twelve hours or so. Jack should be at IdaClare's by now. I'll try to reach him there.''

His tone somber, Stephen asked, ''Is something wrong? I don't mean to be nosy, but you haven't sounded like yourself since we started talking.''

She smiled, hoping it transmitted over the telephone line, and lied, ''I'm a little curious why Jack didn't stop here before he went to IdaClare's, that's all.''

''Now that you mention it,'' Stephen said, ''I am, too.''

''Only one way to find out. Later, gator.''

Suddenly realizing one of the messages she'd ignored could be from David, Hannah punched the answering machine's replay button. Two calls from Jack spieled forth—last night's, and another—wouldn't you know?—left while she was in the shower.

Hetta Caldwell had also forewarned her of the committee's planned offensive, and a telemarketer wanted to speak with "the lady of the house" about lifetime-guaranteed replacement storm windows.

David must be heeding Detective Andrik's communications blackout. Or he hated her for being the strapping tape on the box he was in.

He wouldn't have wanted her to lie. He'd told her she had no talent for it and honest men had a thing about expecting integrity in others. The problem with the truth was its openness to interpretation—the bulwark of the advertising industry.

Hannah doodled a daisy on a notepad, checkmarking the petals, "He hates me. He hates me not."

The pencil clinked on the banker's lamp's brass base. "You told David you trusted him, Hannah Marie. If you meant it, *act* like it."

IdaClare answered her phone as if she'd been sitting on it, waiting for it to hatch. Voice lowered to a whisper, she said, "You're the answer to my prayers. Please, dear, can you come over right away? If you can't talk sense into that son of mine—"

The muffled sounds of hand-to-hand combat proceeded Jack bellowing, "This is your *employer* speaking. Bear that in mind and get up here, pronto."

In the background, IdaClare yelled, "I talked to her *first!* She's on my side—"

Click. Dial tone.

Peachy frickin' keen. I'm the designated rope in a Clancy family tug-of-war. After IdaClare wins, which she will because she's Jack's mother and Valhalla

Springs's largest single investor, I get to tell the loser we're about to be codefendants in an age discrimination lawsuit.

For this, I quit a better paying job? With incentive bonuses *and* a 401K?

7

Jack Clancy's Jaguar Mark II crouched in IdaClare's driveway like a two-thousand-dollar door-ding waiting to happen. He knew Hannah drove a Blazer, not a jellybean mobile she could park on a dime and have change left over.

Muttering her opinion of phallic symbolism and middle-aged boys and their toys, she pulled her truck as far right as the concrete pad allowed.

She also wished she'd remembered her sunglasses. Even on a cloudy day, IdaClare's white Victorian cottage, adrip with fuchsia bargeboarded gables, spindles, balconets, gingerbread, window boxes and shutters, made visitors' pupils whimper, then contract with an almost audible slam.

Pink flamingos, ceramic elves, squirrels and chipmunks frolicked in the barberry bushes along the sidewalk. The clink-a-tinks of abundant wind chimes hooked to the porch's fretwork were as pleasing to the ear as dining at a table just outside a restaurant's kitchen.

Mother and son stood shoulder to shoulder behind the millworked screen door. Their lips were pulled back, exposing two sets of clenched teeth. Fidgeting implied a thumb-wrestling match being waged behind their backs.

"Red rover, red rover," Hannah singsonged. "One of you has to move over."

Jack reached for the latch. IdaClare's hip shot sideward. Her only child disappeared as if snagged by a giant hook and forced to exit, stage right.

The victor claimed the spoil's elbow in possession-is-nine-tenths-of-the-law fashion. "I have a batch of your favorite brownies and I just made a fresh pot of coffee to go with them."

"Which brownies?" Hannah inquired. "The ones with chocolate icing on top or the ones with marijuana baked in?"

"The frosted ones, dear." She heaved a tragic sigh. "I'd have split the recipe, but that colicky detective and that sheriff of yours took off with my entire herb garden. Dirt and all."

"The brute," Jack said, swooping in from the opposite side.

Often as the Clancys threatened to disclaim each other, their sky-blue eyes, stocky builds, pug noses and chin dimples wouldn't allow it. Over the years, Jack's hair had silvered and his waistline had expanded a notch, but he possessed that indefinable quality that caused passersby in airport concourses to later tell seatmates they'd glimpsed Harrison Ford or Richard Gere.

He grinned and opened his arms. "I'm fresh out of chocolate to bribe you with, sweetpea, but hugs aren't fattening."

A familiar tug pulled behind her ribs, a poignant reminder that a man and a woman can love each other and wish on the same star but be powerless to make it come true.

Jack stepped back and twirled an index finger. "Now turn around so I can give you a swift kick in the butt."

"What for?"

"Stephen called in a panic. Thanks to you, he thought I'd wrecked the car and was lying dead in a ditch somewhere."

The sadness that had veiled IdaClare's face lifted so quickly a casual observer would dismiss it as a figment of the imagination. She loved her son too much to condemn his lifestyle or his partner, but would never stop hoping Jack's sexual preference was a phase he'd outgrow.

Hannah said, "Well, if you weren't so famous for blowing the cobs out of that Jag, lots of us wouldn't worry about you so much."

Behind her, a reedy voice said, "Don't listen to her, boss. Fixing your traffic tickets generates half my annual income."

She turned, scoped the portion of the kitchen visible beyond the entry hall, then adjusted downward.

A young man dressed in a camel-hair sport coat, gray sport shirt and pleated trousers gave her a sly smile. The Fu Manchu mustache was for show. The oval, tortoiseshell glasses were not. Neither saved him from looking like a sixth-grader masquerading as an adult.

"Kayak Teel, I presume." She held out a hand. "It's about time I met the man I've heard so much about."

The child prodigy had grown up in Saint Louis's notorious Pruitt-Igore housing project, leap-frogged from grade school to Harvard Law and taken a junior partnership at his hometown's most prestigious law firm.

For years, senior partners had solicited Kayak's advice on trial strategy, declared it brilliant, hailed him as the greatest attorney since Clarence Darrow and kept their in-house genius sequestered in his office.

Kayak resented his banishment from the courtroom, but understood why a four-foot-nine-inch lawyer who relied on Lord & Taylor's children's department for his wardrobe couldn't effectively argue a client's fate before a jury.

Switching from criminal to corporate law, the "Bootstrap Boy Wonder from the Projects" now headed Clancy Construction & Development's legal department.

He clasped Hannah's hand. "I know Jack didn't tell you I came along for the ride. How could you have guessed who I am?"

Hannah's wrist swiveled. "By your class ring. You *are* the only Harvard alum at CC&D, aren't you?"

"My, oh my." Kayak angled his head at Jack. "Why'd you invite this woman to our tea party? She's too quick—"

"He didn't invite her," IdaClare said. "I did and she's on my side, aren't you, Hannah?"

Jack shot back, "Oh no she isn't."

"Oh yes she is."

"She's got too much sense to be on your side."

"She does *not*." IdaClare's face flushed three shades darker than her velour pantsuit. "I mean, she has too much sense to side with you and a shyster." She patted Kayak's shoulder. "Nothing personal. You're a very sweet young man. I just don't like lawyers."

"Damn it, Mother, will you give it up? Kayak and I have been trying to tell you all morning, *you don't have a side.*"

IdaClare's fists ground her hips. In the malevolent tone Eve originated and mothers have duplicated for millennia, she said, "John Patrick Clancy, this is my house and you'll lower your voice when you yell at me or I swear on your daddy's grave I'll strap your butt till you can't sit down for a week."

The fifty-year-old multimillionaire CEO went pale.

"Yes, ma'am."

"Now, y'all take yourselves in yonder and behave, while I see to the refreshments."

In unison, Jack, Hannah and Kayak said, "Yes, ma'am."

IdaClare whirled and marched into the kitchen. Her chastised guests cat-footed into the living room in single-file formation.

The ceiling and walls were papered in a peony pattern so vivid Hannah could smell them. A pink, enameled baby grand piano angled in one corner reflected the gauzy, twinkle-lighted swags festooning the bay window and continuing around the room.

Jack referred to IdaClare's decorating scheme as a blind madam's whorehouse. Hannah fought the urge to hyperventilate.

Kayak gathered a laptop computer, file folders and a tablet from a wing chair, sat down and made a minor production out of rearranging his portable office.

Jack took the far end of the white, L-shaped sofa and glared out the window, as if surveilling the cottage across the street.

Hannah deposited herself at the couch's other end. Well, gee, aren't these spur-of-the-moment get-togethers, great? Almost as fun as hanging out with Theron Pike and Hetta Caldwell.

She should have taken a walk around the lake to ease the aftereffects. Jack was as tense as she'd ever seen him if not more so. Oh, he'd hugged her and seemed happy to see her, but why was he sitting with his back half turned to her?

High-pitched coos from the kitchen were accompanied by the dire tickety-ticks of tiny, prancing toenails. Seconds later, two pink-orange blurs streaked across the carpet and went airborne.

Itsy and Bitsy, IdaClare's teacup poodles, panted and pawed and yapped at Hannah with glee, knowing any retaliation on her part—such as wringing their obnoxious, bejeweled necks—would be bad form.

"My fault," Jack said. "Mother set them loose to get back at me."

Hannah dodged the bouncing wads of fur. "Then why are they *here* instead of over there?"

Kayak suggested, "I guess they know a dog lover when they see one."

For all his smarts, the guy didn't know a thing about animal psychology. Itsy and Bitsy were mutant dust-bunnies not dogs. A dog was big and shaggy and had melty brown eyes. Intelligent enough to pee and poop outdoors, well beyond sneaker range, but dumb enough to unconditionally love its owner, especially when no one else did.

IdaClare entered the room, tray in hand. She beamed at her four-legged, psycho "grandbabies" cavorting in

Hannah's lap. "When I told them their aunt Hannah was here, they begged to come say hello."

As she set the tray on the pink-and-gilt japanned coffee table, Jack and Kayak mouthed "Aunt Hannah?" then snorted under their breath.

IdaClare glanced up. "Did you say something, son?"

"Me? I...ah, yes, I did. I said it's been too long since I had your fabulous homemade brownies."

"It wouldn't have been if you came down here more often. Isn't that right, Hannah?"

"Absolutely." She gave Jack a smarmy smile. "Hardly a week goes by that I don't tell him he should make more effort to spend time with you. Don't I, Jack?"

No response.

Okay, he wasn't in a teasing mood. Whatever mood he was in was a new one on her.

The hostess distributed coffee and confections, took neither for herself and sat down in the second wing chair. Itsy and Bitsy sailed off the sofa and plopped down between her feet.

Thank God.

IdaClare said, "Hannah, this squabble we've put you in the middle of is because Jack insists that Kayak represent me at the arraignment Monday morning."

Her mouth full of brownie, Hannah pantomimed, "What's the problem?"

"I don't want an attorney, don't need an attorney and I truly wish everyone would let me do things my own way."

Jack said, "She has what she calls 'an advocate'"

lined up to plead her case. She won't say who or what this person plans to do.''

His dessert plate clattered on the tray. ''This is not a bunch of unpaid parking tickets, Hannah. We're talking cultivating, possessing and distributing an illegal substance, and she was caught red-handed.''

Kayak said, ''Aside from using a layperson, I'm very concerned about the lack of precedent regarding medicinal marijuana. Court rulings in California, Arizona, Washington and elsewhere it's been legalized—to varied extents—by popular vote are anything but consistent.

''The Missouri legislature is considering a bill to exempt from criminal or civil penalties possession of less than seventy grams of marijuana for those with a physician's written recommendation for its use—''

''But,'' Jack broke in, ''the bill has been stalled for months. Even if it passed—effective today—neither Mother, nor her 'patients' have medical authorization, and cultivation will still be illegal.''

Hannah placed her cup and saucer on the Bombay chest beside the sofa. ''Pardon me for being dense, but I don't understand what any of that has to do with the charges against IdaClare.''

''Nor do I, dear,'' IdaClare said. ''This gobbledygook is exactly why I don't want an attorney.''

''Basically,'' Kayak said, ignoring another jab at his profession, ''since Mrs. Clancy has already pled guilty, she's at the judge's mercy. If Messerschmidt is a hardliner and makes no distinction between recreational marijuana and medical marijuana, gives no consideration to the plaintiff's age, or—shall we say—her humanitarian intent, he could sentence her to a year in the county jail.''

Barred doors clanged shut in Hannah's mind, like the sound track from *I Want to Live* when Susan Hayward is escorted to her cell on death row. IdaClare must have missed Hayward's performance, for she appeared as unperturbed as the fern on the plant stand behind her chair.

Hannah said, ''Well, If the judge is predisposed to lock up anyone and everyone, what difference will it make *who* represents IdaClare in court?''

''Exactly what I've tried to tell them, dear,'' Ida-Clare said.

Jack's and Kayak's eyes met and held.

''Probably none.'' The lawyer sighed in disgust. ''For the record, Jack, I asked you why you wanted her included in this discussion. Tactical error, boss. Big time.''

Hannah knew they were communicating in code, but wasn't prepared for the cold, angry stare Jack leveled at her. ''You're the advocate, aren't you?''

''Me?'' She laughed. ''God, no.''

''An adviser, then.''

''No, Jack, I—''

''A consultant? Mediator? Negotiator? Pick a title, sweetpea.'' A vulgar hiss defiled his pet name for her. ''Any title.''

''What's the matter with you, Jack? I haven't even talked to IdaClare about this, let alone—''

''Bullshit!''

Hannah leaped to her feet. Her dessert plate tumbled to the floor. ''I've been a pawn in somebody else's game since I got up this morning and I'll be *damned* if I'll sit here and be browbeaten by you or your remote-controlled 'learned counsel.'"

She threw her napkin on the tray. "If there's *anyone* who should be IdaClare's advocate, it's *you,* Jack. Hey, now there's an idea. Taking your mother's side, even if you think she's wrong." Her eyes bored into his. "Just like she's always taken yours."

Heart pounding, fists clenched so tightly her forearms ached, she repressed the impulse to storm out and sever a relationship she'd treasured for over fifteen years.

After all they'd been through—especially the painful acceptance that they could be friends and nothing more—how could he believe she'd lie to him, betray him for *any* reason?

Kneeling beside the coffee table, Hannah plucked a crumb from the plush white carpet and dropped it on her plate, then another and another.

Mental scrapbook pages flipped back to the day a tornado roared through the heart of Effindale's business district. After the danger passed, Samaritans and snoops crawled out of their 'fraidy holes to survey the damage. Walking hand in hand with her mother, Hannah gawked at buildings and houses that looked as though a hungry giant had bitten their roofs and sidewalls and a sprawling tree with straw imbedded in its trunk like wispy arrows.

"It'd take six men and a boy with chainsaws to bring that tree down," Caroline had said as if to herself. "Funny how it didn't take nothin' but a gust of wind and some chaff to wound it."

The grand old oak was still standing when Hannah detoured to Effindale to visit her mother and family elders at the cemetery and tell them about her new job at Valhalla Springs. The towering, leafy lollipop she'd immortalized in green and brown crayon had resembled a pie with a slice missing, but it soldiered on, despite the damage that time, acts of God and the electric company had inflicted.

"Sweetpea." Jack's voice was soft now, and remorseful, but it startled Hannah nonetheless.

She retrieved a crumb from behind the coffee table's leg, then sat back on her heels. "The Eleventh Commandment says, 'She who makes a mess of things is obliged to clean them up.'"

Her palms ironed the crease in her slacks. "Of the two I just made... well, this one I knew how to fix. I'm not sure the other can be."

Jack held out his hands to help her to her feet. Unable to look at him, she saw that IdaClare, Kayak, even Itsy and Bitsy, had left the room.

How kind of them to let Jack fire her in private. Tom and Rob Friedlich subscribed to the notion that public dismissals discouraged scenes, like dumping a lover or spouse in a restaurant between courses to nip the dumpee's hysterics in the proverbial bud.

Jack laced his fingers with hers. "You can stop with the pulling away already. I'm not going to let go."

"That implies there's something worth hanging on to."

"You are," he said. "The one person I swore I'd never hurt again, but I did. Sorry doesn't cut it except to describe me."

Tears clouded Hannah's vision. Wounded, yes, but it'd take six men, a boy and chainsaws to bring them down. "Sorry applies to me, too, Jack. I shouldn't have—"

"Gotten so mad you turned into a digital vacuum cleaner?" He made tut-tut noises. "No, you shouldn't have. You robbed the Furwads from Hell of their only purpose in life."

The grin tugging at Hannah's lips was impossible to squelch. "Will you shut up and let me explain?"

"Explain what? You were right. Mother was doing it her way before Sinatra learned the words. If I respect her gumption when I agree with her, I have to respect it when I don't."

"Okay, maybe my tantrum had merit, but the delivery was way out of line."

He caressed her knuckles with his thumbs. "How many times have you seen or heard me lose my temper?"

"That doesn't—"

"How many?"

"A million."

"A conservative estimate. Now, how many times have I seen or heard you lose yours?"

Hannah sighed. "A million and a half."

"Also conservative. I'd have rounded it up to two. The point is, what's so different about today's little tiff?"

"Little tiff? Jeez Louise, that's like dropping a bomb on Baghdad and calling it a step toward lasting peace in the Middle East."

Jack's upraised eyebrows warned against further asides and demanded an answer.

"I told you the truth and you didn't believe me," Hannah said. "I'd never do anything behind your back and you were convinced I had."

"That may have been how it sounded, but I was a runaway train before I asked if you were Mother's advocate. I love her, I'm afraid for her and after Kayak lobbed worst-case scenarios at me all the way down here, I had such a head of steam built up, if you'd told me your name, I'd have hollered, 'Bullshit.'"

They really *had* tried to outshout each other a million times. Free-for-alls were one of the beauties of their friendship. No stops, no gloves, just two stubborn, willful people growling and teasing and baiting each other like puppies at play.

Stress and lousy timing were the real culprits. The shooting, Pike's unexpected arrival and Eulilly What's-Her-Name had primed Hannah's fuse. Jack struck the match. Well, things might as well get worse so they could start getting better.

She sat him down on the couch and told him about David, the interview, the Connor committee, their threatened lawsuit and its basis in fact.

"None of that justifies me losing my cool," Hannah admitted, "but *both* of us were runaway trains."

Jack ran his fingers through his hair. His demeanor intimated the chairman of the board had taken charge. "Well, a court fight would be expensive, bad publicity for Valhalla Springs and could drag on for months."

His jaw cocked sideward. "And I'd sic Kayak on

them in a heartbeat if I thought it'd expose our resident bigots for what they are.''

He looked up. "But it won't."

"I know."

"Any ideas for a counterattack?"

"Several are germinating. I'll call you when—"

"Uh-uh." A finger tapped his chest. "Me, absentee owner." It whipped around at her. "You, manager. Pick one and go with it. That's why I pay you the big bucks."

Twenty-five thousand a year and an almost lakeside cottage did not a *Fortune 500* member make, but big was a relative term. Especially to guys.

"Item two," he continued, "the bind your sheriff is in."

Hannah rolled her eyes. "He is not my sheriff. He's county property."

"Meaning, you haven't done the horizontal boogie yet." He chuckled. "No wonder you're on edge."

"Jack!"

He ducked in case Hannah's right hook wasn't a feint. "I've never met the man, but he has yours and Mother's seal of approval, so that's good enough for me. Tell Hendrickson one of the finest criminal attorneys in the country is at his disposal, if it comes to that. Pro bono. Kayak won't man the defense table, but he'll mastermind the strategy."

A question she'd hardly allowed herself to think lodged in her throat. "It's going to come to that, isn't it? Lieutenant Pike isn't out to prove David is innocent. He's collecting evidence for a homicide charge."

Jack averted his gaze like a doctor faced with informing a patient of a terminal prognosis.

Hannah knew what he was thinking: Innocent until proven guilty is judicial spin. Nor was this a case of matching a list of suspects to motives and opportunity.

David Hendrickson shot Stuart Quince in self-defense. But was the threat real? Or had the stress of the Osborn case, his best friend Mike Rivera's near-fatal injury and the long drive home from Tulsa combined and caused David's imagination to play a deadly, dirty trick on him?

8

The square was downright lively for late Saturday afternoon. There was little traffic to speak of, but pickups with clay mud stuccoed in their wheel wells and a half-dozen cars lined the curb outside the Short Stack Café.

Instead of napping in his barber chair until closing time, Eli Cree was holding court with a couple of codgers in MFA gimme caps and Big Smith overalls. Robbed of his customary forty winks, Eli would be snoring in front of the TV before six o'clock news came on.

No doubt what the topic of conversation was inside both establishments. David wondered which side was holding sway: the Hendrickson-is-a-cold-blooded-killer faction or the Hendrickson-acted-in-self-defense one.

If he were a gambler, he'd say the former. It made for a whopping good story with plenty of room for improvement.

His eyes didn't stray to the courthouse. Peripheral vision assured him the dog-ugly, half-yellow, half-red-brick building was still standing.

Life does go on.

David wondered how Hannah was going on with hers. He'd picked up the phone a hundred times, punched three or four numbers, then cradled it. Cooperating with Andrik's no-talk rule had given the fear of how she'd react a wall to hide behind.

The phone lines ran both directions. Andrik's gag order did, too, but was that why she hadn't called him? Fear of getting David in deeper than he already was?

She cared. More than she let on. More than she wanted to. He knew because he felt the same way. Before they met, they'd decided they were loners. Had taken a strange kind of pride in it, truth be known.

Stumbling on to each other had made *loner* feel like *lonely*. Except admitting it meant one of two things: either they'd been fooling themselves all along or they were fooling themselves now.

Hannah said she trusted him, but that was before she became a witness to a homicide. Sticking "justifiable" in front of it wouldn't change a thing if she'd never be able to look at David again without seeing blood on his hands.

The possibility haunted him almost as much as Stuart Quince's voice, the smell of cordite, the thump of a dead man falling to a dirty, bare floor and the taste of cobwebs and ashes when Andrik told David no gun was found at the scene.

Theron Pike's unmarked Caprice and Andrik's unmarked clunker sat nosed into the curb outside a storefront with a dark-tinted, bullet-proof plate window and door. David parked nearer the corner, careful not to clip the meter with his bumper.

Tourists fed spare change into those municipal piggy banks, unaware that Sanity's city council had declared the square a free parking zone back in 1989. It was a standing joke that Millie Lindhorst, the older-than-rocks meter maid who allegedly died of a broken heart when her job became obsolete, had herself buried with the cash boxes' keys. Nobody'd seen hide nor hair of them since her funeral.

David cadged a look in the rearview mirror. Yep, same smudges and bags under his eyes he'd seen fifteen minutes ago when he left the house. Under the florescent lights in Andrik's office, he'd look as beetle-browed as Frankenstein.

He gave his black, Western-cut jacket, chambray shirt and black jeans a once-over—as if he'd haul ass home to change if they suddenly didn't suit him. He'd felt like six kinds of idiot pawing through his closet in his underpants, debating what to wear to Pike's official 4:00 p.m. nut-cuttin'.

Stamping the wrinkles from his britches, David shut the pickup's door harder than intended. All that dinking around and he'd left his Stetson on the hat rack in the living room. Feeling as naked as the storybook emperor, he started down the sidewalk to the Kinderhook County Sheriff's Department's Detective Division headquarters, otherwise known as "The Outhouse."

He dug out his wallet, the cowhide as satiny and curved as a saddle seat from years of riding his hip pocket. An empty slit with credit cards runged above it gave him pause, before he remembered he'd turned in the security system's key card along with his badge, his gun and a big chunk of his pride.

"Strictly for your own protection," Jimmy Wayne had said, refusing to meet David's eyes.

Jessup Knox, who'd donated and installed the system, was running against him in the August primary. If word got around David still had access to the investigation's files—well, trust a jackass like Knox to make a federal case out of it.

"Better safe than sorry," Jimmy Wayne had said.

David wasn't sure whose backside the chief deputy was covering, but he would bet it wasn't his.

He nodded at a passing sedan, then raised his eyes to the corner windows on the courthouse's third floor. His office looked empty, too.

Count your blessings, son. Be grateful Theron Pike had the good grace not to hold your feet to the fire at your own hearth. Meeting at The Outhouse saved twenty-two departmental employees and their kinfolk the hassle of inventing excuses for being at the courthouse this afternoon.

Saved them the embarrassment of tumbling butt-over-toenails into David's office whenever the door opened, too.

Ignoring The Outhouse's video camera, David pressed the buzzer. A dull throb at the bridge of his nose jagged outward.

Clack. In ten seconds, the lock would reengage. David sucked in his gut, gripped the door's elongated metal handle and pulled.

Flit...tish—tish—bloop.

Amazing how a flat stone skipping across an Illinois farm pond, Lake Michigan or Lake Valhalla Springs sounded the same.

Great-uncle Mort once side-armed a rock eleven hops, by actual count. The best Hannah'd ever done was six. Nowhere near a record, but it had pissed Jarrod off, who threw like a girl. Whereas Hannah threw like the old man who'd taught her the soothing quality of a stretch of water and a handful of skip-rocks to chuck at it.

Laughter and "Sentimental Journey's" smoky melody lilted out the community center's open sliding-glass doors. The Saturday-night potluck dinner dance was in full swing, though the sun hadn't yet slipped behind the hills.

"Got a favor to ask of you," Delbert had called to announce earlier that afternoon. "Put on your glad rags and go to the dance with me tonight. Maxine McDougal is down with the lumbago, and if I show up stag the lonely hearts'll be on me like ducks on a june bug."

"Nice try," Hannah said, laughing, "but you told me about your harem the day I moved in here. Besides, I thought you and Leo Schnur checked out the local action in town every Saturday night."

"Hmmph." For a small man, Delbert packed a ton of disgust into a single grunt. "Leo's all moony-eyed over Rosemary Marchetti, so to hell with me. If I squire another one of my regulars, Maxine'll cut me off for a month."

From what? Surely not the wild thing. Okay, even more surely not Maxine's weekly low-fat chicken casseroles by candlelight. Jeez. Senior sex was a lovely concept, but let's leave it at that, shall we?

"I'm sorry, Delbert," she said. "Really I am, but I'm of the hustle and funky chicken generation. And I haven't hustled or funkied for ages."

"I can have you lindy hoppin' with the best of 'em in five minutes."

She made a face, loving him dearly for trying to dance her troubles away and wishing he'd take no for an answer.

Delbert broke the hum on the line with, "You haven't heard from him, have you?"

"No."

"Baby-sitting the phone won't make it ring."

"Sure it does. It just hasn't been David on the other end. Yet."

"I had an appointment in town this morning. I saw that state police car in your driveway when I went by."

Delbert didn't sound as though he were on a fishing expedition, but Hannah didn't reply.

"Have you tried to call him?"

"Uh-uh. Orders from headquarters, remember?"

His tone sharpened. "That's not what's stopping you."

"Oh?" A defensive low C slid upward a full octave. "Then what is?"

"Not knowing what to say because you're afraid David will hear the doubt in your voice."

"As in, 'Gee, I'd like to believe you, but guns don't sprout legs and walk off'?"

No comment.

"Okay, you're half-right," Hannah said. "I don't know what to say to him, but I not only believe him, I believe *in* him. I may be the only one in the whole stupid county who does."

Another grunt. "Well, now, there's a conversation starter..."

"But what if—"

"Do you love the man?"

"Yes. No. I don't know." She rested her forehead on the heel of her hand. "How I feel or don't feel has nothing to do with whether I believe David or not."

Curses spluttering from the earpiece sounded like a

peeved Donald Duck. Holding the receiver away for a moment, Hannah reeled it in just as Delbert said, "For a half-smart female, you don't think worth a damn sometimes.

"Jiminy Christmas. If you were David Hendrickson, who would you need more right now? Somebody who believed you? Or somebody who believed *in* you?"

Coffee percolated in David's belly, hotter and stronger than the brown sludge in the foam cup he held. How long had he been here? Two hours? Three?

Felt like a month. He'd avoided glancing at his watch—as if that would give away his anxiety more than the sweat glistening his forehead.

It didn't matter where The Outhouse's thermostat was set. The air stayed hot and the mangy, shag-carpeted floor stayed cold. His toes numb, but his upper body on the verge of heatstroke, David cussed the jacket he couldn't shed. He must own a hundred shirts. Naturally, he'd picked a light blue one.

To his left, Marlin Andrik's complexion and sport coat were the same shade of gray. He slouched in a chair, a crossed knee resting against the end of his desk, not happy to be there instead of behind it.

Theron Pike was on the desk's business side. He wrestled a sheaf of typed reports, comparing them to his handwritten notes. A quick statement analysis? No doubt about it.

Whether a statement was written or oral, truthful people almost always used the first-person singular to tell their stories, recounting them chronologically and concisely without hedging.

David wasn't satisfied with his report, but knew it

met the criteria. Though not intentional, each of the before, during and after segments were in almost equal thirds. Experts believed the greater the balance, the higher the probability the statements were true.

Pike said, "Tell me again why you didn't wait for your backup."

"It was Friday night," David said. "The duty roster was short a man already. I thought I'd handle the call and let Cahill go Code 4 instead of waiting on him and tying up two officers."

"Even though you said you felt 'hinky' about the complaint."

"Yes."

"And even though you had an unauthorized civilian in the unit with you."

"C'mon, Pike. I'm the sheriff. Who, exactly, should I have obtained authorization from?"

"Isn't it policy for a rider to sign a liability form?"

Again with the ticky-tacky crap. Again, David explained the circumstances. Admitted he'd fudged on using a county vehicle for personal reasons and how he should be strung up by his thumbs, being the first law enforcement officer in history to ever do such a thing.

"I understand the urgency in identifying Mr. Quince's next of kin," Pike said, "but under the circumstances, ordering your deputies away from the scene looks—"

"Suspicious, in twenty-twenty hindsight," David finished for him. He ditched the empty coffee cup in the trash can. "How many times do I have to agree I contradicted myself?

"Yes, as soon as I reported the shooting, I told Tony I was off the case. Yes, not ten minutes later, I told

Moody to do crowd control and Tom Cahill to canvass the neighborhood. Yes, I should have kept my mouth shut and let Bret Vann, the watch commander, take charge.''

Marlin Andrik broke in, "We all made mistakes, Pike, and shit slides downhill. I broke with procedure, too—namely, regardless of how death appears to have occurred, it's murder until the evidence proves otherwise.''

The detective shrugged. "Hell, some of us are human.''

Technically, Andrik wasn't a participant in the interview. Whether Pike included him out of courtesy, or because it was being conducted on Andrik's turf, Marlin was supposed to be an observer. And he had kept his involvement to observation thus far, to David's surprise.

Pike said, "It seems to me—correction, it would seem to anyone reviewing this incident—that an officer's involvement would foster a stricter adherence to procedure.''

"It should,'' David allowed.

"Except for it being tougher to maintain objectivity,'' Marlin said. "No excuses, but it comes more naturally when strangers are involved.''

David silently agreed. "I can't recall, specifically, what ran through my mind at the time. To a great extent, I was on automatic pilot. The training pounded into my skull took over.''

The marionette creases above Pike's mouth deepened. "You took the precaution of putting on a bulletproof vest, didn't you, Sheriff?''

"Yes. Under a departmental windbreaker, for identification purposes."

"But you left your handset radio in the trunk."

Conscious of the video camera recording his every
twitch, David rectified a tendency to slump in the
molded plastic lawn chair that served as visitor seating
at The Outhouse.

"I was responding to a non-emergency call. I had
backup en route and—"

"You parked well away from the scene," Pike continued, "as a measure of protection for the civilian who
accompanied you. You took the precaution of wearing
body armor. You armed yourself but left your handset
in the vehicle."

"Yes, but—" David's lips flattened. He was volunteering too much. *K.I.S.S. Keep it simple, stupid. You
know the drill. Pike isn't your enemy, but he damn sure
isn't your friend and you're not telling war stories over
a couple of beers in a bar.*

Think before you answer. Make Pike ask what he
wants to know. If ninety-nine percent of the suspects
you've questioned had done likewise, a majority would
have walked.

"Ms. Garvey has stated she heard only one shot
fired," Pike said.

Not a question. Bait. Don't bite.

"Would you agree, Sheriff, considering the time of
day and your position in the yard, the lighting was not
advantageous to you?"

"Yes."

"Mr. Quince could see you more clearly than you
could see him, is that correct?"

David said, "I can't speculate on what Mr. Quince could or could not see."

"Well, it is a reasonable assumption, isn't it?"

Yours, David thought. Not mine.

"According to your report—" Pike licked a finger and riffled several sheets in his folder "—Mr. Quince said, 'I need to die. This is the only way,' as well as other statements alluding to a suicidal frame of mind."

Assumption and allusion. Verbal bear traps lawyers—and highway patrol investigators with law degrees—loved like a wheatfield loves rain.

"Those two statements, in addition to the others in my report, indicated to me that Mr. Quince was suicidal, yes."

"You saw no weapon while Mr. Quince was making these statements?"

"Holy mother of Jesus," Marlin howled. "You think Hendrickson tried to fuckin' *bond* with Quince while the drone was pointing a gun at him?"

Even Pike cracked a smile at that one.

David answered, "Quince opened the door, holding his right arm behind his back. I ordered him to put his hands where I could see them. When he didn't, I pulled my service revolver, took aim and repeated the order to show his hands."

"That's when he displayed his gun?"

"No." David answered. "Quince said, 'I can't do it myself, I've tried.' *Then* his arm—the right arm he'd kept behind his back—came up, gun in hand."

"There was no doubt what he held was a gun."

"None."

"Can you describe it?"

"A Glock nine-millimeter, semiautomatic. Black metal frame. Black plastic grips—"

"The light was poor," Pike said, "you were in fear of your life, but you identified the gun's make and caliber?"

David raised his palm in a staving gesture. "When Quince moved his arm, I saw a gun in his hand."

"Or something shaped like a gun. A shadow—"

"When Quince moved his arm," David said slowly and deliberately, "I saw a gun in his hand."

"And you fired."

"In self-defense. Yes."

"And then what?"

"Holding my Smith & Wesson at ready, I advanced to the doorway of the house." David struggled to block the graphic images scrolling behind his eyes. "I kicked a Glock nine-millimeter semiautomatic lying on the floor out of Quince's reach, then—"

"Did you see the expended shell casing?"

"No, Lieutenant. Not at that time."

"When did you see it? Where was it in relation to the body?"

David stared at file cabinets banked along the wall. "I did a walk-through to make sure no one else was inside the house. On my way out, I saw an ejected shell casing a few inches from Quince's knee."

Cellophane crackled. Marlin's thumbnail flipped the top back on a fresh pack of Marlboros. Butts from the first pack lay like a nest of albino roaches in the terracotta saucer he used for an ashtray.

Pike batted at the fog roiling below the suspended ceiling's stained tiles. "Do you mind?"

Andrik's throwaway lighter clicked. "If I did, I

wouldn't do it." He exhaled with gusto. "This is my office, Lieutenant. Not yours."

David groaned inwardly. Antagonizing Pike was not in his best interests. Nor was it a show of Marlin's loyalty, as much as it connoted tension and his addiction to nicotine.

Resentment motivated him, too. Marlin respected Theron Pike as much as David did, but power struggles existed between branches of law enforcement just as they did between branches of the military.

As the adage went, city cops don't like county cops, county cops don't like the highway patrol, the highway patrol doesn't like the ATF and everybody hates the FBI.

Pike said, "I appreciate your restraint, Sheriff, but you may as well light up, too."

David frowned. "Me? I kicked the habit years ago."

"Oh?" Pike checked his field notes. "Ms. Garvey stated you were smoking at the scene. Inside the police line, I might add."

"Hannah said that? Then she's mistak—"

"Is the name Jay Magalski familiar to you?" Pike asked.

"Yes. He's a paramedic."

"Magalski states he offered you a cigarette, which you took, while the two of you talked at the scene. Magalski states you both extinguished the materials inside the barrier."

David didn't remember. Another black hole he hadn't been aware of. An important one. Another mistake. If it was true, and it must be, he'd contaminated a crime scene.

Pike said, "You saw an expended shell casing on the floor beside Quince's knee, is that correct?"

"A wha—? Oh. Yes, sir."

"Which knee?"

"The left."

Pike and Marlin exchanged a look.

David said, "Yeah, we all know a Glock ejects to the right." Leaning over the desk, he separated the stack of crime scene photographs, then tapped at one. "See how the front door is standing open, at an angle to the frame? My guess is that when Quince's Glock ejected the brass—to the right—it hit the door and ricocheted *left*."

Marlin crushed out his cigarette and eased back in his chair. Pike examined the photo a few seconds longer, returned it to the pile and straightened it. "You're aware that no casing was found at the scene."

"Yes." Sweat trickled down David's ribs. His first lie. He'd prayed it vanished after Marlin had taken photos.

"You're also aware no firearm of any make or model was found at the scene."

"Yes."

"Do you own a Glock semiautomatic similar to the one you described, Sheriff?"

"I do. It's in the trunk of my Crown Vic."

"What color is the frame? The grips?"

"Bla—" Realizing what Pike's questions implied, David's jaw fell, then snapped shut. "You don't just believe I shot Quince in cold blood. You think I panicked. That I overrode the watch commander and sent Moody and Cahill off to get rid of them, intending to plant *my* Glock on the corpse to cover my ass but I didn't have time to do it.''

Slamming back in the chair, he roared, ''What's more, you think I'm so psychologically fucked up, my mind tricked me into believing I *did* plant the Glock, described it down to the grips to Andrik at the scene and now I'm stuck with it.''

David felt as if he was suffocating. His head swung from side to side. He couldn't stop it. Couldn't yank off the noose tightening around his neck.

Vocal cords stretched taut, he said, ''You not only think I'm a murderer, but that I'm one dumb son of a bitch. Why, it's a goddamned miracle I get my boots on the right feet every morning.''

David jumped up and paced the silent room. ''Want to give me a lie detector test? Do it. I'm telling you the God's honest truth.''

He was shouting. He didn't care. Maybe it'd make 'em listen. ''Stuart Quince pulled a gun on me. He fired. I returned fire at damn near the same instant. That's why Hannah thinks she only heard one shot.

''Quince's gun was on the floor in plain sight. The casing was by his left knee when I went to the car to—''

David whirled on a heel. ''Gunpowder residue. Quince's hands *had* to have tested positive. No, I can't explain what happened to the gun, but for Christ's sake, *at least that proves he fired one.*''

Marlin averted his eyes to Pike, then bowed his head.

Pike laced his hands behind his neck and focused on the papers in front of him.

Legs trembling and gall burning up his throat, David came as close to screaming as he ever had in his life.

He swallowed hard. His clenched fists ached for a heavy bag to slam into.

"Marlin, my friend, if you didn't test Quince's hands for residue, you've as good as put me on the shortlist for the gas chamber."

The detective raised his head, but looked at the wall, not at David. "I did test them," he said, his voice graveled and strained. "The result was negative."

9

Sunday morning's gloomy sky and chilliness had no effect on Hannah's mood. She had a mission. Several of them, actually, and a sequential plan of attack.

She'd cleared her desk of all pending managerial tasks. Manila folders were stacked on one side. On the other, the promotional packets she'd mail tomorrow from Valhalla Springs's substation.

Most of the shops in the development's commercial district, a redbrick throwback to the Victorian era with street lamps and boardwalks shaded by awnings, observed the Sabbath until lunchtime. Hannah knew the Flour Shoppe was an exception and could hardly wait to stoke up on a fresh-baked Danish and a cappuccino to go.

First things first, however.

Willard Johnson's reaction to her phone call started out surprised, morphed to apprehension and ended with directions to his garage apartment.

Striking a businesslike posture in her swivel chair, Hannah dialed Hetta Caldwell's number. Salutations aside, she said, "My decision concerning Zerelda Sue Connor will have to be postponed until Monday afternoon. I'll be out of the office all morning tomorrow and have a tour appointment at one."

She'd never heard anyone titter, but Hetta did. "Well, isn't *that* a coincidence? I was about to ring you, for the same reason."

Ring me? Hannah rolled her eyes.

"Our attorney, Terry Woroniecki of Sachs, Woroniecki and Pratt, wants us to meet at four-thirty in the firm's conference room. Will that be convenient for you, Ms. Garvey?"

Oh, sure. She'd much rather drive twenty-two miles into Sanity to an attorney's office than make a five-minute phone call from her own.

"Four-thirty it is," Hannah said.

Her call to Marlin Andrik was no more gratifying. He sounded astonished to hear she'd complied with his gag order, didn't argue when she told him where he could put it, then refused to give her David's home address, which wasn't included in the telephone book's listing.

Going straight to the source for the information didn't work, either. David's answering machine clicked on with an electronic Beethoven symphony, indicating a backlog of messages.

Hanging up without adding her own, Hannah wiggled her eyebrows. "Ah, but ve haf other vays of finding out vat ve vant to know."

Churchgoers in no hurry for redemption doubled the drive time between Valhalla Springs and Sanity. Common sense and Highway VV's miles of yellow double lines prohibited passing, though several drivers put God as their copilot to the test.

Rural became urban with startling abruptness, as if the county-seat community had been dropped by helicopter in the wide valley bounded by rolling hills. At

Sanity's northern outskirts, the crescent-shaped Fountain Plaza Shopping Center was anchored by a Price-Slasher supermarket and a Wal-Mart. Between them, locally owned shops and stores leased at inflationary "location, location, location" rates struggled to survive.

Like similar retail developments named after landmarks that were paved over during construction, Fountain Plaza had no fountain. Nor, for that matter, a plaza.

The cinnamon roll painted on the window of Ruby's Café kind of resembled a frosted cow patty, but the restaurant was David's favorite haunt. Hannah's taste buds quivered at the memory of a chicken-fried-steak orgy a couple of weeks ago that she could have died and gone to heaven after eating.

The café's dining area was dark. A lopsided Closed sign hung in the door. At the back, though, light filled the pass-through in the kitchen wall. Bingo.

Hannah drove around to the center's graveled backlot. Dodging industrial-size Dumpsters and the trash not contained by them, she cruised past unmarked, rust-circled metal doors, then spotted a red, late-'70s Cadillac with fuzzy dice dangling from the rearview mirror. White fake-fur glued to the dash and rear deck, and gold lamé seat covers spelled Ruby Amyx like a vanity license plate.

Ruby answered Hannah's knock with a snarled, "What's your excuse for being late this… Why, flibber my giblets, if it ain't Miz Hannah from out Valhalla-way. Whatchoo doin' out here with the weeds and offal?"

"I have a favor to ask and I've heard beggars are supposed to go to the back door."

"Horsefeathers. Get yourself in here. I got pies fixin'
to come outta the oven."

Despite a tummyful of Danish pastry, Hannah
swooned at the aroma of fresh-baked yeast rolls and
barbecued brisket. Gaining a pound a minute just by
breathing, she said, "I know you're busy, so I won't
keep you, but could you give me David Hendrickson's
home address? I had it written down somewhere and
now I can't find it."

"Uh-huh." Ruby's coal-black beehive and spit curls
were impervious to the heat blasting from a stainless-
steel wall oven. "Hon, I'll thank you not to play me
for simple. The closest thing that man's got to an address is the corner of East Jesus and plowed ground."

Hannah assumed she looked as sheepish as she felt.
"I'm sorry, Ruby. I was afraid you wouldn't tell me
unless I acted as though David already had."

"That's city folks for ya." She jerked a pen out of
her apron pocket. "Always expectin' dung on their
shoes afore they've set foot off'n the porch."

Minutes later, Hannah was armed with a banana-
cream pie, a three-napkin map and directional references such as, "the third sycamore past where the old
McGill house stood till it burnt" and "when ya come
to the trestle bridge down on Turkey Creek, ya know
ya done went too far."

Ruby waved goodbye from the back door. "You tell
that sheriff his knees is welcome 'neath my table anytime. Yours, too, hon, for that matter of fact."

Thankfully, Willard Johnson had a normal street address on the south side of town. Hannah parked in front
of his parents' trim, post-World War II bungalow,

which would fetch an easy two hundred grand in Chicago.

The part-time fitness instructor, part-time science fiction novelist greeted Hannah before she reached the top of the stairs attached to the side of the garage.

"I hope I'm not interrupting your writing schedule," she said.

"Not at all."

She knew she was, but wouldn't for long.

His apartment's combined office, living room and kitchen showed signs of a hasty attempt at housekeeping. Hannah waxed nostalgic at the sink's towel-covered mountain of dirty dishes and clothes kicked under the sofa bed.

Star Trek and *Star Wars* posters balanced thumb-tacked paperback book covers. Noting the author's name, she asked, "Who's Corey Parcival Spoon?"

"Me and six or seven others—two of them women—who write under it." He pointed at an empty, double-matted frame. "That's reserved for a jacket with Willard Johnson on it. Depending on what mood I'm in, it's motivation, inspiration or a bully."

"Well, if you don't know where you're going, you're sure to get there." Hannah grinned. "Mortimer Galen Garvey, 1898-1969."

"I'll, uh, keep that in mind." Willard tugged on an earlobe, furrows creasing his brow. He'd had an hour to wonder why Hannah had asked to see him. The faster she laid out her scheme, the faster she could get lost trying to find the corner of East Jesus and plowed ground.

His expression reflected disbelief, anger, anguish and resignation as she explained her reasons for firing Zerelda Sue Connor, the committee's intentions to sue and the closeted few's hidden agenda.

Hannah mentioned no names other than Connor's. It rankled not to identify Eulilly Thomlinson—the surname supplied by tenant files—as the ringleader. But doing so would be as divisive as telling a wife that her husband had copped a feel while she was out of the room.

Willard said, "So, I guess I'm out of a job, huh?"

"Not unless you want to be."

"With all due respect, Hannah, and you're due plenty, from where I stand, duking it out in court won't accomplish anything besides making the lawyers rich. Especially since age isn't the discrimination you'd be fighting."

"I'm talking compromise, Willard, not court. If you're willing to hang in there, come what may, for a month—six weeks at the outside—I think this situation will resolve itself."

"I don't know..." He rubbed his chest, as men do before committing themselves to something they'd sooner avoid. "Last time I saw that gleam in your eye, I got rope-a-doped into teaching tae kwon do to the world's oldest Mighty Mite division."

"And the sign-up sheets filled up in one day, too."

He fidgeted. He hummed. He said, "Much as I'm going to regret asking this, what do you have in mind?"

Hannah outlined her idea, admitting that Connor would also have to agree to it. "I don't see how she can refuse, if I demand a take-it-or-leave-it answer. Tomorrow's meeting at Woroniecki's office may work to our advantage. Make it seem more official."

"Yeah, but what if Ms. Connor and the others don't react the way you expect them to?"

"We go straight to Plan B."

"Which is?"

Hannah laughed. "I don't have one, but trust me. I'll think of something."

Confidence wasn't radiating from every fiber of Willard's being when she left, but he didn't know her that well.

Anticipation tingled in her midsection. The man who did, often beyond her comfort zone, was a few miles away. Hannah reviewed the squiggled lines on the napkins lying on the passenger seat. "Luck, don't fail me now."

It didn't. Roads intersected and forked just where Ruby Amyx said they would. Buckled concrete slabs traversed dry creeks that "a good rain swells faster'n a boil."

Farther on, amid a tumble of briars and brush, the ruins of a chimney pointed at the clouds like an obscene gesture. By golly, that's where the old McGill house stood before it burnt.

Hannah stopped at a field-rock post supporting a weathered RFD mailbox. Stick-on letters spelled out D. M. Hen-r-ckson on its door. A break in the trees marked a grassy lane angling off Turkey Creek Road.

Her head tilted back against the Blazer's built-in rest. The impulsiveness that had brought her this far drained away.

Maybe David wasn't answering the phone because he wasn't home. Which made her a trespasser, and that could be a felony when a sheriff owns the property. Large, trespasser-eating dogs were also a possibility.

Alternative: what if David were home? Who was she to barge in uninvited and unannounced? What if he gave her the Mount Rushmore face and told her to go home the way she'd come?

Her mental jukebox growled to life, as it did whenever emotional pushes came to shove. The Lettermen's "I Believe" dropped onto the turntable.

Hannah bolted upright. "All right, all right. I never liked the song, but I get the drift."

The lane less traveled's wheel-troughs guided her tires like an automatic car wash's conveyor through an arbored cathedral. The track sloped downward, curved to the right and rumbled over a cattle guard. Beyond a banked leftward bend, the forested hills seceded to a meadow teeming with wild hyacinth, Dutchman's-breeches, bluebells and primrose.

Hannah didn't know such beauty, such serenity, existed, except in margarine commercials. Working for over half her life in an industry devoted to illusion was like the joke about French philosophers: if everything nonphysical is real and everything of substance is not real, then sorrow exists, but escargot does not.

The pitched vee of a house being built by hand and financed with sweat equity rose from a rocky promontory. David's dream house. The one he'd sketched in a spiral notebook when he was a teenager. He'd set it aside when a wife and a career in Oklahoma didn't jibe with a secluded A-frame home in the Ozarks, but he'd never stopped hoping to have it someday.

Hannah's gaze descended from the dream coming true to a saggy, moss-shingled barn with a red pickup parked inside. No blue-and-white Crown Victoria on the premises, but the front door to a single-story farm-house with a sheet-metal roof was open.

Boondocks or not, David wouldn't have gone some-where and left his house unsecured. Maybe his cruiser had broken down or a deputy had borrowed the sher-iff's wheels.

A rottweiler scrambled to his feet and stood on the porch as resolutely as a four-legged Sherman tank. He didn't bark or rush her vehicle. He was content to let her bring her jugular to him, rather than exhaust himself chasing her down before ripping her to shreds.

Watching the dog watch her, Hannah held Ruby's pie in both hands and wriggled out of the Blazer.

Bur-bur-burf.

The aluminum tin shot straight up. Meringue parted company with banana-cream, hovered, then fell—*ka-splot*—more or less from whence it had come.

The dog panting up at her was not the auxiliary rott-weiler Hannah expected when her life had flashed be-fore her eyes. Her best guess at this dog's breed was a cross between a giant Airedale and a wildebeest.

His curly, gray-and-tan coat straightened into a thick, blondish ruff. Matching feathers fanned from the tail whapping her truck's sidewall. An anvil-shaped head, one black cocked ear, another floppy tan one and quar-ter-size-shaped spots on his rump indicated a canine genome project gone awry.

Being a dog, he sniffed her crotch and sneezed, then slinked in front of her, slumping against her thighs. Balancing the pie in one hand, Hannah scratched be-tween his asymmetrical ears.

"You're not mean like that bully on the porch, are you, big guy? You're a sweetheart. Oh, yes, you are."

Dutch-chocolate eyes stared into hers. They expressed undying affection and not a glimmer of native intelligence.

No violins or moonlight backdropped the scene, but it was love at first sight. Naturally, it was with a dog. And not just any dog—a huge, genetic Mixmaster of a dog.

"His name's Malcolm." David entered her peripheral vision. "He's yours if you want him. I'd planned to bring you out and introduce you to him after dinner the other night."

The knife-edge in his voice kept Hannah's head lowered.

"Why are you getting rid of him?"

"He was picked up in a raid on a puppy mill that also procured lab animals. Being ugly and stupid, nobody wanted him. The county humane society can't keep strays forever."

And you're a bigger sucker for ugly, stupid dogs than I am, Hannah thought, returning Malcolm's grin.

"I'd hoped him and Rambo would be buddies," David said, "but rottweilers aren't keen on sharing their territory." From his monotone, he might as well be talking to a stranger about a used car. "Rambo wouldn't hurt Malcolm. He just won't let him within ten yards of the house. The mutt deserves better than being a barn dog the rest of his life."

Hannah deliberated fleas and ticks versus companionship. Shedding versus somebody to talk to who couldn't talk back. Veterinary bills versus a home security system versus an in-house, barking burglar alarm.

Let's not get carried away. A dog named Malcolm and "burglar alarm" are antonyms.

David removed the pie from her hand and set it on the hood of her Blazer. Fingers sliding beneath her hair, his thumb massaged a spot at the back of her neck.

Mmm…oh, yeah. It's about time you acted as though I looked somewhat familiar. She said, "You know a dog is, uh, a big responsibility. Mind if I, um—that does feel good—take a few minutes…or an hour…or the rest of the afternoon to think about it?"

David's hand slipped to her shoulder, then wheeled her to his chest. He sighed as though he'd been afraid she was a mirage. His wash-worn shirt smelled of dryer sheets, sawdust and a musky maleness all his own.

Malcolm's body blocked Hannah from behind, his rib cage pressing against her thighs. Big, warm dog. Big, warm man. Woman squashed between them. A love sandwich. Add fries and a soft drink and you'd have a really happy meal.

"I should have called," David said.

"I should have, too, a lot sooner than this morning."

"I didn't know what to say to you. Didn't know what you'd say to me. I was afraid to find out."

"You didn't trust me."

"No sense denying it, sugar. For the past couple of days, if somebody told me the sky was blue, I'd look up before I agreed."

She nodded, despising herself for waiting for him to reach out to her. In any other circumstance, he'd have Marlin Andrik, Jimmy Wayne McBride—any number of comrades-in-arms and friends willing to listen, commiserate and advise.

Not this one. Like a fool, she'd failed to realize it, beginning the moment his actions became suspect.

"Then," David continued, "as of yesterday afternoon, I didn't see any point in talking to you at all."

He tensed, holding her tighter, but the impersonal note in his voice had returned. "The break was already clean. Best to leave it go at that."

She stepped back, stumbling over Malcolm. He yelped and scuttled off with his tail between his legs. Her first good look at David wrenched her heart.

His face was stubbled, pale beneath his tan and creased with exhaustion. Dull gray, bloodshot eyes were steadfast in their refusal to meet hers. The man who'd taken her in his arms had retreated behind an emotion-proof rampart.

"When I heard your vehicle," he said, "I thought it was Marlin coming to arrest me. Glad it wasn't, for Malcolm's sake, but I expect a warrant with my name on it any time."

"On what charge? Defending yourself against a—"

"Second-degree manslaughter. No gun at the scene. No shell casing. No gunpowder residue on Quince's hands. My word against the evidence doesn't mean shit."

He chuckled, a hopeless, humorless rattle. "Hell, they've about convinced me that I hallucinated the whole damn thing. Killed a drunk that aimed a finger at me over thirty bucks' worth of pizza."

Teeth gnashing as anger surged through her, Hannah jammed her hands in her jeans' pockets before she grabbed him and shook the life into him.

Bitterness she could understand. Withdrawal? Sure.

A personal favorite. But capitulation? The "throw in the towel 'cause you're beaten before you start" crap?

Caroline Garvey had lived and died by it. Her daughter rebelled against that handy hereditary excuse for blaming the world and everyone in it for your mistakes and weaknesses. Breaking the cycle didn't mean Hannah was better than her mother or the Garveys, et al. Only that she'd learned from them.

"Well," she said, "I guess this is where the woman you don't want anymore is supposed to load up the dog you don't want anymore and leave you in the dust so you can finish memorizing *How To Be a Martyr In Ten Easy Steps* before they take you to jail."

David grimaced. Whistled backward. Worked his jaw.

"You're the last person I expected to kick me in the balls when I'm down."

Hannah's laugh sounded a bit maniacal, even to her. "Oh, it's *a lot* worse than that, Sheriff. Present company included, I'm the last person who still believes in you."

A dandelion died a violent death under the stacked heel of her boot. "Evidence? All I need is right in front of me—or would be, if the self-appointed victim who looks like David Hendrickson would get the hell out of the way."

Hannah's lips pursed, then smacked apart. "Character may be a tissue-paper defense against a manslaughter charge, but ya know what? I'm idealistic enough to believe the truth, and the man telling it, are worth fighting for."

A ruddy hue suffused his skin. The stoic, defeated posture gave way to squared shoulders, a bullish stance.

Attaboy, Hendrickson. C'mon. Rev 'er up, pal. Yell at me. Cuss me. Get in my face and lemme have it.

"Damn right they are." He snagged her arm and yanked her to him, the act forceful but not rough. As his lips descended to hers, she danced away. "Huh-uh-h-h. I don't kiss strangers."

"Kiss *me,* then. That other guy I was hiding behind doesn't need anybody. This one needs you."

"Oh yeah? Why?"

She thought her heart would burst when that glorious, sexy, pure-David grin appeared. "Among other things, to kick me in the balls when I'm down."

"Hmm." Hannah's arms wound around his neck. "I guess that'll do. For starters."

His mouth brushed hers, his usual luscious tease and prelude to hold desire at bay for an exquisite few seconds...except this time she traced his lips with the tip of her tongue, then nibbled at his full lower one, sucking it gently between her teeth, thrilling at the groan thundering in his chest.

They kissed as if it were their first and their last, the unknown future suspended in a wondrous swirl of passion, tenderness and hope.

Knuckles stroking her cheek, David whispered, "Let's go inside, sugar."

"Yes. Let's."

Arms clasping waists, they ambled across the yard, gazing at each other spellbound, expectant...

"Oh, guh-*ross.*"

Hannah's head jerked up. She tripped over her own foot, then David's. A young girl wearing cutoff, acid-washed overalls, a football jersey and leg warmers sneered at them from the porch. "Wait'll I tell Mom you were doing sex right in front of me."

"Shit." David's arm fell away.

"Who is she?"

"Polly Burkholtz, my chief dispatcher's oldest. I forgot she was here."

They were too near the house for Hannah to ask, "Can you make her go away?"

"We were *not* doing sex, Miss Priss," David said. "We were just kissing."

The freckled blonde threw a leg over Rambo as if he were a pony. She crossed her arms and looked from David to Hannah. "Huh-uh. We *saw* you and you were sex-kissing like Leonardo DiCaprio and Kate Winslet before they *did it* in that car."

"Well, we don't have a car and we dang sure missed the boat, so I reckon you and Rambo'll have to find something else to do besides spy on us."

"We were *not* spying on you. Lunch is almost ready and I'm hungry and you said you'd be right back."

Hannah hadn't met Claudina Burkholtz, but would bet Polly's tone and no-prisoners attitude mirrored her mother's to a T. Come to think of it, the girl reminded her of another nine-going-on-twenty-five-year-old who had been wise to the difference between guff and gospel.

David made introductions, including Rambo. The caramel-eyed hit-dog regarded Hannah with disdain, either for being an exhibitionist sex fiend or giving her heart to Malcolm, who was leaning forlornly against the Blazer's front tire.

First IdaClare's French Furwads turned up their snooty little noses at her, then started playing the Aunt

Hannah routine to the hilt. Now a German porch-pooch was giving her the canine equivalent of *der griffbrett*. Okee-fine. A melting-pot, all-American mutt loved her.

"So, do ya want to stay and eat with us?" Polly said, skipping into the house. "It's just sandwiches and stuff. He says I'm too little to cook on the stove."

Hannah caught the screen door. "Then I'll let you cook on mine sometime. Maybe I'll learn something."

The girl looked back at her, brown eyes agog. "You mean you don't know how to cook?"

"Not very well, but I think I can manage helping with sandwiches..."

Hannah gaped at the parlor's forest-green walls, off-white trim and refinished hardwood floors. Two flame-print sofas angled at a walnut wardrobe housing a TV, VCR, stereo equipment, videotapes and CDs.

"David, it's...it's beautiful."

"I dusted," Polly reported.

"Yeah, and I mopped up the Kool-Aid you spilled from here to yonder, too."

She countered, "I heard you say the S-word. Twice."

David muttered others in his repertoire.

Hannah started toward the kitchen, but Polly shooed her away. "You're company, so you don't have to help. I only have to make one more sandwich and finish setting the table."

Taking a step, she spun around and shook a finger at David. "And you keep your hands where they belong or I really will tell Mom."

"*Scat.*"

Laughing, Hannah said, "She's a doll."

"When she's not being a pain in the butt, which is

most of the time. I take her, Jeremy and Lana out for pizza and a movie now and then, to give their momma a break."

"Where are the other two?"

"Home." David lowered his voice. "Polly took a notion to run away this morning."

"Why?"

"She overheard Claudina talking to a neighbor about the shooting and decided I needed a mother hen." Chafing his neck, he added, "I wouldn't hurt Polly's feelings for the world, but I don't want her here when Marlin shows up. It'd upset her too much."

Hannah agreed. The girl obviously adored him. No references to a Mr. Burkholtz implied that David was, to some degree, a father figure to all three of Claudina Burkholtz's children.

An idea hatched as she surveyed the full-wall bookshelves and photos displayed with them. "Were you serious about giving Malcolm away?"

"Yep. He needs a good home and you need a watchdog."

In violation of the no-hands rule, David hugged her spoon-fashion and smooched the side of her head. "Your cottage is too close to the highway and too far from the others."

Hannah snuggled against him. "True, but what thoughts I'd had on the subject centered on puppy, then on housebreaking a puppy, then on not in this life, thank you very much."

"Well, Malcolm's a coupla tacos short of a combo plate, but he does know to take his business outside."

"All of his business? All of the time?"

"So I was told by the gal at the humane society."

A buck-pass if Hannah had ever heard one. "Then how about if I take Polly home after lunch? I'll say I need her to keep Malcolm occupied in case he's skittish about riding in my truck. Which could turn out to be true."

"She'll see through it like a window, but she'll go along with it." David squeezed Hannah tighter. "The only part I don't like is you leaving."

The part indicating his desire for her to stay pressed hard and hot into the back seam of her jeans. Hips rising, arousal flooding through her, she heard Polly's tennis shoes yip on the kitchen linoleum.

"Why are you torturing me?"

"You're torturing me right back, sugar."

"You started it."

"I'm even better at finishes."

"Then either handcuff Polly to the stove or she's *really* going to have something to tell her mother."

He chuckled, "That bad, huh?"

"Why, you—" Mouth curving into a wicked grin he couldn't see, she retaliated with the ol' bump and grind. "No, David. That *good.*"

Growling, he nipped her shoulder. "One of these days, we're gonna put 'good' to shame before we even get warmed up."

He loosened his hold. Hannah shivered from the drop in temperature. God, he was dangerous. So was she, around him. Think about something else. Anything else.

Photographs on the bookshelf shimmied into focus. "Your parents?"

"Uh-huh. They're in a travel-trailer somewhere between Florida and Toronto. For people who used to think a day trip to Kansas City was a big deal, they've kept the road hot ever since Dad retired."

A younger edition of the Nookie Monster and three look-alikes hammed it up in another shot. "The brothers Hendrickson, I presume?"

"Daniel, Darren and Dillon. If one of us had been a girl, she'd have been named Diane. God knows why the folks were so high on D's."

"Where do your brothers live?"

"Scattered from California to Ohio. That's some of the reason Mom and Dad went mobile. In the old days, they had circuit preachers. The folks are circuit grandparents."

Hannah frowned. What was the use of having two living parents and three siblings if they were too far away for moral support?

That's the way it worked in books and on TV. A crisis occurred, the family swooped in without regard to their own jobs or lives, everybody gang-hugged, cried a lot and formed a united front. A secondary hullabaloo arose when one of them confesses he's gay, but in the end they all said they love him unconditionally and think it's peachy when he inherits the entire estate from dear, old, homophobic dad, who—miracle of miracles—made amends before he croaked.

David's sigh ruffled Hannah's hair. "If you're worried about me being by my lonesome, don't be. That other guy side of me is bound to pay a call again, whether I am or not. I'll just have to do my best not to let him get under my skin."

Her head tipped back and she closed her eyes. Manslaughter. Nasty word. As vicious, if not more so, than murder.

Semantics didn't matter. What did, was that appearances do deceive. Evidence speaks for itself—its presence as well as its absence. In David's case, the latter defied logical explanation.

Nor were detectives exempt from the third law of management: No one in an executive position devotes time and effort to proving himself wrong.

"Don't, sugar."

"Don't what? I'm not doing anything."

"When you get all scowly and quiet, it means you're thinking."

David turned her around and cradled her face. "I know you're itching to dig me out of this hole I'm in, but you can't. Neither can I, and let me tell you it's hell standing in it hog-tied and helpless. All I can do is keep reminding myself I've spent half my life being part of the system and believing in it."

Hannah said, "And I've spent most of mine fighting it."

"That's what made me nervous when you clammed up." His eyes searched hers. "I've called Marlin and Pike every name in the book, but bottom line, I trust them. Promise me you'll leave the investigating to the professionals this time."

Hesitate. Give him the basic pained expression. Gnaw a lip. Exhale. "All right, David. If that's what you want, I promise."

Four fingers uncrossed behind her back before he thought to peek over her shoulder.

10

Hannah braked at the lane's junction with Turkey Creek Road. "Which way, Polly?"

The girl's thumb jerked to the right. "I hope you drive fast, like Sheriff David."

Hannah smiled. "Are you in a hurry to go home?"

"Uh-huh." She pinched her nose. "Malcolm stinks."

The melting-pot mutt sitting in the middle of the Blazer's back seat cocked his head. Saliva dripped from his tongue like a faucet with a bum washer. If he were any more adorable, he'd be edible.

"Sheriff David gives Rambo a bath every week. It makes a big, yucky mess in the tub, but he smells real nice after."

Hannah's cottage had an oversize shower, not a bathtub. A soap-and-rinse in the lake? No. Eau de Bass would not be an improvement over whatever Eau de Let's-Not-Think-About-It Malcolm had rolled in.

Showering with an Airedale-wildebeest. What fun. At least he couldn't tell anyone what she looked like in a swimsuit.

"How far is it to your house, Polly?" she asked, assuming it was nearby.

"You mean, like, miles?" Her head wobbled. "Oh, prob'ly about, um…fifty-four."

An estimate worthy of the IRS. Kinderhook County measured less than seventy-two miles, diagonally. "Do you live on this road?"

"Nuh-uh. Mom has to win the lottery before we can move to the country. She's gonna buy us a mansion on the hill. She sings about it when she irons."

Hannah feigned patience. "I need a little help here, sweetie. How about an address? Do you have one?"

"Sure. It's 218 Fort Street." Polly hesitated a beat. "You know where that is, don't you?" Her tone suggested a no-confidence vote, as if an adult who didn't know how to cook might not be well versed in geography, either.

She went on, "Everybody knows a two-number means it's two blocks from the square on the side where the Short Stack Café is, 'cause if it was on the other side, it would be a seven-number and if it went crosswise it'd be an avenue, not a street."

A shrug preceded, "You'd have to be a real dummy to get lost in Sanity."

Uh-huh. If the child had sailed with Columbus, he'd have rowed the boats ashore in Australia.

"My mom works at the café, too, 'cause my daddy left us high and dry and she needs two jobs to keep a roof over our heads." Polly's face rumpled. "*I* have to baby-sit Lana and Jeremy for free 'cause I'm the oldest, but Mom pays Lisa Vermeer to baby-sit us in the summer and all *she* does is paint her toenails and talk to her boyfriend on the phone."

Gently, Hannah asked, "Is that why you ran away this morning? Because you don't like to baby-sit?"

"No-o-o. 'Cause it's Sunday."

Well, of course. How stupid of me. State statutes must prohibit running away on Monday through Saturday.

"And I didn't run away," Polly said. "I left a note telling Mom I was going to Sheriff David's. She got mad anyhow 'cause she's a dispatcher and they get bulletins about child abductions and murders and stuff, so she borrowed Mrs. dePriest's car and went looking for me."

The girl bowed her head. "I didn't mean to scare her. Honest. I just didn't want Sheriff David to be alone and I've got to go to school tomorrow. When Mom found me, she took me as far as the lane 'cause she said my heart was in the right place, but I'm grounded for two whole weeks for not using my head."

A lump grated Hannah's throat as a thirty-five-year-old memory belied the adage "time heals all wounds."

When her mother's affection and attention had diverted to yet another in a parade of boozer boyfriends, Hannah snuck out one morning, leaving a note saying not to bother looking for her.

With a library copy of *Huckleberry Finn,* a peanut butter sandwich and canteen of water in her Roy Rogers lunchbox, she'd climbed a tree at the edge of Tin Can Alley to wait for her frantic mother to pound on neighbors' doors, begging them to help search for her beloved daughter.

It was late afternoon before Caroline and her boyfriend emerged from the trailer. They sashayed to his car as if unaccustomed to dry land after months at sea.

Dressed in her cocktail-waitress outfit—stretch pants, a midriff top and sneakers—Caroline slid to the center of the front seat and draped an arm over her lover's shoulders. They drove off in a cloud of purple-black exhaust.

Tears had streamed down Hannah's face. Her mother hadn't noticed she was gone, much less seen the note. She envisioned Caroline pausing at the door to slur a "Bye, sweetheart. Love you," and a reminder not to fall asleep on the couch with the TV on unless Hannah wanted to pay the electric bill next month.

She'd shuffled back to the trailer and packed two shopping bags with food, clothes, a blanket and Bojangles, her stuffed, work-sock monkey doll, before realizing that going where nobody cared about her was no different than staying where nobody did.

Years later, just before she died, Caroline had spoken of that day and how frightened she'd been when she read the note. "I was staring out the window trying to decide whether to start looking or get to a pay phone and call the police when I saw your red shirt shining like a big ol' cardinal on that branch.

"I thought you'd get tired of sitting up there before I went to work. When you didn't, I figured to teach you a lesson on making me dance to your tune. Hardest thing I ever did was leaving you to stew in your own juice, but I was right to do it."

Her mother's thin, bluish lips had curved into a smile.

"You never pulled a trick on me like that again, did you?"

No, Momma. I learned my lesson. Like so many others, it just wasn't the same one you thought you'd taught me.

Malcolm's cold, wet nose nuzzling Hannah's ear

jolted her back to the present. Thrusting his head between the seat backs, he whimpered as if to ask, "Are we there yet?"

She turned onto the street—er, avenue—leading to the square, then scratched him under his flop-ear. His muzzle lifted in ecstasy. She refused to speculate on the hard things matting his fur. Whatever they were, they felt smaller than the holes in her shower drain.

Polly said, "Rambo would've stayed in the seat until Sheriff David told him he could get up. Rambo has had K–9 training."

"Well, Malcolm doesn't need K–9 training. He already knows how to be a dog."

Lame though it was, the joke was lost on Polly. "How come you like him so much?"

"For the same reason you went to Sheriff David's. Malcolm's a good guy and I don't want him to be alone anymore."

Hannah surveyed a street sign mounted on a steel corner post. She'd entered the square on the south side, hoping to zero in on Fort's opposing intersection, then cruise around to the north.

Hallelujah. Fort Street it was, in all its three-inch reflective-lettered glory. Only a real dummy could get lost in Sanity.

"Do you have kids?" Polly asked.

Hannah shook her head.

"Then if Malcolm goes to live with you, you won't be alone anymore either, huh?"

Yowser. Out of the mouths of babes. "Has anybody ever told you you were too smart?"

"My teacher said I was precocious. Her face squinched up weird when she said it, so I looked it up in the dictionary 'cause I thought it was bad. It took me hours and hours to find, 'cause it isn't spelled a bit like it sounds.''

Polly snorted. "All it means is 'to exhibit mature qualities at an unusually early age.''' A finger twirled the air. "Big whoop-de—Hey! Slow down—that's my house. The crummy brown one.''

A tired chain-link fence stockaded the asphalt-shingled house and mostly dirt front yard at 218 Fort Street. Lawn chairs, bikes, toys and a chest freezer crammed the slab porch, sheltered by an awning with missing ribs.

A towheaded boy not much younger than Polly and a frail-looking girl of about five clung to the fence, the diamond-shaped mesh framing their noses and eyes like oversize goggles.

Malcolm galumphed onto the back seat. He bashed his snoot on the unexpectedly solid window glass, gave a mucus-intensive sneeze, then *burfed* hello to them.

"Do you know my mom?" Polly asked, unlatching her seat belt.

"No, I—"

"Then you have to come in and meet her. I'm not allowed to take rides from strangers.''

Hannah hesitated. The sheriff's department's senior dispatcher might be a prime information source, but, "What about Malcolm? I hate to leave him cooped up in the car.''

Polly hopped out and easily plied the seat-release lever that had taken careful study of the owner's manual for Hannah to find and operate. "I'll baby-sit him for you.'' She tossed a weary glance over her shoulder at her siblings. "I gotta baby-sit *them*, anyhow.''

Yodeling with joy, Malcolm leaped from the Blazer and promptly careered into the gate Jeremy opened for him instead of through it. Trajectory adjusted, the Airedale-wildebeest streaked for the backyard, the two younger Burkholtzes chasing after him.

Polly poked her head inside the battered aluminum storm door. "Mo-o-m-m-m. I'm ho-m-me. C'mere, will ya? Sheriff David's girlfriend wants to meet you."

"I am *not* Sheriff David's girlfriend."

Polly graced her with a prim "I saw you sex-kissing, remember?" look.

A woman with curly, dishwater-blond hair, wearing a polka-dot muumuu and jelly-shoes, filled the doorway. Her outfit neither maximized her five-foot stature nor minimized the two-hundred-plus pounds she carried on it.

"Mom, this is Hannah. Hannah, this is Mom." Polly darted off the porch, calling, "Thanks for the ride," and disappeared around the corner of the house.

"Little Miss Manners," the woman drawled, her voice low and honeyed. "I'm Claudina Burkholtz, alias Mom. Come on in, girlfriend."

The interior was a shotgun arrangement. The dining room divided the living room from the kitchen, with two bedrooms and a bath directly off the living room.

Claudina apologized for the mess, but the birch-paneled front room was as spotless as a single mother of three could hope. A rabbit-eared console TV was the focal point for a harvest-gold sofa, side chair and striped recliner whose footrest was locked in an upright position.

An electrical cable spool painted enamel yellow had been given a second career as a coffee table. Walnut-stained crates served as lamp tables and held cartoon videocassettes. Carpet samples in sundry colors quilted the floor like a horizontal rainbow.

Hannah walked around the dining room's picnic table, marveling aloud at Claudina's ingenuity. She might sing about a mansion on the hill, but she'd transformed a dreary, cramped house into a bright home for her children.

"It'd take dynamite to improve it much," Claudina said, "but it's cheap and convenient, except to the grocery store, now that Price-Slasher put Neehring's Market out of business on the square."

She motioned at an ice-cream table and chairs tucked into a windowed corner of the kitchen. "We'd better do our gossiping in here. Jeremy and Lana have whined all day about Polly going to Sheriff David's. They might gang up on her if they think I'm not watching."

Hannah looked out at the children romping with Malcolm. "I hope you don't mind having a dog-shaped horse in your backyard. Polly volunteered to baby-sit him, but I should have asked you before I turned him loose."

"Anything that keeps the rug rats out there instead of in here is okay with me." Claudina opened the refrigerator door. "Let's see, the Kool-Aid of the day is grape and I have three orange sodas, two colas and a lemon-lime."

Shoulders sagging, she added, "I don't know about you, but I'd sin on dirty sheets for a cold beer."

Hannah laughed. "If I wasn't Malcolm's designated driver, I'd spring for a six-pack. Since I am, a cola sounds great."

An enclosed utility porch tacked onto the kitchen

appeared when Claudina moved to the cupboards for glasses. Stacks of red, white and blue-striped yard signs, posters and bumper stickers urged Vote David Hendrickson for Kinderhook Country Sheriff.

Following Hannah's gaze, Claudina sighed as she placed their drinks on the table and sat down. "I'm his campaign manager. Not that there'll be any campaign to manage unless he's exonerated, and quick."

Hannah admitted her worries had concentrated on David's personal future more than his professional one.

"For him, they're one and the same," Claudina said. "He's a natural-born lawman. If this goes to trial, even if he's acquitted, he's through. A black mark on his record would be a liability for any department he applied to."

"Why, if a jury finds him innocent?"

"Common misconception." Claudina's finger snaked down the condensation on the side of her glass. "The verdict is *not guilty,* not *innocent.* You know the 'guilty beyond a reasonable doubt' thing, right?"

"Anyone who doesn't was in a coma during the O.J. trial."

"Well, the flip side is 'not guilty,' which may be nothing more than a shitload of reasonable doubt." Claudina looked up, as if her choice of description might have offended her guest. "It doesn't necessarily mean the defendant didn't do the deed. Only that the prosecution couldn't prove it."

Hannah's stomach churned. "And reasonable doubt clings to the defendant like a foul odor, forever."

"Maybe not so much in a big city, but here?" Claudina laughed. "Small towns have long memories and they get riper with age."

"I know. I grew up in one, too. My family was living on the wrong side of the tracks fifty years before the railroad came through."

A mischievous grin plumped Claudina's jowls. "Hey, it's cool to be trashy. If you get in trouble, nobody gets their panties in a wad. If you don't, mouths drop so wide, you can count their fillings."

"But *everybody* backstabs rich people," Hannah said, "including the other rich people, just because they're rich."

"Only fair." Claudina stretched across the table to raise the window. "Jeremy, turn that hose off before you flood the yard."

"Polly told me to give Malcolm a drink. He's thirsty."

"One...two..." Pipes rattled under the house. Claudina shut the window and sat down. "My kids could count to three before they could walk."

Hannah's gaze returned to the signs in the utility porch. "Would David have won the election if Friday night hadn't happened?"

Claudina gestured *comme çi, comme ça.* "Not by a landslide. I don't have to tell you, he's a hummer to look at, his appointment to office is second to being an incumbent and he's done a great job."

"I hear a 'but.'"

"Personally, I'd rather talk about you and him moonin' and spoonin', but you're company, so if it's a civics lesson you want, I can give you one."

Hannah arched an eyebrow.

"Okay, civics it is, only first I'd appreciate hearing how the boss is holding up."

"I don't know how to answer that, Claudina. Polly's

visit helped a lot, I'm sure. She's crazy about him and since she's a child, he didn't have to put up a front for her like he would an adult.''

"I'd hoped it would go that way. That's why I dropped her at the road instead of taking her to the house.''

Claudina's hands splayed on the table. "No, it isn't. I didn't want to see him because I didn't know what to say to him.''

"Believe me, there's a lot of. that going around.'' Hannah leaned back in her chair. "David is depressed, hopeful, scared, guilty, angry—everything you or I would be, only to the tenth power because he's male.''

Claudina snickered. "The testosterone curtain. Makes the iron one they tore down in Europe seem as flimsy as toilet paper.''

"Bingo. David came out from behind it eventually, but I hated leaving him alone again. Not that he needs me hanging around doing my Chuckles the Clown impersonation, but...''

Claudina literally went tongue-in-cheek. "Take my advice. Go for Sheena the Slut next time.''

Yes, well, for a hot, heavy, very frickin' short moment, she'd had visions of turning David's toes inside out. Sheena the Slut? More like H. Garvey, Girl Nookie Monster.

"Mom!'' The back door banged behind Polly. "Can we have some cookies? Please? Malcolm, too?''

"None for Malcolm, okay?'' Hannah said. "He already helped himself to a whole banana-cream pie.''

"He wouldn't have,'' Polly said, "if you hadn't left it on the hood of your truck.''

The kid was definitely too smart.

Claudina chanted, "Cookies in the zip-bag in the pantry, Kool-Aid in the fridge, foam cups on the porch. Don't let the dog eat the cups. Bye."

Polly's eyes widened. "That's it? No hassle?"

"No snacks, either, if you're still in my sight ten seconds from now."

The door slammed well before the deadline.

Claudina winked. "Where were we?"

"Civics 101."

"Still?" She rooted around in her chair, then leaned her elbows on the table. "People in this county will vote for a candidate's mother's maiden name as much as his party affiliation. Republicans outnumber Democrats, with the Dems more apt to go straight-ticket.

"Jessup Knox is opposing David on the Republican side. If Knox had filed Democrat, he'd take a majority of the yellow-dogs, but would have to beat David in the November general election. As a Republican, all Knox has to do is knock off David in the primary because J. D. Oglethorpe, the Dem's other candidate, loses every time he runs."

Jessup Knox, the paunchy Elvis wanna-be who owned Fort Knox Security, was as oily as his black-dyed pompadour. To boost his company's profit margin, he'd fed the rumor mill erroneous, exaggerated "facts" about Kathleen Osborn's violent death. Sidebar comments questioned David's competence, youth and judgment.

Hannah had met Knox once. If forced to say something nice, she'd mention he displayed no outward symptoms of venereal disease.

Claudina went on, "The primary is barely two months away. Knox couldn't have sold his soul to the devil and gotten better timing for the Quince investigation. He's already switched from ragging about an increase in crime—statistically, it's down twenty-seven percent—to bragging he doesn't have a law enforcement background so won't be inclined to shoot first and ask questions later.''

"Aw, come on, Claudina. You have *got* to be kidding. That's not only slander, but who'd want a sheriff who doesn't know his badge from his butt? Ye gods, aren't candidates *required* to have law enforcement training?''

"Uh-uh. Have no felony convictions and live in Kinderhook a year and you, too, can be sheriff.''

Unbelievable.

"We'll play *Jeopardy* with your other question,'' Claudina said. "What cop topic has the media shoved down our throats for the last year or so?''

She doo-dee-dooed the game show's theme song.

"I, uh, jeez—give me police brutality for five dollars.''

Claudina's shoulders rose. "Well…generally speaking, I guess. Rogue cops, minority profiling, corruption—most of all, target practice on somebody which, in the bright light of day, maybe might not look justifiable, even if the deceased had a million priors. A fact, by the way, the media seldom reports.''

Hannah said, "So, the alternative is electing a sheriff who promises not to shoot *anybody,* even if the bad guys shoot first?''

"It doesn't just apply to county mounties,'' Claudina said. "I'm not saying slimeball cops don't exist, but in the U.S. of A., there are three hundred million people, two hundred and twenty-five million firearms and three hundred thousand law enforcement officers. Care to make book on your odds of getting shot by a cop *by mistake?*"

Lana scooted into and through the kitchen, her arms stiff and knees locked in the dire need of rest-room facilities.

Lowering her voice, Hannah asked, "Does all this mean David has no chance of beating Jessup Knox in the primary?"

"No. It's becoming more of a Truman versus Dewey, though." Claudina's face was beyond glum. "That's why I can't manage David's campaign anymore. It makes me sick to my stomach, but if I'm too gung-ho for Hendrickson and Jessup Knox wins, I could lose my job.

"The pay sucks, but I've got three kids and can't afford to gamble with my benefits. Lana has asthma. Jeremy is on a first-name basis with the emergency-room docs. If Polly hears 'strep throat,' she catches it."

Hannah reached across the table and patted her arm. "You know David would never put you in the position of choosing between him and your children."

Tears rimmed Claudina's eyes. Lana started through the kitchen, then paused. "Are you okay, Mom?"

"Sure, baby. Hannah is bringing me up to date on *Days of Our Lives*. Austin was in a car wreck and not expected to live."

"Oh, *yuck.*" The little girl hastened outside as though soap-opera plots were a leading cause of cooties.

Lana's muffled report of the topic under discussion drifted through the window glass. All three children lay spread-eagle on the grass, making snow angels without benefit of snow. Malcolm twitched on his back, *argh-arghing* with glee.

Hannah asked, "Does divided loyalty apply to other departmental personnel? The noncivilians—Marlin Andrik, for example."

Claudina frowned, her curly head atilt. "Well, the sheriff appoints his chiefs of staff, but Knox wouldn't dare demote Andrik. He's too good."

She took a drink of cola, then munched an ice cube. "I don't see him bumping McBride, either. Knox can't be dumb enough to ignore how badly he needs a second-in-command who knows what he's doing."

"Isn't it possible Knox would want a handpicked yes-man?"

"Anything's possible, Hannah, but Jimmy Wayne wouldn't sit still for a demotion." Claudina sucked in a breath. "Except...he might have to, or get out of the cops-and-robbers biz. The Sanity Police Department is out. In county parlance, that's scraping the bottom of the barrel. And McBride's about as fond of the highway patrol as he is of being sheriff."

"Why doesn't he want to be sheriff?" Hannah asked.

"Because Jimmy Wayne's into kissing babes, not babies. Between you and me, if he ever wised up and wanted a lotta woman to love, I wouldn't throw him out of the sack."

She flapped a hand. "I'm making him sound horndoggy and he isn't. I think Jimmy Wayne's seen too many deputies get divorced, remarried and divorced again to try it himself yet."

Interesting. The soap-opera context wasn't altogether off base. Maybe nothing more than womanly intuition was ramping into high gear, but Hannah's sixth sense had pegged the motive behind Kathleen Osborn's murder, hadn't it? Okay, *pegged* might be a little strong...

"This afternoon, before David's mood improved to normal," Hannah said, "he mentioned something about no gunpowder residue on Stuart Quince's hands."

Claudina blanched. "That's worse than the disappearing Glock ever thought of being. My knowledge of forensics and ballistics comes from eavesdropping on the guys, but I'm pretty sure you can't fire a gun barehanded without the skin showing traces of gunpowder. Like Marlin said, 'The drone didn't take a slug to the heart, wash up in the john, then fall dead in the doorway.'"

"Then I assume he and Pike believe the gun didn't disappear, but that it simply didn't exist."

"Uh-huh."

"Haven't they found *any* evidence in David's favor?" Hannah asked. "I'm biased and as far from an expert as Jessup Knox, but it seems beyond pat that every finger points at him."

"Well, girlfriend, evidence comes in two flavors, conclusive and circumstantial. The more conclusive, the better, but forty pieces of circumstantial evidence equal one piece of conclusive evidence. You with me so far?"

"Yes."

"The majority of the evidence against David is circumstantial. It usually is. So far, David's side is totally circumstantial."

"I understand that, but—"

Ignoring her, Claudina went on, "At the beginning there were a few X's in his favor. His title and character, for two. Plus, a records search showed a nine-millimeter Glock registered to Stuart Quince. Then Lydia Quince told Andrik that the gun, a Walkman, some tools and a CD case were stolen from hubby's truck a year ago.''

"Maybe she's lying," Hannah said. "Or Quince did."

"I'll admit, the theft wasn't reported, but what does that prove? Nothing either way."

"It looks suspicious to me." Hannah translated Claudina's expression. "Yeah, I know. I'm not a cop and suspicions aren't evidence."

"I also heard on the wind that Quince was an alcoholic, couldn't keep a job and was flat broke. Lydia—aka his meal ticket—left him in January and filed for divorce last month."

Hannah slapped the table. "So, he decided suicide-by-cop was an easy solution and David's story bears that out."

"Sounds righteous to me, along with the fact Quince was worth a hundred thousand life-insurance dollars dead and not a red cent alive."

Hannah sputtered, "Well, then what's—"

"Except," Claudina emphasized, "there's no evidence to go *with* David's story and Jimmy Wayne swears Stuart Quince didn't have the guts to set up his own firing squad, then stand in front of it."

Hannah leaned forward on an elbow. "Are you saying Chief Deputy McBride *knew* Stuart Quince?"

Claudina looked surprised, then smiled. "I keep forgetting you haven't lived here very long. Sure, they knew each other. Jimmy Wayne and Lydia are first cousins."

11

"Since you played with the kids for a couple of hours," Hannah lectured to the passenger seat, "you'd better behave while I'm in the store."

Malcolm growled a yawn. He licked his side whiskers, then stared sphinxlike out the windshield, oblivious to passing motorists' double takes.

"I mean it, Malcolm. I have enough on my mind without you using the upholstery for a chew toy."

Moompf. Which was mutt-speak for either "Okeydokey, heart of my heart" or "Jeez, will ya give it a rest?"

Hannah already knew the Airedale-wildebeest was a dog of few words and fewer subtleties. Depending on pitch, volume and repetitions, *burf* denoted a greeting or a warning, whereas *argh-arghs* indicated pleasure, the onset of an itch or a plea for attention.

And Dr. Doolittle thought he was hot stuff?

Her whirlwind spree through Wal-Mart's pet department netted two bowls large enough to hand-wash lingerie, rawhide bones, canned dog food, a fifty-pound sack of the dry kind, a collar, leash, car restraint, an economy-size bottle of doggy shampoo and a Scooby-Doo beach towel.

Equipped for parenthood, Hannah resisted the gravitational pull back to the farmhouse tucked in a peaceful valley. Sex wouldn't achieve anything except fabulous, mind-numbing, multiple and mutual orgasms and Andrik would probably get there before she and David did, anyway.

"Among about a thousand other things I don't understand, Malcolm, what's with this gangway to justice? Yes, it's damage-control time when an elected official is suspected of a crime, but this is ridiculous."

Malcolm sniffed at the sour-mash smell of dog food wending from the cargo bay, then absently gnawed on the nylon harness securing him to the seat.

"What this investigation needs is someone who doesn't think like a cop. Not that cops are stupid or have no imagination, but they have to *prove* everything.

"Well, life isn't geometry, my friend. Who cares if the shortest route between point A and point B is a straight line? Show me someone who can make it through a day without an off-ramp and I'll show you someone overdue for detox."

Malcolm slouched against the door, seemingly incapable of remaining in an unsupported, upright position for more than a few minutes. Polly had kept her ear tuned for the quiet gurgles that presaged carsickness, but if ever there was a dog who appreciated effortless, forward momentum, that would be Malcolm.

His liquid brown eyes telegraphed compassion for David's plight. Or maybe gratitude for her shutting up.

"I love you, you big doofus. I'm just tired, and worried, and…" An inrushing tide of emotion blocked the words to express it.

A relationship—any relationship, let alone one with a younger man—had been the absolute last thing Han-

nah wanted when she severed all ties to Chicago and
her career, Jack Clancy being the sole exception.

She'd accepted the manager's job on the assumption
a retirement community would be as free of romantic
entanglements as a convent. Her track record had been
as pathetic as her mother's. So what if Hannah's lovers
had been far fewer, farther between, sober, better
dressed and gainfully employed? Caroline never gave
up believing in and wanting forever. Hannah did, the
day Jarrod Amberley walked out of her life.

Or thought she had, until David Hendrickson walked
into it.

She missed him. Missed talking to him about anything and everything. Missed the moment-to-moment,
push-me, pull-you uncertainty that comes from your
head saying the chance of getting hurt is no less than
it ever was, and your heart not giving a damn what
might happen tomorrow or next week or six months
from now.

Argh-argh. Argh.

Hannah laughed. "First I talk too much, then I go
into the zone, huh?"

For about fifteen miles, judging by the power substation screened by razor-wired fencing. Scary, driving
that far on half a brain—if that much.

"We're almost home, which means bath time for
Malcolm, then something to eat for both of us, then a
nap for Hannah. Agreed?"

The happy cadence of tail thumping against console
accompanied their cruise through the gates. A grounds-
and-greens employee on a stand-up mower zipped
along as though surfing on grass. Another worker pitch-

forked mulch from a lawn cart into doughnut-shaped berms at the bases of trees.

"Look over here, Malcolm. That's our..."

Hannah's fist banged the steering wheel. "Oh, no. Jeez Louise. Not *again*."

Delbert's Edsel, IdaClare's Lincoln and Leo Schnur's orange "Thing" convertible were parked bumper-to-bumper in the driveway.

The elderly amateur gumshoes had confiscated Hannah's cottage for their headquarters the night they'd launched their anything-but-private investigation of Kathleen Osborn's murder. Hannah's locks were changed twice before the case was closed, but IdaClare not only obtained keys for her own use, she supplied her colleagues with duplicates so they could come and go without bothering Hannah with a lot of tacky knocking and doorbell ringing.

Hannah told Bob Davies his gonads were history if he ever let IdaClare coerce him or any Maintenance Department employee out of another key. Bob thought Hannah's predicament was amusing, until he noticed the look on her face.

If IdaClare's advocate failed tomorrow morning, Jack needn't fret about his mother being sent to the Big House. Stone walls do a prison make and iron bars a jail, but if IdaClare was as talented at breaking out as she was at breaking in, she'd escape in ten minutes flat.

Malcolm loped around the yard, his nose vacuuming new scents and landmarks, pausing here and there for the ritualistic hike-and-whiz on whatever he deemed worthy of baptism.

In keeping with the idiotic idea that back-and-forthing between vehicle and house expended more effort than hauling everything in one spine-wrenching load, Hannah jettisoned the rawhide chewies, then staggered up the back steps juggling the dog-food sack, plastic shopping bags and her purse.

She kicked the door's brass plate, the irony of knocking for assistance from a bunch of geriatric burglars not lost on her.

Delbert peeked out the miniblinds, then shot the dead bolt. "Give me that plunder before you hurt yourself," he ordered, trying to yank the sack from her arms.

Yanking back, the weight skewing her balance, she said, "I got it, I got it. Just move over before I drop everything."

Shuffling into the utility room, Hannah saw Marge, Rosemary and Leo leaning over in the breakfast room's chairs, staring at her. Opposite them, IdaClare's cotton-candy head bobbed and weaved above the bar counter.

Halfway into an orthopedic squat to divest herself of her burdens, with the ever-gallant Delbert trying to pry the bags off her wrist, Malcolm galloped inside, a new rawhide bone the length of a brontosaurus femur clamped in his teeth.

Toenails skidded on the tile. Four giant paws tacked to different compass points. Lips curled and body steeled for impact, Malcolm sent Hannah sprawling.

Delbert staggered backward into the dryer. "Mayday! Mayday!" Detergent jugs and spray bottles clattered to the floor. "Killer dog on the loose!"

In mortal terror, Malcolm clambered to his feet, clopped Hannah upside the head with his bone and ran pell-mell into the kitchen.

Delbert hurled a box of dryer sheets at the yelping menace. "Run for your lives!"

Chairs banged table legs. Rosemary and Marge screamed. Leo's German expletives boomed off the walls. Hannah collapsed on the dog-food sack, laughing so hard she couldn't breathe.

Above the racket, IdaClare yelled, "Y'all get down off the furniture this instant. That's no killer dog— that's Malcolm. The poor thing's retarded not vicious."

The mental image of Marge, Rosemary and particularly Leo, who bore an uncanny resemblance to Mr. Potato Head, huddled like shipwreck victims awaiting rescue did nothing for Hannah's self-control.

"Are you sure?" Rosemary's quavery voice was surely accompanied by hand-wringing.

"Of course I am." IdaClare explained how her "hot tip" to Sheriff Hendrickson had closed down the puppy mill/lab-animal operation and saved Malcolm from a gruesome future.

Brushing dryer lint and dog hair from her sleeves, Hannah looked up at Delbert's beet-red face and almost lost it again.

"Glad you think it's funny. Coulda busted a hip, you know."

"Nah-h," Hannah teased. "It would have taken more than a softener-sheet box in the rear end to do that."

"I mean me, damn it. Jehoshaphat, if you wanted a dog, why didn't you get a pretty one?"

"Beauty is in the eye of the beholder." Hannah started into the kitchen. "My great-uncle said, no matter how lousy you feel when you wake up, an ugly dog always looks a helluva lot worse than you do."

Delbert muttered something, then bent down to collect the scattered cleaning products.

"Where'd Malcolm go?" Hannah asked the other Mod Squad members, straightening what panic had wrought on the tableful of files, paper goods and coffee cups.

"The living room, dear," IdaClare said. "Marge and Rosemary's caterwauling scared the liver out of him."

"We scared *him?*" Marge protested.

"Mercy sakes," Rosemary said, "that dog had a bone in his mouth bigger than my leg."

"No, not so big as that, liebschen," Leo said in a croony tone.

"Oh, *really?*"

"The bone, I meant. It was smaller than—" Leo clapped a hand to his forehead.

Delbert chimed in, "Leo means the mutt's jaw would've locked up hoisting one of your gams, Rosie."

"What!"

"No, that is not…"

Hannah went on into the living room, having developed an immunity to IdaClare and Company's squabbles, insults and unveiled threats.

The room wasn't huge and Malcolm was, but no Airedale-wildebeests could be seen or heard. She crouched to peek under the dining/conference table, the sofa and club chairs, in the event there was some truth to "shrinking in fear."

"Malcolm?" No telltale tail thumps, but ruches in the area rug testified to his escape route and cornering ability.

She found him scrunched in the kneehole of her desk gnawing on his bronto-chewie, the swivel chair having been appropriated for additional seating in the breakfast room.

Mindful of warnings about disturbing a dog with a bone and assuming he wasn't permanently traumatized, Hannah murmured sweet nothings, then rejoined her unwanted guests.

The five Sherlocks had settled their differences and their posteriors in their respective chairs. With the tabletop blocking gamma-ray emissions from Delbert's madras slacks, his checked gingham shirt and brown vest verged on color coordination.

Since Hannah saw her last, Rosemary's jet-black hair had been cut in a short shag, with bordeaux highlights. Jaunty silver hoops swung from her earlobes, silver-lamé stirrup pants encased her bounteous lower half and a scoop-necked tunic exposed an acre of cleavage.

The nouveau vamp held hands under the table with a bald, besotted Leo Schnur, whose horn-rimmed spectacles were fogged from ganders at her goodies.

IdaClare had opted for a peach skort and a sweater with multifloral crewel embroidery, while Marge's burnished cheeks and navy windsuit said she'd spent her day on the golf course.

"I can't wait to tell Itsy and Bitsy you've adopted Malcolm," IdaClare gushed. "Why, they'll be tickled pink."

Though still smarting from her calling Malcolm "retarded," Hannah stifled a remark about the Furwads already being the approximate color of Merthiolate. Defensiveness about one's pet was not exclusive to tea-cup-poodle owners.

"I apologize for the way Malcolm barreled through here," she said, "but we didn't expect a houseful of people when we got home."

Everyone forgave Malcolm's rambunctiousness. No

one took the hint. None ever had, but there was supposed to be a first time for everything.

"The *reason* neither of us expected a houseful of people," Hannah continued, homing in on IdaClare, "is that we thought we were the only ones with a key."

"Don't need a key, ladybug."

Delbert reached down beside his chair. An object that looked like a hybrid of a pricing gun and a five-speed drill clunked on the table. "The stuff I ordered from Private Spy Supply finally got here yesterday. Night-vision binoculars, surveillance sunglasses, a couple of field manuals and this handy-dandy tool of the trade."

He caressed his new toy. "A genuine, professional-grade lock-pick gun."

"The gadget," Leo said, "it is amazing. A click here, a click there and voila. Open the says-a-me."

Rosemary said, "Delbert was up half the night practicing on our locks. He wouldn't let me have a turn, but I'll bet I could do it, just from watching him."

Hannah's posture deteriorated until she could have scratched the backs of her knees without bending backward. Now nothing, save installing steel brackets and bars on her doors would keep the gumshoe gang from barging in whenever they pleased. And as David had informed her a few days earlier, the damn deck doors opened *out*.

"Is that thing legal?" she asked. A trivia mote floated up from her vast storehouse of useless information. "Don't locksmiths have to be licensed and bonded? In fact, I know I've read that possession of burglary tools is a misdemeanor—maybe a felony."

Delbert waved away her protest. "Next time you

lock the keys in that femi-Nazimobile of yours, don't call me.''

She wouldn't anyway. She'd seen Mr. Fix-It in action. As soon as he tripped the lock, her transmission would fall out.

Rosemary nudged Leo. "I'll slice you an extra-big piece of cherry cheesecake if you'll help me serve."

Rapture suffused his moon-shaped face. His lips parted and trembled with desire. The man would crawl across ground glass for dessert.

Marge said, "I'll do the coffee." For Hannah's benefit, she added, "It's the real thing, not decaf, since we're meeting earlier than usual."

Hannah surrendered and took her regular seat at the bar. Principles were one thing. Cherry cheesecake and coffee were quite another.

Thus far, every meeting's agenda had included refreshments of the homemade, hideously fattening variety. As long as they did, it would be selfish of her not to let them use her house for their headquarters.

Besides, if they met somewhere else, she'd have no clue what the snoops were up to other than no good.

IdaClare tapped Hannah's shin with a file folder. "This is yours, dear. We're just getting started on the Hendrickson case, so we don't have any dossiers yet."

A gummed label affixed to the tab read Code Name: Beta. Well, of course. The "Osborn case" had been Code Name: Alpha. If God answered prayers, there'd be no Code Name whatever-the-heck "C" was.

"How about the Clancy case?" Hannah asked. "As in, shouldn't you be preparing for your hearing before the judge tomorrow morning?"

IdaClare shook her head. "I pressed the blouse to

my favorite suit this afternoon. You know, the rose one? With the satin piping? I haven't decided which shoes to wear, but I will, before I go to bed.''

From the kitchen, Rosemary said, ''Marge and the other girls paid their fines and were home in an hour. Weren't you, Marge?''

''That's right.'' She set a mug of coffee at Hannah's elbow. ''Don't worry, this one's in the bag. Dixie Jo at the Curl Up and Dye couldn't work IdaClare in yesterday, but I'll go over early to poof her hair.''

She winked. ''Mark my words, Judge Messerschmidt will sit up, take notice and turn her loose in five seconds.''

Leo passed dessert plates, forks and napkins to Hannah and IdaClare. ''The victory, we will celebrate tomorrow night, yes?''

''Wait a sec,'' Hannah said. ''I thought you pled guilty, IdaClare. The hearing is to determine your sentence.''

''Well, I couldn't very well plead innocent, could I? Not after that Detective Andrik butted in on our card party.'' She popped a cherry in her mouth. ''After my advocate and I speak our piece, I may have to pay a fine too, but that'll be the end of it.''

Lord love a duck, Hannah thought. It had better be, or the next person throwing herself on the mercy of the court will be me. Then, when Jack finds out, I'll not only be unemployed, I'll be deaf from the nuclear explosion.

Silence descended, broken by smacking lips, *mmm's* and clinking forks. Recalling a remark IdaClare had made the day of her arrest, Hannah said, ''Pardon my curiosity, but telling the judge he could kiss your keister in the middle of the courthouse square at high noon isn't included in that piece you plan to speak, is it?''

IdaClare looked at her as though she'd announced she'd been impregnated by an alien. ''I cannot for the life of me imagine where you got the idea I'd *ever* say such a thing to a judge.''

''Uh-oh,'' Marge teased, ''maybe Hannah's hearing voices in her head now. Owen was forever saying you told him this or that when you didn't.''

''Stress,'' Leo diagnosed. ''The circuits in the brain, they overload. *Bzzt-bzzt.*''

''Sounds just like something IdaClare would say,'' Delbert commented. ''All flash and no pan.''

''It does not and I am not.''

''Never mind.'' Hannah waved her napkin. ''Let's move on. I'm sure all of us have other things we need to do tonight.''

Delbert checked his watch. ''Hmmph. Already missed my fishing show, and *The Wonderful World of Color* starts in an hour.''

''It does?'' IdaClare's fork tapped her coffee mug. ''I call this meeting to order. First order of business is for Hannah to tell us everything she knows about the Hendrickson case.''

''What?''

Marge said, ''I'll take notes.''

IdaClare gave Hannah a perky smile. ''We're already behind on this one, dear, and it isn't fair for the other investigators to know more than we do.''

''Gotta get to brass tacks, ladybug, or the sheriff'll be a gone goose before we get deployed.''

Five pairs of ears swiveled expectantly, including Leo's, who was seated with his back to her.

Voices in her head? Darn tootin' Fig Newton. A whole choir was belting out "Rescue the Perishing." In the deeper recesses, another advised, *You're stone-walled and you know it. You need to brainstorm, to let the wild hares loose and see which ones don't sound so wild after all.*

Hannah laid her plate on the bar, grateful for their eagerness but missing David as her backboard. Hesitant at the beginning, the pertinent facts, speculations and perceptions as she knew them tumbled forth.

Marge's pen scratched, her notebook's pages crackling as they turned. When Hannah finished, the sleuths sat transfixed, exchanging glances, their expressions alternating between thoughtful, pained, perplexed and sympathetic.

Quietly, Delbert said, "Everyone makes mistakes. Big ones, small ones. Can't live a day without 'em. But you don't believe Hendrickson made one, do you?"

"No."

"Then that's our jumping-off point."

Rosemary's brow furrowed. "I'm not sure what you mean by that."

Delbert gave her a 'Boy, am I glad you asked' look. "This book I got yesterday, *Trade Secrets from the Masters of Criminal Investigation*, says a gumshoe needs a premise—a hook to hang his fedora on. Usually, the client provides it, since he's paying the dick to prove he didn't do something or to find a missing person or some such."

Elbows propped on the table, Delbert's shrewd blue eyes flicked from comrade to comrade. "The cops are operating on the premise Hendrickson is lying or loco in the cabana. Our premise for Code Name Beta is that he's telling the truth.''

Hmm, Hannah thought. A visual scan deduced that nobody else knew what the hell Delbert was talking about, either.

''A good premise,'' Leo said. ''The truth, it is the best premise of all, yes? Except what about it will we investigate?''

''Excellent question.'' Delbert sat back in his chair. He folded his hands in his lap. Time marched on.

''Well, do you intend to answer it?'' IdaClare inquired. ''Or just sit there like a toad on a flat rock?''

''Hmmph. I was being democratic. I figured one of you might pick up the ball and run with it.''

''We don't play golf the way you do,'' Marge said. ''We play the ball where it lies.''

Rosemary whispered, ''I think what he said is a football thing.''

''Hah! Ever see Delbert take a drop when his tee-shot lands against a tree? He winds up and pitches it like Sammy Sosa.''

IdaClare said, ''Sammy Sosa isn't a pitcher,'' then looked at Hannah. ''Is he?''

''I play the sport of kings by the Marcus of Quizzenberry rules,'' Delbert said. ''Set forth in 1492 by Marcus himself.''

IdaClare warned, ''I've heard all the blarney I care to, Bisbee. Finish what you started or hush up.''

''Well, it's so dadblamed simple I shouldn't have to give chapter and verse.'' He grasped his vest's neck-ribbing. ''If truth is the premise, that equals somebody else having a motive and the opportunity to swipe

Quince's gun and frame Hendrickson. What we have to figure out is who that somebody is.''

If life were a cartoon, the table would have been illuminated by lightbulbs aglow over five elderly heads. Hannah stared into the middle distance. She'd pecked at the edges of the oh-so-obvious for days. The questions she'd asked Claudina followed that path. Why hadn't any bells rung?

Compensation. *Over*compensation. She'd distrusted her instincts, assuming her closeness to David invalidated them.

Fool me once, Hannah thought, shame on you; fool me twice, shame on me. Bipolar inference aside, her error in judgment would not be repeated.

Malcolm slunk in, groggy but leery of the group seated at the table. Padding around them, he squeezed behind Leo's chair, then drooped against Hannah, his muzzle in her lap.

Moomph.

She petted her brave soldier, promising him silently that his patience would soon be rewarded.

Referring to her notes, Marge suggested, ''Two people have what I'd call a motive. Jessup Knox and Lydia Quince.''

''Knox more than her,'' IdaClare said, ''if that dispatcher knows Kinderhook County politics as well as it sounds like she does.''

Delbert harrumphed. ''No, as little use as I have for Jessup Knox, my money's on the widow, with an assist from cousin Jimmy Wayne.''

''Now, that's a shock,'' Rosemary said, chuckling. ''A gold digger *and* a conspiracy theory? The only thing missing is a Russian spy.''

Delbert collected conspiracies like a numismatist did coins, but this one wasn't as far-fetched as his last, which involved a congressional plot to reduce Social Security expenditures by bumping off a percentage of its recipients.

"Their kinship and the life insurance policy bothers me, too," Hannah said. "Except there's no doubt David shot Quince, so why frame him? Suicide usually voids a policy, but Quince's death wasn't suicide. The insurer may balk, but it'll have to pay survivor's benefits eventually."

Delbert pointed at Leo. "What say you, Schnur? You hawked insurance for what, forty years?"

"Maybe yes, maybe no."

"Well, that's helpful as all hell."

"The carriers, they differ," Leo said. "The clauses, they differ. Many are the similarities—is boilerplate, to some extent. If, however, the Quince policy had a felony clause? A motive for the frame that would be."

"Do they *usually* have one?" Delbert asked.

"More common it is than not."

Hannah's heart quickened. "What's a felony clause, and why would it be a motive?"

Leo turned in his chair. "The insured, if he is committing the felony at the time of death, and the policy, it has the felony clause?" He made a gagging noise, then a throat-slitting gesture. "The beneficiary, she gets bupkis."

Delbert added, "And coercing an officer of the law into a draw-down shoot-out is a felony, ladybug."

That damn gun again. Stolen gun, according to Lydia Quince. Could be she'd fudged the date a bit. Maybe it was stolen, only not a year ago, and not from Stuart's truck. Maybe as recently as last Friday night, from the living room of her former residence at 5406 Skyline Drive.

With or without cousin Chief Deputy Jimmy Wayne's help, a hundred thousand dollars would go a long way toward financing the fresh start Lydia mentioned to church carolers last Christmas.

12

On the fourth ring, the answering machine broadcast its outgoing message, then the Beethoven concerto.

"David, it's Hannah. I—" She faltered at the thought of an empty living room and her voice echoing off its walls.

A high-pitched beep punished her eardrum. "Hey— it's me. Don't hang up."

"David?"

"Well, it ain't Rambo. He's about mastered 'hello,' but his paw is too big to punch the buttons."

Her head sank back in the bed pillows. God, he sounded almost normal. So why was she ransacking her brain for a comeback?

The eternal eighth-grader within said, because it's almost ten o'clock and he's home, not in custody or in jail; so why didn't he call before you gnawed off every fingernail on both hands worrying about him?

"How's Malcolm doing?" he asked, sidestepping the issue as though unaware of its existence.

The all-American mutt lay snoring on the Scooby-Doo beach towel he'd dragged from the bathroom and deposited beside her bed. He'd loved the shower, endured the brushing and blow-drying and *burfed* at the back door twice to go out, as if they'd been roomies for years.

"We've had several frank discussions about the sofa being off limits and that my desk isn't a doghouse," Hannah said. "Other than that, *his* behavior has been a solid A+."

A sitcom's laugh track nattered in the background. *Sorry to interrupt your viewing enjoyment, Sheriff.* She glowered at the ceiling bumps, hoping for a cutaway to a feminine-hygiene spray commercial.

"Uh, Hannah?"

"Yes?"

"Are you mad at me?"

"Gee, David. What makes you think I'm mad?"

The correct answer would be: Because after caring enough to deliver yourself, Ruby's banana-cream pie, a lecture, the hottest, most erotic, tongue-intensive kiss I've ever been on the receiving end of and some X-rated bumping, I didn't call and I should have and I'm sorry and I'll make it up to you somehow, and I'll be naked when I do and you'll need CPR afterward.

What David said was, "I dunno. You just sound kind of ticked off."

Kind of? The Federal Communications Commission would censor the responses thumping between Hannah's temples.

"You are mad. You said, 'What makes you think I'm mad' instead of 'Oh, David—' he warbled in falsetto voice '—I could never be mad at a wonderful man like you.'"

Hannah pulled the receiver away so the dork wouldn't hear her laugh. At the same time, a cavern opened in her belly because he truly was wonderful and life sucked.

"Hannah?"

"I'm still here."

"That's the problem, sugar. You're there and I'm here."

The blanket's nubby weave tickled her palm. It didn't seem possible that only five days had passed since he'd brought her breakfast the morning after her life-and-death struggle with an assailant.

Pastry, coffee and David's irresistible bedside manner had led to snuggling, then drifted into the languid kisses and caresses that prelude lovemaking—until Marlin Andrik got on the radio and ruined everything.

"Distance never bothered us before, David. I hate that it is now."

"So do I." He hesitated. "This may not make a helluva lot of sense, but the second I heard you on the machine, the other side of me did his level best to stop me from picking up."

"Why wouldn't it make sense? There's no reason to put your guard up when no one's invading your space."

"Yeah, except he doesn't do it with just anybody. Not to say I haven't been a prize prick around Marlin and Pike and Jimmy Wayne, but that's a different kind of self-defense."

His chuckle only implied humor. "Much as I'd like to believe a little thing like alleged malfeasance wouldn't curdle my attitude toward them, I'd be as skink-eyed and angry as they are if I were in their shoes."

Hannah smiled at the allusion. Andrik did project a lizard-like demeanor now and then.

"But other than when I'm singing the blues to my-self," David went on, "it's you that makes the other me pull back on the reins."

Wadding the blanket in her fist, Hannah fought the crush of helplessness and frustration. "I can't think of a thing to say besides repeating 'It's going to be all right,' but it *is*, David. It has to be. You haven't done anything wrong."

"I'll admit, nobody banging on my door with a war-rant yet has me wondering what's cooking down at the courthouse."

Oh? Hannah's temper flared again. *Then what have you been doing all evening besides not calling me? Rotating your tires?* Another possibility availed itself. "Why do I have a feeling you took a drive into town this evening?"

"Because that's what you'd have done."

"And?"

"Want to hazard a guess?"

Not particularly, but in the interest of keeping the dialogue chugging, she replied, "Either unmarked cars and lighted windows indicated a powwow in progress, or not a creature was stirring, not even a mouse."

"That's two guesses, but you clinched it with the powwow in progress. Kind of like the one at your cot-tage."

Hannah's mouth formed a capital O. "You were here? Why didn't you stop?"

"With Delbert's Edsel and IdaClare's Lincoln out front? A twenty-mule team and log chains couldn't have dragged me inside."

A fuming, fussing tirade ended with, "You're a wuss, Hendrickson."

"Better a wuss than a masochist. Though it's fair to warn you, the last person who called me a wuss got carried off the football field on a stretcher."

She rolled her eyes. "Am I supposed to be impressed by that?"

"Well, it impressed the dude I was scrimmaging with at practice. Leastwise, my little brother's never called me a wuss again, not where I could hear him."

Pity David's long-suffering mother, giving birth to one giant economy-size son after another in the vain hope of winning the chromosome lottery. Outbreaks of sibling rivalry at the Hendrickson house must have resembled the Vandals sacking Rome.

Malcolm grunted, his legs paddling as if escaping a bad dream or hastening to a sweet one before it vanished. At a farmhouse occupied by a lonesome county sheriff, trumpets blatted a newscast's intro.

"A minute ago, when I said the problem was you're there and I'm here?" David's baritone sliding to sultry had a ripple effect on areas far removed from her ear.

"Uh-huh." Her heels pummeled the mattress. Oh, you *go*, girl. That ought to send his Lust-o-Meter into orbit.

"Well, maybe it's better this way, because there's something I need to say and I'm not sure I could if we were together."

Hmm. Sex might not be on tonight's program, but his voice implied something was up…so to speak.

"Hold the phone a sec." She slid the extra pillow behind her, plumped both with her fist, then wriggled into a seated position. "Okay. I'm listening."

"What did you do?"

"If it's bad news, I wasn't going to take it lying down."

She could almost see his eyebrows change from upside-down check marks to an elongated line. "You're on the couch, right?"

"No-o-o." A fingertip traced across her favorite scuzzy nightshirt. It followed the curve above her breast, then upward to the tip of Wile E. Coyote's left ear. "I'm in bed."

"You were just faunching to tell me that, weren't you?"

"Of course. If you've taught me anything, it's the importance of honesty in a relationship." She snickered. "Wanna know what I'm wearing?"

Or will be, when you get here. Think floor-length black silk. Lace side panels. A smile.

"No."

"Wanna know what I'm not wearing?"

"*Hell* no."

"Want me to shut up so you can tell me why you're so happy you're not here with me?"

"Yes, ma'am, if it won't strain you unduly."

Guessing he'd penned a new verse to the "We Have No Future Together" song, Hannah pulled the covers to her chin so they'd be handy to stuff in her ears.

She'd composed a thousand dirges on the subject long before this ordeal with Stuart Quince forced them apart. Had she heeded any of them? No. Had David? No. Well then, by God, she wasn't about to start now.

"This afternoon," he began, "if Polly hadn't been here, we would have made love. If you'd been alone when I drove out there, we would have made love."

Forget her ears. She crammed the blanket in her

mouth to keep from screaming, *And we can be making love thirty frickin' minutes from now if you'll stop talking and start driving.*

"Interruptions being the rule so far," he continued, "it seemed like a conspiracy was afoot, till I realized why today was different. Maybe the other guy side of me is doing us a favor and I think we'd be wise to let him."

He took a deep breath and exhaled. "We were attracted to each other from the get-go. Stronger for me, I know, but you've felt it all the same."

No, David. It was never any stronger for you than for me. I just fought it harder.

"Last week," he said, "before Andrik put the kibosh to it, we were about to make love for all the right reasons. The only thing in this world keeping me here tonight is knowing if we were together we'd make love for all the wrong ones."

A huskiness resonating in his voice, he said, "I want our first time to be a beginning, Hannah. Not something we rush into because all of a sudden we're afraid that if we don't we might not have another chance.

"I may be crazier than everyone in the county thinks I am, but I suspect that's why I'm wearing armor around you. I need you in plenty more ways than physical, but if I let my guard down, I'm a goner and it'll cheat us both out of something we can't have twice."

Batting tears from her lashes, Hannah tried to feel guilty about tormenting him earlier, but couldn't. Teasing, flirting—even arguing—had been as much a part of their relationship as mutual respect, trust and an intense emotional and physical hunger they'd resisted but couldn't stop.

"We'll have our someday, David," she said, the words as much a promise as a prayer. "And when we do, it will be for all the right reasons."

The Kinderhook County Courthouse's enameled concrete floors amplified every clop and shuffle of foot traffic. Hallway conversations, ringing telephones, the jittery screech of computer printers and violent flushes of public rest-room commodes converged at the intersection of the building's compass-point entrances.

Hannah stood less than a yard from the epicenter, her eyes ratcheting down the glass-enclosed, wall-mounted directory. Plastic-lettered lines on a grooved felt background divided county governance by the floor each branch occupied. Lawbreakers, lawmakers and enforcers were billeted in the nosebleed section.

The rotunda's mahogany staircase spiraled upward around a space-age brass and Plexiglas elevator, a conspicuous example of two centuries colliding, with both sustaining permanent injuries. Hannah chose the fanned, concrete steps rather than be launched to the third floor like a deposit slip in a bank's pneumatic tube system.

She regretted it midway to the second level's landing. Sunlight pierced the locked casement windows, dehydrating the six air molecules that survived the journey upward from the main floor. Feeling as though she'd scaled a subtropical version of Mount Everest, she paused at the stairway's summit to catch her breath and her bearings.

IdaClare's fate would be decided in Courtroom C, wherever that was. No familiar faces were among the groups of three and four milling outside closed office doors. None of them appeared to be in the mood to play docent.

Hannah turned, hoping to spot a friend, another directory or a Cub Scout a couple of good deeds shy of his citizenship badge. Her eyes riveted on a pebble-glass door marked Kinderhook County Sheriff's Department. Beneath it, smaller, black script read David M. Hendrickson, Sheriff.

The artist who'd painted the chipped, faux-gilt letters identifying the office had probably retired his brushes two decades ago. A rag and turpentine could erase David's name in minutes.

A shadow-figure loomed behind the opaque glass. She whirled like a spy about to be caught reconnoitering an enemy camp and blundered into a man rounding the bend from the other direction. As she bounced off his air-bag belly, he snagged her arm to steady her. "'Ey, where's the fire, li'l lady?"

"Fire" rhymed with "tar." That and the sobriquet identified him even before she took in the capped teeth, swarthy complexion and black pompadour.

"Why, if it ain't Miz Hannah Garvey," said the pitiful excuse for an Elvis impersonator. "Must be my lucky day bumping into a purty gal like you."

Resisting the urge to ralph on his ostrich-leather boots, Hannah extricated her arm. "I apologize for not looking where I was going, Mr. Knox."

"Glad to be of service, but everybody and their

brother's dog calls me Jessup. Mr. Knox always has me checking to see if my daddy's behind me, God bless and keep his immortal soul.''

If father resembled son, the elder Knox's soul was roasting not resting. "If you'll excuse me—"

"What brings you to the hall of justice on such a fine April morn?" he inquired, the patois as thick as his waistline. "If it's a traffic ticket, it'd be my pleasure to talk to the judge on your behalf."

Tempted to tell him what she'd rather he put where, sideways, she hadn't formulated a more courteous response when he said, "'Course, you wouldn't need my help if ol' Dave hadn't got himself in such a bind."

She'd never heard anyone call David 'Dave.' Familiarity bred contempt.

Knox clucked his tongue. "I can't understand what got into that boy the other night. Him being fresh from the city and all, I suppose he didn't have time to learn how we do things around here."

Hannah weighed the possibility of pumping information out of the repulsive son of a bitch *before* she grabbed him by the cojones and bad hair and hurled him down three flights of stairs. But discretion was the better part of malicious wounding. "Since I'm new here myself, I'm curious how you would have handled the situation—" she gulped "—Jessup."

"Well now, li'l lady, I'm from the old school that says a man with a gun strapped to his hip can't rightly call himself a peace officer. Seems to me, having deadly force at your fingertips makes a fella quicker to use *it* than his head.

"Seeing as how folks in these parts say I can talk to a stump and carry both sides of the palaver," he continued, "I'd have conversated with Mr. Quince till he fell asleep standing up or sunrise, whichever come first."

Plastering on a mournful expression, he added, "Like they say, it's always darkest before the dawn. Why, it's plumb tragic ol' Dave didn't let that young man live to see another one."

Hannah's molars ground obscenities to dust. Knox wasn't fit to wax David Hendrickson's car, much less second-guess him. "You'll have to excuse me. I have an appointment to keep."

"Don't you be late on my account." He pointed over her shoulder. "Just follow the balustrade that-away and take a turn at the hall. Traffic court's the third door on the left."

Her nod sufficing as "Thanks for nothing, you pompous ass," Hannah strode toward the opposite hallway, rounding its corner just as Knox called after her, "Do give ol' Dave my best regards. Hear?"

Her unspoken reply bristled with F-words functioning as a noun, a pronoun, a verb, an adjective and a suffix. She stalked past a pair of recessed double doors before her brain registered the Courtroom C engraved on the lock rails' brass plates.

The windowless, paneled room was smaller than she expected, austere and cold despite its stuffiness. A carpeted platform raised the judge to a lord-of-the-realm altitude, while the jury box's antiquated theater seats would cure narcolepsy. The court stenographer's and clerk's desks faced each other, the latter positioned farther from the judge's bench and adjacent witness stand.

Photographs and documents hung in framed effigy above the sidewalls' wainscoting. Unlike the courtroom where Perry Mason outfoxed Hamilton Burger, no blindfolded statuette balanced scales of justice in an outstretched hand.

IdaClare was alone at the defendant's table on the business side of the bar. She'd forbidden Jack's attendance, threatening to bequeath her estate to Itsy and Bitsy if he crossed the county line, but who and where was her advocate?

The prosecution was represented by a thirty-something woman in a tailored, charcoal power suit. Her razor-cut pageboy excluded her from the Curl Up and Dye's clientele.

Velma Billingsly and Marge Rosenbaum occupied the bench behind IdaClare. Marlin Andrik coughed and fidgeted in his seat across the aisle.

"You're in my place." The speaker, a woman in a baggy cotton dress, crocheted shawl, crew socks and vintage Earth shoes, didn't look a day over a hundred and twelve.

Waggling her cane at Hannah, she said, "Are ye deaf? Scoot over and make it snappy."

Hannah did both.

The woman slid in to the space Hannah vacated. Positioning the cane between splayed knees, she lowered herself by increments, hovered a moment, then dropped onto the uncushioned bench.

Cane dispensed with and straw hat adjusted, she pulled a corduroy pillow from a Rainy Day Books shopping bag and stuffed it behind her back. She then fished out a ball of red yarn skewered by knitting needles, a cellophane-wrapped sandwich and a thermos.

Hannah, who'd stared in rapt fascination throughout the procedure, watched her seatmate unscrew the cup from the thermos and fill it with hot tea. The aroma of strong Earl Grey joined forces with eighty-proof Jim Beam.

She hoisted her cup at two matrons and a wizened gent scowling at her from the other side of the room. The trio sniffed, thrust out their chins and looked away.

"Sore losers. There'll be a blizzard in h-e-double-hockey-sticks afore Sophonia Pugh can't tell a hung jury from one herding kittens till they get their free lunch, then vote guilty and go home."

"Excuse me?"

"I don't go in much for hearings." Sophonia tossed back the last shot of tea and screwed the cup back on the thermos.

"No drama in 'em. But it's folly to think a humdinging, blood-and-guts trial comes along every day, like on TV."

Hannah blinked, sensing her role in the commentary was peripheral.

The court groupie pointed at IdaClare. "What's her story? You kin to her? Never saw such hair in all my born days. Looks like she stuck her head in a cotton-candy machine at the fair."

Hannah related the particulars, but could offer no explanation for IdaClare's hair coloring.

Sophonia snorted in disgust and started repacking her bag. "I should have known better than settle in when I saw *her* at the prosecutor's table."

She glanced up. "What *is* that girl attorney's name— Alice? Andrea? Something with an A." She shook her head.

"Mack and his big guns are too busy with the grand jury to fiddle with small potatoes. Lo, I'd give my uppers to be a fly on the wall for one of them. They don't call 'em grand for nothing, they don't.''

Hannah mentally unraveled yet another stream of semiconsciousness. Mack Doniphan was the county prosecuting attorney, thus Ms. A. Whatever with the great haircut must be an assistant handling scut work in the absence of Doniphan and his first team.

Could that have any bearing on the outcome of IdaClare's hearing? Hannah was about to ask Sophonia, when the double doors burst open like bat wings on a frontier saloon.

Pausing at the threshold, the man whisked a golf cap off his head and smoothed his hair. Attired in a white swallow-tailed coat, knife-creased trousers, a yellow French-cuffed shirt and turquoise tie and spats, he strolled to the empty chair beside IdaClare, leaving a slipstream of camphor and Old Spice in his wake.

Hannah clapped a hand to her mouth. Oh... my...God. Why didn't I guess he was IdaClare's advocate? He never said a word—snide or otherwise— about her hobby or the hearing. Who else, in all the land, would leap at the chance to be Jay-Gatsby-does-Clarence Darrow?

''Who's the hunk?'' Sophonia asked, an awestruck quality to her voice.

''Delbert Bisbee. He's a retired postal supervisor, born-again Renaissance man, buttinsky extraordinaire—''

''Is he married? Aw, he must be. The sexy ones always are.''

Ye gods. Was someone dumping hormones in the water supply or what? ''As it happens, Delbert is between wives at the moment. The fifth and sixth, to be specific.''

Sophonia's shopping bag thunked on the bench.

The court clerk and stenographer preceded Judge Cranston Messerschmidt's entrance through a side door. The magistrate scaled the steps to his perch, looking from the defendant's table to Ms. A. Whatever and back again.

Once seated and sorting papers while Ms. A. recited the charges against Mrs. IdaClare Belinda Clancy, the judge's eyes repeatedly flicked to Delbert, poised in his chair like a track star awaiting the starter's pistol.

''Do you understand the seriousness of the charges levied against you, Mrs. Clancy?'' Messerschmidt inquired.

IdaClare stood. ''Yes, Your Honor.''

Delbert popped up. ''I object.''

''Who are you, and what precisely are you objecting to, sir?''

''Delbert Bisbee, Esquire, Your Honor, acting as Mrs. Clancy's legal advocate. As for my objection, the question was leading, irrelevant and immaterial. Maybe even prejudicial—I didn't study up on that one much— but if my client didn't take this seriously, she wouldn't be here.''

The judge folded his hands. ''Objection overruled. You and Mrs. Clancy may be seated.''

''But—''

''Your Honor.'' Ms. A. shot Delbert an exasperated look as she stood. ''Might I point out that, despite a *three-hour* discussion with Mr. Bisbee on Saturday, I failed to convince him that his participation is neither warranted nor necessary? That my office, Sheriff Hendrickson and Detective Marlin Andrik, the arresting officer, have already submitted written recommendations for your consideration?''

"Dag-nab-it, I object." Delbert vaulted upright. Behind him, Velma and Marge jumped several vertical inches.

"This—this *child* knows good and well, me and IdaClare have a couple of rip-snortin' orations to deliver. As a taxpaying citizen of this county, I demand my First Amendment right to be heard, whether Miss Wet-Behind-the-Ears likes it or not."

Face buried in his hands, Andrik keeled sideward in his seat, his shoulders shaking uncontrollably.

Sophonia murmured, "Mmm-mmm-mmm, you better stuff a sock in it, handsome, or Cranston will put you in the pokey for contempt."

"Mr. Bisbee," the judge intoned, "much as I admire your, er, enthusiasm, the court has no intention of entertaining a filibuster."

Delbert planted his fists on his hips. "Does that mean I'm overruled again?"

"Permanently."

"We beg your pardon, Your Honor." IdaClare yanked Delbert into his chair. "We feel certain a man old enough to have one foot in the grave, the same as we do, wouldn't want a poor, defenseless widow to spend what hours she has left on earth in prison for growing a few teensy little herbs to ease her dearest friends' pain."

Hannah didn't realize she'd groaned aloud until Sophonia jabbed her in the ribs with an elbow.

Messerschmidt's steepled fingers were either a pause for thought or a barricade to hide a grin. Presently, he addressed IdaClare, who stood, as did Delbert Bisbee, Esquire, and Ms. A. Whatever. "The efficacy of marijuana as a treatment or alleviant for various conditions and/or diseases is an issue yet to be fully studied by the medical community. However, the possibility this substance may, in fact, have benefits—if only perhaps psychological ones, by virtue of a placebo effect—has complicated adjudication on local, state and federal levels. Currently, there is no standard..."

Hannah's attention strayed to the stenographer recording Messerschmidt's ungodly boring treatise. The woman's features were slack and her eyes appeared to be closed.

"...this court thereby sentences you to serve five years in the state penitentiary and pay a fine in the amount of two thousand dollars."

IdaClare staggered against Delbert. Hannah gasped, her heart sliding to her ankles. Five *years?* Why not make it life, since that's what it was.

Sophonia squeezed her arm. "Now, now, don't panic. Cranston's famous for scaring the whey out of defendants. He isn't done till the gavel falls."

"However," Messerschmidt continued, "in light of the recommendations submitted, though the fine shall stand as read, the court hereby suspends the prison sentence and institutes a five-year probation period.

"In addition, the court orders the removal of the defendant's greenhouse within thirty days. Said removal will be verified by an officer of the Kinderhook County Sheriff's Department. The construction of another like facility by Mrs. IdaClare B. Clancy, or her propagation or distribution of cannabis by any means whatsoever will be deemed a violation of probation and result in the court's immediate reinstatement of the prison sentence.''

The judge's eyebrows arched. ''Do you understand the terms and limitations imposed upon you, Mrs. Clancy?''

''Well, I don't see why the court saw fit to churn my bowels to butter imposing them, but yes, sir, I do.'' IdaClare jutted her chin. ''Except for one.''

''And which might that be, Mrs. Clancy?''

''Ordering me to destroy the sweetest little greenhouse ever there was.'' She stamped a foot. ''For heaven's sake, Judge. What would you do if I'd been making gin in my bathtub? Order me to rip the plumbing out of the walls?''

''Yes, Mrs. Clancy. That is *precisely* what I would have done.'' The gavel whapped the block on his desk. ''This hearing is adjourned.''

Hannah blew out a breath she wasn't aware she'd been holding.

Sophonia tucked her legs under the bench. ''Slip out and wait for me at the corner by the water fountain. I want to powder my nose before you introduce me to that Bisbee fellow.''

Oh, boy. The wild thing was bursting out all over, Hannah thought. Present company excluded.

Velma, Marge, IdaClare and The Hunk were arguing about something. Surprise, surprise. Not inclined to referee, Hannah hastened from the room.

She was trying to cadge a mouthful of lukewarm, metallic-tasting water dribbling from the hallway's fountain when a commotion near the stairway piqued her curiosity.

Lieutenant Theron Pike and David, both dressed in

business suits, strode toward her in lockstep. Neither acknowledged the calls of "Howya doin', Sheriff?" and "Hey, mister—is Hendrickson under arrest?" Chase Wingate captured the scene on film for all the county to see in the *Sanity Examiner's* next issue.

David's eyes met and held Hannah's, then lowered. He and Pike disappeared into the sheriff department's office entrance.

She stared after them, too stunned to think. A glimpse of a herringbone sport coat weaving between three scruffy teenage boys and a man carrying a brief-case jolted her from her stupor.

"Detective Andrik," she called, rushing after him.

His back stiffened, but he didn't stop.

Dodging around a young woman and her toddler, Hannah cried, "Marlin...please?"

His hand flipped a "follow me" gesture, then he clattered down the stairs as if the building were being evacuated.

Hannah found him outside the courthouse's east entrance, sitting on an empty bicycle rack, smoking a cigarette. Strain showed on a face not known for happy-go-luckiness. The tremble in his hand could be from caffeine overload and nicotine deficiency, but Hannah doubted it.

"Your friend Bisbee is a loony tune," he said.

"You have to admit, he has style."

Andrik studied the tip of his Marlboro as if the ember were an augury. "What did you want to see me about? As if I didn't know."

"Is David under arrest?"

"No."

"He looked like he was in Pike's custody to me."

"Anybody seeing us out here shooting the breeze could get the wrong idea about that, too."

Hannah cocked a hip, the toe of her shoe swinging like a metronome. "You don't do coy any better than I do, Marlin."

"I don't appreciate being cornered, even by a pretty woman." He squinted up at her. "Bar none, this has been the worst week of my entire career. The next may top it."

Telling him David's and hers hadn't been rosy either was ludicrous. "If David isn't under arrest, why is he here dressed like a pallbearer?"

Marlin took a drag, exhaled and aimed his remarks at the ground. "Mack Doniphan has enough for a second-degree manslaughter charge, he just doesn't want his office to file it. We met last night with Jake Waycross, the assistant state attorney general. He recommended Mack add Hendrickson to the grand jury's docket. Let them hand down an indictment."

"Waycross has to be back in Jefferson City this afternoon, but wanted to interview Hendrickson. Pike went out this morning to tell David he'll have to testify before the jury Wednesday—Thursday at the latest—and bring him in for the interview."

Hannah's tongue traced her teeth. "Why doesn't the county prosecutor want to file the charge? Isn't that his job?"

"The sheriff isn't an everyday Joe, Hannah. I think Mack's doing himself and Hendrickson a favor. Doniphan ducks accusations of foot-dragging and Hendrickson has a little more time before the shit really hits the fan."

"Forty-eight hours? At most, seventy-two?" She shook her head. "Chinese water torture."

Andrik crushed his cigarette under his heel. "There are two ways of looking at everything, toots."

Isn't it ironic for you to say that, Detective. "Yes, there are, Marlin. At least two."

He smiled, which was to say the corners of his mouth moved. "Been playing this one cagier, haven't you?"

"What do you mean?"

"You jumped into the Osborn murder with both feet. This is the first I've seen of you since Friday night. I've heard your name mentioned a few times, but other than wanting Hendrickson's address, my phone isn't ringing."

It will be, Hannah thought. Maybe sooner than you think.

Andrik opened his jacket, exposing the shoulder holster strapped to his chest. Removing a pen and a business-card wallet from the inner pocket, he jotted three numbers on the back of his card. "This is privileged information. Home phone, pager and the yuppie-ass cell phone I'm lugging around, as of today."

"Thank you, Marlin."

"Don't mention it. To anybody." Starting toward the courthouse, he paused beside her, their shoulders almost touching.

For a moment, the dark, hooded eyes of a professional cynic lost their case-hardened sheen, then he nodded and walked away.

14

"**D**eath Benefits Division?" the heavyset insurance salesman repeated.

Hannah nodded solemnly.

"Awful Johnny-on-the-spot, aren't you? Clients tell me they have to stand on their heads to get Social Security's attention."

"Reform is our rallying cry," Hannah said. "These preliminary reports are among many directive improvements we've instituted to minimize suboptimal episodes. Like the Internal Revenue Service, we're striving to be a kinder, gentler bureaucracy."

"Land o' Goshen," he muttered. "You work for the government all right."

Eldredge Randal wadded the fast-food wrappers on his desk, conferring new grease and ketchup stains to the combination blotter and calendar. If titled and framed, it would qualify as a masterpiece in avant-garde circles.

"I apologize for interrupting your lunch, Mr. Randal."

"You wouldn't have if my wife had brought it nearer noontime." He snorkeled the dregs of a bonus-size diet soda up a straw. "I'm glad for the company. Not a soul has called or come in since my secretary left for a dentist's appointment.''

He peered at the wall clock. "That girl better be getting a root canal, too, long as she's been gone.''

Billboards along Highway VV proclaimed the Randal Insurance Agency had been "serving the citizens of Kinderhook County since 1966.'' Plaques and trophies on bracketed shelves behind him denoted salesmanship and a devotion to civic and charitable activities.

Randal slam-dunked a waxed cup and picnic leavings in the wastebasket and camouflaged a belch as clearing his throat. "Now, what can I do to help Lydia? I probably shouldn't say this, but she deserves every dime coming to her and more. It's too bad about Stuart dying and all, but it isn't like he was ever the breadwinner.''

"How long did Mrs. Quince work for you?''

"Let me think.'' Concentration brightened the spidery veins in his cheeks. "Four years? Or was it closer to five?''

He pushed back in his chair and lumbered to the file cabinets along the opposite wall. Extracting a manila folder, he skimmed a sheet stapled to the cover as he returned to his desk. "Would have been five years next month if she hadn't quit last December and moved home to Richland to put a few miles between—''

His hazel eyes, magnified by invisible bifocals, narrowed by half. "Being separated from Stuart doesn't make any difference in her benefits, does it?''

Careful. Behind that virulent blue tie beats the heart of a businessman wise to owners who claimed their year-old, fully insured vehicles with three-digit payments were stolen by joyriders, then totaled at the bottom of a ravine.

By his tone, Randal also already knew the answer.

Hannah worried her lower lip, her expression a picture of uncertainty. "Gosh, Mr. Randal, I'm so new at this, my business cards haven't arrived from the printer yet."

His sympathetic smile belied David's opinion that she couldn't lie her way out of a paper sack. "I did kind of wonder why you're scribbling on a tablet instead of the forms you people are so fond of."

"These are, uh, field notes. To be transcribed later into our computerized formatting. Faster, easier, more efficient."

"Computers." Randal cast a disparaging glance at a monitor where a Dilbert screen saver trudged through a maze of cubicles.

"Before Mrs. Quince came to work for you, she was employed by…" Hannah let her voice trail off, flipping pages as if in search of a prior notation.

"Re-Nu Industries, Inc.," he said. "It's an engine remanufacturing plant here in town, but Lydia wasn't there more than two or three months.

"She quit a good job working for an attorney in Richland to move here when Re-Nu hired Stuart to drive long-haul. Lydia earned more on their assembly line than I could pay her, but she couldn't take the salty language and every tomcat in the plant knowing when her husband was on the road."

"Sexual harassment?" Hannah asked.

"We-l-l, Lydia's real timid, you know? The kind ya-hoos pick on because they know she won't stick up for herself. Some folks are just born victims and a bully can smell them a mile away.''

''Stuart included?''

Randal grunted. ''That's why she stayed with him for years, waiting for him to straighten up and fly right.'' His palm raised. ''Now, don't misunderstand. Lydia's as sharp as cut glass. She just isn't a fighter.''

He offered Hannah the file folder. ''I doubt there's anything here you don't already know, but you're welcome to look.''

As Delbert would say, *hot-ziggety*.

Except he'd have to retract it. The contents were a nonprovocative array of federal and state tax forms, letters from customers grateful for Lydia's kindness and copies of medical claims, primarily Stuart's, for prescription-drug reimbursements.

No handy-dandy copy of Quince's life insurance policy with a highlighted felony clause. She prayed a subtle way to ask Randal would present itself.

Backtracking to Lydia's job application, Hannah calculated the widow's current age as twenty-eight. High school graduate. A year's technical-school training in office management, i.e. Secretarial 101.

For general principles, Hannah copied the names and telephone numbers listed as references, Lydia's Social Security number and her forwarding address in Richland. For someone desirous of a new life, Lydia hadn't ventured farther than her hometown.

Handing back the folder, Hannah said, ''It isn't compensation for a bad marriage, but with survivor benefits and your agency's hundred-thousand-dollar life insurance payout, Mrs. Quince should have no problem supporting herself.''

"It'll help, but whoever told you I brokered the policy is mistaken."

Hannah frowned down at her notebook. Silence really is golden. If given the opportunity, most people will fall over themselves trying to fill it. Eldredge Randal, included.

"Shortly after Lydia and Stuart eloped," he explained, "her daddy marched her down to his insurance agent. I never met Mr. McBride, but as a father myself, I figure he saw his new son-in-law for what he was and didn't want Lydia and his grandchildren left without a pot, nor a window to throw it through."

Great news, that. A ten-year-old policy also threw a premeditated, short-term death-dividends scam out the window. Odd that the premiums were kept up so long, though, despite the Quinces' paycheck-to-paycheck existence.

Had Mr. McBride originated the policy and maintained it? Perhaps fathers were like that. The paternal identification on Hannah's birth certificate read John Doe, which had led her to believe she was somehow related to Bambi.

"I wasn't aware the Quinces had any children," she said truthfully.

"They didn't. Lydia wanted a houseful, but having them was a Hobson's choice."

"In what way?" Hannah flinched, then brushed the question away. "Don't answer that. I'm a disgrace to myself and the bureau, being so nosy."

"No harm in it as long as it isn't mean-spirited."

Could posing as a government official because you suspect a former employee is framing the sheriff for murder be interpreted as 'mean-spirited'?

Tough.

Randal said, "When Stuart went off the pills the doctors prescribed—which was whenever they started doing him some good—he wasn't fit to live with. Drank too much. Holed up in the house, a walking zombie. If he took his meds, he, uh…well, that type of medication has side effects, if you know what I mean."

Impotence too, huh? On top of mental illness, chronic unemployment, alcoholism and a refusal to help himself? The ten years Lydia stood by her man must have felt like a century.

Deputy Cahill and his wife were caroling when Lydia told them she was leaving Stuart. Couldn't she face another Christmas with no money to spare? Or did Stuart spend it like there was no such thing as a January billing cycle?

A divorce would have ended the joint accounting, but wouldn't wipe the red ink from Lydia's side of the ledger. A hundred grand in one nontaxable chunk?

Goodbye, Skyline Drive. Hello, Easy Street.

Hannah patted her bosom. "What that poor woman has endured is enough to break my heart. If there's any justice in this world, she'll find someone who'll appreciate her instead of taking advantage of her."

Randal pointed a thumb at a family photograph on his desk. "My Robby worships the ground Lydia walks on. He's the assistant baseball coach at the high school—busier than a cranberry merchant right now—but I suspect he's going to pop the question before somebody else beats him to it."

The bespectacled, prodigal white whale stood behind two fleshy younger women. One cradled an infant in the crook of her arm; the other vise-gripped a toddling girl's shoulder. Robby Randal's buttoned oxford shirt and tight smile shrieked "math wonk" without a hint of athletic interest.

"These days, being a coach is the same as holding down two full-time jobs," his father boasted. "Robby teaches advanced algebra, trig and calculus, too."

Imagine that.

Hannah mulled the possibility of Robby-the-Roly-Poly and Lydia-the-Mouse's affair being the catalyst for bailing out on Stuart-the-Loser.

Well, maybe not an *affair,* as in hot, adulterous sex in the high school dugout. Not with a guy who probably still slept in pajamas with a horsies-and-lassos motif. But, to a woman too meek to save herself, Robby might represent the legendary light at the end of a long, painful tunnel.

Did Stuart know about Robby? Had Stuart called Lydia and told her he had nothing to live for as a desperate attempt to get her back or a last goodbye? Maybe even told her how he planned to coerce a cop into being his executioner?

Realizing Stuart was going to save her the cost of a divorce by screwing her out of the insurance money, Hannah theorized, Lydia snuck into the house and removed all evidence of a felony while David was in his cruiser.

After a few weeks of widow's weeds, condolence cakes and casseroles and waiting for the check, Lydia would become Mrs. Coach Math Wonk in a quiet, family-only ceremony, then get pregnant on their wedding night.

She still could, with Hannah's blessing—minus the money—after Lydia confessed to Pike and Andrik. She hadn't framed David intentionally. She couldn't have known who'd respond to the restaurant manager's complaint any more than Quince had.

If prosecuted at all, the jury would surely understand and be sympathetic. Jeez, the scenario had *Movie of the Week,* starring Farrah Fawcett, written all over it. The suspenseful closing scene would cut from the hatchet-faced foreman handing the verdict to the bailiff, to closed double doors identical to the courtroom's, then Farrah and...Drew Carey—yes!—would burst through them in a hail of postnuptial bird seed.

Hannah's bullshit detector drowned out the Mendelssohn sound track. Would Lydia know about gunpowder residue? Even if she did, could she have bent over her dead husband's corpse to...

Not Lydia-the-Mouse. Not for a million bucks.

Well, hell.

"Mr. Randal," Hannah said, offering her hand. "Thank you for your time and for answering my questions."

Startled by her abrupt departure, he struggled to his feet. "Oh, well—it, uh, it was a pleasure meeting you, Ms.—" He winced. "Gad, where is my mind? It isn't like me to forget a name."

Retreating into the reception area before he remembered Hannah didn't give one, she bid him a nice day and marched out the door.

Traffic circling the square mimicked the thoughts in her head. She stomped to the Blazer, a revised cast of characters flashing in her mind's eye:

Jimmy Wayne McBride tampering with the evidence, instead of Lydia.

Lydia and Jimmy Wayne cotampering, with him taking care of the gruesome, but imperative, posthumous hand-wiping.

Lydia and Robby in similar cahoots. Or Robby acting alone. Or Jimmy Wayne and Robby.

For Christ's sweet sake, why not make it a full carload? Lydia pocketed the gun. Robby plucked up the shell casing. Jimmy Wayne swabbed away the powder residue, then they all went out for a beer to celebrate.

Delbert would love it.

A plumber's panel van, an SUV and a Datsun were parked where his turquoise aircraft carrier, IdaClare's Lincoln and Marge's car had been earlier. If the gumshoes were following last night's battle strategy, Leo was dog-sitting Itsy, Bitsy and Malcolm. Rosemary, who'd been crowned Operations Manager for a Day, was touring Mr. and Mrs. Dinoto of Warren, Michigan, around Valhalla Springs.

Delbert was pestering the bejesus out of Chief Deputy McBride, if Sophonia hadn't bopped him with her cane and dragged him off for a nooner.

IdaClare was chatting up Coroner Junior Duckworth or his younger brother, Ozzie, principals of the family funeral home—disregarding LaVada, their spooky old mother.

The visit, as IdaClare termed it, was a "two-fer." While finalizing arrangements for Kathleen Osborn's memorial service, IdaClare had been enchanted by a casket with a golf-course mural called "Fairway to Heaven." On the pretense of buying one—if it *was* a pretense—she'd weasel insider information from the mortician, then hang around for Stuart's viewing and eavesdrop on the attendants.

Last but not least, Marge and Velma were getting

manicures at the Curl Up and Dye, where the air was saturated with equal parts super-hold hair spray and gossip.

Hannah's fingers *rat-tatted* the Blazer's steering wheel. Every instinct told her they were all just futzing around, which included her interview with Eldredge Randal and another she'd have to hustle to make on time.

Adding Robby to the suspect list lengthened it instead of shortening it. Adding him to Lydia's list of motives was asinine. What, the woman needed a hundred and *one* thousand reasons to get serious about insurance fraud?

As if via shortwave radio from the Great Beyond—or the Not-So-Great Below—Great-uncle Mort said, "You can't jump a hedgerow flat-footed, girl. Sometimes the best way to go forward is to back up and take a running start."

Hannah keyed the ignition. "Want to help me out, Uncle Mort? Stuff the homespun philosophy and tell me who's trying to destroy David Hendrickson."

Riverside Road's glass-smooth asphalt belied its degree of incline, giving Hannah an eerie sense of levitation. On the right, crumpled guardrails bolted to posts separated terra firma from two seconds of airborne terror and a crash landing in Sanity's city park.

She wondered why she'd never noticed the antebellum mansion on the bluff, visible from First Street's northbound lane, or to southbounders more interested in where they'd been than where they were going.

A mental doorbell rang. Oglethorpe Park. Jefferson Davis Oglethorpe's ancestral home overlooked said park. Donate a hundred acres you have lying around doing nothing for a public amenity and the city council will name it after you, institute a tax increase to fund its maintenance and mutter under their breaths about the whopping tax write-off you received for your generosity.

God bless America.

An evergreen waterfall and fuschia azaleas banked the brick steps leading to Oglethorpe's double-columned portico. A wrought-iron railed balcony softened the imposing entry and balanced the upper and lower levels' wide shuttered windows.

Near the bluff was a bronze statue of a mounted soldier. Not the typical lawn ornamentation, but it had more panache than a fountain with cherubs taking eternal whizzes in the bowl.

The Democratic candidate for sheriff answered his own front door. Of slight build and medium height, with white, shoulder-length hair and a dagger-tip goatee, Jefferson Davis Oglethorpe should have been holding a mint julep in one hand and a sword in the other.

He bowed at the waist. "Ms. Garvey, I am at a loss to remember when such a lovely young lady came to call. Please, do come in."

Hannah shrugged off an impulse to curtsy. "I appreciate your agreeing to meet with me on such short notice."

The entry hall smelled of age—the home's and its owner's—along with fried onions, pipe tobacco and linseed oil. Hannah took in the authentic Aubusson carpet, majestic grandfather clock, side tables and framed portraits, then lingered on a curving walnut staircase.

"Gorgeous."

"Gone are the days when I took those steps three at once." Oglethorpe chuckled. "Riding down them on a cookie sheet was a gimcracker, till Papa and a business associate arrived for dinner just as I achieved, ah...cruising altitude. Papa excused himself and me for a brief but memorable sojourn to the woodshed."

"And you never did it again?"

He lofted a hand. His index finger twined with its neighbor. "On my word as a gentleman."

Her host escorted her into the library, where his forebears must have retreated for after-dinner cigars, brandy and talk unsuitable for delicate ears. Hannah's breath caught at the ceiling-high bookshelves, the way other women's do at a shoe store's wall-to-wall clearance sale.

Marrying Oglethorpe was out of the question, but maybe he'd adopt her. He could leave the house and furnishings to his cat for all she cared, as long as she got her mitts on all his beautiful books.

He motioned her to a wing chair by the fireplace. "May I ring the maid to bring you a liquid refreshment? Sweet tea? A glass of wine, perhaps?"

"Thank you, but—"

"You don't have the time," he finished, then smiled. "Nor did I when I was your age."

He clasped his liver-blotched hands in his lap. "Ms. Garvey, I am aware of the reason behind this visit and assure you if I chose to, I could bring about the ruination of Sheriff Hendrickson in swift and sundry ways."

Oglethorpe's expression remained benevolent, but gooseflesh tickled up Hannah's arms.

"Ah, but did I?" The rhetorical question echoed in the stillness. "The price of my answer is a few moments' indulgence in the lost art of listening." A woolly eyebrow arched. "Will you pay?"

Hannah crossed her legs and settled back in the chair. "I'd be happy to, Mr. Oglethorpe."

He stared off into the middle distance as if gathering thoughts, then said, "My family and another, whose name has not been spoken within these walls for over a century, emigrated from Tennessee in 1842, settling where the city of Sanity now stands and extending their holdings well beyond its surrounds."

Glancing at Hannah, he added, "The parcel known as Valhalla Springs was Oglethorpe land."

Still is, in his mind, she realized.

"I derive as much joy from the fact the nameless one's last descendant is a spinster as I do sorrow from my failure to acquire a bride and beget an heir." His chin clefted. "Not a particularly Christian attitude, I'm told, but I take comfort in the hope the Almighty prefers honesty to hypocrisy."

Hannah said, "Would it be rude to ask what caused the rift between your family and the other one?"

"My dear Ms. Garvey. A rift is when two gentlemen disagree on a matter of minor consequence. What Josiah Oglethorpe and the blackguard whose name is blasphemy instituted was a feud of historic and durable proportions."

Passion gleamed in his rheumy eyes. "When news of Tennessee's secession reached Josiah, he formed a militia devoted to the cause of states' rights.

"Let not the history books deceive you. The War of Northern Aggression had naught to do with slavery. It inflamed righteous indignation in the common man, but Yankee industrialists conspired to destroy the South's audacious expansion from agriculture to manufacturing.''

Hannah said dubiously, ''Kind of a barbaric way to put the brakes on your competition, isn't it?''

Oglethorpe nodded. ''Indeed it is, but effective. The Confederacy is the only nation to have declared and lost a war with the United States and not receive reparations. To date, the South remains on the hind teat—pardon my crudity—of any economic scale you'd care to examine. Had my ancestors not repaired from Tennessee to Missouri, they would have been ravaged.''

Before Oglethorpe launched a verbal reenactment of Gettysburg, Hannah said, ''I assume the nameless family were, er, Yankees?''

''Bluebellies to the marrow. Oh, they prospered, as did we, but with no grasp whatsoever of the civic responsibility wealth and influence enjoins on its possessors.''

''Is that why you've run for sheriff so many times?'' Hannah asked. ''Civic duty?''

''That, as well as reasons of a personal nature.''

''Personal enough to disqualify an opponent?''

Oglethorpe threw his head back and laughed. ''When I could have bought any or all the elections I've deigned to enter? Really, Ms. Garvey. I do have the distinction of having lost three unopposed races to write-in candidates.''

And proud of it. What a strange, charming, disturbing old man. Hannah rose to her feet. ''Thank you, Mr. Oglethorpe, for the most fascinating 'no' answer I've ever received.''

"Pity you can't stay longer." He rocked forward in his chair, then leveraged himself upright. By the contempt on his face, he detested evidence of infirmity as much as he did Yankee sympathizers. "I was about to tell you how Jessup Knox will also be stricken from the ballot if Hendrickson is forced to resign from office."

Why, you sly old fox. "Making you the winner."

A hand clamped his chest. "Can honor take away the grief of an egregious wound?"

"Is your honor as flawed as your Shakespeare, Mr. Oglethorpe?"

"If it were, I would do nothing to prevent a dunderhead from capitalizing on Sheriff Hendrickson's malfeasance."

God, how Hannah despised that word and the inflection Oglethorpe put on it.

"In the event of a resignation," he said, "the county commissioners will name a temporary replacement until a special election can be held on or before the tenth Tuesday after the vacancy occurs."

A melodramatic pause, then, "I trust you will understand the need for confidentiality when I tell you Jessup Knox will be named as Hendrickson's replacement."

"What! Why? You call Knox a dunderhead, then manipulate the commission into appointing him *sheriff*?"

"Please, Ms. Garvey. If you will refrain from further interruptions, I will gladly elucidate."

Her fingernails gouged her palms. "Go on."

"There is no doubt in my mind, and I assume in

yours, that Jessup Knox will accept the temporary appointment with the alacrity of a buzzard to carrion.''

She nodded. Once.

"And in his glee, he will not bother to read the document drawn by the commission prohibiting his candidacy in the special election."

Hannah's eyes went from wide to a squint. Simple. Devious. Brilliant. "Is it legal?"

Oglethorpe splayed his arms. "A lawsuit would not endear Mr. Knox to voters and couldn't be resolved before the election."

His expression softened with what appeared to be genuine regret. "Nor, if Sheriff Hendrickson resigns and then is vindicated, will there be time enough to redeclare his candidacy."

"David hasn't been charged with anything yet, Mr. Oglethorpe. Much less convicted."

He lowered his gaze and sighed. "I'm afraid, dear lady, that, too, is only a matter of time."

The law offices of Sachs, Woroniecki and Pratt were in a rose-brick, mansard-roofed house along a section of First Street where rezoning had allowed the conversion of historic, residential white elephants to commercial use.

The paved parking area was scored to resemble brick and fenced on three sides by the black posts and swagged chains common to national monuments and mortuaries.

Hannah brushed her hair and slicked on a coat of lip gloss. Not much help, thanks to Oglethorpe's little bombshell. Angst wasn't a good look for anyone.

Stowing her basic black pumps in a shopping bag,

she slipped on a pair of four-inch spike heels. Eulilly Thomlinson might not be intimidated by an Amazon on stilts, but height advantage applied as much to conference rooms as basketball courts.

Art deco meets Office Depot summed up the law office's decor. Blush-beige walls, plume-sculpted carpet and a rattan, square-pretzel sofa with parrot-print cushions and tied-back window curtains fraternized with a computer desk, credenza and swivel chair.

The receptionist pointed a pencil at a set of curtained French doors. "Right through there, Ms. Garvey. The others have been waiting for you."

The kitschy starburst clock on the wall read four-twenty. "I thought I was ten minutes early."

"Oh, but I left a message on your machine that the meeting had been rescheduled for four o'clock." Her coppery lips drew into a pout. "I'm *so* sorry you didn't receive it."

Let the games begin, Hannah thought. I should have anticipated Blackstone's variation on the bait-and-switch.

She recoiled as she entered what must have once been a sunroom. The windows' lower row of shutters were latched, blocking the light at chair level. The upper ones were open to blind the late arrival.

"Ms. Garvey?" A medium-size blob rose at the head of the table. "Terry Woroniecki. Glad you could make it."

They shook on it, then she took the seat at his left, as indicated. A ladylike genuflection ended in an awkward plop, like Goldilocks testing Baby Bear's chair. Hannah would have laughed at the idiocy of it, but had left her sense of humor in the truck with her other shoes.

Woroniecki was older than she'd expected, for no reason other than his nickname. A fringe of grizzled hair and full beard placed him in his late fifties or early sixties. She declined his offer of coffee or a soft drink. The cup would undoubtedly have a dribble hole punched in the bottom.

The opposition sat across from her like broody hens with Grade-A jumbos stuck up their respective butts. Eulilly resembled a Madame Alexander doll. Hetta's mummified tan, dandelion frizz and stark white tunic top gave a cotton-swab-dipped-in-iodine effect. Zerelda Sue Connor's turtleneck shirt emphasized her earlobes' proximity to her shoulders.

"Now that we're all here," Eulilly said, "let's get down to business. I do believe poor li'l ol' Zee has been on pins and needles long enough."

As Hannah imagined a neckless voodoo doll, Woroniecki inquired, "Have you discussed this matter with Mr. Jack Clancy, the development's owner?"

"Yes, I have."

"Directly?" Hetta asked. "Or did his mother do the talking for him, as usual?"

Irrelevant, immaterial and bitchy. "Directly, Mrs. Caldwell."

"And he, er, Mr. Clancy, is amenable to your acting as his agent, Ms. Garvey?"

By Woroniecki's tone and wording, a tape recorder was spinning its little reels off somewhere. Illegal, unless all parties to a conversation were aware of it, but one needn't abide by the law to practice it.

"Jack Clancy and I have been business associates

and friends for many years, Mr. Woroniecki. He trusts my judgment implicitly.''

Zee paled and looked at Eulilly, who feigned indifference. Miss Candied Yam, 1944, hadn't done her homework.

''Isn't that what Mr. Clancy told you, Mr. Woroniecki?'' Hannah asked, suspecting what had inspired the juvenile appointment-time switcheroo.

''Excuse me?''

''When you spoke with Mr. Clancy this morning. He pledged full support for any decisions I make as the development's operations manager, didn't he?''

Knowing Jack, he'd suggested the attorney perform an anatomically impossible sex act, but the essence was the same.

''Yes, er, yes, he did.'' The attorney wrenched his jaw as if his collar had shrunk.

Checkmate. Hands splayed on the table, Hannah pushed up from the chair and leaned forward, spotlighted, rather than hampered, by the glare from the windows. ''This is the deal, Ms. Connor. Same thirty hours, same pay per hour, effective next Monday.''

Hetta and Zee gasped in unison. The former beamed a triumphant smile. The latter tried, but her facial muscles had forgotten how.

Hannah thought, wait till they hear the catch: a Pick-Your-Instructor Program giving participants a choice between Zee and Willard. May the best man win. And he would. Then, if Zee had an ounce of pride, she'd quit. No more verbal abuse directed at residents or military-style drills. No more lawsuit.

Eulilly's head slanted to one side. An index finger tapped her chin. ''Does that mean you have informed

Mr. Willard Johnson that his presence is no longer desired in our community?''

The other two and Woroniecki caught the inflection in her voice. Anyone would, who'd lived through the civil rights era, or seen a documentary about it. They squirmed, eyes downcast and mouths compressed, but said nothing.

To realize Eulilly's real motivation and not intervene was worse than despicable.

Hannah straightened, her hands gliding backward over the polished ebony tabletop. She was angry, sure. Vengeful. Disgusted. And ice-cold certain of what Plan B entailed.

''Rather than relate the conditions attached to the offer to rehire Ms. Connor,'' she said, ''I am retracting it. *In toto.*''

Hannah's eyes shifted from one stunned face to the next, her smile as frosty as her gaze. ''Mrs. Caldwell, if you and your committee decide to file suit, Jack Clancy and I will see you in court—in what, Mr. Woroniecki? A couple of years? Or would a more appropriate estimate be in two or three hundred billable hours?''

Whisking from the room, Hannah pulled the door shut, then paused to listen. If she accomplished nothing else today, she'd left Miss Candied Yam, 1944, speechless.

15

"A psychogenic fugue," Marge repeated, inserting verbal hyphens between the syllables in the first word; the second sounding like the horn on a Model T. "That's what the girls at the Curl Up and Dye think Sheriff Hendrickson had."

"Some operative you are." Delbert said. "Your assignment was to dig up dirt on Lydia Quince."

"And I would have, if there'd been any to dig, besides Dixie Jo not liking her because she goes to Mister Scissors instead of her salon."

Rosemary patted her new 'do' with the hand not attached to Leo's under the table. "I don't trust franchise places to understand my hair." She poked a spot near the crown. "See that funny little whorl—"

"For the love of Mike," Delbert howled.

"Be quiet," IdaClare said. "Marge, that psycho-thingamajigger. What is it?"

"Sort of like amnesia, except the person doesn't know he doesn't know who he is."

IdaClare cupped a hand behind her ear. "Run that past me again?"

Marge did. IdaClare appealed to Hannah. Hannah made a "you got me" gesture.

Marge continued, "The blackout can last a few

minutes, or…well, forever, I guess. Dixie Jo said a man downstate had one a couple of years ago. When he didn't come home one night and nobody answered the phone at his business, his wife went to check on him."

She lowered her voice to a ghost-story whisper. "The back door was standing wide open. His office looked like a tornado had hit it. Papers all over. A blood smear on the light switch. One shoe lying beside his desk."

Rosemary gasped. "The woman must have been terrified."

While Marge dropped the story's other shoe, Hannah swiveled on her bar stool. Something had nagged at her since Great-uncle Mort paddled into her stream of consciousness that afternoon. Whatever it was, it flitted just beyond cognitive reach, like a friend's name you can't dredge from your inner Rolodex because the circuits are overloaded trying to make lucid conversation and do word-association exercises at the same time.

An "ooph-mooph" diverted her gaze to Malcolm, sprawled in the doorway between the breakfast and living rooms, sound asleep. Itsy and Bitsy, also deep in the land of nod, huddled on his back like humps on a camel. Deeper, actually, since they were drugged out of their tiny minds.

When IdaClare had come by earlier to take them home after their "playday" with Malcolm, the Furwads had thrown a yipping fit. Operating under the idea he was a three-pound, psychotic poodle too, Malcolm had leaped onto, off of, around and clunked headfirst into furniture he couldn't dive under.

IdaClare placed an emergency call to her veterinarian, who diagnosed the poodles' problem as acute separation anxiety. Whacked out on his prescribed double dose of Valium, neither Itsy nor Bitsy would have twitched a whisker if their pouffy little tails were excised from their pouffy little butts.

Marge fumed at Delbert, "I never said *I* thought the sheriff had a psychogenic fugue. I'm just reporting what Dixie Jo and the girls said."

IdaClare said, "Well, if you ask me—"

"Nobody did," Delbert shot back. "You gals keep yammering about fugues and the rest of us won't have time for our preliminary reports."

He looked up at Hannah, again elected moderator by a five-to-one vote. She said, "You don't need me to tell you who's next. Go for it."

Weary as Delbert must have been after a full day of advocating, snooping and whatever else he'd done between, he bounced to his feet as if his magenta disco shirt and kelly-green pants were as electrostatically charged as they appeared.

Hands thrust in his trouser pockets, he told a ceiling corner, "As you may recall from last night's meeting, the fact-finding mission I was to undertake—after freeing our colleague, Mrs. IdaClare Clancy, from the jaws of jurisprudence—was to ascertain whether Chief Deputy Jimmy Wayne McBride had the opportunity to conspire with Mrs. Lydia Quince, since we already established this individual had the means and motive."

Hannah took semantic exception to McBride having *the* means and motive, as opposed to *a* means and motive, but kept it to herself. To interrupt Patrick Henry Bisbee's oratory would wreck his timing.

He teetered on his Hush Puppies. "Now, this ascertaining of a person or persons' whereabouts vis-à-vis direct questioning is not the best modus for an investigator to operandi. Why, you ask?"

"I didn't ask." IdaClare winked at Marge. "Did you?"

"Not me. Must have been Rosemary."

"Who, sir? Me, sir? No sir, not I, sir." Rosemary nudged Leo. "Was it you, sir?"

Anger rashed Delbert's cheeks, but there was hurt in his eyes. He was equally comfortable being the arrow or the target of their barbs, but private investigation was his baby. Without intending to, they'd called it ugly.

Hannah said, "As soon as David is in the clear, I'd love for Delbert to do an evening workshop on all these techniques he's learned."

Visually surveying the others, she prompted, "What do you think, gang?" Her eyebrow dipped a meaningful fraction when she got to IdaClare. "Wouldn't that be *great?*"

"I...uh, a workshop? Oh, my heavens, yes, dear. It would. Tell me when and I'll make special folders to keep our notes separate from our case files."

Rosemary said to Marge, "If you'll bring the dessert, I'll fix a seven-layer dip to snack on."

"Ah," Leo moaned. "The dip, it is my favorite."

Delbert sawed a finger under his nose. "Okay, then, I'll, er, be discussing the whys and the whereto-fors of professional ascertaining during the workshop, so we'd best move on to McBride's alibi for the night in question."

A sigh of relief breezed through Hannah's lips. Diplomacy, par excellance. Eat your heart out, Madeleine Albright.

"What it boils down to is, Jimmy Wayne doesn't

have much of an alibi, because he wouldn't tell me the names of the ladies he was with between the hours of 6:00 p.m. and 8:00 p.m."

"Ladies?" Rosemary echoed. "More than one? In two hours?"

Delbert hitched a shoulder, indicating it was common practice among the bon vivant set, himself included. "Except I think he was lying through his teeth."

IdaClare sniffed. "Well, I should hope."

"I had to step up to the plate and swing six ways of Sunday before Jimmy Wayne would tell me that much. I understand a man being cagey about his love life, but why didn't he say he had a date or two from the start?"

Leo said, "A law enforcement officer, he must be discreet, yes? Above the reproach."

"Then why hem-haw around?" Delbert said. "He could have said he was home watching the tube. It isn't like I had a *TV Guide* in my pocket to quiz him with."

Marge frowned. "Not knowing for certain is no better than not knowing at all."

"Hannah could ask Claudina Burkholtz who his girlfriends are," Rosemary suggested.

"Oh, no, Hannah could *not*." Although Hannah would love to know herself, just for the heck of it.

Delbert boasted, "I'll have the goods on McBride soon enough. I'm having breakfast with his aunt's best friend's daughter's next-door neighbor. Sophonia's forgotten more scuttlebutt than most ever knew."

True enough. Sophonia Pugh probably remembered when Missouri achieved statehood.

"Lastly," he went on, "I stopped by Mama Leoni's pizza joint for a beer on my way home. The delivery boy, Kenton Neeb, doesn't work weeknights, but the manager told me Quince grabbed the food from the kid, shoved him off the stoop and slammed the door in his face.

"Kenton banged on it, hollering for his money. Quince yelled back along the lines of, 'If you don't like it, call the cops,' then told Kenton to scram or he'd blow him away."

Hannah reiterated, "The delivery boy told his boss the door was *closed* the whole time?"

"Uh-huh. Kenton changed his original story some when Lieutenant Pike interviewed him on Saturday. The manager thinks what Quince said, and probably how he said it, convinced the kid he had a gun, but Kenton never saw one."

Well, the little shit said he saw one that night. Tony, the dispatcher, relayed the restaurant manager's skepticism, but David's initial reluctance to take Hannah along was because a gun was mentioned. The tape of the radio transmission would bear that out.

In hindsight, did it matter? No. Not if Quince threatened Kenton through a closed door. Testifying to the grand jury how effing "convinced" he was would be as helpful to David as...

Cold sweat prickled the nape of Hannah's neck and chilled her spine. I'm a witness, too. I'll be subpoenaed to testify. She closed her eyes and shuddered.

Was that the real reason David wanted them to keep their distance until this nightmare ended? Had he lied, or just wrapped the ugly truth in moonbeams and stardust to hide it from her or himself.

Andrik had cited a conflict of interest when he'd issued his gag order. The term was accurate for his purposes, but what continued to divide her and David

physically and emotionally was a conflict of circumstances.

As long as David stood accused of a crime she had
witnessed, they couldn't have someday—couldn't even
talk and flirt and laugh and hold hands, couldn't tell
themselves they were just friends and not falling in love
because it would spoil everything.

"Hey, ladybug. You okay?"

Realizing she was the center of concern, she at-
tempted a smile. "I guess I shouldn't be surprised that
Kenton's corroboration on the gun went kablooey.
Nothing's gone in David's favor yet."

Marge said, "Then he's overdue for a break, isn't
he?"

"Darned right he is." Rosemary turned to IdaClare.
"I don't suppose Lydia walked into Duckworths', took
one look at her departed beloved and confessed, did
she?"

"Law, wait'll you hear what she did do." IdaClare
rolled her eyes. "I had tea with LaVada—a sweet
woman, but funny-turned. She is beside herself over
Lydia bringing her dead daddy's hand-me-downs for
Stuart to wear for the viewing.

"LaVada said they had to split the suit jacket's seam
down the back before it would button, but couldn't do
a thing about the sleeves hiking above his wrists."

"Disgraceful." Rosemary clucked her tongue.

"Disrespectful, too. I wouldn't send my worst enemy
to his heavenly reward dressed in rags."

"I might," Marge said with a devilish grin. "If the
casket was closed."

Hannah's eyebrows scrunched. When Caroline died,

she'd have stolen the money for a proper outfit before she'd have buried her mother in hand-me-downs.

Either Lydia's finances were beyond dire or someone, probably Lydia's mother, had chosen Stuart's wardrobe; an unspoken, subtle denouncement of the man who'd never given her daughter anything but heartache. If Lydia had protested at all, she'd given in, like she always had.

"What about the casket, IdaClare?" Marge asked. "Was it decent?"

"The same bronze loaner the funeral home let us use for Kathleen's memorial. Quince is being cremated, too." IdaClare's lips crimped. "Lydia didn't buy an urn for his ashes, though, and LaVada's terrified she'll hand her a sandwich bag to put him in, after."

Hannah tried not to laugh and failed. Imagining the wraithlike matriarch, who spoke of the deceased in present tense, as though they'd spoken to her in present tense, toting Quince's remains around in a plastic bag would make a howler of a *Saturday Night Live* skit.

"How'd Lydia act at the viewing?" Delbert asked. "Bet she played grieving widow to the hilt."

"I didn't tarry long. With only five or six people in the room, I felt conspicuous, but really, the poor girl looked ill. From a distance, you'd mistake her for a teenager, but she carried herself as though she had the weight of the world on each shoulder."

Delbert harrumphed. "Getting her mitts on that hundred grand'll straighten her up in a hurry."

"Did you have a chance to talk to Junior Duckworth?" Hannah asked IdaClare.

"No, he was out somewhere, but Ozzie told me the preliminary autopsy results showed Quince's blood-alcohol content was way high. Point-zero-three-one something. Or maybe it was zero-point-one-three something.''

Her hand waved dismissal. ''Whatever the numbers were, Ozzie said a normal person would have been grabbing the curb to keep from falling off the sidewalk, but Quince was a boozer and held it pretty well.''

''He say anything else about the autopsy?'' Delbert asked.

''Yes…'' IdaClare's finger ran down her notes. ''Oh, here it is. The state medical examiner ruled that Quince died of a gunshot wound to the heart.''

If Academy Awards were given for askance looks, Delbert would be a shoo-in. ''Well, I'll be damned. I figured the bullet went in through his big toe and worked its way up.''

IdaClare retaliated with a ''Don't truck with me, Shorty'' glare. ''Ozzie also said an old box of nine-millimeter cartridges was found under the seat of Quince's truck, but…'' She turned to Hannah. ''Oh, I do wish I wasn't the one who has to tell you, dear, but Quince didn't leave a suicide note.''

A meaningful disclosure. Dreadful, even. Except Hannah had not the slightest clue why.

''It's one of the main reasons Lieutenant Pike believes Sheriff Hendrickson is, well, mistaken about what happened,'' IdaClare said. ''It seems Stuart threatened suicide three or four years ago. He wrote a long letter telling Lydia she was better off without him and how he was going to wreck his truck and make it look like an accident.

''Lydia showed it to their boss—she and Stuart both worked for Re-Nu Industries then—and he alerted the highway patrol. When they pulled Stuart over, he acted as though he didn't know what they were talking about. Both the Quinces were fired because of it.''

A deviation from Eldredge Randal's account, but either he didn't know otherwise or had glossed over the details.

IdaClare continued, ''Pike thinks it's odd Quince didn't leave a note this time because he did before and wrecking his truck and suicide-by-cop are similar behavior patterns.''

''Similar?'' Rosemary said. ''What does a truck wreck have to do with getting shot?''

''It confused me, too, at first,'' IdaClare said, ''but as I understand it, the 'accident' Quince planned to have corresponds with suicide-by-cop because both are premeditated and they depend on something besides him physically causing his own death.''

''The truck,'' Leo said in a thinking-aloud tone, ''it would be the weapon and so would be the policeman who shot him. Thus, the pattern. Yes?''

''*Yes.*'' IdaClare stabbed the air with her finger.

''But a note should be part of the pattern, too. Pike went so far as to confiscate the mail at the post offices in Sanity and Richland, but didn't find one.''

''Mail doesn't zip straight from one town to the next,'' Delbert said. ''The note could still be at the sorting facility in Springfield or maybe Kansas City.''

IdaClare said, ''I suppose it could, only you'd think Pike would have checked there too.''

''Yeah, well, note schmote,'' Delbert blustered. ''Maybe Lydia packed all the pencils when she vamoosed. Quince looks around while he's waiting on his pizza and can't find anything to write with. What's he going to do? Tell the delivery kid to come back later?"

Marge chuckled. "Shocks me though it does to admit it, I have to agree with Delbert."

"Me, too," Rosemary said. "Note or no note, Lydia is still that insurance policy's beneficiary."

Hannah said, "But if Lydia didn't know in advance what Stuart planned to do, how would she know to rush over there and tamper with the evidence so she'd collect on it?"

"Hmm," the gumshoes droned collectively.

A wily grin crinkled Delbert's face. "There you go thinking too much again, ladybug. Quince called in his last sayonara, the same as did his pizza order."

Well, duh. Where better to have a senior moment than with a bunch of—"Hey, hold the phone, so to speak. Isn't it a toll call between Sanity and Richland?"

"Yes, it is," IdaClare allowed, "but I don't believe Stuart would worry overmuch about the bill, dear."

"What I mean is," Hannah said, "Pike wouldn't check the mail and not check long-distance telephone records."

Marge prodded Delbert with an elbow. "See what you've done? You've got her talking in circles now."

"No, I'm not. If there were a record of Stuart calling Lydia that evening, would Pike be as concerned about the lack of a suicide note?"

Rosemary said, "Because he'd assume that's why Quince called her. To tell her goodbye."

"Right," Hannah said. "More importantly, if he had, there's no doubt in my mind she'd have alerted the sheriff's department immediately." Thoughts clacked into place like ball bearings in a Pachinko game. "Stuart cried wolf at least once before, but to gamble he was doing it again? And have to live with it if he followed through this time? Lydia wouldn't risk it. No way."

Marge asked, "Could Stuart have worn her down until she didn't care what happened to him? Until she hated him? Don't forget, the man's laid out at Duckworths' in a hacked-up old sport coat."

"She may have hated him," Hannah said, "but there's an enormous difference between wanting a guy out of your life and doing nothing to stop him from taking his."

Delbert pantomimed an air violin and deedledummed a tune famous for denoting tragedy before movies had sound tracks.

"If you're trying to piss me off, you're succeeding," IdaClare warned. "Don't you dare make sport of Hannah. I won't abide it, especially when she's making sense."

He whipped his imaginary bow to finis position. "So does Lydia not being home when hubby called. No connectee, no chargee. Later, Jimmy Wayne hears about Quince on the police radio or a scanner—the same as I did—and does get ahold of her. Lydia tells him about the moolah at stake, then one, the other or both of 'em tear over there to monkey with the evidence."

Leo's shiny head ticktocked. "Or if McBride, he did not reach Lydia, but knew of the felony clause, he did the monkey himself."

"Pick your poison," Delbert said. "Motive. Means. Opportunity. Plain as daylight for those two."

"Now, all we have to do is prove it," Rosemary said.

Sliding her hands behind her neck, Hannah wadded her hair into a frowzy ball. "I must say, I'm in awe of these logical explanations for everything."

IdaClare beamed. "Why, thank you, dear."

"Except I don't believe Lydia Quince or Jimmy Wayne McBride were within a mile of Skyline Drive last Friday night."

"You did yesterday," Delbert reminded her. "Did that Randal fellow say something to change your mind?"

She shook her head. "In fact, it seems there's a new man in Lydia's life, which I interpreted as yet another motive for insurance fraud, plus a pinch hitter for the conspiracy-theory softball team."

"If the boyfriend is a Russian spy," Marge said, "that clinches it."

"For pity's sake." IdaClare tossed her pen on the table. "Will y'all hush and let her *talk?*"

Hannah let her arms drop to her lap. "Basically, I have a problem applying logic to an illogical situation, and evidence disappearing from a crime scene five minutes after the crime occurred is *not* logical.

"Neither is Lydia, and/or Jimmy Wayne, and/or the boyfriend being obvious candidates for tampering, but David taking the fall for a homicide. Add to that, the complete illogic—not to mention stupidity—of Marlin Andrik and Theron Pike overlooking two or three tailor-made suspects and *letting* David take the fall for a homicide."

Brows corduroyed in thought. The refrigerator's compressor cycled. Malcolm snuffed and shifted position. Itsy, or perhaps Bitsy, slid to the floor. Had the telephone rung, six amateur sleuths would have splattered the ceiling like bugs on a windshield.

"Lieutenant Pike, I have not met," Leo said, "but Detective Andrik? A stupid man he is not."

Rosemary added, "Which means they must have suspected Lydia, too, for the same reasons we do."

"Then crossed her off the list," Delbert admitted.

"Most likely because she has an airtight alibi."

IdaClare took up the devil's-advocate gauntlet. "That still leaves McBride. Like Leo said, he could have known about the felony clause and swiped the evidence to protect Lydia."

"Was he at Duckworths' this afternoon?" Marge asked.

"Not when I left." IdaClare bolted upright. "Maybe *that's* why Lydia looked so punk. What if—purely on impulse, mind you—McBride took the gun and that bullet-thing so she wouldn't lose the money. Later, he got greedy or realized he'd put his neck in a noose and demanded she make it worth his while."

Delbert chafed his hands. "Now we're cookin', yessiree-bob. Conspiracy after-the-fact and blackmail."

Rosemary looked over her shoulder at Hannah. "Is that illogical enough for you?"

"It'll do till something else comes along."

"What's the matter?" Delbert bellowed.

Rosemary rested her chin on her knuckles. "You want us to believe Jimmy Wayne McBride had enough energy to have sex with two women in two hours, drive to Quince's house, tamper with the evidence under the sheriff's and Hannah's noses, then track down Lydia and blackmail her?"

Delbert hmmphed and sat back in his chair. "I never said he had sex with 'em."

"But if Lydia and Jimmy Wayne and the boyfriend didn't do it, who did?" Marge asked. "It didn't matter to anyone else whether Quince pulled a gun on the sheriff or not."

Hannah froze. The discussion surrounding her receded. Her vision narrowed, as if hurtling backward into a tunnel. "It's the other way around. The evidence tampering had nothing to do with Stuart Quince. It's *David*. David was the target all along."

Her gaze swept around the table. Conviction leavened her voice. "How many people are going to vote for a sheriff who's under indictment for second-degree manslaughter?"

16

Hannah stood on the deck hugging herself, elbows cradled in her palms. The air had an almost metallic aroma, as if the stars were near enough to smell.

She thought back to nights she'd gazed out of her apartment's picture window at Chicago's skyline, the heavens awash in a man-made bronze glow, the traffic twenty-two floors below reduced to Hot Wheels in slow motion, and how she'd felt like the queen of the world surveying her domain.

Never, in all those years, had she realized how rare it was to see the moon, much less the stars, from her concrete, steel and glass tower. What was that Jim Croce song? Something about a king who worked day and night to build a castle for his queen, but the queen said he'd built her a jail.

The cold settled over her, invigorating and invasive. Forty-eight degrees, someone had said. Not unseasonal for an Ozarks spring. It had been known to snow in April. Only the impatient or come-heres planted gardens by the heat of the sun, not the signs and phases of the moon.

Snaps and rustles from the dark maze of trees blazed Malcolm's trail into his private patch of wilderness. He seemed to understand this was home and that it came

with boundaries, but he was a teenager in dog years.
Bad idea to let a boy his age roam at night unsupervised.

Voices snuck through the patio doors; the patter of
revised schemes pitted IdaClare and Company against
a conspiracy and the clock. Hannah hoped Malcolm
hurried and wished it were warmer so he needn't rush.

Jessup Knox was the culprit of the hour. Delbert was
devising strategies to trap "that sidewindin' son of a
bitch." Proving Knox the villain presented a two-birds-
with-one-stone proposition for Sam Spade Bisbee.

In his oily, inimitable way, Knox had turned a sales
pitch for a development-wide security system into what
Delbert took as an insult to his manhood. The memory
of Delbert with an upraised golf club, chasing Elvis up
and down Valhalla Springs Boulevard, had Hannah
chuckling to herself all over again.

"Shame the old fart missed him," she said through
chattering teeth. "If Knox set David up..."

If. Tiny word, infinite permutations. It inspired every
invention, every scientific discovery, every expedition
by land, sea or air—every *everything*—and a billion
more failures.

Malcolm clomped onto the deck. His lolling tongue
expressed the relief, pride and pleasure of a dump well
taken. He snuggled against her, a barrel-chested space
heater that ran on affection not electricity.

Scratching the sweet spot under his ear, Hannah's
eyes were drawn heavenward again. Heredity, she supposed. Great-aunt Lurleen had called Mort a "stargazing fool."

Mort's freezing to death in a tree during the winter
of '69 lent credence to her rant, but when Hannah was

little, her uncle had pointed out constellations and told wondrous stories of minotaurs and dragons and wizards.

"I forgot to look up for too long, Uncle Mort. I don't remember most of what you taught me." Vapor slipstreamed through her lips. "I always listened, though. If I hadn't, your riddles, like that 'back up to go forward' thing, wouldn't have bugged me."

A growl burbled up Malcolm's throat. Hannah knelt, arms encircling his ruffed neck. "It scares me, too, big guy. I don't want to believe someone hates David that much. At least we're on the right track now. If I hadn't been so dense, we wouldn't have wasted another day on the wrong suspects."

Moomph.

Palm gliding down his back, she patted Malcolm's speckled haunch. "C'mon. My toes are numb and the Mod Squad needs more supervision than you do."

Reaching for the patio door's knob, she said, "Just keep your paws crossed Knox doesn't have an alibi. We don't have time to play whodunit—"

She stopped short. Whodunit? That wasn't it. *How*dunit was the key. Figure out the how and the who would fall into place.

Malcolm bumpity-shoved past her and hung a left to the utility room, aka his local watering hole. IdaClare and Company had adjourned to the kitchen. Marge was brewing a fresh pot of decaf. At the sink, Leo and Rosemary were making a romantic interlude out of rinsing forks and dessert plates. IdaClare bounced on the balls of her feet, crooning jabberwocky to the groggy poodles in her arms.

"Here she is," she announced as though Hannah had

just returned from one of the Crusades. "You were gone so long, we decided to take a break."

"Where's Delbert?"

"In the powder room, dear." Creases tined above IdaClare's pug nose. "Is something wrong?"

"Not anymore."

Hannah entered the living room just as the half bath's commode flushed. She scurried to the sitting area rather than appear as if she'd been waiting in ambush outside the door.

Water splashed in the basin. A happy tune—the theme to the *Andy Griffith Show,* if she wasn't mistaken—whistled from within.

Ye gods, and men say women spend half their lives in the bathroom?

His watch face shone neon green in the darkness. "Fifteen more minutes, then I'm out of here."

He'd levied the same deadline twice already. This time he meant it. Shouldn't be here in the first place. He had better things to do than sit in his truck freezing his ass off, staring at Hannah's cottage and waiting for the coast to clear.

He could've talked to her when she'd called earlier. She'd hung up without leaving a message, but he'd known it was her. Even Rambo had looked at him cockeyed when he'd stood there with his hand on the receiver, letting the phone ring and cussing himself when it quit.

Could have called her back, too, instead of shooting the shit with Claudina, Polly and his brothers, then bellyaching to Mike Rivera for an hour, long distance.

His eyes scanned the cottage's front windows, the

cars in the driveway, his watch. Thát's it. I never featured myself any kin to Job and I ain't gonna start now.

Thirty more minutes, then I'm out of here.

Delbert sauntered from the bathroom, his face
scrubbed, his thick, white hair damp and comb-tracked,
a snip of shirttail caught in his zipper placket.

He motioned at the door. "It's all yours, ladybug,
but hurry up. We've got a skunk named Knox to lay
traps for."

"No, we don't. What we need to do is stick to your
original premise."

His eyebrows met at center.

"Instead of trying to figure out who framed David,"
Hannah said, "we should be proving he told the truth
about what happened."

"That's what we're doing."

"No, it isn't."

"Is so."

Yeah, well, my daddy can whip your daddy and your
momma's daddy, too. Sheesh. She held up her hands.
"Just bear with me, okay?"

"Hmmph."

On that note of enthusiasm, Hannah asked, "If two
guns were fired at virtually the same instant, could it
sound like one shot?"

"Yea-h-h, prob'ly. Though I suspect it'd be louder
than a single." He sucked his teeth. "Might not be,
either. Sound waves are tricky bastards."

Hannah pointed at the living room's far corner. "If
you shot at me from about that distance, I'd be pretty
hard to miss, wouldn't I?"

"Fifteen feet? IdaClare could plug you with her eyes shut and her mouth open."

So far, so good. "When David described the shooting to Andrik, he mentioned a shell casing near Quince's left leg. David seemed puzzled by that, then said the shell must have ricocheted—"

"Great Caesar's ghost!" Delbert sucker punched the air. "I see what you're getting at. Quince didn't just aim at Hendrickson, he *fired* or there wouldn't be any shell casing."

Like love, a hunch—when it paid off—was also a many splendored thing. Or would be, if her three-parter held up.

"Now, I think I already know the answer," she said, "but why would David have been puzzled by the casing landing where it did?"

Delbert considered the question. "Expert I'm not, but most handguns expel brass to the right, the same as rifles, because most people are right-handed." He grinned. "Back in the forties, when I was in basic training at Lackland, this southpaw city boy nearly gelded himself when a hot one fell in his lap and set his pants to smoldering."

Hannah said, "But if David imagined Quince's gun, as Andrik and Pike apparently believe he did, would he also have imagined seeing an ejected shell on the floor and on Quince's *left* side?"

"Why would he?" Delbert's face flushed with excitement.

"Quince didn't have to fire to justify the sheriff using deadly force. Why complicate things when there's no reason to?"

Hannah gripped his arm, as much to steady herself

as emphasize her final supposition. "Quince and David were no more than fifteen feet apart, Delbert. They fired at the same time. Quince missed intentionally. He wanted to commit suicide by proxy, not murder."

Comprehension shone in his eyes. "And we know where David's bullet went."

"Unfortunately, we do. But how about Quince's?"

Delbert paused for thought. "He could have fired straight up, ladybug."

Well, hell. So much for blind faith. A nod to Longfellow's "It fell to earth, I know not where" was not an appropriate substitute. Think...*think.*

"Muzzle flash," she said. "David said he saw one. Would he have, if Quince fired up?"

"Hmm. I dunno." Over his shoulder, Delbert yelled, "Hey, Leo. C'mere a—"

"The powder flash, yes. The muzzle flash? No."

Hannah and Delbert yelped and staggered backward. Leo, Rosemary, Marge, IdaClare, Itsy, Bitsy and Malcolm stood not two yards away, huddled as though Scotty had just beamed them down from the *Enterprise.*

"Goddamnit, Schnur. What are you trying to do? Gimme a heart attack?"

"You shout 'Hey, Leo,' I answer. What should you have me do?"

Delbert enunciated through clenched teeth, "What you should have been is in the kitchen."

"In the kitchen, I was. Then in here, I came."

While Delbert made noises peculiar to those in need of respiratory therapy, Hannah asked, "What's the difference between powder flash and muzzle flash, Leo?"

His thumb and forefinger stiffened into pretend pistol position. The latter was designated the muzzle; the tip of his finger, the bore. "A gun, it is a little cannon. Pull the trigger and the firing pin, it strikes the primer, the primer, it ignites—"

Leo whipped the pretend muzzle around and scowled down the pretend bore as if it had misfired a pretend bullet. "Is not good. No pizzazz."

He pressed a button on the metal reel clipped to his belt, releasing the wire cable attached to the key ring in his back pocket. Why it was on a leash and stowed aft, not fore, was clarified by the rabbit's foot, nail clippers, Swiss Army Knife, Mace canister, identification tag and mini-penlight dangling from the ring, along with three actual keys.

"Watch closely." Leo aimed the penlight at Hannah. The switch flipped on and off like semaphore. "The muzzle flash, eh? Bright and the pinpoint at the bore."

"Gotcha."

Raising it ceilingward, he repeated the demonstration. "The powder flash. Not so bright, not so pinpoint."

"Well, I'll be... David wouldn't have said muzzle flash for powder flash, either. They're too different." She snapped her fingers. "I want to try something."

Positioning herself in the corner in a shooter's stance, she leveled a double-fingered pretend pistol at Leo's chest. "Hold the light higher and more like a gun and do it again. Two flashes each time."

She focused on Leo's shirt pocket. The penlight winked twice and distinctly. When he raised it, the beam was visible but diffused.

"Leo, my man," she said, "you are a genius."

"Flash us, too, Leo," IdaClare said. "We couldn't see what you showed her."

Hannah looked at Delbert. "Quince didn't fire into the air. It had to have been almost straight on for David to remember the muzzle flash."

At his nod, she added, "If you guys would rather hassle Jessup Knox tomorrow, fine. I'm going to find that bullet."

Skeptical didn't begin to describe Delbert's expression.

"Didn't you tell me there was nothing but open field across from Quince's house?"

"I'll search every inch on my hands and knees if I have to."

Delbert examined the fringe edging the area rug for a long moment. "The sooner we call it a night, the sooner me and Leo can get on the horn to our Treasure Hunter's Club buddies. Ought to be a couple willing to help. Those with better things to do can loan us their metal detectors."

He dodged her outstretched arms. "Before you go to smooching all over me, here's the rest of the bargain. I'll cancel out on Sophonia so's we can meet at Quince's place at oh-eight-hundred, but come noon, we pack it in, if we last that long.

"Metal detectors are heavy and awkward as hell and we're none of us as young as we used to be. Quit early and me, Leo and the girls can redeploy for some afternoon skunk hunting."

Hannah grinned from ear to ear. "Anything else? Or is it okay to smooch all over you now?"

Every excuse he'd dreamed up for being on her porch this late at night stuck in his craw. She stared at him, then squeezed her eyes shut and took a deep breath.

The screen swung open. She reached out, her hand closing around his wrist. Inner door shut, the dead bolt latched, she took his Stetson and sent it sailing like a Frisbee into the rocking chair in the corner, then turned and slipped her arms inside his barn coat, her hands sliding up his back, her cheek pressed against his chest.

He pulled her close, burying his face in her hair, his body absorbing her strength, her warmth, all the while wondering how she could know what he needed most.

"You feel so good," she whispered.

"So do you, sugar."

"I thought I was dreaming when I saw you standing there."

"I wasn't sure what you'd do when you opened the door."

"Umm." She hugged him tighter. "Well, I guess that's because you're a dork."

He chuckled. She chuckled. They burst out laughing, clinging to each other, shoulders shaking, cackling and gasping for air and neither wanting to let a little thing like suffocation separate them.

"I'm not here because I changed my mind about what I told you last night," he said. "I just need to talk to you a while."

"You are determined to state the obvious, aren't you, Hendrickson?"

"No." He shifted his weight. "More like denying what's getting kind of obvious."

"Gee," she murmured, low and silky. "I hadn't noticed."

"Liar."

Control, he thought. Have some. Well, then, fake it, for Christ's sake. Don't think about hands and mouths and tongues and filling and being filled and touching heaven because you promised her and there's a reason the easiest ones to break are the hardest to keep.

All-time leading rushers. Walter Payton, four-point-four average. Dorsett—uh, uh, a T—first name starts with T...

Burf.

David's head snapped up.

Bur-bur-burf.

"Sheriff Hendrickson, I can't tell you how much safer I feel having a watchdog on duty."

David sneered at Malcolm, parked on his haunches, looking pleased with himself. "Dumb mutt. You're supposed to bark *before* somebody comes into the house."

"Don't you dare call him dumb." Hannah eased from his arms. He curbed the impulse to gather her in again. "Malcolm knows you're not a burglar."

Nah, just your common ordinary homicide suspect with a two-by-four in his pants. "Then why'd he bark at all?"

"Because we're paying attention to each other and not him."

Sympathy laced Hannah's tone. They'd been insensitive to Malcolm's needs. Maybe scarred him for life. Next thing they knew, he'd get his navel pierced and whine to Limp Bizkit CDs.

"Coffee?" she asked.

"No thanks." David draped his coat over the office nook's railing. "I'm counting sheep by the herd as it is."

"It's decaf. IdaClare and Company's private stock. I used to hate the stuff, but I'm beginning to get used to it."

Coffee with no kick was on a par with soybean burgers and no-yolk eggs. "I'm not likely to, but okay. Black, no sugar." He winked. "Sugar."

She rolled her eyes, in an as-if-I-didn't-know-how-you-take-your-coffee manner. With Malcolm the Wonder Dog padding behind her, she sashayed to the kitchen, another genuine article for which there was no substitute.

Sweat suits became her. The classy outfit she'd worn to the courthouse became her. Jeans, dressy stuff and oh, man, that skimpy, purple satin number she'd had on the morning he brought her breakfast in bed—everything he'd ever seen her in became her.

Groaning, David shook off the image of her wearing nothing but him and a smile. Fools rush in and all that crap. They probably died with big stupid smiles on their faces, too.

Quince had.

David's gut tightened. *You got what you wanted from me, you son of a bitch. One hour. Quit messin' with my mind for one lousy, damn hour.*

Tipping the carafe away from the mugs she was filling, Hannah glanced over her shoulder as David pulled a bar stool from the counter. "I like kitchens," he said as if she'd asked why he hadn't availed himself of the couch in the living room.

"My grandmother Garvey said there were two kinds of people in this world." Hannah sat down next to him, near enough for comfort, far enough away to give a good listen. "Kitchen-sitters come to visit you. Parlor-sitters come to visit your house."

"A lot of truth in that." He took a sip of decaf. It wasn't as awful as some he'd choked down to be polite. "I don't recollect setting foot in our living room at home except when Mom hustled everybody in there for a Kodak moment."

Hannah's finger circled the rim of her cup. He knew by the tilt of her chin that the only scrapbook she had was in her mind not her closet. There weren't any baby pictures of her cuddled to the bosoms of relatives and family friends. No naked-toddler-in-the-bathtub shots, none of her standing as stiff as the historic monument beside her, or series of birthday parties, Halloweens and Christmases.

David tried to tell himself it didn't matter. He didn't give the albums on his shelf a thought until packing them for a move. Then he'd sit on the floor, turning pages and chuckling at the toothless boy with the burr haircut and feel guilty for not recognizing several people in the backgrounds and foregrounds of his childhood.

Clear as air was the memory of Hannah telling him "My mother was an alcoholic. Pink-collar trailer trash, unwed mother, hopeless romantic with an unerring eye for Mr. Couldn't Be More Wrong and I loved her as fiercely as she loved me."

Any rookie who'd responded to a half-dozen domestics would hear the fallacy layered in willing delusion. David wished Hannah had grown up as sheltered and clueless as he had, but he didn't feel sorry for her. It was Caroline Garvey he pitied.

Malcolm staggered in from the bedroom, an oversize

towel clamped in his teeth. With each step, a forepaw caught the cloth and jerked his head downward.

Brilliant animal. If he were any smarter, he'd have to be sprayed for bagworms.

Failing to wedge himself between the bar stools, Malcolm nosed his towel upside Hannah's, then collapsed as though his legs had given out on him.

"My hero," she said. "A rock star should have such a devoted bodyguard."

"Uh-huh." David calculated how many sheets of plywood he'd need to build a Malcolm-size doghouse.

She leaned away and rested her head in her hand, her expression pensive. "Did I tell you I resigned from Friedlich & Friedlich before Jack offered me the job here?"

David shook his head.

"Well, I did, and over the last few days I've wondered where I'd have ended up if he hadn't." She smiled. "Years ago I went to a retirement party for a brokerage house's head honcho. He and his wife were talking cruises and pilgrimages and gushing about the Vermont farmstead they'd bought.

"Before the year was out, he was the CEO of another brokerage house. When I asked what happened, he said, 'Just because you stop running the rat race, you don't stop being a rat.'"

"Meaning, you can kick a cop out of the courthouse, but you can't kick the cop out of a cop?"

"Exactly."

"It isn't that simple."

Hannah didn't flinch at the harshness of his voice. Unfair as comparisons were, Cynthia had taken every change in tone as a personal affront. He'd learned to

watch what he said, how he said it and apologize for
both when he crossed her internal Maginot Line whose
boundary shifted depending on her mood. In time, communication was reduced to nothing much and nothing
meaningful.

Hannah slid her other hand across the counter. It offered an anchor to grab on to while he loosed his de-
mons, instead of a "there, there, honey, let's talk about
it later when you're not so upset" pat.

His rough, broad hand smothered her small, soft one,
careful not to squeeze too tight. God, how he loved her.
He was no more ready to tell her than she was to hear
it, but...

Someday. A promissory note invested of equal parts
joy and despair, with no guarantee of which half would
come due and payable.

Twirling his coffee mug for a southpaw grip on the
handle, David raised it to his lips, thinking some guys
really did have all the luck. Him, for example.

Still a bit wary about pressing his, he asked, "Are
you sure you want an orchestra seat for a piss-and-
moan concert?"

"As opposed to what? Watching you argue with
yourself and nurse a cup of bad, lukewarm coffee?"
Hannah sucked air through her teeth. "Boy now, that's
a tough one."

Strange how a smart-ass remark pushed the gate
wider than a yes. Setting the mug and his reticence
aside, he said, "The reason my situation isn't as simple
as your rat-racer friend's is because I'm still the Kinderhook County sheriff, except it's in name only.

"Jimmy Wayne McBride is doing the job I was hired
to do, want to do and can't, while I draw a paycheck

for being the last person to see Stuart Quince alive and the first to see him dead.''

David tamped down the resentment simmering inside. He'd have taken light desk duty, shuffled paperwork, manned the phones—anything to keep him climbing those three flights of stairs every morning. Understanding the politics and public relations behind his exile didn't alleviate his bitterness.

Earlier, Claudina had said, ''When things get back to normal,'' as if sameness were a place with metes and bounds on the far side of forty miles of bad road. For him, whatever might constitute normal from one moment to the next, the past would forever haunt his present.

You can kill a man, but you can't kill his shadow. Quince would throw one for the rest of David's life.

Hannah's fingers wriggled under his. He repeated his thoughts aloud, surprised and concerned he'd reverted to brooding without realizing it.

''As for the investigation itself, sure, I hate being benched when it's my life on the line, but knowing how Pike and Andrik work and from the questions I've answered umpteen times, I could reproduce eighty-five percent of the reports in their case files.''

He took a deep breath and blew it out. ''And have, as a matter of fact. Yeah, once a cop, always a cop, and routine is a fine diversion. I also thought it'd give some distance and objectivity, maybe jog my memory and...well...''

Hannah finished, ''Good as Pike and Andrik are, there's always a margin for error.''

''Eh, I prefer to call it a margin for oversight. No insult intended, but your intuition about Miz Osborn would have been compromised somewhat if she'd been a close friend or co-worker."

"Absolutely. IdaClare and Company's theories weren't so much wrong as they were based on preconceived notions." Hannah grinned. "They are, however, being much more open-minded about the Hendrickson case, aka Code name Beta."

David made a face. "No details, please. I'm in enough trouble without tacking 'accessory before the fact' to whatever Delbert's dreamed up."

A whisper of pink at her cheekbones could be dismissed as imagination. The bland expression? He'd give it a B+; a marked improvement over the solid C's she'd scored in the past when a hunch teetered between possible and proven.

She said, "I don't suppose you'd let me take a peek at the files you put together."

"Nope. As long as I'm a county official, they're official county documents."

Implications clicked behind her eyes. "Is it an official secret where Lydia Quince, Deputy McBride and Robby Randal were at the time of the shooting?"

What had she done? Bugged Marlin's office? Tailed Pike from interview to interview? "Are you fishing," David asked, "or confirming what Eldredge Randal told you this afternoon?"

"How did you know I—" Her mouth pulled back at one corner. "For the record, he's a nice man and I didn't enjoy fooling him."

"Well, you didn't for long and Eldredge sure enjoyed looking at your legs while you were trying."

"I should have gone for cleavage." She laughed.

"But Rosemary, who has some, was busy touring tenants this afternoon."

A reconnaissance of Hannah's bustline verified no basis for complaint. Brains to Reeboks, the lady had it all, in all the right places and in just-right proportions. All she needed was convincing.

"Jimmy Wayne, the widow and the wonk," she reminded. "Any truth in the rumor that one, two or maybe the three of them are framing you for murder?"

"I've heard rumbles," he said, the sources being Andrik and Pike's giveaway questioning, "but none of them were in the neighborhood that night."

"Was Jessup Knox?"

David squirmed in his seat. The bar stool's creaky spindles alerted Malcolm, who sniffed, sneezed, then stretched out on his side.

Had Hannah and the Mod Squad taken a crash course in deductive reasoning? Or had Pike's investigation sprung a leak? Marlin had been late for the meeting with Jake Waycross that morning. Said he'd gone outside for a smoke, which was undoubtedly true, but Hannah was at the courthouse at the same time.

David hedged, "Knox leads an evening bible study group at his church on Fridays."

"Ah, but who's to say he did last Friday night, huh?"

"You promised you'd stay out of the investigation."

"I lied." She sat upright. "And you're not making it easy to save your butt."

"Too many people after it, Hannah. I suspect some may be within the department."

David curled a finger under her chin and turned her face to his. "I trust you. Don't doubt it for a second.

But the longer this drags on, the less I trust everyone else. Could be I've let paranoia saddle up and ride off with my horse sense, but I feel like a target and I don't know who's got me in their sights. I have to assume everyone does."

"A wise assumption," Hannah said, "and a shitty way to live."

"Yep."

She bumped his shoulder. "Care to change the subject a little?"

"Do I get to pick?"

"No."

He leaned closer. "How come?"

She started to say something, then frowned, looking at David as though he should know why and was being obtuse to annoy her.

"Okay." Her tone suggested a dare. "Go ahead and kiss me and I'll kiss you back because you're the world's best kisser and it's been too damn long since we have, then we can rip each other's clothes off and just do it on the floor and get it over with so we can stop thinking about howling multiple orgasms and concentrate on how to keep you from going to prison."

David stared at her, his mouth agape, his mind struggling with the concept of "world's best kisser," "howling orgasms" and "prison" being in the same sentence.

"Or," she went on, "the target can explain why he declined Jack's offer to have Kayak Teel represent him."

"Those are my choices?"

"Uh-huh."

David surveyed the perimeter. Tile floor. Ugly, large dog. Hannah, naked. It just didn't quite parse.

"There're two reasons I turned Jack down," he answered. "Around here, hiring a Saint Louis lawyer is as good as admitting you're guilty. Worse would be firing Lucas Sauers after he agreed to work on the cuff until my place sold."

"Oh, David." Hannah looked as sick as he felt when he signed the Realtor's listing agreement that afternoon.

"I have to sell it, sugar. If the grand jury indicts me, I'm out of a job. Defending myself against a manslaughter charge will cost the moon. My truck's the second most valuable thing I own and it wouldn't cover Luke's retainer."

Her expression was as readable as neon. David kissed her cheek. "No, you're not going to put down earnest money on it or ask Jack or IdaClare or anyone else to, either."

"But—"

"No, Hannah."

"God, you're stubborn."

"Yep." He brushed the hair from her neck, marveling at how she never shied away. "I reckon it's a blessing you aren't. Be hell to pay if we were both bullheaded."

She laughed, shaking her head at the ceiling.

"Hendrickson, you—"

The phone interrupted. Something always did.

Malcolm sprang to his feet. His muzzle jerked left, right. He tore out for the living room, barking his stupid head off.

David inquired, "What's he do when the doorbell rings? Bite the phone?"

Ignoring him, she grabbed the kitchen wall unit's receiver. "Valhalla Springs, Hannah Garvey speaking." A sly grin. "No, I'm still up. Uh-huh. You did? Terrific!" She drooped. "Oh, it is? What if it does? Okay. Yeah. Oh-eight-hundred. I will and you'd better, too. Right. Bye."

Replacing the receiver, she began, "That was—"

"Delbert." David pushed his bar stool under the counter.

"You two are meeting to do something—probably illegal—at eight bells, if it doesn't rain too hard, and he told you to get some sleep."

"Show-off."

"Not yet." He wriggled his fingers. "C'mere. Walk me to the door."

Tucking herself under his arm, she wrapped hers around his waist. "You don't have to go."

"Yes, I do."

She'd take it wrong if he told her the strain of a long day had shown on her face even before she took his troubles upon herself, doubling her burdens and halving his.

The image of cuddling her to him was so clear, he could see her hair fanned on the pillow. Hear her breathing slow, and deepen as she fell asleep.

Reality was Malcolm's tail thumping the railing around the office nook. David reached for his coat, watching Hannah cross to the rocker for his hat, wishing she'd stop, turn around and tell him to stay.

She smiled up at him, Mona Lisa with a pinch of Meg Ryan. "If I call tomorrow, will you answer the phone?"

"Yes'm, and I'll hang up if it's bail money you're after."

"It might be me—" Her lips flattened. "Never mind."

David laid the Stetson on the desk behind him. "Kiss me."

"Uh-uh. Too dangerous." She slid into his arms, head tilted, eyes sending the opposite message. "Have I ever told you you're the world's best kisser?"

"Not often enough."

"'Fraid it'll go to your head. Or somewhere."

"Might could."

A soft hum slid from alto to bass. "Okay, Hendrickson, half a lip. That's all I can stand."

17

A figure waved at Hannah from Skyline Drive's far shoulder. Groggy after staying up late to finish the bi-monthly payroll and her sleep disrupted by hot 'n heavy fantasy lovemaking, alternating with dreams of David trading rifle fire with the bad guys out to steal his ranch, she hoped her eyes were playing tricks on her.

Short, skinny old fart. Desert-camo shirt. Voluminous, chest-high, rubber waders. Pith helmet.

No tricks. That would be Delbert.

She parked the Blazer behind his Edsel, leaving a gap between its overshot continental kit and her bumper. *Hatari* meets *A River Runs Through It* appeared in her side window. Lowering the window halfway added audio to his in-motion mouth.

"...didja bring that mutt for? You can't watch him and the ground at the same time."

"Well, good morning to you, too, Gunga Din."

Malcolm started when the passenger window slid downward, then thrust his head through the breach. A soft *argh-argh* implied contentment.

"Nobody has to watch him." Hannah shut off the engine and unfastened hers and Malcolm's seat belts. "He'll be perfectly happy in the truck watching us."

"He damn well better be." Delbert opened the door

for her. "The others are over there testing equipment. Me and Leo came out early to mark the search perimeter and found a couple of things in our favor."

"Such as?"

"The land lies higher on the field side than the house side, so the bullet should have gone to ground faster than if the vice was versa. Plus, there's a decent chance the scrub ceders along the fence line might've slowed it down."

"What if it ricocheted?"

"Could've, but they're puny trees and we didn't see any gashes or busted limbs. No marks on the fence posts, either."

The police lines were gone from the house across the street, as were the semitractor and stock car. Repossessed, or towed away for scrap, Hannah supposed. If possible, the property was shabbier in their absence.

Delbert said, "Understand, this is a by-guess and by-golly operation, since we don't know David's exact position."

"I thought I told you, he was about fifteen feet from the door and about three feet right of it."

"The 'abouts' are the problem, ladybug. Plays Billy Ned with the trigonometry."

He swung around, indicating two handkerchiefs tied to the barbed-wire fence. "One marker jibes with the center of the front door. The other, as far left as we think Quince could aim without winging the sheriff.

"Best me and Leo can figure, Quince fired straight on or slightly to his left. If he'd aimed much to his right, David would have seen powder flash not muzzle flash."

Hannah looked from the door to each flag, mentally

drawing an isosceles triangle. Or maybe a trapezoid. Whatever.

"Makes sense to me."

"That's 'cause you're female. The only trig women can cipher is the closest distance between two malls."

She'd have called him a chauvinist, but he'd have thanked her for the compliment.

They joined the rest of the ground crew milling beyond their parked vehicles. Leo was a rotund vision in gray sweats, a fanny pack worn frontward, black socks and wing tips. IdaClare's duds of the day ran to a plastic rain bonnet, a pink, pouf-quilted rayon jacket and matching jeans.

"Love the shoes," Hannah said, eyeing the pink high-top tennies with glittery laces.

IdaClare swiveled a foot. "Aren't they the cutest things you ever saw? Nineteen ninety-nine at Bev's Head-to-Toe."

"I'd give her twenty-five to burn 'em," Delbert muttered.

In mustard-drab coveralls, Walt Wagonner's gangly frame resembled a tongue depressor with legs. Face graven in a constant dour expression, he stuck out a hand. "Walt Wagonner. One g, two n's. W-a-g-o-n-n-e-r."

"Thanks for volunteering, Walt." Hannah ignored his consistently odd manner of introduction. According to Delbert, the retired *Encyclopedia Britannica* associate editor would revert to a "Hi, how are you?" eventually.

"Move it, Tubby," a raspy voice demanded, "and make it snappy."

Leo jumped as though he'd been goosed. Cane in

hand, Sophonia Pugh scuttled past him. "Bet you're surprised to see me here, eh?"

Hannah's eyes averted to Delbert. "Less so than you might think."

Leo ducked the cane Sophonia whipped toward the field. "The government granted my daddy this land after the Civil War. I won't sell and I'm too old to plow, so I rent it out to keep the taxes paid."

"Any objections to us trespassing for a few hours?" Hannah inquired.

Sophonia squinted one eye shut. "I could charge you a few bucks a head for the scenery, like they do at Silver Dollar City down in Branson."

Yeah, Hannah transmitted on the woman-to-woman frequency, and I could have charged you a few bucks to meet Delbert "The Hunk" Bisbee, too.

"Not that I don't admire you all for wanting to help the sheriff," Sophonia continued, "but my jury's still out on that boy. Seems to me, if he can't come up with a better story than he's telling, he ought not have tried."

Caroline had used the same line many times during Hannah's childhood. It contradicted "truth is stranger than fiction" and provided scant incentive for "honesty is the best policy." Punishment received when the truth wasn't believed had a more hurtful, lasting effect than those meted out when caught in a lie.

"But," Sophonia went on, "the Good Book says it's a sin to prosper from another's travail, so go on and get after what you're here for." To Delbert, she added, "My hip says rain's acomin' and a gullywasher will fill those rubber pantaloons faster than a bucket under a downspout."

He peered up at the clabbered sky, down at the gape in the front of his waders, then blanched.

"A metal detector," Leo said to Hannah. "Have you used one before ever?"

She shook her head.

"Is simple." His thumb and fingers splayed. "Five minutes and an expert treasure hunter you will be."

A quarter-hour later, the only thing Hannah knew for sure was that Leo Schnur was an optimist. The machine looked like a length of bent tubing with a forearm cuff at one end, a plastic plate stuck on the other and an electronic box clamped to the middle.

After Leo twiddled knobs and cautioned her not to touch them—as if she would have, on a dare—he told her to ease the plate-thingie toward the fence. Rapid-fire beeps sent her heart up to her tonsils, but Leo said Hannah was "the natural."

Equipped and as ready as they'd ever be, Hannah, Leo, IdaClare and Walt shuffled in place, knowing their otherwise-occupied fearless leader would have a tantrum if they started without him.

In advertising industry vernacular, an actor who impersonates a migraine or indigestion sufferer is known as a "Merry Andrew." Delbert could have nailed an acid reflux shoot in one take when Sophonia hiked her posterior onto the hood of his Edsel and unloaded a lap robe, her knitting, thermos, a pineapple Danish and paper napkins from her shopping bag.

"Now, don't you fret, sweetie pie." She hooked her cane on the antennae post. "If it comes a sprinkle, I can picnic inside the car as easy as out here."

Arms conducting an invisible orchestra, Delbert stammered, "Th-that upholstery's genuine leather. Original. So's the paint. From the factory. Not a stain, not a scuff on it.''

"Don't I know it," Sophonia said. "Why, when we were coming out here, if I laid my head back and closed my eyes, I'd swear I was sitting on a two-hundred-dollar, spanking-new, vinyl davenport down at Sid's Factory Furniture Universe.''

Red face clashing with his ensemble, Delbert whirled and stomped off, pith helmet bobbling above his ears. To the treasure hunters, he yelled, "All right, by God, ten-hut for Operation Needle-in-the-Haystack. Line up on t'other side of that fence. Six feet apart. Detectors at ready. Move it—*move it.*''

Galvanized into action, Walt pushed down the top strand of wire to step over it just as Leo swung a leg over the second to squeeze between.

"Eee-yaaah! *Mein gott, mein gott, ich kann nicht mir helfen.*'' By his frantic crotch-grabbing, Hannah translated it to mean "mine balls, mine balls, the barbs have got me by mine balls.''

Walt jerked up the wire, his apology lost in Delbert's blue-streak cussing, Leo's wails and IdaClare and Hannah whooping so hard their stomachs cramped.

Cows, some with spindle-legged calves at their sides, sauntered over to see what the commotion was about. A black dowager with an auction tag clipped to one ear mooed her opinion of people who had nothing better to do than disturb the peace.

Order was restored when Delbert threatened to take the women's loaned metal detectors and go home. Finally, the troops were assembled as directed. Delbert asked, "Machines set for a shallow sweep?''

Affirmative.

"Power switches on?"

Ditto.

General Bisbee nodded approval. "Now, the primary objective for this operation is to cover a lot of ground and be thorough about it. Stay in formation. No dawdling. No jackrabbiting. One stops to check a hit, everybody stops. Any questions?"

Hannah cast a backward glance at the street. Sophonia, who'd added a straw cowboy hat to her outfit, gestured "Godspeed" with her pastry. One vehicle back, Malcolm's nose vacuumed the air. Being a dog, he was probably deliberating which of the soft, warm, organic substances he smelled would be the nicest to roll in.

Hannah patted her coat pocket for her keys. Aw, forget it. If the window's down too far, I'll give him a bath when we get home. Outside. With the hose.

"Forward…" Delbert fell in beside her. "March!"

Two steps later, Walt's machine crackled like a Geiger counter. He scuffed the dirt with his boot. "Nail."

IdaClare halted next. "Oooh, I found a penny! That's good luck."

Go. Stop. "Bolt," Leo said.

Go. Stop. "More nails."

Inch by inch, their progress was measured in battery-powered, electronic chatter; the detritus above and below the spongy, grass-cobbled earth strewn as though tractors, tools and spare change grew from metal seeds.

Beep. Hannah called, "Screwdriver."

Forward march. Stop. "Baling wire."

The air smelled like rain, loamy and oppressive. In

the distance, a streaky gray veil hung between the darker clouds and the hilltops.

Beep.

Buzz.

Eh-eh-eh.

Stop. Look. Discard.

Thrills of discovery had long ago fallen victim to routine. Itemizations, too. "No" was specific enough.

Birds swooped down to prospect for worms and flew off with their prizes wriggling in their beaks. Now and then a cow craned her neck at the Magnificent Seven, except there were only five of them and magnificent applied to their effort not the results.

"No."

"No."

A muscle stitched between Hannah's shoulder blades. Her fingers tingled. Her forearms ached. And her wrists. And her Achilles' tendons. Most of all, her heart. Needle in a haystack, my butt.

Buzz. Toe-dig in the dirt. "No."

More like finding a hat pin in a needlestack. A pebble in a sand dune. A Kennedy in Jefferson Davis Oglethorpe's foyer. A puddle in Death Val—

Buzz-zzzz. Heel-dig. Hmm. Stoop. "No."

"How're you holding up, ladybug?"

I'm depressed and bored and tired of schlepping this dumb, awkward machine. "Fine," she said. "How about you?"

"Fit as a fiddle."

One lame lie deserves another.

Leo and IdaClare scored dual hits. Delbert propped his detector on his hip and did neck rolls like a boxer staying loose between rounds.

Hannah looked back at the handkerchief drooping on the fence. How far had they come? Fifteen yards? Twenty? How far can a bullet travel? Better question: How much more can you expect of your friends?

"Heads up," Delbert said. "We're off to the races again."

Hannah blew out a breath, and winced at the icepick stabbing her spine. Eyes tracking her machine's monotonous arc, she said to Delbert, "See that feed bunk, about ten feet ahead of Walt? When we're even with it, we about-face."

"You sure?"

A fist closed around her stomach and wrenched it. *I'm so sorry, David, but we tried our best.* "Positive."

Beep. Leo kept on walking. "No."

"Here, either."

IdaClare stumbled. "Damn clodhoppers. I don't know what possessed me to buy the silly things."

"No."

"No."

Buzz. Hannah looked closer and recoiled. "Shit."

Delbert glanced at her. "Whatcha got?"

"Just what I said I had." She pointed at a hideous greenish-brown blob.

"Give it another pass."

Buzz.

Delbert swiped a hand across his mouth, as if the grin would disappear. "Well, you know what they say. Leave no stone unturned."

IdaClare, Leo and Walt crowded in. They frowned at the ground like archaeologists at a shard of Egyptian pottery.

"Is nothing," Leo said. "Probably."

"Yes, but," IdaClare whispered, "what if it's... something?"

Walt waved his machine over the cowpatty. *Eh-eh-eh.* The other two followed suit. *Be-beep-beep.*

Delbert reached for Hannah's detector. "Ladybug, you've found yourself the mother lode."

Funny, funny man. She gulped. Shuddered. Turning her head away, she drew back her foot—

"W-a-i-t," IdaClare shrieked, waving frantically. "Don't you *dare* kick that. Lord have mercy, we'll be picking cowflop out of our ears for a week."

Good point, Hannah thought, especially coming from a cattle rancher's widow. Except if I don't kick it out of the way, how am I going to see what's under...

Oh no. Oh, *ick.*

Drops of rain tatted the field. Hannah squatted on her heels, lips curling in disgust. Delbert knelt beside her. "Okay, joke's over. Let me do the dirty work."

"Thanks, but—" she shrugged "—finder's keepers."

Contrary to Sir Walter Raleigh's Rules of Gentlemanly Behavior, Delbert didn't insist, leaving Hannah no second chance to give in. Instead, he looked up at Leo. "Gimme those sandwich bags in your field kit."

Leo rifled through the frontward fanny pack. A giant pair of tweezers, cellophane tape, twine, rubber bands and a marker-pen tumbled out before he produced two crumpled plastic bags.

"Brought 'em to seal the evidence," Delbert explained.

"Wish I'd thought to bring gloves."

She slipped her hands inside the flimsy shields. Just

close your eyes and it'll all be over in a second, Hannah reassured herself. Kind of like having sex with Jarrod.

Nose squashed against her shoulder, Hannah probed and massaged the fragrant muck and pretended she was eight years old again, sculpting an ashtray from modeling clay for her mother, who would use it, thinking that showed how much she cherished it, while Hannah wished she wouldn't for the exact same reason.

Something hard. Cylindrical. Just a bolt, she thought, praying the cosmos were suckers for reverse psychology. Rolling it between thumb and forefinger, she felt a flat end. Her heart sank. Lifted at its smooth, unthreaded sides. Soared as she pressed down on its blunted tip.

Turning her fist palm up, her voice muffled by her coat, she said, "Delbert?" and opened her fist.

Silence. Tears welled in her eyes. Damn. She knew she couldn't get that lucky. Garveys never did.

"Eu-reee-kaa!" IdaClare hollered. "She found it!"

Hannah's pulse tripped a beat, then raced. "I did?" Scrambling to her feet, she crowed, "I did, I really did," laughing and crying and clasping the bullet cupped in folds of slimy, smelly plastic to her chest.

Leo and Walt locked arms and do-si-doed. IdaClare yanked off her rain bonnet and twirled it like a lasso. The Edsel's horn blared. Delbert aimed crude, nonverbal signals at Sophonia. She tooted back "Shave and a Haircut, Two-Bits" just to annoy him.

Hannah hugged her helpers, giving each a close-up view of the small piece of brass that would prove David Hendrickson wasn't a cold-blooded killer.

"Don't touch it," Delbert warned.

Leo's hand retracted. "Ach, too happy I am, to think straight. The fingerprints, yes?"

"Maybe the lab'll find Quince's all over it, if we don't smudge 'em." To Hannah, Delbert said, "Best just peel that plastic bag off inside out and stick the mess in your pocket."

How fingerprints would be on what constituted the inside of a bullet, Hannah didn't ask and hoped no one else did. Delbert was in his element. She wouldn't embarrass him for the world.

"All of you, listen to me." IdaClare's tone was as stern as her expression. "Bend down slow and steady and pick up your detectors, then start walking backward to the fence."

Delbert snorted. "What are you jabber—"

"Hush, fool." IdaClare nodded to her left. "Look yonder."

A horned, brockled locomotive on legs stood not five yards behind them. Twelve-hundred pounds of nostril-flared, devil-horned steak on the hoof.

IdaClare said, "He has a herd to protect and the racket we made didn't set well with him."

Let me live, Hannah thought, and I'll never eat beef again, I swear. Veggies all the way.

Walt stammered, "Wh-what are we going to do?"

"Take our leave nice and easy and quiet. As long as we don't rile him, I don't think he'll charge." IdaClare looked from one frightened face to the next. "Unless he does, whatever you do, *don't turn tail and run.*"

Following her example, they knelt, eyes locked on El Toro, fingers scrabbling for their detectors' handles.

Spasms quivered up the bull's foreleg. He stamped. Shifted his weight. Pawed at the turf.

"He's just feeling his oats," IdaClare assured, as if such were possible. "Now, let's spread out so as not to trip each other, and get the hell out of here."

Jelly-muscled and stiff-kneed, their machines gripped like flagstaffs, they backward marched over rain-slick rocks and grass tufts.

Leo's spraddled gait wasn't geared for reverse. In desperation, he opted for a semisidle. Walt's boot-dragging shuffle sounded doubly loud heel first. Delbert's waders squeaked, their oversize soles as awkward as swim fins. Surefooted IdaClare had the benefit of experience.

Hannah tromped her shoelace. Staggered. Caught herself an instant before she fell. *Klutz.*

The bull broke into a trot. Bowed his head.

Half-turned to run for the fence, Hannah froze in her tracks. IdaClare, holding her metal detector like a lance, charged the animal.

Hannah screamed, "No-o-o-o!"

Hooves churning, the bull bore down on IdaClare.

"Yah! Yah!" She jabbed at him. "*Git,* you wind-bellied son of a bitch. Gi' back. *Back.*"

Head rotating, horns almost vertical, the animal swerved away at the last possible second.

IdaClare took off running. Hannah started after her, watching the bull over her shoulder. He stutter-stepped. Bellowed. Wheeled for another charge.

"Go—go—go."

Delbert cursed. Sprawled facedown in the mud, skidding.

Sprinting toward him, Hannah screamed, "Get up," and threw her detector at the bull.

A blur streaked across the field. Snarling, teeth bared

and snapping, Malcolm lunged at the bull's forelegs, shoulder and head, dodging hooves, ducking a horn an instant before it ripped his throat.

An elderly woman trying to clout him with the business end of a metal detector was one thing. Being attacked by a ferocious Airedale-wildebeest was more than the bull could take. He cut upfield, Malcolm galloping behind him, barking like a fiend.

Panting from terror and exertion, Hannah slicked the wet hair from her face. "Oh, Delbert, weren't IdaClare and Malcolm fantas…"

Her eyes slid from the lumpy, headless, torsoless waders to the upturned pith helmet lying a yard or so from them. "Delbert?"

She turned around. IdaClare, Walt, Leo and Sophonia were cheering Malcolm from the fence's street side. Delbert wasn't with them.

Turning back, she crouched to peer through the Edsel's side windows. Uh-uh. No de-pantsed, Renaissance men huddled up in the back seat. Then where the heck—

The waders convulsed and flopped over. Hannah shrieked and backpedaled. Two arms, then a drenched, white head shot out.

"Wha-whassamatter? Is the bull comin' back?"

Hannah patted her chest to keep her heart where it belonged. "You scared the crap out of me."

"Well, pardon me all to hell, which it was hotter than in there." He yanked up the waders' shoulder straps. "If I'd had a thermometer stuck in my butt like a goddamn Butterball, it would have popped up a couple of minutes ago."

Hannah helped him to his feet. "I should know better

than ask, but why did you hunker down in them in the first place?''

"Rodeo clowns dive into barrels when a bull goes loco," he said with a sniff. "I did the next best thing."

18

If you're driving through town and need to call someone, no pay phone will appear, except the one bolted to the outside wall of Wild Bill's Tattoo and Adult Video Parlor.

If you're driving through town and trying really hard *not* to call your probably someday-lover because he won't believe his worst nightmare is over until he hears it from Marlin Andrik or Lieutenant Theron Pike, pay phones with giant, flashing arrows pointing at them materialize at six-foot intervals.

"We've got to stick with protocol on this one," Hannah told Malcolm.

The Blazer's muddy, cow-poop-perfumed copilot gave her a "you wouldn't know protocol if somebody served it to you on a plate" look.

Flaunting local tradition, she clicked on her turn signal. "Okay, so scratch protocol. Common sense says it isn't smart to show a suspect proof of his innocence before showing it to the cops. That's like sitting your daughter down for a frank discussion about sex after you find birth control pills in her purse."

Moomph.

The rain had decreased to a drizzle, enough moisture to warrant windshield wipers, but not enough for the blades to *shoop* across the glass, instead of *dr-r-ragging*.

Hannah joined the carousel orbiting the square in search of a parking place. Search being the operative term, as finding one increased in difficulty in proportion to the decline in the weather.

A jaywalker halted between the bumpers of two vehicles. He scrunched his shoulders and scowled at Hannah as though it were her fault he'd left his umbrella at home. She braked to let him cross in front of her, but he swatted her on.

So much for random acts of kindness, Hannah thought. Might even be why they're random.

Andrik's unmarked Chevy was in its reserved space. Hannah continued onward around the square's south side, her mind's eye seeing the detective pull on his sport coat, straighten his tie, reach for his keys on the desk...

"This is insane, Malcolm." She throttled the steering wheel. "Here we are, driving in freakin' circles with evidence of a justifiable homicide burning a hole in my freakin' pocket and we can't find a freakin' parking place anywhere in this stupid, freakin' town."

The surly jaywalker had disappeared. Some people had all the luck. Back-up lights winked just ahead. Like me, for instance.

Hannah braked to wait for the departing car. An oncoming delivery-van driver stopped, too. His piggy eyes darted from the reversing Intrepid to Hannah. She pointed at the car, at herself, made a slash motion at her throat, then pointed at him.

His head wobbled a snide, "Oh yeah? That spot's mine, lady, and there's nothing you can do about it."

The Intrepid's wheels straightened. Hannah inched forward, issuing an unheard apology for being pushy, but war was hell and the jerk in the van started it. Clearing the adjacent pickup's back bumper, she cranked the Blazer toward the slot…and stomped the brake pedal.

Curses as blue as the handicapped logo on the parking meter's sign blistered Malcolm's tender ears. Hannah drove off, frustrated but virtuous, only to glimpse the van whipping into the space.

"All right, that's it. No more Ms. Nice Girl."

A visual one-eighty confirmed the only vehicles in motion were the same five she'd been following, plus the three that had trailed the delivery-van driver, who would die a slow, painful death if there was a God, or if Hannah's knee ever found itself in the vicinity of his groin.

"The odds are against us, Malc. Crisis management time."

After assessing her options, Hannah decided to ramp her truck onto the sidewalk at the next corner—which was just lying there doing nothing besides soak up rain—and almost missed the Bondo-mobile humping backward into the lane of traffic.

In less than a minute, she was smushing her hair in the reflection from the video monitor guarding the Kinderhook County Detective Division's door. At a metallic *clack,* she entered the noisy, smoke-hazed cavern David had called "The Outhouse."

He hadn't been kidding. He'd been tactful.

Detectives Josh Phelps and Cletus Orr were seated at their desks, both holding telephone receivers to their ears. Phelps, the squad's rookie, raised an index finger to signal he'd be with her in a minute.

Hannah shook her head, mouthed, "Andrik" and headed toward the back of the room.

Andrik tossed his pen on the blotter, and leaned back in his chair. He clasped his hands on his belly, as if visits by wet, odorous women with mascara rings around their eyes were an hourly occurrence.

Come to think of it, in his line of work, maybe they were.

"Have a seat."

She didn't want to sit. She wanted to slap the small plastic bag on his desk and gloat, "You wanted evidence? Well, there it is, Mr. Hotshot Chief of Detectives."

She sat.

"O. C. Algeyer has been trying to find you since before eight this morning," Marlin said. "I never thought to tell him to check out the livestock arena."

"Algeyer?" Hannah repeated innocently. "I don't know anyone by that name."

"Older guy, medium height, thick glasses, subpoena in his hand?"

A blush warmed her face. "It isn't smart for a woman living alone to answer the door to strangers."

"Yeah. Especially process servers with picture ID's clipped to their lapels." He tilted forward and snatched his cigarettes and lighter. The Thank You for Smoking placard on his desk said it all.

With his lower lip pooched to aim carcinogens at the ceiling, his gaze returned to her. "I understand why you don't want to testify before the grand jury—any jury, for that matter—but if Hendrickson finds out

you're ducking service, he'll deliver *you* to the subpoena instead of the other way around.''

"I'm sure he would.'' The wadded plastic rolled off
Hannah's fingers and onto the desk blotter. She
squelched a "Ta-da,'' but just barely. "Except thanks
to that, he won't have to.''

The bag unfurled like a Sea-Monkey tablet in a dish
of magic growth serum. Marlin sniffed. "I've heard of
shittin' a brick. Shittin' a bullet's a new one.''

"We found it under a pile of manure in the field
across from Stuart Quince's house.''

Heart drumming in her ears, Hannah struggled to
contain her excitement. "It proves Quince fired at David, at the same instant he fired at Quince. That's why
it sounded like one shot.''

The detective took a long pull on his Marlboro. He
exhaled, then balanced the cigarette on the rim of his
makeshift ashtray. Lowering the desk lamp's goose-
neck, he examined the bullet through the smeared plastic.

"We?'' he asked.

"Delbert Bisbee, IdaClare Clancy, Walt Wagonner,
Leo Schnur and myself. Delbert scrounged enough
metal detectors for all of us. Well, for me and IdaClare.
He and the other guys have their own. They belong to
a treasure hunter's club. At Valhalla Springs.''

Hannah raked her fingers through her hair and fisted
a hunk to tick-a-lock her runaway mouth. Now, if Andrik would use his for something besides breathing...

"Leo says it's a nine-millimeter.''

"Uh-huh.''

"The same caliber as the gun registered to Quince,
right? And the box of ammunition in his truck.''

Andrik's head raised. "Who told you what we found in his rig? Hendrickson?"

Uh-oh. She met his hard stare. "Not hardly. David has kept me about as well informed as you have."

"Then who did? Somebody in the department? That's not public knowledge."

"You may not think it is," she said, "but if I heard it thirdhand, which I did, Chase Wingate might as well have printed it in today's edition of the *Sanity Examiner*."

"Surprised he didn't." Andrik ironed the bag with his palms. "You owe me, by the way. I told him Friday night to bug off on interviewing you."

Watching him smooth the crumpled plastic, displaying no outward interest in its contents, a hard knot began to form under Hannah's ribs.

He went on, "I figured Chase took me seriously, when there weren't any quotes from you in—"

"Don't jerk me around, Marlin." She slid to the edge of her seat. "I bring you evidence Quince fired a gun at David and you go off on a tangent about the newspaper?"

His hands came to rest on either side of the bag. In a tone as weary as he suddenly appeared, he said, "This bullet doesn't prove anything, Hannah."

"Why." A demand, not a question.

He winced. "You want it no frills, huh? Hell of a waste of the sensitivity-training seminar I slept through last February, but here goes.

"Without being too technical, the interior barrel of a handgun or rifle has grooves and lands that are impressed on a slug when it's fired. No two patterns are identical, so they're basically the weapon's fingerprint. You follow?''

Hannah nodded.

"If we had Quince's pistol, we could do a ballistics comparison and determine whether this bullet was fired from it. Without the gun, this could have come from any one of a million that use nine-millimeter ammo.''

Andrik's forehead creased. "And if the pistol surfaced and we matched your bullet, it still wouldn't help Hendrickson.''

Too stunned to respond, she sat rigid as hope splintered and fell around her like glass.

"I'm sorry, Hannah, but if you'd left the slug where you found it and called me, I could have taken pictures, done a sketch-and-measure—Christ, you know the drill. Still couldn't prove when it was fired and from what and the prosecutor would've screamed at entering it under the scintilla-of-evidence rule and probably gotten it thrown out, but...''

His cheeks plumped, then flattened like bellows. "Since you didn't call me to the scene, I can no more testify to where this slug was found than I can fly.''

"Well, *I* can." She leaped from the chair. "And so can Delbert, IdaClare, Walt and Leo.''

Andrik pushed himself up from the desk and slid his hands in his trouser pockets. "Do you want to leave here hating me a little or a lot?''

"You mean, there's more?" A chuckle rattled out. "What the hell. Go for broke.''

"If Mack Doniphan asked why the five of you were in that field with metal detectors, what would your answer be?''

We were looking for the bullet Stuart Quince alleg-edly fired at Sheriff David Hendrickson.

"Yeah." Andrik grunted, having read her expression with his typical accuracy. "Toast."

Arms hugging the Blazer's steering wheel, Hannah's wrenching sobs echoed loud in the small space.

"David hasn't done anything wrong. I can't do any-thing right. It's not fair. It's just not fair."

Tears burned down her cheeks. She didn't care any-more. She'd let herself care too much. Let David care too much.

"If he'd never met me, none of this would've hap-pened." Pain ripped through her, shredding her inside-out. "I'm a Garvey. A jinx. Happiness is for other peo-ple. Why did I think this time would be different?"

She slumped back against the seat, head rocking back and forth, weeping and laughing like the fool she was. "Blood will out, Hannah Marie. Always has, al-ways will. You've heard it since the day you were born. God Almighty damn, what'll it take for you to believe it?"

Eyes squeezed shut, she surrendered to the hurt, hopelessness and inevitability crushing her from all sides. In a day, two at most, the grand jury would indict David on the strength—no, *weakness*—of her's and Andrik's and Pike's and who knows how many others' testimony.

David would resign from office; the letter would more than likely be written in advance and carried in his suit coat's inner pocket throughout the proceedings.

Jefferson Davis Oglethorpe, the county chess master,

would chafe his hands and manipulate his political lackeys, as had his father and grandfather before him.

Before spring yielded to summer, David would be tried, convicted and imprisoned for a crime he didn't commit. Hannah would pack another rental trailer, say her goodbyes and leave the only real home she'd ever known, because it would harbor more memories, more what-might-have-beens, more if-onlys than she could bear.

"And there's nothing," she said, anger chipping away at melancholy, "*nothing* I can do to stop any of it from happening."

Whiskers tickled her face. A warm, wet tongue lapped her chin, then slurped upward to her hairline.

"Oh, Mal—" *Slu-rrp.* Hannah winged an arm to fend off another sloppy smooch. "Yes, yes, I love you, too, you big doofus. Now, will you heel, already?"

He gave her a long, unblinking look, then settled back in the seat. Any conscientious Airedale-wildebeest owner would interpret the curt *moomph* as "If you're through with the gloom, despair and agony thing, let's grab a burger and get on with the program."

Typical male reaction. He fades into the wallpaper while you cry yourself sick, then when your tear ducts dry up, he lays on a couple of kissy-wissy-make-you-feel-betters and *shazam,* God's in his heaven, all's right with the world, so whaddaya say we get something to eat.

The console's tissue box was as empty as it was the last time Hannah needed it. She banged the lid shut and mopped her face with a reeking, muddy sleeve.

"Finding that bullet *was* the program, Malcolm.

Lands and grooves, my ass. That sucker came from Quince's gun and Andrik knows it as well as I do."

She skimmed her hair back behind her ears. "Okay, I should have called him. Let him scoop the poop and play freeze-tag with Ferdinand the Bull. Except I'd have *still* heard the 'Gee, Hannah, I'm real sorry' speech and walked away feeling like I'd just had a full-body mammogram, so unless you have any bright ideas on where that blasted gun is or how to—"

Well, speak of the devil. One hand in the pocket of his unbelted trench coat, the other awning a cigarette pinched between forefinger and thumb, Marlin Andrik gave no indication of noticing Hannah's vehicle as he walked to his own.

Turning and flipping the butt into the gutter, he rounded the Blazer's front bumper. Hannah sensed he'd scanned the square before his casual change in direction. She keyed the ignition to lower the window.

Shoulder presented and eyes downcast, he asked, "You okay?"

"No."

He nodded, as though he'd anticipated her answer. "Have you, uh, talked to Osborn's next-door neighbor lately?"

"No…" The question wasn't out of left field—it wasn't within a mile of the park. "Why do you ask?"

A sidelong glance, then a shrug. "The way the two of you hit it off, I, uh…you know…thought you might've."

Hannah gawked at him, mystified.

"Well." Andrik tapped the Blazer's quarter-panel. "Got a gang of baby drones and a receiving stolen property I'm working. Guess I'd better give the tax-payers their dime's worth.''

"Baby drones?"

"Juveniles, aka preemie felons. Punk burglars, in this case. Can't do much to them till they're eighteen.'' He shook his head. ''The mini-dirtbags couldn't read *Red Fish, Blue Fish* because of the big words, but they know their civil rights down to the statutes and who versus whom.''

"You're a cynic, Marlin."

''Uh-uh.'' He started off. ''I'm a realist with a piss-poor attitude.''

At a few minutes before noon, the sunlight angling through the clouds set off a golf cart stampede to Valhalla Springs's clubhouse. On the roof, a red flag waved from a pole, signaling the course was still too wet for play, but not for duffers to converge in the pro shop and offer opinions on improving drainage.

The community center's parking lot was three-quarters full. Willard Johnson's car was parked in its usual place. No sign of Eulilly, hooded marchers or of any crosses staked on the lawn awaiting the flick of her Bic.

Power walkers and bicyclists vied for ownership on the streets and cedar-chipped paths. Shoppers and lunchers strolled Main Street's boardwalks, making up for time lost to a rain delay.

Hannah tried to feel satisfied by her whirlwind mobile inspection tour. When Jack offered her the job, he'd said the development practically managed itself. He'd been lying, but it didn't relieve her conscience. If he asked what she'd done to earn her paycheck the past few days…well, the prospect was enough to give her a psychogenic fugue.

Plastic Dollar Store bags rustled on the floorboard, their contents shifting when Hannah turned into her driveway singing, "To-morrow, to-morrow, I'll chain myself to the desk to-morrow." What it lacked in key and tempo was compensated for with volume and sincerity.

Malcolm galloped off to his relief station. She toted the supplies for Operation Grease the Skids into the kitchen, then gathered up his towel, bowls and brontochewies and carried them to the garage.

Eyeballing the interior found no hazards that Malcolm could avail himself of or create—other than the jillion-volt battery charger attached to her gadabout golf cart. Hannah shivered at the memory of Lightning Bolt Bisbee's demonstration on connecting and disconnecting the cables. The *do's* had increased her wariness. The *don'ts* had left her an incurable fry-me-phobic.

At the moment, the charger wasn't doing anything besides emitting silent, boogety-boogety rays. Malcolm would have to flip the power switch, then chomp down on the cord before he could electrocute—

The three-pronged plug came away from the wall outlet without turning Hannah into a human torch. It would not be replaced, barring an Act of Delbert.

At her call, Malcolm caromed through the garage's side door and zeroed in on his food dish, as if he hadn't wolfed down a deluxe double-cheeseburger, jumbo fries and a vanilla ice-cream cone an hour earlier.

"Hey, uh, Malcolm? You know, figuring out what Andrik was hinting about means I have to go back into town."

Kibble crunched in two-beat syncopation.

"And you can't go with me."

If the news were a crushing blow, he hid it well.

"The problem is," Hannah explained, "anyone I'd ask to watch you would want to know where I'm going. I'm afraid to let you run loose and I won't chain you to a tree. That leaves two safe places, but you're too smelly and gross to lock in the house and I don't have time to bathe you and me both, so…"

Hannah zipped out the door and pulled it shut, telling herself it was for his own good.

According to the answering machine, Delbert had decided to go ahead with harassing Jessup Knox that afternoon. Not good news. Sanity had few roundabout ways of getting anywhere. If the gumshoes were out and about instead of sleeping off the morning's running of the bull, one of them might take a notion to return to the scene of the crime.

Cross that bridge when you come to it. Burn it if there's an Edsel behind you.

David had called twice. Ignore him, Hannah instructed herself. He'll drag the bullet fiasco out of you in five seconds, then you'll blab about Operation Grease the Skids and he'll say Andrik was only making conversation and you'll have to promise not to go through with it, so forget about talking to him until it's *fait accompli*.

Willard and every departmental supervisor had left an unspecified request for a callback. None mentioned an emergency.

Hetta Caldwell's chipper recorded voice informed Hannah that the lawsuit had been dropped. *Nothing more than a tempest in a teapot. We all simply must have lunch together soon. Have a nice day. Ta-ta.*

Hannah said, "Don't hold your breath. On second thought, take a big one and hold it till I get back to you on that, 'k?"

Her shower was comparable to a Caribbean honeymoon: hot, relaxing and a month too short. Later, she mirror-modeled the heathered tangerine power suit and taupe DKNY slingbacks that had once been a uniform and declared it good.

The doorbell rang as she was tightening the lid on the last of a dozen travel-size bottles she'd bought and filled from a jug of two-bucks-a-quart hand lotion.

She recognized O. C. Algeyer from a sneak peek through the window earlier that morning before her rendezvous with the Mod Squad. This time, a UPS mailer was wedged under his arm. If his intent was to trick a subpoena recipient into opening the door, the polyester sport coat and black slacks didn't cut it.

"Ms. Hannah M. Garvey?"

"Yes."

He presented her with a trifolded sheet of paper. "You are hereby summoned to appear before, and offer testimony to, the Kinderhook County Grand Jury at 9:00 a.m. tomorrow. Failure to appear will result in a warrant being issued for your arrest for contempt of court."

Fighting to maintain composure, Hannah slipped the subpoena behind her back without looking at it. "Do I need to sign anything?"

"No, ma'am. I keep a log for the court as proof of service." The mailer slipped. "Oh, hey, this is yours, too. The driver left it on the mat where you'd have stepped on it before you saw it.''

Algeyer waved toward the far side of the porch. ''I threw your paper over there when I was here this morning. S'pect it'll dry afore next week's comes out.'' A gold tooth glinted when he smiled. ''S'pect you won't miss much if it don't.''

''Thank you, Mr. Algeyer. That was very thoughtful of you.''

''Pshaw. Just being neighborly.'' He hesitated at the steps. ''Don't you be late tomorrow.''

Better never than late, Hannah amended.

Noting Eulilly Thomlinson as the packet's sender, she held it to her ear in the event that it was ticking, then ripped it open.

The single sheet of perfumed, pale blue stationery had a silver-inked header and a notary's stamp at the bottom. The salutation read: Dear Operations Manager.

Sweet.

This notification constitutes notifying you of Mr. and Mrs. Chet Thomlinson's (hitherto known as The Tenants) intent to vacate the premises in which they currently reside at 1903 Larkspur Lane within 30 (thirty) days of the date at the top of this duly notarized notification.

After skimming the rest of Eulilly's attempt at legalese, Hannah threw back her head and laughed. Mr. Thomlinson's signature was absent, but screw policy. An X on the dotted line would have been good enough for her.

Gee, would it be tacky to offer to help them pack?

Load the moving van? Bust a bottle of champagne over Eulilly's bow and wish them bon voyage?

IdaClare had prevailed in court; okay, *prevailed* might be exaggerating, but she wasn't enrolled in License Plate 101 class, either. Eulilly had surrendered rather than haul Hannah, Jack and his corporation into court.

Two for two.

Three times is charm.

Hannah knocked on the office nook's railing.

19

Have you to talked to Osborn's next-door neighbor lately?

There were two interpretations for Andrik's remark: either he'd lost his mind somewhere between his desk and her vehicle, or he was suggesting Hannah chat up Quince's neighbors, as she had Kathleen Osborn's.

People do say the darnedest things to a stranger—especially a female stranger. It's apparent to anyone who's stood in a long supermarket check-out line, occupied a waiting room or had frequent-flyer miles.

But pin a badge on that stranger and some clam up, some embellish accidentally, or on purpose, and others waffle because they don't want to get involved.

Andrik wouldn't ask Hannah outright to stick her civilian nose into an official investigation. All he'd done was customize his business card, then inquire after a Valhalla Springs's resident's well-being.

Exhilaration tingled through her as she neared the Whispering Pines subdivision for the second time that day. Marlin believed David. He'd telegraphed it repeatedly, in his obtuse, inscrutable way. Like David, he trusted the system, but the system required evidence and cops had to play by the rules. Andrik would also laugh himself into a truss at the mere mention of Operation Grease the Skids. The Delbert Influence had inspired the name, but its strategy was on Hannah's home turf: advertising.

Door-to-door test marketing had existed as long as there had been products to sell and people to coax into buying them. The survey results foretold success or failure about as accurately as a coin flip, but build a better mousetrap and its marketers will beat a path to your door.

To encourage customers to open theirs, surveyors provided free samples, the industry's favorite redundancy. Hannah had applied an extra tweak of the trade to the bottles of lotion she'd remanufactured as giveaways.

For some strange psychological reason, inexpensive containers and plain, black-on-white labels reading Survey Sample: Not For Resale, with no brand-name or ingredients list, often inspired thoughts of movie stars' secret formulas.

When marketing and advertising agencies got wise to this version of "less is more," some package redesigns became so schlocky customers literally threw samples back at the givers. To counteract that possibility, Hannah had a pocketful of mint-crisp dollar bills for vigorish. A buck didn't buy much these days, but new ones had great tactile appeal.

The pièce de résistance was the uncirculated fifty she'd use to swing conversations toward Lydia Quince's sudden widowhood. Andrik and Pike's interviews had relied on truth, justice and the American way. Hannah's approach keyed in on the three G's: greed, gullibility and gossip.

Deceitful? Well, not on a Tricky-Dick Nixon scale.

Or even Michael Milken. But yeah, if you wanted to be anal about it, it might be…sort of…fraud.

Turning onto the development's main road, Hannah told her inner Goody Two-shoes, "Look, everyone gets a free bottle of lotion and a buck out of the deal, so we're talking major gray area here."

She parked in front of the vacant lots adjacent to the Quince house. Ignoring thoughts of déjà vu all over again, she slipped a clipboard in the crook of her arm and laid a bulging, silk cosmetics bag on top of it.

Birds squawked and took wing, flushed from their perches when the Blazer's door slammed shut. *Jeez, why not toot the horn while you're at it, Einstein? If anybody recognizes your truck from this morning, it's endgame time.*

A corollary risk was more worrisome. What if someone recognized her? Aw, c'mon, Hannah reasoned. The suit, the makeup, a half a can of mousse in your hair? Pygmalion wouldn't recognize you.

Probably.

She didn't remember if any lights were on Friday night at the house whose driveway served as a roundabout, nor did anyone appear to be home, now. Garages attached to crackerboxes seldom had space for vehicles with their engines, transmissions and tires intact.

Midway to the door, a rap song's bass track vibrated in her chest. The compact car it thumped from blew by her and screeched to a halt as though physics didn't apply to interlocking brakes.

The goateed driver and younger passenger bailed out, hitched their gangsta jeans, then gave practiced tugs so the world needn't wonder if they were boxer-shorts kinds of guys.

Hannah nodded at the house. "Do you guys live here?"

"Yes, ma'am." By the driver's slow-blooming grin, the graduation from braces to an orthodontic retainer was recent. "But I reckon it's the lady of the house you're after."

He looked like one of Andrik's baby drones. Sounded like a baby David Hendrickson. And she called Marlin a cynic?

The shotgun passenger said, "Mom's a nurse at the hospital. She doesn't get off till eleven."

Big brother gave him a "shut up" glare across the top of the car.

"I'm not supposed to leave a sample and cash bonus without talking to the customer." Hannah unzipped the case.

"But as sure as I come back, I'll disturb her when she's trying to rest."

Bottle and dollar bill inches from the older boy's grasp, she suggested, "Unless tomorrow is her day off? I'll be out of the area after that."

Younger Sib said, "Naw, she's only off Saturdays and Sundays. She'd make more money if she worked—"

"Buzz off, jerk face. The lady's talking to me, okay?"

Having confirmed Mom hadn't been home Friday night and the boys probably hadn't, either, Hannah left Big Brother to lecture Little Brother on latchkey-kid safety rules.

Head bent over her clipboard, she dawdled until they went inside, for fear they'd warn her away from the Quince house, then wonder why she ignored them.

She couldn't skip 5406. If she did, neighbors on the other side might question her cover story.

Hannah touched the doorbell but didn't press it. Wiping her finger on her skirt was childish, irrational and necessary. The smell of decaying wood and uncollected garbage invaded her nostrils. Bad karma rustled in the shrubbery. She gripped the bottle of lotion, the nails of her other hand ticking off seconds on the back of the clipboard.

Surprise, surprise, no one's here.

She walked away, the creepy-crawlies prickling at the bends of her knees, rippling upward on spider feet. Imagination whispered, *he's watching from the window. Turn around if you don't believe me.* Common sense scolded her for reading too damn many Stephen King novels.

"Nobody lives there anymore."

Hannah gasped, choked. The bottle smacked the pavement. Lotion splattered her instantly favorite pair of shoes, the tops of her feet, her shins.

"Omigosh. Oh, I am *so* sorry." A young woman pushing a stroller materialized from behind an overgrown forsythia hedge. "I swear, if my husband doesn't chop down those ratty ol' bushes, I'll put a match to 'em, just see if I don't."

Tissues and an empty bread bag materialized from the stroller's go-pocket. Giving Hannah the former, she chucked the drippy bottle in the latter. "First thing a new mommy learns—don't go anywhere without something to put messes in."

Hannah grinned. "And Boy Scouts get all the credit for being prepared?"

"Why, sure they do. They've got den mothers to

show 'em how." Sack rolled and returned to its pocket, she dug a little deeper and came up with a billfold. "Now, how much is it for two bottles—the busted one and one for myself?"

"Not a penny." Hannah took a dollar from her jacket pocket and wrapped it around a fresh bottle. "The lotion is free and here's a little bonus for you for trying it."

"No, no. If that's a sample for true, I'd love to have one, but I can't take your money." Her gaze averted to the glop moisturizing the asphalt. "It just wouldn't be right."

Funny thing, the R-word. In theory, it was an absolute. In practice? Baskin-Robbins should have as many flavors.

"Some sales rep I am," Hannah said with a chuckle. "What people never have enough of, I can't give away today."

"Beg pardon?"

Hannah removed the fifty from the cosmetics bag. "My company draws names at random and awards a cash prize or a month's supply of our products. Mrs. Lydia Quince is today's winner, but no one answered the phone or the door."

"No, I'd expect not." The young woman shivered and tucked the quilt tighter around her child. "You not being from around here, I guess you don't know..."

Arms crossed, she nodded at the house. "Lydia and Stuart split up a while back, then the other night, he...well, it depends on which story you hear, but...he either killed himself right in front of the sheriff, or tried to kill the sheriff and got himself shot dead, or the sheriff killed him in cold blood."

She went on at a clip IdaClare Clancy would envy. "Me and Joe Donald—that's my husband—we heard the shot, only we thought it was Kyle Earley's car back-firing. He lives at the end of the street and it does that sometimes when he slows down at the corner and the clutch slips.

"I was thanking my lucky stars the noise didn't wake up Cora Ann 'cause me and Joe Donald were…" Eyes widening, she let out a squeal. "Well, you know, it *was* Friday night and all…then, my Lord, there was lights and sirens and deputies at the door and Stuart laid out on the undertaker's gurney and that was the end of what me and Joe Donald had in mind."

Hannah said, "I'd have been scared to death."

"Still am." The woman stared ahead toward the Earleys.

"This is the first time since that me and the baby have gone for our walk. I like taking her this way, 'cause once the Earley boys go by after school, there's no cars to watch out for."

Looking up at Hannah, she said, "Shames me to tell you, but the thought of walking by that house had me all goose-bumpy again. Then what'd I go and do? Gave a yell and scared you worse'n I was."

"Follow me around the neighborhood," Hannah teased, slipping the grand prize back in its hiding place, "then when I drop another one I can blame you instead of my clumsiness."

"Really? You want me and Cora Ann to tag along?"

Oh, great. Wonderful. Ever think of doing stand-up, Ms. Garvey? With a mouth like yours, you could go places.

"Gosh, miss, that's awful nice of you, but Joe Donald says if I let spooks keep me from my pleasure walks, next thing, I'll be sleeping with the lights on.''

Her eyes darted to the house and back again. "Truly, it isn't ghosts I'm afraid of.'' Her fingers curled around the stroller's pushbar. "It's renting *Lethal Weapon* 'cause it's Joe Donald's favorite, then whoosh, it's like the movie is playin' in my yard and a deputy's tellin' us the sheriff killed the guy next door and that we should go back inside where it's safe.''

The stroller's wheels cheeped into motion. Voice quavering, she said, "Except it doesn't feel safe anymore, and if it isn't, no place else is.''

Her tennis shoes struck the pavement heel first, as though it was the enemy she was determined to conquer.

IdaClare and Company had been founded on the same vulnerability, anger and resentment. Catching a murderer was supposed to restore the sense of security they'd felt at Valhalla Springs, but fewer cars passed Hannah's cottage at night, foot traffic ceased when dusk fell and Malcolm wasn't the only four-legged new resident in Paradise.

Sad, but... Hannah cocked her head, then turned.

"Excuse me, but did you say a *deputy* told you 'the sheriff killed the guy next door'?''

The woman slowed, squinting over her shoulder at Hannah.

"That's what he told Joe Donald when he went outside to see what was going on.''

"The same deputy who questioned you later?''

"No, it was...'' She stopped, a fist landing on her hip. "Hey, why all the questions? Who are you anyway?''

"Just curious." Heat raced up Hannah's neck and face, the curse of the auburn-haired and fair-complexioned. "It seemed like an odd thing for a deputy to say, that's all."

If strollers had clutches, the woman's would have slipped and backfired on takeoff.

Interesting. Maybe even a pattern, unless coincidences came in threes, as well. Could it be that pieces of pieces of the puzzle had lurked in every theory and supposition she and the gumshoes had batted around her breakfast room?

Pertinent mental pictures scrolled by. Motive? Fuzzy, but if correct, it teetered between absurd and brilliant. Opportunity? Absolutely, unless an alibi proved otherwise. Fifty bucks cash said whatever it was, it couldn't be corroborated.

No time for tangents. No conclusion jumping. Save them to brainstorm with David later.

A berobed, middle-aged woman clung to 5402's doorframe like a shipwreck survivor to flotsam. Her bowels were irritable, her tinnitus maddening and if tachycardia didn't do her in, the horseshoe kidneys she was born with would.

Backpedaling for all she was worth, Hannah bid her a good day, which, for a hypochondriac, would be a severe allergic reaction to the lotion.

The question of whether to ride or hoof it around to the next street was answered by Cora Ann's mother turning into the Earleys' driveway. Hannah suspected the notes they'd trade wouldn't be of the automotive persuasion.

There was no stream within miles of Streamside Circle, which wasn't circular. Houses on the far side faced

the back of the Quinces', but proximity won the toss.
Hannah swung open the door for another knees-
together Gumby-slither to the ground, demonstrating
why skirts and trucks were diametrically opposed.

The hypochondriac's back-door neighbors had
moved without benefit of selling their house, which
seemed oddly significant. The gridlocked driveway of
5405 should have tipped Hannah off to a canasta game
in progress.

"Free samples and money, too?" the hostess
squealed, unscrewing the lid for a sniff. "Ooh, doesn't
that smell lush? Gimme four of them, sweetie. The
girls'll be thrilled to have them for table prizes."

Well, hell.

"Lydia Quince?" She tapped a finger on her lips.
"Sure it isn't Quincy? I went to school in Little Rock
with a Kathy Quincy, but I don't know any Lydias."

Rosie O'Donnell's laughter met Hannah at the walk-
way to 5407 and leaped ten decibels when a one-armed
man opened the door. "Holy moley. Hang up on a
telemarketer and I'll be jiggered if the Avon lady don't
ring the bell."

Hannah explained who she wasn't. He grudgingly
aimed a remote at the television, then holstered the de-
vice in his suspenders. "Jes' what the wife needs—
more junk clutterin' up the bathroom. Ain't got nowhere to set my shavin' cream as 'tis."

The Lydia Quince spiel didn't improve his disposi-
tion. "If that don't beat all. Whiniest creature God ever
stuck mammaries on. Ups and goes home to momma
right when Stu's 'bout to get himself straight, then he
bites a bullet and she wins fifty smackers for
breathin'."

Hannah gasped. "Do you mean Mr. Quince is...?"

"Ye-ap. Ol' Stu met his maker 'long about eight, eight-thirty Friday night. The cops was still pawin' 'round when me and the missus got home from bowling."

He shook his head. "Why, if I'da known Stu was gonna check out, I'da called for a beer frame in his honor."

"Stuart Quince was a no-account, money-grubbing leech," said the exhausted-looking mother of twin girls at 5409, "and if you ask me, Lydia's one of those enablers. *Ladies' Home Journal* had this article a while back, I just *know* was them. It didn't use real names and Lydia wouldn't admit it when I asked her, but it *was*."

At the rumble, screech, ba-room of a schoolbus wheeling around the corner, the twins made a break for the door. Not missing a beat, their mother jailed them with her legs. "I felt sorry for Lydia for a time. Always fretting over Stuart's 'disability.' Making excuses for his drinking, for losing another job—you name it."

She clucked her tongue. "I could have told her he'd do something crazy. Not because he was, mind you. For the attention. If you ask me, it's a miracle he didn't take her with him."

Hannah said, "From what I've heard, Friday night must have been awful for all of you. Gunshots and sirens and..." She widened her eyes. "Your children must have been terrified."

"Uh-uh, it was cool." A blond, chocolate-mustachioed boy of about seven slam-dunked his backpack on the stoop. "I'm gonna be a policeman when I grow up."

"Last week it was a baseball player."

"Billy, Billy," the prisoners chanted. "We wanna play wif Billy."

"Was not," he told his mother. "I said I *might* be a baseball player, *then* I'd be a policeman." The stare he'd leveled at Hannah narrowed to a squint. "How come you're here talking to my mom?"

"I'm giving away samples of hand lotion." She smiled.

"Sorry it isn't something good, like candy."

"Candy, candy. We want candy, Mommy, ple-e-e-ase."

"Oops." Hannah grimaced. "Poor choice of words."

"Believe me, if you'd said rat poison, they'd be begging for it." She pushed the storm door wider. "C'mon, Billy, get your backpack and go play with your sisters. I'll fix you a snack in a minute."

Eyes locked on Hannah, he folded his arms at his chest. "That's okay, Mom. I'm not hungry."

"I didn't ask if you were hungry." A threat edged the tone mothers resort to in front of company. "I told you to come in and play with Ashley and Erica."

Billy stomped past her and she mouthed, "He's gifted," over the top of his head, as if that explained anything.

Hannah made the requisite "That's wonderful, how proud you must be" nods and smoothed her hair, her mind rummaging for a prompt to resume the conversation.

The house sat diagonal to the Quinces'; its backyard abutted the undeveloped lot. The windows at the back had been lit when Hannah was waiting in David's cruiser, griping to herself about being bored and left out.

The trickle-down theory as it applies to family dynamics guaranteed that Billy-the-Oppressed would pick a fight with his smaller sisters.

"I'm sorry, you'll have to excuse me," their mother said as the phone rang in the background. Gesturing exasperation, she whirled around, barking orders. The storm door's pneumatic hinge baffled the melee, then contained it.

Hannah stepped away, studying her clipboard as though an excuse to pester the woman further would reveal itself. The best she could divine was to ply her wares at the last two houses, then return to search for her bracelet—a family heirloom with a fickle clasp. A segue to the shooting would be tricky, but she'd already aggravated one Whispering Pines mother today. May as well give the grapevine plenty to buzz about.

Whoever ordained sidewalks an unnecessary amenity in the burbs clearly didn't consider or didn't care about children forced to skateboard and ride bikes in the street—or spies disguised as salespeople pounding the pavement in lotion-gooey high heels.

A feeling of being watched invaded Hannah's thoughts. She glanced back. Nothing. *Jeez, will you get a grip? You hate sleeping with the lights on.*

Senses on red alert, she strode toward 5411, masking a sudden self-consciousness with feigned nonchalance.

Muffled footsteps. Glimpsed movement. Hmm. Awfully solid for a spook. Slowing, turning, scanning her backtrail, Hannah stopped—and grinned at a lidded, rubberized garbage can. It had not only transported itself from beside 5409's garage door, but a cute little blue-jeaned butt was sticking out from behind it.

Two steps into a stationary moonwalk and a blond head emerged like a prairie dog from its burrow. Again, there was a stare, the scowl, arms akimboed and the hip cocked.

Detective Andrik, I have seen the future and its name is Billy.

"You're a cop, aren'cha." Statement, not a question.

"A cop?" She chuckled. "No, I'm just a sales—"

"I saw you in Mr. Quince's yard with that deputy and the sheriff." The boy's lips pursed. "You leaned on his race car, too. If Mr. Quince hadn't been dead, he'd have yelled bad words at you. Nobody touched that car, 'cept him."

Hannah sucked in a deep breath. "Is it okay if I come closer so we can talk?" She raised a palm. "You have to promise it's just between us though."

His "okay" had a sore lack of conviction.

Squatting down to his eye level, she said, "I'm not a cop, Billy, but I am a very good friend of Sheriff Hendrickson's. He's in a lot of trouble because of what happened the other night and I'm trying to help him."

"How come you lied to my mom?"

"Well, since I'm not a cop, I have no authority to ask questions," she answered. "I guess I could have lied and said I was, but…well, that seemed like a much worse lie than the one I told your mom."

His head waggled, signifying he understood the finer points of prevarication.

"And just because cops are the good guys, doesn't mean people are as comfortable talking to them as a door-to-door saleslady."

"Grown-ups are dumb sometimes if you ask me." Blue eyes half-hidden by thick lashes, said Hannah was no exception. "When Josh—I mean, Detective Phelps—came over after? My dad kept going 'eh-eh, eh-eh,' like he had strep throat or something."

Hannah sneaked a glance at the house. Ashley's and Erica's silhouettes darkened the storm door's lower panel. Hell hath no fury like a little sister scorned. In stereo.

"What did your dad tell Detective Phelps?"

"I dunno." Billy sawed a thumb in his jeans pocket.

Other than having been one, Hannah didn't know anything about children. Her friends' kids were either squirmy, nonstop noisemakers or could have starred in *Return of the Body Snatchers.*

"I got grounded to my room," Billy said, "'cause I didn't come in when Mom called, 'cause I couldn't find my catcher's mitt. She was talking on the phone to Grandma and it got dark, then Dad got home and asked Mom where I was."

He drew lazy circles on the dusty lid of the garbage can. Voice quieting as if thinking aloud, he said, "How was I s'posed to know dumb ol' Ashley hid my glove in the playhouse? I was looking and looking, then a man said something kinda loud, then *ka-kaboom.*"

Creases etched his forehead. A gunshot was reverberating in his mind, as it had in Hannah's, except she was a grown woman and he was just a little boy. "I'm sorry, Billy. I never should have asked—"

"I played possum," he said. "That's what our D.A.R.E. officer said to do if somebody came to our school with guns."

Jesus. When Hannah was his age, it was civil defense

drills and mushroom-cloud nightmares. Now it was school-shooting drills and six o'clock news nightmares.

"It was real, real quiet for like, an hour? And I thought it was okay to get up, then that policeman ran out of Mr. Quince's house, so I waited till he was gone 'cause he'd tell Mom I was outside and I'd get in trouble."

Billy made a face. "Then my dad came looking for me and I got grounded anyhow."

Hannah's pulse tripped over itself. "You're sure it was a policeman that ran out of Mr. Quince's house?"

"Well, yeah." He gave her a "just because I'm a kid doesn't mean I'm stupid" look. "He had on his suit and everything."

"His suit? Do you mean he was in uniform?"

"Uh-huh. Except for his gun. I think that's why he was running. 'Cause he forgot it or something."

"You're sure about that, too?"

"Y-ees-s-s."

"I *believe* you, Billy."

"No you don't."

"Oh yes I do." How do you convince a child who caught you lying that you're telling the truth? "What you're telling me is very, very important. That's the only reason I keep asking if you're sure."

He frowned and picked at his pants leg. "Mom and Dad always believe Ashley and Erica 'cause there's two of them. It's not fair, never having anybody on my side."

Dish towel in hand, his mother started from the house, her expression a stew of concern, curiosity and anxiety.

Hannah asked, "The policeman you saw, do you think you'd recognize him if you saw him again?"

Tipping his head, he looked at her warily. "Do I have to be sure again?"

"As sure as you can be, Billy."

"What's going on here?" his mother demanded.

"How come?" he asked. "You know him. He was the policeman you were talking to in Mr. Quince's yard."

20

Hannah's foot rode the brake pedal as she drove down MacMillan Street.

Three uniformed deputies had been in Quince's yard the night of the shooting. One of them had framed David. She didn't know why. *How* was a plausible guess. *Who* was a stone-chiseled certainty.

All she needed was proof.

Andrik had been out of the office when she'd called, after a long talk with Billy's mother. Hannah had thumbed more coins into the pay phone and was punching the detective's cell-phone number, when she'd stopped, clapped the receiver on the hook, and reached for the directory chained to the carrel.

A hunch and a seven-year-old child's observations weren't enough to stay a grand jury proceeding. Andrik and Pike would investigate, but denial was the suspect's ace in the hole.

"I need a trump card," she said, straining to read a street sign obscured by a branch, "and I don't give a damn what I have to do to get it."

Grassy parkways, majestic trees and concrete retaining walls dated the neighborhood as early 1950s. Detached garages were built in an era when wives tied scarves around their pin curls and jitneyed husbands to work on days they borrowed the family car for errands.

By the rearview mirror decorations and the type of vehicles snugged against the curbstones, Mom and Dad still had dibbies on off-street parking. Intent on counting off house numbers, the green Toyota and the man bending over its trunk didn't register with Hannah for a moment.

When it did, she gulped, whipped a left onto Sixth Avenue, then made an illegal U-turn at the next intersection. Approaching MacMillan Street again, she halted when the Toyota's roof was in sight.

Her fingers drummed the window ledge. Give me thirty minutes. You can get lost for that long, can't you? C'mon, be a sport.

A disembodied head bobbed above the roof of the car, looked left to right, then vanished, as though he'd stepped into an airshaft. Hannah inched forward as the Toyota swung from the curb. When its taillights shrank to red hyphens, she crossed MacMillan and parked at the corner.

Time for the Lotion Lady's final performance, this one, for all the marbles. Condors took wing behind her waistband. Oh, good, Hannah thought. You're supposed to be psyching yourself up, not psyching yourself out.

With lip gloss replenished and a practice smile for the mirror, Hannah put the fifty-dollar bill in her wallet, then changed her mind. Her ''where's Lydia?'' intro was null and void, but the cash might come in handy for her new cover story. It was hard to say, since she didn't have one yet.

Favoring blistered pinkie toes and heels, she called

on the corner house for appearance's sake. Mail in its ribbed glass box and two newspapers yellowing in the yard informed both salespeople and burglars of its un-occupied condition.

Chin high and hoping her expression was closer to friendly than a death rictus, Hannah marched up the shallow steps from the sidewalk to the next house.

Immaculate green AstroTurf carpeted the porch. No dust would begrime a gloved finger swiped across the lifetime-guaranteed siding. Hannah twisted the Swedish doorbell's key, envisioning furniture shrouded in plastic slipcovers and industrial-strength cans of Lysol stockpiled in the pantry.

"Yes?" The lady of the house's jowly smile was as counterfeit as Hannah's. With crimped, postmaturely brown hair, a lick of gray at the crown, trifocals, a lawn-chair print top and navy slacks, she looked like a teacher known to generations as the Dragon Lady.

Hannah held up the sample bottle and dollar bill and was in her pitch's second stanza when the woman said, "Your solicitor's permit. Show it to me."

"Excuse me?"

"Door-to-door hucksters have to register at the clerk's office and pay ten dollars for a permit. City ordinance number 265-74." Her nostrils flared.

"The penalty for scofflaws is a five-hundred-dollar fine or thirty days in jail."

Pleading ignorance didn't work on those who lived life as though their panties were three sizes too small. Hannah said, "Well, actually, I'm not selling anything. Just giving away free—"

Lotion and cash disappeared. *Slam.* Lock tumblers clicked. Panes rattled in the windows' frames.

Staring at the steel-reinforced door as if it were a mirage, a pathetic little "hey" tiptoed out of Hannah's mouth.

The old bat had ripped her off. In broad daylight. In front of God and everybody. Hannah turned around in search of witnesses. Okay, in front of God and nobody. It was still petty larceny. Eight'll get you ten, the thief's guest bathroom had a toilet-paper cozy embroidered with the golden rule, too.

Hinges squeaked behind her. The snatch-and-run artist reappeared in the doorway, massaging lotion into her dishpan hands. "The best lessons are the hardest learned, I always say."

Um, such as, the hand is quicker than the eye?

"Just so you won't think I'm a mean old woman, the law is no trifling matter in this house." She struck a regal pose. "My boy is a deputy with the Kinderhook County Sheriff's Department."

Her "boy" was an unpaid reservist and at least a decade beyond puberty, but Hannah couldn't have acted more impressed if he'd been president-elect. "You and your husband must be very proud of him."

"Hah! *That* worthless excuse for a man left us when the child wasn't but three years old. I'm the one that saw to his raising." She gazed heavenward. "I don't mind telling you, whatever he makes of himself, he has me to thank for it."

"Oh, there's no doubt about that." Hannah relaxed her stance and switched on a high-octane smile. "I'm a single mother, too, and—"

"Hmmph. Easier these days than it was in mine. Nobody'd ever heard of day care. The government didn't dole out checks and food stamps then, either."

Ye gods. If they'd burned this woman at the stake with Joan of Arc, she'd tell Saint Peter her side of the fire was hotter.

"As I was about to say, my son, er, Malcolm, is also interested in a law enforcement career."

"Oh, he is, eh?"

"I don't know how serious he is, but—" Hannah made a fluttery gesture "—I'm terrified of guns. The idea of sitting down at the dinner table with Malcolm wearing one scares me to death."

"The boy's under your roof?"

"Uh…yes."

"Mollycoddled him, haven't you? And folks wonder why young people aren't worth the powder it'd take to blow 'em up. Spare the rod, spoil the child."

Hannah bristled at the insult to her parenting skills. Reality checked in with a belated reminder her son was a dog.

Smug understated the woman's expression. "No firearms of any kind have ever been allowed in my house. Not that I'm afraid of them. Fear is an excuse for cowardice. I simply will not abide the filthy things, any more than I'd keep the lawn mower in my boo-doy-yeh."

A thoughtful pause was needed to convert "boo-doy-yeh" into *boudoir*. With it came a keener understanding of how *Aux Arcs* had transmuted into *Ozarks*.

"Of course, if I'd had my way," she went on, "Rudy would've been a doctor. Came home from school every day crying like a girl about being bullied, then says he wants to be a deputy? That's the Moody side for you. Dreamers, every one. Want what they can't have and deaf to what's good for them."

Hannah said, "Medicine is an honorable profession, but so is law enforce—"

"Honorable?" She laughed, a bitter cawing sound. "You aren't from around here, are you?"

"Southern Illinois." Nice to be truthful now and then.

"Well, you can take it from Chlorine Moody, there's no honor in it in this county. Not since Larry Beauford went to Jesus and Mr. High-and-Mighty Hendrickson took his place—as if he could, on his best day."

Hannah's toes curled under inside her shoes. *Careful. Don't trump yourself. Keep your mouth shut and let Mrs. Moody vent her dirtiest.*

"Really? How did this Hendrickson fellow get the job?"

"I hear his daddy bought his promotion from chief deputy. Can't say it's true, but why else would the commissioners hire an outsider, when there's better men here at home?"

Removing her glasses, she huffed on the lenses. "Lord, it almost broke Rudy's heart the night he found Larry slumped over the steering wheel in his car."

The hem of her overblouse substituted for a cleaning cloth. "The boy idolized that man since he was little, playing cops and robbers in the yard. Larry promised to make him a deputy when he grew up and Rudy stuck with the academy until he graduated." She chuffed. "Closest thing to ambition the boy's ever shown.

"You'd have thought he'd won Powerball when Larry took him on as a reserve. Said Rudy needed more experience—time to learn the ropes before he hired him outright. I tried to tell him Larry was stalling, but did Rudy listen? Hah."

Glasses replaced, her eyes softened from rusted iron to the crayon shade kids used for tree trunks. "That night, Rudy got Larry to the hospital as fast as he could, but..." She shook her head. "A massive stroke, the doctor said. If they'd saved him, Larry'd have been a vegetable."

Alarms tolled in Hannah's mind, some loud, others audible but indistinct. "Is that when—what was his name? Hendrickson?—took over as sheriff?"

"Took over is right. Started running things like it was the academy again. Weight training. Obstacle courses. Missing church to go to the firing range. Told Rudy he had to shape up or ship out."

Hannah said, "And your son put up with all that? I can't imagine."

"Oh, Hendrickson made up to Rudy at first. Called and invited him to go jogging or target practicing. Rudy thought he was taking a special interest—like Larry Beauford always had."

Mrs. Moody sneered and tapped her bosom. "I knew better. All Hendrickson was doing was showing Rudy up. Making him look foolish in front of the whole town, hoping he'd quit. The harder my boy tried to please him, the more that man hounded him. Said there was no room for mistakes in his department."

The vile laugh rattled out again. "Right he was. No room for the sheriff to make mistakes, either. It'll be somebody else's department soon enough. A born-here, not a strutting, trigger-happy foreigner."

Hannah's jaw ached from the pressure being exerted on it.

"Like I tell Rudy, with Beauford gone and Hendrickson about to be…'' Chlorine smiled. ''Well, you ever hear of 'third time being charm' up Illinois-way?''

''Absolutely.'' Hannah couldn't care less if vindictiveness showed in her face, her voice, her slitted eyes. ''In fact, I'm counting on it.''

A rubber-soled oxford planted itself on the Blazer's floorboard. A hand clenched the seat belt's buckle like a pommel. Delbert bounced on his land-based foot, then heaved himself into the passenger seat like Dudley Do-Right mounting his horse, Horse.

He grunted something about femi-Nazis. Fidgeted. Adjusted his knitted cap. Yanked the shoulder harness. ''I wouldn't have a car I needed a ding-danged step-ladder to get into.''

Hannah shifted into reverse. ''Neither would I.''

His scowl lacked conviction. ''At least you had sense enough to leave that cow dog at home and wear black, like I told you to.''

They passed her cottage, which a bathed, sweet-smelling Malcolm had to himself. She'd left the TV on for company, with strict orders to sit on the floor to watch it. Visions of Malcolm stretched out on the couch with a beer in one paw and the remote in the other floated through Hannah's mind. He was, after all, a guy dog.

As for her clothing choice, the black turtleneck sweater and stirrup pants were already laid out on the bed when she'd phoned Delbert to propose a couple of felonious activities.

He, too, was in basic black. Hannah said, ''We look like father and daughter cat burglars.''

''Ever see *To Catch A Thief?*''

"About as many times as I've driven Highway VV to and from Sanity today."

"Well, there're two differences between us and the movie."

She grinned. "You're no Cary Grant and I'm no Grace Kelly?"

"You're half-right, but that's not what I meant." Delbert pulled his duffel bag from the floorboard into his lap. "First off, this caper's at ground level. No chance of breaking our necks falling off a roof."

"A definite plus."

"Ah, but here's the kicker." He flipped down the sun visor. "We're not gonna get caught."

Hannah wished he hadn't said that. Too much was at stake to tempt fate.

The passenger-side visor thumped against the headliner. He angled the rearview mirror toward him. A shallow gold tin glinted in the dash light.

"Delbert." Oncoming traffic demanded her attention.

"Quit messing with my mirror."

"Just watch where you're going, Grace," he said out one side of his mouth. "Where we've been will take care of itself."

How Zen. Also true, considering their downhill approach to a stretch known as the Devil's Backbone. Hannah's grip tightened on the steering wheel.

An eon ago, when David's first name was Sheriff and her best guess at the middle one was Ticket-Happy Jerk Face, he'd called her a "flatlander." For reasons either egregious or erotic, she'd never remembered to ask why more natives than passers-through got their clocks cleaned between Valhalla Springs and the county seat.

A familiar, rather pleasant but not quite identifiable smell drifted from the passenger seat. *Ominous* was always attached to *silence* when it applied to Delbert.

Her sidelong glance was less than edifying. Highway department statistics showed that outright head-turning looks at fifty-some miles per hour, particularly on dark, roller-coasterish roads, had the nasty habit of being fatal.

"What *are* you doing over there?" she asked.

"What do you *think* I'm doing?" Delbert's tone suggested her IQ had shrunk. "I'm adapting my physiognomy to a low-light surveillance environment."

Well, of course. How silly of her. The sweetish, waxy aroma was shoe polish and where else would Delbert be putting it than on his goofy old kisser?

"You expect me to drive through town with you in blackface?"

"Why not?" A two-beat pause. "Nobody's gonna see me, ladybug."

Oh, Lord. Buddha. Allah. Ra. Somebody, anybody, save me.

"Probably ought to keep a lip-lock on the conversation, though," he added. "Might draw too much attention if people think you're sitting there talking to yourself."

Forget the traffic rounding yonder bend. Her initial single take compelled a double, then a triple. A pair of eyes googled back at her like Ping-Pong balls.

Her mouth snapped shut. Choo-choo sounds puffed out her nose. Vital organs threatened to rupture. Don't laugh. *Do not laugh.* Thousands live long fruitful lives without their spleens.

"Are you laughing at me?"

"Um-um."

"You sure?"

"Um-hmm."

Sanity's mercury-vapor-lit aura rose and fell with the pavement's gradation. Hannah would have given anything for a dash-mounted video camera. The townies' expressions when they scoped the Invisible Geezer would be worth maxing out every credit card she owned.

The shoe-polish tin clanked into the duffel. "Plenty of goop left for you when we get there." Delbert twisted the rearview mirror toward her. "That about right?"

"Uh-huh." The argument about her lily-pale physiognomy staying that way could wait.

As if it weren't disappointing enough that no one along the main drag seemed to notice the almost sexagenarian throwback to minstrel shows, a cruise down MacMillan Street revealed a marked absence of Toyotas.

After circling the block, Hannah shoehorned the Blazer into a motorcycle-size gap at the corner, opposite from where she'd parked earlier that afternoon.

Delbert proferred the can of shoe polish before she'd switched off the ignition. "Thanks, but I'll take my chances au naturel."

"You're going to duck every time a car comes by?"

"Yes," she answered. "And so are you."

"The hell I will." He waved a pair of sunglasses.

"I slip these on and the whites of my eyes won't even show."

Hannah jerked a thumb at the side window. "Hate to tell you, but headlights from that direction will outline us like shadow puppets on a blank wall." She pivoted her wrist. "Then there's the ever-popular, head-on windshield view."

Delbert leaned forward, peered past her, then sat back. "Correct-o-mundo, ladybug. You aced the Perimeter Sweep Appraisal on the first try."

What an amazing recovery. When it came to CYA, Delbert Bisbee had few equals and no betters. A legend, no doubt, in the annals of postal service history.

"While you do the lookie-looing, I can get in some practice." He removed the lock-pick gun and a bracketed cylindrical object from his bag of tricks. "Hubert Montague's Camry is a newer model, but beggars can't be choosy."

Hannah's gaze shifted from the lock assembly in his hand to his stygian leer. "You didn't... You wouldn't..." A gentle throb commenced at her brow. "You did, didn't you?"

Tumblers clicked and clacked with purloined glee. Delbert said, "I'll put it back on Hubie's trunk before he ever knows it was missing."

She plopped an elbow on the window ledge and tried not to think of the irony in exonerating David and spending the next, say, twenty to twenty-five years of her life in jail.

He'd called earlier, waking her from a surprisingly dreamless nap. A prehearing strategy session with his attorney had started at midmorning. An assistant was due back any minute with carryout orders of cashew chicken for supper.

"I just needed to hear your voice, sugar."

His own plowed into her like a fist. "You've given up, haven't you?"

"Gotta be realistic. Lucas says we have a decent shot at an acquittal when the case goes to trial, but an indictment is as sure as sunrise."

"No, it isn't, David. I don't believe in sure things, forever or coincidences."

"I'm with you on the first and third. Forever, I wouldn't mind believing in again." A weary chuckle preceded, "There's a thing or two I'd like to exclude from it though."

"I refuse to dignify that with a response, Hendrickson."

Male voices echoed in the background. One of them called David's name. "Be right there," he said away from the receiver, then spoke into it. "How do you always know what I need to hear when I need to hear it most?"

Because I'm definitely in like with you, and maybe, just maybe, a little in love with you, you big, dumb, wonderful dork snagged on the lump in her throat. She'd managed to say, "The same way you do."

"Same way I do what?" Delbert asked.

Hannah started. "Nothing. Just thinking out loud."

"Guess that explains why you didn't let out a peep when those two cars went past."

She bolted upright. The space in front of the Moody house was still vacant.

"Both came from the other direction," Delbert allowed, "but if they'd turned this way..."

"I'm sorry." She scrubbed her face with her hands. "It won't happen again."

They hit the deck five times in the next hour, the last due to the corner house's residents' homecoming. From back to front, light splashed out windows onto bushes, trees and porch boards. Curtains whisked shut behind some but not all.

Delbert spoke for them both when he said, "That, we didn't need."

A pair of halogen high beams pierced the darkness to Hannah's left. "Prepare to submerge, Captain. And for variety's sake, can we do it without conking heads for once?"

The car progressed at a breakneck five miles an hour. A brilliance akin to an alien mother-ship docking suffused the cab of the Blazer. Cheek pressing Delbert's fossilized hipbone, Hannah flipped unseen birds at the vehicle on behalf of everyone who'd been blinded by those miniature kliegs.

Which included her. Certainty struck with almost physical force. Quince's driveway. Deputy Cahill hooking her arm, pulling her out of harm's way.

"It's Moody." She confirmed her sixth sense with a peek over the passenger window's ledge.

Delbert said, "Stay down till he starts for the house," which begged the question how would she know when he did if she wasn't watching?

The car eased into the open space at the curb with a finesse she grudgingly envied. Upon exiting, the driver rolled his shoulders. He looked south, then north, as though broadcasting Mr. Badass was here and ready to rumble.

Doubt seeped into Hannah like a sodden gray fog.

The reservist was a dull-witted, brown-nosing buffoon. A mama's boy—of the indentured servitude kind, not the doted-on Prince Charming, Valiant and William combined.

Framing David for manslaughter was not a premeditated act. The perpetrator needed cunning and guts to capitalize on a split-second opportunity.

Hannah's prime suspect tripped over the curbstone, then ambled across the parkway. She shoved herself upright.

"Okay, so, now how long do we have to wait?"

Delbert's shoe-blacked eyebrow arched at her tone. "We don't."

"Oh." Her adrenal glands responded instantly. "But he just got home."

"Well, since somebody didn't bring her scanner to plug into the cigarette lighter, we don't know if he's taking a break or in for the night, either."

"I'd have brought my scanner if somebody had told me to." Hannah fumbled in the console for her gloves and penlight. "I might even have thought of it myself if somebody had told me it had an A/C adapter."

"My mistake." The lock-pick gun clunked on the dash. "I keep forgetting you're an amateur."

A long-barreled flashlight joined his illegal burglary tool. The shoe-polish tin brinked the bag's placket. Delbert glanced sideward, shook his head and dropped it back inside. The bag slid from his lap to the floorboard.

"Ready?"

"10–4." Hannah reached for her keys.

"Uh-uh. Leave 'em in the ignition. Keep your finger off the door-lock button, too."

Pulse and respiration broke from a trot to a dizzying gallop. "Gotcha."

"While I jimmy the trunk, you watch the house. Once it's open, I'll bird-dog for you. Anything happens, run like hell. *Capiche?*"

"But what if—"

"Get your butt out of the truck, Grace." He cringed at the overhead light. "And don't slam the goddamn door."

By his example, Hannah bent double and jogged behind him down the sidewalk. Leaves rustled in the breeze. A radio announcer took exception to an umpire's strike call. Windows in surrounding houses glowed like jack-o'-lanterns. Up and down both sides of MacMillan, telephone keypads chirped 911.

She swiped a glove across her forehead. *Jeez Louise, will you cool it already?*

The Moodys' porch light was off. A stroke of luck, that. Curtains closed. Ditto. Toward the back, light shafted from a higher side window, probably the kitchen.

Delbert crouched behind the Toyota's rear bumper. Hannah stepped to the driver's side and flicked on the penlight. A supernova burst off the glass.

Holy crap. You have a brain. Use it, for God's sake.

Cardiac arrest arrested, she pressed the penlight's rim against the window, shielding it with her hand. A case of moist towelettes shared the back seat with a box of Moon Pies, a pair of binoculars and a three-ring binder.

Metal snicked and rattled. Delbert cursed under his breath.

The front-seat area was as showroom clean as it had been Friday night. The half-dollar-size beam lingered on the glove box as though it were a cyclops X-ray machine. Didn't she wish.

No change at the Moodys' domain. Mark McGwire went down swinging somewhere in baseball-land. A block down, a pickup made a rolling stop at the corner, then passed through the intersection. A disembodied voice called, "Here, Sparky. C'mere, boy."

Thirty seconds. Sixty at the outside, before she peed her pants or started screaming. Maybe both.

Click. "Hot-ziggety."

Light gushed from the trunk. *Crunch.* Darkness fell. Delbert whispered, "Watch that glass while you're poking around."

"What'd you do? Smash the bulb?"

"Worked, didn't it?" His flashlight banged her knuckles. "Here. Go for broke and make it fast."

One pan of the larger, brighter beam and Hannah forgot how to exhale. A wooden rack subdivided the trunk into compartments. Light played over an assault rifle. A machine pistol. Not one, but *four* revolvers. Shit.

Delbert examined them with the penlight. "A .22. Two .38s. Another .22. Wrong calibers."

Clips. Cartridge boxes. A carton stamped Pepper Spray. Night-vison scopes. Audio- and visual-monitoring devices. Video cameras from handheld to palm-size.

Delbert's fingers curled clawlike over the equipment. "Might as well be hanged for stealing a horse as a mule."

She swatted his hand. "You're supposed to be bird-dogging for me, remember?"

Unmarked boxes held more electronic gizmos, paintball cartridges, batteries of sundry sizes. Why didn't he set up shop with all this stuff?

The porch light flipped on. Hannah froze.

"Let's get outta here," Delbert commanded.

Beam probing the corner of the trunk, Hannah plundered the last boxes, tossing catalogs aside and yanking oily rags from a bucket shoved against the quarter-panel.

The Moodys' front door opened a few inches. "What'd you say, Mom?"

Delbert pushed down on the trunk lid. "C'*mon*."

"No—look." At the bottom of the bucket, partially concealed by a handkerchief, a handgun lay atop sheets of paper ripped from a spiral notebook.

Dear Lydia...

"Grab it and let's go."

Hannah gripped the handle and pulled. *If you'd left the slug where you found it and called me...*

"I'll do it later, Mom, okay? I've got to get back on patrol."

The trunk lid closed with a soft *whump*. Hannah took off a step behind Delbert. No time for stealth. Their every footfall echoed double along the quiet street. Any second, Moody would yell, "Hey, you. Stop or I'll shoot."

They darted around the evergreens smothering the retaining wall at the corner. Delbert reached for the Blazer's door handle.

"No, don't, Del—"

The dome light switched on. Swerving away, Hannah clenched a fistful of Delbert's sleeve. Hauling him around the back of the truck to the street side, she whispcrcd, "Stand even with the tire. Keep your head down."

Scurrying beside the front wheel, Hannah bent at the waist, hands on knees, sucking wind. Terrific safety feature, touch-sensitive door handles, except when you're trying to sneak into your truck without the whole friggin' neighborhood seeing you do it.

No ignition whir gladdened her heart. Moody must have seen the Blazer go Viva Las Vegas—which it still was, God bless General Motors. Had to be curious why, too, since obviously there was no one in it.

The dome light kicked off. Hannah could feel Moody eyeballing the truck. Sensed his indecision. Could be a grand theft auto in progress. Could be faulty wiring. Could be nothing.

It's nothing, she thought—hard and loudly. Who'd steal a vehicle right around the corner from a reserve county deputy's house? The dude'd have to be crazy. You're late going back on patrol anyhow. You can always swing by later. Good plan. *Excellent* plan.

A car door shut. A four-cylinder engine cranked. Delbert tapped Hannah on the shoulder. She went vertical and launched as the Toyota rolled off into the night.

"Pretty smart, lining up with the tires," he said. "Where'd you learn that one?"

"You—" Waste of breath. "In my past life, I was a juvenile delinquent."

He looked down at her hands, then the pavement. "Where's the bucket?"

She pointed south. "It went thataway."

"What! You left it in the car?" A pale blotch appeared where he smited his forehead. "What in the name of Judas Priest did you do that for?"

"Because taking the gun is the same as taking that bullet—only ten times worse. Andrik's got to find it in Moody's possession."

"And how's he going to do that? Tell him it's in the trunk and you have to tell him how *you* know it's there. Then he's got to tell how *he* knew it was there, then the prosecuting attorney says you planted it and your evidence goes *kawoosh*, right in the toilet."

"Yeah, well…" Hannah gnawed a lip. "Then we'll just have to arrange things so Andrik finds it on his own."

Delbert bent backward and googled at the sky. "How? There's no way he can get a search warrant without probable cause."

"I'll call in an anonymous tip."

"That's not enough for a judge to waive the Fourth Amendment." He added helpfully, "The one about illegal search and seizure."

"I know, Delbert." She pondered a moment. "What about all those guns? I don't care if Rudy is a reserve deputy. It can't be legal to have an arsenal in his trunk."

"Same problem. I'm not sure if it applies to cars, but the Supreme Court has ruled a tip that somebody is carrying a concealed weapon isn't probable cause for the cops to search."

"What'd they do that for?"

Delbert gave her a "beats me" gesture. "Without that bucket to show Andrik, David's sunk, ladybug."

"The hell he is." Hannah jerked on the door handle.

"I'll think of something."

"Hmmph." Pin floppy ears on him and Delbert could have been mistaken for a basset hound. "I was afraid you'd say that."

21

Hannah scowled out the windshield. It would be simpler, and less of a pain in the brake pads, to tail Rudy Moody on water than on land. If they were in boats, she'd have an anchor to drop for drag.

Nibbling at a hangnail, she pondered why she wound up with toothmarks on *her* butt every time she tried to take a bite outta crime.

She'd found the bullet. Learned from her previous mistake when she'd found the gun that had fired the bullet. She should be deciding what color convertible she wanted to ride in for the ticker-tape victory parade, but oh no. Now she had to choreograph a Close Encounter of the Andrik Kind with a bucket hidden in the right rear corner of Moody's trunk.

The Blazer's dash clock read 12:24. The grand jury would convene in eight and a half hours.

Pain stabbed her cuticle. She tasted salt. All right, Vampira, Hannah admonished herself. Think faster than the Schmoo in Blue drives or go home and get some sleep before your court appearance.

Delbert snapped his fingers. Sweat and scratching had altered his twinship with Al Jolson to a mildewed, albino-tiger look.

"How 'bout this, ladybug? You give Andrik an

anonymous tip about a methamphetamine lab out in the boonies. Then Leo—no, not with his accent...*IdaClare* can tip our boy Rudy. I'll lay in wait to shoot out Andrik's back tires. When Moody gets there, he'll have to open the trunk to loan him an extra spare.''

Hannah knew she was desperate when she realized she was considering the idea. ''A little drastic, don't you think? Besides, the closest thing you have to a gun is that lock-pick gizmo.''

He swatted air. ''Rosemary'll let me borrow hers.''

''Rosemary Marchetti has a gun?''

''A .345 Magnum long-barrel,'' he reported. ''Her late husband gave it to her on their fortieth wedding anniversary.''

Hannah's breath stitched. Her *late* husband? Memory provided the factoid that Ilario Marchetti had died of complications from diabetes. May he rest in peace. Thank God.

''We've spent hours talking about pistols and shell casings and bullets and Rosemary just sat there, acting as ignorant as the rest of us?''

''She's never fired it. She just keeps it in her nightstand as a deterrent.''

Against what? An Iranian expeditionary force?

''Well?'' Delbert pressed. ''What do you say?''

''No.''

''Why not?''

The Toyota stopped for a flashing red traffic light, the last along Sanity's white way. Hannah veered into a dry cleaner's parking lot. ''Because it's felonious assault on a police officer, property destruction, illegal discharge of a firearm and anything else Andrik could dream up to put you away so long, you'd have to be reincarnated twice to be eligible for parole.''

Delbert folded his arms. "Got any better ideas?"

"No." Hannah ripped off the sock hat and threw it in the back seat. Scratching her scalp, tangling, wadding her hair and not caring how hideous the result, she said, "No better ones. No worse. None whatsoever."

The green vehicle chugged through the intersection. Anger parched her mouth; frustration soured it. Rudy Moody was a shining example of a crappy childhood. Too bad, so sad. Destroying David's life and career weren't divine retributions for the stork dumping Rudy on Chlorine Moody's doorstep.

Except life wasn't fair; the good guys didn't always win or else the bad guys would have found another line of work by now. People got away with murder and lesser crimes every day.

Snatching herself bald-headed wouldn't stop him. She ought to just ram the pudgy little son of a bitch—

The Toyota's left taillight blinked. Hannah stared as though hypnotized, then her eyes slid to the coppery-pink, sodium haze where he was bound.

The Pump 'n Munch was Sanity's only twenty-four hour convenience store. A gold mine, David called it. The owner had contracted with the city police and sheriff's department to supply gasoline at a nominal discount.

Hannah pulled back out on First Street. "How much change do you have on you?"

"Huh?" Delbert made a noise common to the rudely awakened who were unaware they'd nodded off. "I don't have any. Didn't want it jingling, if we had to make a run for it."

She reached behind his seat for her shoulder bag. "Dig out my billfold. There's plenty in the coin compartment and Andrik's business card is in there, too."

Moody glided into the convenience store's driveway.

"Slow down or he's—"

"Be quiet, Delbert. Please. I don't have much time."

The Fountain Plaza's deserted parking lot hoved into view on her right. "I'm dropping you at a pay phone. Call Andrik. Use the numbers on the back of his card. Tell him it's an emergency. Tell him to get to the Pump 'n Munch as fast as he can, but no lights and sirens. Repeat—no lights, no siren."

Price-Slasher's indented facade was a-clutter with newspaper vending machines, nested shopping carts, barbecue grills chained together, stacks of molded-plastic lawn chairs, and—thank God—two phone kiosks that better, by everything sacred and right, be in working order.

"Tell Andrik he *must* act like he's out on an errand," Hannah said. "Needed milk or something. Then you stay put—*I mean it*—until he's on the scene."

She whipped a tight one-eighty. Both of them canted sideward like crash-test dummies. The truck fishtailed to a halt beside the rowed parking blocks.

"Holy mackerel." Delbert grabbed his duffel bag. "Okay, I'll call Andrik. But what if—"

"Get your butt out of the truck, Cary." She grinned. "But you can slam the goddamn door, if you want."

The window glass rattled in its frame.

She pulled away, a dozen emotions chasing through her, none strong enough to withstand an onrushing fear of failure.

Timing was crucial and out of her control. The risks

were off the scale. Why Moody had kept evidence of his crime, Hannah couldn't fathom, but one hitch and he'd know she was on to him. Quince's gun would disappear. David's fate would be sealed.

Truck jouncing through the ruts behind the shopping center, she thumbed the thermostat's slide to heat and the fan toggle to high. Delbert should be delivering the SOS to Andrik by now.

Goosenecked fixtures illuminated every steel-reinforced rear entrance. The lighting satisfied insurance requirements and burglars probably appreciated forgoing the awkwardness of juggling flashlights and lock-picks.

Andrik had better be home. He had *to be home. What if he's out on a call? Then you're screwed. Slam, bam, thank you, ma'am, for finishing what Moody started.*

Let's dispense with the mind games, shall we?

Her knuckle zipped the thermostat lever to max/air.

Industrial-size Dumpsters and Price-Slasher's cardboard baler loomed large. She doused the headlights. Darkness amplified the sound of tires grumbling over rocks and gravel sluices, the cap-gun pops of beer bottles shattering.

Crimson flared in the side mirrors, splashing the supermarket's concrete-block wall. Hannah gasped, cursed and wished she knew which fuse powered the taillights.

Erosion troughed the service alley's sloped, wide-open exit onto First Street. She shifted into park without applying the brakes. The truck clunked, skidded, rocked to a stop. Contrary to what she'd always heard, no parts dropped off, fell out or bayonetted the firewall.

Across the street, Moody was filling his tank on the

county's nickel. She visually scouted for a place to lay her trap.

Bingo.

Sweaty palms chafed her thighs. Anticipation prickled her skin. Her lips bowed into a sly smile. She had Rudy by the short and curlies and he didn't even know it. She couldn't wait to see the look on his face when his world crashed down around—

Hannah's hand fluttered to her mouth. Oh, God. He'd thought the same things, Friday night. Waiting. Watching. Quivering like a cat tensed for the perfect moment to pounce on an unsuspecting bird.

What goes around comes around; a figurative hex on dirty doers. Moody had put a literal spin on it, to punish David for demanding competence. She was about to reverse the helix.

The correlation was discomfiting. Eerie. Necessary.

A Re-Nu Industries semi thundered past. A Windstar. A motorcyle. Moody holstered the nozzle. No unmarked county cars in sight. Hannah looked over her shoulder at Price-Slasher's sidewall, as if Delbert might have spray-painted a high sign on it.

Well, stranger things had happened when Barney Fife Bisbee was left to his own recognizance.

Moody walked toward the store, tugging his billfold from his back pocket. He was in uniform. Surely, he needn't show an ID for the logbook. It must be snack time. Good-o.

Hannah drove across to the parking lot. The clerk and Moody were yukking it up. With the Blazer hugging the far edge of the pavement, she scrunched down in the seat, in accordance with the misbegotten notion that making oneself smaller reduced the size of one's vehicle, as well.

Concrete gave way to hard-packed red clay. Steering wide around refuse bins, barrels and generic, out-of-sight, out-of-mind refuse, she yelped when motion-detector lights mounted under the eaves blindsided her. She floored the accelerator, whipped around the corner of the building, jammed the gearshift into park again and shut off the ignition.

No tattletale brake lights, no engine noise to give her away if the clerk looked out the back door. Smart move for an amateur, she told Delbert, in absentia—to which he countered, in that snide Master Detective tone, "Unless motion detectors are connected to video monitors, ladybug."

Perish the thought.

The Toyota sat refueled and unoccupied. From his post in front of the supermarket, Delbert waved "mission accomplished." Andrik was en route, ETA unknown.

The ignition clicked; the battery indicator glowed like a square-cut ruby. Kill the a/c. Hannah pressed her thumb against the starter ring, thinking, a quick flick of the wrist and we'll have liftoff, lady and gentlemen.

Seconds crawled into a minute. Two. Four. Her head swiveled from the road to the pumps. Travis Tritt's "If I Were a Drinker" whistled through her teeth.

Keys jangled at Moody's sudden appearance. He listed to starboard, intubated by the straw from a giant soda. A jumbo candy bar was cradled in his other hand.

The Blazer's driver-side window slid down. A maroon sedan wheeled into the lot, adding three teenage witnesses to her plot. Oh well.

The Toyota's door slammed. Hannah turned the key the necessary fraction of an inch. Moody stowed his drink. Peeled his candy bar. Started his car.

She shifted into drive.

His headlights snapped on. A fist closed around the gear lever. He eased forward, steering with one hand.

She waited, praying her brake lights didn't trip his peripheral vision.

Moody swung toward the inclined exit. The Blazer humped onto the parking lot. Steering wheel gripped at ten and two o'clock, she gunned the engine, eyes boring into her quarter-size, silver target.

Moody's taillights flashed a millisecond before the Blazer plowed between them. The shoulder harness sliced Hannah's neck, stung her collarbone. The Toyota lurched a yard on impact. The trunk lid creased...and stayed closed.

She sat rigid, paralyzed. *No* screamed in her mind; died in her throat.

Moody's car rolled backward toward the Blazer. A timid kiss of metal on metal. Slowly, his trunk lid yawned open. Bounced on its hinges. Held.

Hannah shut her eyes. Peeked through her lashes. No optical illusions. Yes. *Yes.* Oh, David—

He's not home free yet. Play the hand you dealt.

Shutting off the engine, numb fingers grappling with the seat belt, Hannah hopped out of the truck, rubbery knees almost buckling beneath her.

Moody stumbled from his car, face mottled, expression morphing from shock to fury to fear.

"Officer Moody? Is that you? Omigod, I'm so sorry." Hannah clasped his doughy biceps. "Are you hurt? Please, tell me you're not hurt. We didn't hit that hard, but my truck is so much bigger than your cute little car.''

He shrugged her off, eyes darting to the trunk. "I'm okay.'' He sidled a step.

She blocked, patting his chest with gentle concern, gasping, "Are you sure? You know, a friend of mine was rear-ended once and thought she was fine until a day or two later, and—well, I know it sounds crazy, but it's true, I swear, she wound up in the hospital with a fractured vertebra in her neck.''

"I'm not hurt.'' He edged around her.

C'mon, Andrik.

Beaming a smile, Hannah cut him off at the pass. "Oh, I'm so relieved, but I *insist* you go to the emergency room and be checked over by a doctor. That's what insurance is for, right? And I am. Insured. Full coverage. Major medical. The works.''

Brakes squealed on the adjacent street. Gray Chevy. A Sanity patrol unit riding its bumper. Hurry, damn it.

Moody shoved by her. "Don't worry about it.'' He slammed the trunk. "I'll take care of it myself.''

Hannah yanked his sleeve. "I can't let you do that.''

His hand slipped. The trunk lid raised. "You hit me on purpose, didn't ya? *Didn't ya?*'' He jerked free. *Slam.* "Say one word and I'll kill you, I swear.''

Hannah's eyes met his. He meant it.

Andrik nosed his car into the concrete riser fronting the store. The cruiser parked alongside.

Arms raised in traditional "stick 'em up'' position, the detective groused, "'Go pick up some milk,' the wife tells me. 'Won't take five minutes this time of night.'''

Both his thumbs jerked backward. "Couple of blocks

from the house, Adam–12 gets on my ass for speeding. Pull in here and what do I see? Hannah 'Demolition Derby' Garvey has stomped a deputy with her lean, mean, too-big-for-her machine.''

Pillow-mussed hair stuck out the sides of Andrik's ball cap. A poplin windbreaker, stonewashed jeans, wrinkled, untucked dress shirt and flip-flops completed his attire. "Anybody hurt?"

"I'm not," Hannah answered, "but I'm *very* concerned about Officer Moody. Can you call an ambulance from your car?"

"No!" Moody paled, then wiped his mouth on his shoulder. His splayed left hand trembled with the force he applied to the trunk lid. "I'm fine, okay? No big deal."

He chuckled, machine-gun style. "Been thinking about buying a new car. Now I've got an excuse, right?"

Andrik's expression gave nothing away, but Moody's agitation and his awkward, stiff-armed stance hadn't escaped notice.

The city cop walked up. "What's with you, Rudy?" He assessed the damage. "She smacked you pretty good, boy. I'd be madder'n a wet hen."

Moody's reply was lost in Andrik's murmured, "Nice outfit."

Hannah said, "Black is supposed to be slimming."

"Who called?"

"Who called whom?"

The city cop pivoted. "Ma'am, if this wasn't private property, I'd write you up for careless and imprudent."

"Since it is," Andrik said, "how's about I take it from here?"

"You're out of your jurisdiction."

"Oh? When did this joint secede from Kinderhook County?"

"Anything in the city limits is my territory, Andrik, until and unless assistance from your department is requested."

The veteran detective advanced on the rookie, one hundred and sixty pounds of rumpled, bad-tempered authority figure. "Listen up, _kemosabe_. I'm a _county_ law enforcement officer. One individual involved in this 10–76 is a reserve _county_ deputy. The gasoline sloshing in said deputy's vehicle is financed with _county_ tax money."

Andrik scratched a stubbled jaw. "That adds up to county—three, city—zip. Hit the showers, sport."

The younger man blustered, "Chief Rhodes will hear about this from my watch commander."

Andrik gestured an unmistakable "Like I give a shit." Aloud, he said, "Hey, let's be careful out there."

He fished a lighter and a pack of Marlboros from his jacket pocket. "Okay, Ms. Garvey. You admit to being a woman driver, is that correct?"

"Yes." He'd pay for that later.

Exhaling, he asked, "Tried starting your vehicle?"

She frowned, thinking, what's _my_ truck got to do with anything? "No, but I'm sure it will. It's barely scratched."

"Humor me. And back 'er up while you're at it."

She complied as instructed, stepping from the cab just as Andrik said, "Your turn, Moody."

He fidgeted. Licked his lips. Stammered, "I—I don't need to, uh, sir. The, uh, engine's in the fro—"

"What is it with you two? Maybe you don't have

anything better to do than stand here all night, but I do.'' Andrik crushed his cigarette under a flip-flop. "Get with it, Moody."

His chest heaved. Fresh sweat greased his face. "I'm telling you—"

"No, kid. I'm tellin' *you*. Either show me your car is driveable or I call a tow truck to haul it out of here."

Moody pushed hard on the trunk and stalked off.

Open. C'mon, Hannah thought. You did a minute ago, damn it. *Open.*

The car tilted when Moody hurled himself under the steering wheel.

Hannah's steepled hands tapped her chin. Oh, please. *Please.*

Exhaust broomed up a tiny cloud of dust and grit. Engine running, Moody swung around in the seat, one foot braced on the concrete. "See, I told you..."

His voice trailed away. He watched, horrified, as the trunk lid raised in glorious, miraculous slow motion. Lot-lights bathed the center of the compartment where guns, ammunition and rags had been disarrayed by the impact.

Hannah felt Andrik's "you knew about this" look, though his eyes inventoried the cache. Jaw muscles working, he peered into the bucket. Extracting a pen from his shirt pocket, he nudged the handkerchief aside, then consulted the small spiral notebook he wrested from the same pocket.

Elbow on one knee, Moody cradled his head in his hand and began to cry.

Hannah hugged herself, her sorrow directed at the boy-dreamer whose reach had always exceeded his grasp, not at the despicable, self-serving Judas he'd become.

Whether he had rushed Larry Beauford to the hospital or waited until he was beyond medical help would never be known. That he'd almost succeeded in destroying David Hendrickson was fact.

Andrik rounded the Toyota, shut off the ignition and removed the keys. "We both know you don't have federal permits for those assault weapons."

"N-no. I keep forgetting to fill out the—"

"We also both know the serial number on that Glock matches the one registered to Stuart Quince."

Hannah grabbed at the Blazer's fender like a child, punch-drunk from a merry-go-round ride.

Tears glistening on his cheeks, Moody blubbered, "I didn't mean to. Swear to God. It's like I blacked out. I was watching Hendrickson trying to reason with that guy, then..." He dissolved into racking sobs. "I don't know what came over me. It was like it was somebody else."

Andrik's sidelong glance at Hannah transmitted disgust, along with a warning. Moody wasn't the only one with plenty more explaining to do.

The city cop reappeared beside her. "Are you sure you're all right, ma'am? I'd be glad to go inside and get you a soda or something."

She added two plus two and got five. "You're Andrik's backup, aren't you? That boundary dispute was an act for Moody's benefit."

"Not officially. Marlin had no idea what he was getting into, didn't want anything going out on the radio and flagged me to follow along." He grinned. "Yeah, the county boy, city boy thing was hoorah, but danged if he didn't trip my trigger all the same.''

''Marlin has that effect on people.''

''I heard that.'' Andrik nodded at Moody, slumped against the car. ''Nice of the dirtbag to loan me his cuffs. 'Preciate it if you'd keep an eye on him and the stash while I call this in.''

The city cop inquired, ''Is that a formal request for interagency assistance?''

''Funny, Cornelius. Real funny.'' Andrik took Hannah's elbow. ''Step into my office, said the spider to the fly.''

Midway to his unmarked car, Leo Schnur's flame-orange Thing putt-putted into Fountain Plaza's lot. A small, black-clad figure, white hair standing on end for want of a comb, scampered from Price-Slasher's entry and dived into the back seat. The Volkswagen chugged toward a side exit to an access road, a meandering route that eventually connected with Highway VV.

''Who—or what—the hell was that?''

Hannah attempted a noncommittal shrug.

''Smile while you can, toots. There's a drawerful of rubber hoses and bamboo shoots in my desk at the office.''

Andrik ducked into the car and grabbed the microphone.

''Baker 2–03.''

Go ahead, 2–03.

''Grab a pencil, Santa Claus. I've got a long list of stuff I want for Christmas.''

A groan emitted from the speaker. *Go ahead, 2–03.*

''Send me a uniform, Code 3, to the Pump 'n Munch for a transport. Roust Josh Phelps out of the sack and dispatch him, same 10–20, pronto, plus a tow truck to haul a vehicle to impound. Then call Lieutenant Pike and Sheriff Hendrickson. Tell them to meet me at The Outhouse in an hour. You copy?''

10–4.

"Oh, yeah." He winked at Hannah. "Tell Hendrickson the citizen who saved his bacon will be there, too. I'm clear."

Static crackled for several seconds. *Clear.*

Andrik tossed the microphone on the seat. Leaning on the car door, he shook out a cigarette. "Okay, so how'd you know?"

"About Moody? I didn't, for sure." A true statement, technically. Until Marlin identified the pistol as Quince's, it could have been any ol' Glock paperweighting what Hannah assumed was the deceased's suicide note to his wife.

She related her saleslady M.O. and the young mother's remark, reminding him that David had ordered the reservist to keep spectators away from the scene.

Little Billy's account followed, along with the memories it revived: that Moody wasn't wearing a sidearm the night of the shooting and that he was the only officer on the scene she spoke with who didn't remark on hearing her Mayday dispatch on the police radio.

Moody's motor-mouth and lead foot when he took Hannah home contradicted the tight-lipped, snail's pace IdaClare described when he drove her to the courthouse two days prior to the shooting, as well as when Hannah had tailed him earlier. The strong body odor Hannah had noticed after the shooting signalled Moody's extreme nervousness and fear of getting caught.

"After Chlorine Moody said she didn't allow fire-arms in her house," Hannah continued, "I guessed the only place Moody could have hidden Quince's gun—if he took it—was in his car."

Andrik snorted. "There are plenty of squirrel nests in a vehicle, besides the trunk."

"If you were Moody, where would you have put it?"

"Are you kidding? I'd have dug a hole halfway to China and buried it."

"Want my theory on why he didn't?"

"No."

A mini-raspberry escaped her lips. "Why not?"

"If you're right, it'll go to your head, which is six sizes too big already."

"It is not. Besides, I could be wrong."

"Oh-ho, I've been married too long to fall for that hustle." Andrik kneed the door shut. "Women are *never* wrong. Men just don't always hear 'em right."

22

David sat on a cast-off desk, hands clasped between his thighs, looking through the one-way mirror into the Detective Division's interrogation room.

Theron Pike, all neck-tied and fashion-plated despite the lateness—make that earliness—of the hour, leaned in a corner; his arms crossed and his face as inflexible as scrimshaw.

Rudy Moody, who alternately slumped in a chair or slumped over the small table separating him from Andrik, resembled the Pillsbury Doughboy left out of refrigeration too long. Like a poorly dubbed foreign film, his mouth movements were a click ahead of his words, amplified by the speakers mounted on the wall behind David.

It wasn't premeditated. It was all my idea. Gee whiz, how many times do I have to tell you guys before you'll believe me?

Damned if he didn't sound like the Doughboy, too.

Marlin said he'd suspected Moody all along. Marlin would. It might even be true. What David wanted to hear was that Marlin had believed him all along. If he ever said so, that might even be true, too.

The Outhouse's dark-filmed windows enhanced the noirish, otherworldly effect of first light. It wasn't going to be Mack Doniphan's day. David shook his head, grinning. It's mine, praise the Lord and the pretty lady catnapping with her feet on Marlin's desk.

He still didn't believe it. Friday night's freight train had blown out of his life as fast as it had blown in and wrecked everything he held dear. David felt the same way now as he had then. Shell-shocked. Disoriented. Leery.

It wasn't over. It never would be, entirely. Oh, in time, complacency would slink back in, but as the saying went, once burned, twice shy.

Until last week, he'd thought all that meant was being slow to give your heart away after it had been stomped on, chewed up and spit out. He'd have gladly gone to his grave without learning its other interpretation.

For a while, the same folks who'd shunned him would make an effort to say hello, their voices a tad too loud and their faces a little too earnest. Then things would simmer down to what everybody'd call normal, except he wouldn't have a "same old, same old" to go back to.

David stared through the glass at Moody, trying to hate him. A reputation, trust, integrity—call those into question and the outcome didn't matter. The damage was done and the taint was permanent.

He wanted to rip the uniform off Moody's back. Wanted him convicted and punished to the fullest extent of the law. Wanted him gone from Kinderhook County for a good long while. But hate him?

Well, truth be known, David wasn't above wishing he could haul him out back and beat the shit out of him, but even that'd take more effort than the bastard was worth.

Hannah stirred, then stretched, her arms winging upward, her lips curving into a languid smile. David watched her, a sensuous, sinuous beauty, wakening from sleep.

A poet or a painter could find inspiration in every nuance, every fluid motion. Her socked toes pointing, flexing. How she whisked the hair from her face. Her dancer's legs reeling in, swinging to the floor, feet sliding into her shoes. The lilt to her voice when she moaned, "God, do I ever feel grotty."

Probably what the princess said in the fairy tale, too, before it was edited out. "Want some coffee?"

"I'd love some," Hannah said, "but not that diesel fuel Marlin makes."

"Don't blame you. As soon as we get out of here, I'll take you to a place where the pot gets washed more'n once a year and there's breakfast to go with it."

"Deal." She held up a hand. "Just don't say any more about it, or my stomach will start growling 'Gimme, gimme.'"

He butt-walked backward on the desk and opened his arms. "You weren't asleep very long."

"Didn't you know? I invented the power nap. Kind of like Al Gore invented the Internet."

Snuggling between his legs, her back spooned to his chest, he wrapped his arms around her, feeling her sigh of contentment as he exhaled his own.

Soft. Warm. Peaceful. Her curves fit his angles. Her faith in him, her gutsiness, her amazing instincts and the intelligence she had to act on them, humbled him.

Inside and out, she was everything he'd ever wanted, everything he'd given up hoping he'd find. Now that he had, he was afraid he wasn't anywhere near good enough for her and sooner or later, she'd reach the same conclusion.

"They're still at it, huh?" she asked.

"They won't be much longer. A clerk at the courthouse is typing up Moody's confession. Andrik and Pike'll escort him over there directly to sign it."

She listened for a moment. "Did I miss much? The last thing I remember is Moody saying he'd kept the evidence in the event Jessup Knox was elected and refused to hire him. Insurance against history repeating itself."

"Knox is a brass-plated jackass, but he wouldn't have put Moody on the payroll, either. He's a liability waiting to happen. And does, over and over again."

"Yeah," she said, "but the scary thing is, Moody's idea might have worked. Plant the gun and other stuff on Knox, then 'discover' it. You'd have been exonerated after-the-fact. Then out goes Knox and in comes another sheriff, who'd be hard-pressed not to make Rudy the Hero a full-fledged deputy."

David's stomach rolled. "Marlin says Moody would have cracked under the strain in a day or three."

She snickered. "Marlin would."

"That's kinda what I thought, too."

"But to give credit where a ton of it is due, he was there when I needed him. A few minutes too early or too late and—" she pressed her cheek to his "—we wouldn't be here."

David kissed her temple. "Nope."

"Lieutenant Pike didn't seem too happy when Marlin let me read Quince's note."

"Well, to be honest, knowing Andrik as I do, he'd have done it just to piss Pike off, but I suspect he considered it a second cousin to professional courtesy."

"I'm flattered."

"You shouldn't be. Marlin respects you, but you earned it."

David sensed her mulling the remark. A fair number of women would argue, for no reason other than to keep the compliments spilling down the chute.

Not Hannah. When she didn't, he didn't know whether it was because she agreed, wasn't in the mood for a debate or was thinking about something else altogether.

"Moody isn't the only villain in this nasty ordeal," she said.

Ah. The "something else altogether" option.

"Me and the gumshoe gang had Lydia Quince at the top of our suspect list for quite a while, due to the felony clause in most life insurance policies."

She chuffed in disgust. "The part in Stuart's note where he gloated about suicide-by-cop putting him out of his misery and keeping Lydia and Robby Randal from living it up on the benefits was as cruel as it was diabolical."

"Well, I'm not exactly prone toward silver linings," David said, "but from what I hear, Lydia is eaten up with guilt about pushing Stuart over the edge. It'll hurt to read what he wrote, but maybe it'll convince her he was scum from the get-go."

Hannah's tone had a singsongy, brittle edge when she said, "The best lessons are the hardest learned."

"I gue—"

"So sayeth Chlorine Moody."

His lips curled back. What a piece of work she was.

Hannah asked, "What's the scoop on Moody, Senior, anyway?"

"Royal? Rumor has it, he was an easygoing traveling salesman for a Chicago novelties company. Folks felt bad for Rudy when Royal took a hike, but nobody blamed him for ditching Chlorine."

He chuckled. "Of course, if he'd stuck it out another year or so, he'd have gotten a cut of the million she made off that card game she invented."

"Oh, *really?*"

An uptick in Hannah's voice spelled trouble with a capital T. "What, oh really?"

"Shh."

...the blackout I had. A lawyer can use that for proof I got a mental defect, couldn't he? Get me probation and I dunno, three, four hundred hours of community service or something. Ya think?

She stiffened. "Promise me Moody can't plea-bargain his way out of this."

"I can't, sugar." The admission made David ill.

"Doniphan will charge him with everything he can. The feds'll have a go at him on felony firearms possession. A lot depends on how he pleads. 'Guilty' puts him before a judge. 'Not guilty' and a jury decides. Solomon himself wouldn't hazard a guess on what either will do."

"Which would you pick if you could?"

David shook his head. "Moody's such a fuck-up— pardon my French—a jury might take pity on him. So could a judge."

After a moment, Hannah said, "What I want to know is what happened to the gunpowder residue on Quince's hands? That was so far out of my league, I made a concerted effort to ignore it."

"Moody's germaphobic, like Chlorine. Hated to shake hands and went squeamish if anyone sneezed around him. He carried a pocketful of those moist towelette-things on him at all times."

Hannah looked back at him. "They can wipe off all trace of gunpowder?"

"It's a new one on me, too, Nancy Drew. The alcohol content in the brand Rudy used was the topper, along with the model of Glock Quince had being tight—meaning it didn't expel much powder when fired."

"Hmm." She faced forward. "Do you think Moody knew that?"

"Nope. I think stressing out over the test results explains the toxic sweat pouring off him that night."

David laced his fingers in hers. "I noticed it at the scene, but thought it was because I took his service revolver away from him and told him to hang up his uniform and stay off the streets, pending further review when I got back from Tulsa."

Anger flared. "Hopalong Dipshit had the smarts to set me up, but couldn't savvy the danger to himself, toodling around in uniform with no sidearm. Bungle into the wrong place at the wrong time and what was he going to do? Throw rocks at the bad guys if they started shooting?"

Hannah's body shook with laughter. David's temper cooled instantly. Another part of him heated up just as fast. He cocked a hip, trying to ease the guillotine effect of taut-stretched Levi's on his manhood.

"I know it isn't funny—"

He winced, thinking, no, ma'am, I guarantee, having your nuts in a vise ain't any man's idea of comical.

"—but why'd you take his gun away from him?"

Aw, hell. Maybe she wouldn't laugh again. Maybe if she did, he'd pass out and that'd take care of the problem. "Moody, uh…well, he *said* he was checking to make sure the safety was on, which it apparently wasn't, on account of it went off—" David clenched his teeth "—and busted The Petal Pushers' front window to smithereens."

Hannah whooped and clapped a hand to her mouth. Bending double, she broke David's embrace, shuddering from head to—

He wrenched his head away. You lucked out, horndog. Do *not* feast your eyes on that fine derriere jiggling inside those skintight britches.

Adjustments accomplished, he couldn't, for the life of him, think of a single, all-time leading rusher. Another new one on him.

Lemme make a short-distance call first, Andrik said through the speakers. *Make sure the concierge at Hotel Hoosegow has that private room available.*

Still motorboating, Hannah straightened and stepped to one side.

Moody protested, *I know my rights. Once I'm charged and I post bail, I can go home.*

Who said anything about charging you? Yet. Theron Pike sounded like a bemused Darth Vader. *By law, we can hold you for another thirteen hours if we so desire.*

Andrik banged the door shut behind him. "What we oughta do is call Momma and lock 'em up together."

"Great idea," David said, "except there wouldn't be enough left of Rudy to charge when she got through with him."

"Are you really about finished with him?" Hannah asked.

"For now." The detective massaged his neck. "We're meeting with Mack Doniphan in his office at eight."

Hannah said, "Then why don't you and Lieutenant Pike have breakfast with us? Kind of a celebration. Definitely a celebration."

David looked hard at Marlin. *I am one selfish son of a bitch, pard, but please, I beg you, make up an excuse to say no.*

"Wish we could, Hannah, but I've gotta go home and change clothes and Theron has to pick up that dweeb from the attorney general's office at the airport in Richland."

David slid off the desk and stuck out a hand. "I owe you, man. More than I can ever repay."

"Just doing my job, Sheriff." Andrik clapped David's upper arm. "Damn, it feels good to say that."

"No better than it does to hear it."

"Tell you what, you want to start on that 'repaying' horseshit, how about a steak-and-kegger at your place soon as we all catch up on some zzz's?"

"You got it."

"Is this a cop-only thing," Hannah asked, "or coed?"

"What do you care, toots? You're covered either way."

Caught by surprise, Andrik "oomphed" when she bear-hugged him. "Thank you, Marlin, for doing more than just your job."

If David hadn't seen Andrik blush or the "Aw, shucks, ma'am" expression on his face, he'd never have believed them possible.

"Jesus criminy, will you two get the hell out of here? I've got a detective division to run, a drone to walk across the street and refrain from throwing under a milk truck, fifty jillion reports to write—"

The plate-glass door closed on Andrik's bellowing. David squeezed Hannah's hand, sucked in a lungful of morning air and gazed up at the courthouse's third-floor corner windows.

No, things would never be quite the same again, but there wasn't any law against them being better, sweeter. In fact, things were downright promising from where he stood right now.

Hannah smirked up at him. "If I could sing, I'd give 'It's A Beautiful Morning' a shot. Then again, that one's probably before your time."

"Lord above, woman. I haven't had my Get Out of Jail Free card five seconds and there you go with the age-difference crap."

"I was just—"

"I figured out the whole thing when I was in Tulsa, but didn't have a chance to tell you."

"David, I—"

"No, no, you started it, now hush." A finger raised for emphasis, he lectured, "In the first place, seven years ain't squat. I piled on about seventy-two of them in less than a week."

His middle finger made a V. "Second of all, it's a

bona fide fact, women live eight years longer than men, so since we'll both kick the bucket at about the same time, what we actually have is as near perfect, age-wise—well, not *just* age-wise, by any means—as a man and a woman can get.''

Laughing, she looked at him as if he'd left home so fast, he'd forgotten to bring his mind along. ''Hendrickson, how you *do* go on.''

''Well, I've heard all I—''

''I was just teasing you, to get your attention, to ask if we were going to the Short Stack for breakfast.''

''Oh.'' David's boot sole scuffed the sidewalk. She wasn't arguing with his actuarial idea. God only knew what that meant.

''No, I had a nicer, quieter place than the café in mind.'' He ignored her arching eyebrow. ''You can ride with me. I'll bring you back to your vehicle later, or you can follow me.''

She stretched on tiptoe and kissed his cheek. ''I lead. You follow.'' Skipping around the Blazer's front bumper, she added, ''Life expectancy or no, I've got seniority on you, Sheriff.''

He knew he was on autopilot before they left the square. Why shouldn't he be? He knew where he lived. Hannah had only been there once, but was heading straight for it without his help. Might as well relax, feel the wind on his face and enjoy the view.

His nerves started to unravel when they turned onto Turkey Creek Road. He wouldn't admit it to anyone except himself, but he'd never felt like Mr. Slick in those awkward moments between the ''Want to come in and have a nightcap or something?'' and the actual or-something.

Hang it all, she *was* older, which translated to maybe more experienced. Not in the wrong way—she wasn't that kind of woman—but he wanted to be the best lover she'd ever known, the most skillful, the...

His bridged knuckles tingled from gripping the steering wheel. I want to send her over the moon and past the stars and when she floats back to earth, I want her to open her eyes and look into mine and say, "I love you, David."

That's the sum total of it, David realized. What I've dreamed about since that morning on Kathleen Osborn's porch. I'm just not sure...

The significance of the Blazer's blinking left taillight yanked him back to reality. He slammed on the brakes, the interlocking rhythm pulsing against his instep. His pickup screeched to a halt an inch from Hannah's back bumper.

Yeah, why not bash her tailgate in about a foot and a half, David thought as her vehicle juddered and rolled into the lane. Wouldn't that be romantic.

If I were Romeo and she were Juliet, you could count on me to recite "What light from yonder window breaks," then clock her upside the head with a rock when she looked down.

Turning in behind her, he expected Hannah's vehicle to accelerate, only to holler "Shit!" when the brake lights flashed red and she stopped dead-bang in front of him.

Her door swung open. She hopped out, grinning like a little kid in a big puddle.

Forearm resting on the wheel, David's head wobbled as though palsied while she wriggled between their bumpers and scampered back to the road.

David craned his neck to watch her out the cab's rear window. It was hours too early for the mail. What in the world was she up…to.

Oh, my. Oh, my darlin' Hannah. *That's* why you wanted to lead, not follow.

David's eyes stung at the corners. Fingertips rubbed his brow, his chest swelling tight enough to crack ribs as he watched her jerk and push and heave the For Sale sign out of the rocky Ozarks ground that was as much a part of him as the blood in his veins.

The sign clanged into the pickup's bed; the loveliest racket he'd ever heard, bar none. Hannah dusted her hands, gave him a "so there" nod and jogged back to her truck.

The next time she stepped from it, David swept her into his arms and spun her around, kissing her neck, her jaw, her cheek, then set her down and kissed her, gently, tenderly, praying he was telling her what words couldn't possibly express.

"See, I told you everything was going to be all right," she whispered, her eyes shining.

"Thanks to you, it is."

"Not just me, David. Besides Marlin and maybe Pike, there's Delbert and IdaClare, Leo, Rosemary, Marge, Sophonia Pugh, Walt One g, Two n's Wagonner, little Billy—"

A finger to her lips stopped the roll call. "I want the whole story, from top to bottom…later."

"Over breakfast."

"Right."

Rambo grunted "Good morning" as they strolled arm in arm across the porch and into the house. David tossed his keys on a side table, looked down the hall to the bedroom, then at the kitchen. *Okay, Mr. Slick. Now what?*

Hannah tapped her thighs, her mouth pursed and, unless he was sorely mistaken, as ill-at-ease as he was. "How about that coffee?" she said at the same instant he said, "I'll make us some coffee."

Weight shifting to the other foot, she held up her hands. "If I ask you something, will you tell me the honest truth?"

"I always have."

"Do you suddenly feel as completely and totally dorky as a fourteen-year-old? Or is it just me?"

"Whoo-eee, girl." Relief clattered through him like a marble down a pipe. "I reckon this cancels the age difference once and for all."

"Life after high school is still high school."

"Amen."

She raked her hair back, as he'd noticed she did when shyness, uncertainty or agitation nibbled at her. "Okay," she said, "I, uh, really do feel like one of the Great Unwashed. If you wouldn't mind me using your shower, how about if I do, while you fire up the coffeepot?"

David fetched clean towels from the linen cabinet, then bowed out and left her to her ablutions.

The hiss of water spraying from the nozzle began seconds before the coffee carafe filled. David poured a cup, held it chest high, leaned against the fridge, stared at the kitchen wall and imagined the water rinsing over her, her hair darkening with moisture, lather frosting her skin...

Coffee sloshed on the counter. He toed off one boot, then the other. His shirt came to rest on the arm of the living-room sofa. Butt propped against the bedroom wall, he peeled off his socks, unzipped his jeans and shucked them. Briefs took wing and fluttered down on the bed.

He walked into a vaporous cloud, pausing to admire her silhouette undulating on the shower's opaque glass. The bathroom door, he shut with a firm *thump*.

Neither of them moved for what seemed like minutes, then she said, "Better hurry before the hot water runs out."

Spray drumming his back, he pulled her to him, her breasts plump and soft. Eyes closed, her tongue tracing her lips, she tipped back her head and he kissed her, feeling hunger and desire and need and want surge through her as it did him.

Thumbs circling her swelling nipples, he lost himself in the taste of her mouth, her tongue, the erotic sensations of water and steam and bare skin.

A soapy, velvet palm glided down his chest, his belly, stroked up and down the length of him, fingers curling around him one by one—

Bam-bam-bam.

Dizzy, breathless, they looked at each other, then the door, then back again.

"Not again," she said. "This can*not* be happening again."

"No. It isn't. Forget it."

Arms curling around his neck, she arched her back, head slanting to receive his lips—

Bamety-bam-bam-bam.

"Damn it to hell and gone." He clasped her shoulders.

"Don't move. Whoever that is only has about three seconds to live, then I'll be right back."

He punched the shower door with his fist. Snapped a towel off the vanity cabinet. Storming and dripping down the hallway, he cinched the towel around his waist. One hand protectively cupping his erection, he flung open the door.

"Surprise!"

David gaped at the gray-haired woman and white-haired man grinning at him from the porch, his mind flashing images of Hannah, naked and waiting in the shower, and the blood draining from everywhere, including his face.

"Mom...Dad. *You're supposed to be in Canada.*"

* * * * *

To be continued...NORTH OF CLEVER

*Mira Books invites you to turn the page
for an exciting preview of*

NORTH OF CLEVER.

*Join Suzann Ledbetter as she takes
readers back to the mystery and mayhem
in Valhalla Springs.*

Available in paperback December 2001.

Until five minutes ago, Hannah Garvey had never considered the advantages to being the sole surviving member of a family small enough to have held reunions in a convenience store's rest room.

Amazing how getting caught in flagrante delicto with the Kinderhook County sheriff when his parents dropped in for a surprise visit could change one's perspective.

Her great-uncle Mort had often said some things were funny "Ha-ha," while others were funny "Hmm." Being horny, naked and trapped in a shower recently occupied by an equally horny and likewise naked David Hendrickson wasn't destined to be funny "Ha-ha" anytime soon.

In this lifetime, for instance.

From what she'd overheard, neither Ed nor June Hendrickson had explained how they'd set out from Florida for Toronto in their dually pickup and fifth-wheel travel trailer and wound up on their eldest son's porch in the central Missouri Ozarks at the freaking crack of dawn.

Only fair, Hannah supposed, since neither had inquired if David was in the habit of answering his door wearing nothing but a homicidal expression, a towel and a woody the size of a Louisville Slugger.

She further supposed she couldn't fault him for not shooting the then-unknown intruders as he'd promised when he stormed out of the bathroom. Taking his parents out of the world they'd brought him into thirty-six years ago because their timing sucked worse than their ability to read a road map might have been a little excessive.

After pulling on the black sweater and stirrup pants that had been de rigueur for the previous night's semi-felonious activities, Hannah wiped the steam from the mirror.

Shoulder-length, towel-dried hair about six shades darker than its natural brownish-auburn and mascara rings around her eyes completed the peri-menopausal Goth look.

Whimpering softly, she squatted on her heels and yanked open the vanity cabinet's doors. A visual survey revealed that male sheriffs with quasi-military haircuts don't own hair dryers. Male sheriffs who've been divorced for three years and had no children don't have bottles of baby oil lying around, either.

In the process of discovering that Vaseline Intensive Care lotion stings like hell but does a creditable job of removing waterproof mascara, she jumped at a knock on the bathroom door. A familiar baritone asked, "Are you decent?"

"No."

Two-beat pause. "Well, is it okay if I come in?"

Her gaze flicked to the mirror. "Yeah, but it's risky, unless you have a cross in one hand and a wooden stake in the other."

The undaunted, living, breathing, albeit no longer naked epitome of Michelangelo's statue waltzed through the door. Not that a T-shirt and jeans shaved any points off this David's overall Lust-o-Meter score. She just wouldn't have minded another peek at six feet three inches of original sin.

For posterity, if nothing else. After all, on at least three occasions experience had shown that God had taken the vow of celibacy she made three years ago more seriously than she had.

David snuggled up spoon-fashion, pressed his head to her and squinted into the mirror. "Okay, so your hair's a little damp and mussy. I think it's kind of sexy."

"I think you ought to trade Rambo in on a seeing-eye dog," she said, referring to David's rottweiler, who was trained to snack on strangers who thought Beware Of Dog signs didn't include them. "Come to think of it, why didn't Rambo bark when your parents drove in?"

Better yet, why hadn't he treed them for an hour or two?

"I suspect he barked like sixty, until he recognized them." A lazy grin crawled across David's face. "Can't imagine why we didn't hear him."

The memory of David's slickly wet, hard-muscled body shimmied behind her eyes. Steam swirling around them...his arms crushing her to his chest...the hungry tenderness of his kiss...the water channeling erotic paths of least resistance...

Leaning back into his embrace, her voice deepening to a husky whisper, Hannah asked, "Are you thinking what I'm thinking?"

"Yep." He retreated a step. "Mom's probably pretty close to having breakfast ready by now."

This from a man who'd demonstrated an uncanny and annoying ability to read her mind? Either David's internal satellite dish was malfunctioning or Mother Hendrickson was scrambling signals, along with the eggs.

Turning from the sink, Hannah braced an arm on her chest and propped an elbow on it. An index finger tapped her chin. "You know what this bathroom needs?"

"Huh?"

"A window. It'd be ten times brighter, if it had one."

David stared at her as though she'd switched from English to Serbo-Croatian.

"By golly, if this were my house, I'd fetch a saw and get right on it. Really, how long would it take to—"

"Only one problem, sugar. All the walls are of the interior variety."

"Oh. Well, then..." She gandered at the ceiling.

David shook his head. "Old farmhouses with sheet-metal roofs aren't prime for skylights, either."

Frowning, she asked herself, *What would Steve McQueen do?*

David rested his hands on her shoulders. "Look, I realize this is sort of embarrassing—"

Sort of?

"But I figure a gal who's been involved in two murders, three burglaries, an assault with a deadly weapon, a pot bust, a bogus second-degree manslaughter charge against me and willful destruction with a motor vehicle ought to be able to take it in stride.''

"Stride is precisely what I'd like to do. Straight out the front door to my Blazer and outta here.''

"We're adults, Hannah.''

"Speak for yourself. I may be seven years older than you are, but I feel like I'm about fifteen.''

"Same here.'' He kissed her forehead. "But bear in mind I'm the one who's gonna get razzed by my folks, all three of my brothers and every aunt, uncle and cousin in creation from now until doomsday.''

Her smile hid a tug of sadness. She'd never had any siblings. Gossipy relatives hadn't been a problem for a long, long time. "Okay, Sheriff. Onward and upward.''

"Attagirl.''

A fluttery sensation, like pterodactyls taking wing, commenced in her midsection as David steered her down the short hallway to the living room and toward the kitchen. Normally the aroma of bacon frying would send Hannah's taste buds into orbit. Instead, she wondered if asking for a glass of Maalox on the rocks would be too obvious.

June Hendrickson, a statuesque woman with bone structure rivaling Maureen O'Hara's, and Ed, a white-haired, slightly stooped, somewhat shorter version of his eldest son, greeted her as though she'd just dropped in—via the front door.

"Pull up a chair,'' Ed said, folding the newspaper he was reading and laying it aside.

"How do you take your coffee?'' June asked. "Black? Well, that's simple enough.''

In a blink, steaming mugs appeared before Hannah and David. June topped off hers and her husband's, then rinsed the carafe for a fresh pot. "Bacon and toast is a poor excuse for breakfast, but there's only one egg in the fridge and I couldn't find a speck of flour to make biscuits."

Hannah would need more than eggs and flour to whip up a batch of biscuits from scratch. Divine intervention, for starters.

Being treated like an instant member of the family didn't put her completely at ease—nothing short of a tranquilizer dart could have done that—but piano-wire nerves were beginning to slacken when she noticed Ed's gaze slide from her face to her ensemble and back again.

"You work undercover, do you?"

Coffee whooshed down her windpipe. Coughing and slapping her chest, she croaked, "Excuse me?"

"Hannah isn't in law enforcement, Dad. She's the operations manager at Valhalla Springs."

"That retirement village out on Highway VV?"

Hannah's respiration not yet having stabilized, a nod sufficed as confirmation.

Ed's woolly eyebrows rumpled. "Why would a pretty young lady like you want to ride herd over a bunch of old geezers?"

Hannah had posed a similar question to herself when Jack Clancy offered her the job. Which was within hours of her resignation from the Friedlich & Friedlich Agency in Chicago, where she'd spent twenty-five years crawling up the career ladder from receptionist/ grunt to advertising account executive.

Her professional relationship with Jack, a renowned resort developer headquartered in Saint Louis, had evolved into a close friendship. When she called him to announce her departure from the agency, she'd expected a string of expletives, allusions that the black cohosh capsules she snorked morning, noon and night weren't working worth a damn, then long-distance sniffles and promises to stay in touch.

To the contrary, Jack somehow—and to this day, she wasn't sure how—had coerced her into managing the retirement community he'd built twenty-two miles south of Sanity, the Kinderhook County seat.

In answer to Ed's question, Hannah shrugged and said, "I was tired of living in Chicago and tired of the advertising industry rat race. When Jack Clancy made the offer, I couldn't think of any reason to refuse."

June set a platter of crisp bacon and buttered toast on the table. "Jack Clancy?" She waggled a finger at Ed. "Didn't Patrick and IdaClare have a boy named Jack?"

"You know IdaClare?" David asked, before Hannah could.

Ed gestured an affirmative. "Me and Patrick used to swap lies at cattle auctions, here and yonder. Most of the big ranchers wouldn't tip their hats to a pharmacist with ten or twenty Herefords grazing behind the house. Clancy didn't care who you were, as long as your check was good."

June added, "We didn't know Patrick had passed away until Ed saw a handbill about the ranch being for sale." She sighed and patted Hannah's hand. "And here you are, working for their son and sleeping with ours."